code

Kathy Reichs

& Brendan Reichs

code

arrow books

Published by Arrow Books in 2013

2 4 6 8 10 9 7 5 3

Published by arrangement with the original publisher, G.P. Putnam's Son's,
an imprint of Penguin Inc.

First published in Great Britain in 2013 by William Heinemann
The Random House Group Limited
20 Vauxhall Bridge Road, London, SW1V 2SA

www.randomhouse.co.uk

Addresses for companies within The Random House Group Limited can be found at:
www.randomhouse.co.uk/offices.htm

The Random House Group Limited Reg. No. 954009

A CIP catalogue record for this book
is available from the British Library

ISBN 9780099571469

The Random House Group Limited supports the Forest Stewardship
Council® (FSC®), the leading international forest-certification organisation. Our books
carrying the FSC label are printed on FSC®-certified paper. FSC is the only forest-certification
scheme supported by the leading environmental organisations, including Greenpeace.
Our paper procurement policy can be found at:
www.randomhouse.co.uk/environment

Printed and bound by CPI Group (UK) Ltd, Croydon, CR0 4YY

Brendan Reichs would like to dedicate this book to
his beautiful wife, Emily, his perfect newborn daughter, Alice,
and his thunderbolt of a son, Henry.
You are the point.

Kathy Reichs would like to dedicate this book to
her beautiful Irish and Latvian families.
Tá grá agam duit. Es jūs mīlu.

PROLOGUE

97 days earlier

Light breezes swept the dunes of Turtle Beach.

Gentle gusts that spun eddies in the bone-white sand before whistling into the dark woods beyond.

The sky was enormous, black and moonless. Though well past sunset, the air remained muggy, thick, and warm.

Another quiet night on Loggerhead Island.

But *not* business as usual.

Just past the tree line, beneath the looming hulk of Tern Point, a monkey troop clustered high up in the branches of a longleaf pine.

Silent.

Observing the forest floor.

Below, in a small meadow bordering the tree's massive roots, a shovel rose, fell, rose again. Fresh dirt landed atop an already knee-high pile.

The digger wore a thick brown cloak, incongruous in the stifling heat. The billowing garment engulfed its owner, hung to the tips of battered black boots.

Sweat glistened on a crinkled brow.

The figure paused, smiled up at the simian audience, content to share the moment.

Years of waiting, then months of meticulous planning.

It was finally time.

The Game was about to begin.

The digger resumed, patient, persistently gouging the rich, black soil. The pit was three feet deep, and growing.

Almost finished.

The digger halted again. Stretched. Breathed deeply, inhaling a heady bouquet of loamy earth, wet grass, and honeysuckle.

A giggle escaped — shrill and birdlike, it lingered for long moments before dying with an atonal squeak.

Above, the primates shifted, nervous, alert to danger. Two young males scampered higher into the shadows of the canopy. But the group stayed. Spellbound. Watching.

Abandoning the spade, the digger reached into a canvas bag and removed a small bundle. Kissed it once. Reverently placed it inside the hole.

The Game was afoot.

"Come and find me," the digger whispered, heartbeat loud enough to still the frogs.

Humming tunelessly, the digger filled the hole and covered the surface with dead leaves. Stepped back. Located a wristwatch button with one trembling finger. Pressed.

Ding.

The childish giggle sounded once more.

It's done. The key is buried.

"Time to play."

Hefting the bag and shovel, the digger stole into the shadows.

PART ONE:

CACHE

CHAPTER 1

The reel screeched, nearly jerked the pole from my fingers.

"Whoa!" I death-gripped my rod. "Got a live one!"

"Go easy." Ben's dark brown eyes radiated caution. "The line'll snap if you're not careful."

Tern Point. Loggerhead Island. Ben Blue and I were perched upon a wide stone ledge twenty feet above the Atlantic Ocean. We'd been there an hour, with no bites.

Until now.

"WhatdoIdo?" First time on a spinner, and my mind was blank. I wiped a sweaty palm on my gray polo shirt.

"Both hands on the rod!" I could tell Ben itched to take over but was suppressing the urge. "Let the fish run a bit, reel back slowly, then let it run again. But stay alert. That tackle isn't designed for sportfishing."

I followed his instructions, letting my catch tire itself out. Finally, a wiggling silver streak flashed in the surf just below.

Ben whistled as he ear-tucked his shoulder-length black hair. "That's a big boy. Nice haul."

"Thanks. Tag in?" My arms were burning from the extended tug-of-war. "This monster's not a quitter."

Ben took over, muscles straining beneath his black tee and cutoff khakis. Of all the Virals, he was strongest by far. And the most connected to nature. Ben spent most of his free time outdoors, and had a deep, coppery tan to prove it.

The Blue family claims to have descended from the Sewee tribe, a local Native American group that disappeared from the pages of history three centuries ago. There's no way to prove it, of course. Just don't tell Ben that.

Ben's small boat, *Sewee*, was our primary means of transportation. He'd used the old sixteen-foot Boston Whaler runabout to explore dozens of Charleston's barrier isles. And learned the best fishing spots, like this one.

Moments later a gleaming, flopping captive dangled from the end of my line. Ben reeled it up to eye level.

My catch was silver, a foot and a half long, and covered with small, loose scales. A thin trail of blood leaked from its mouth.

"King mackerel." Ben removed the hook and lifted the fish by one gill. "Twenty pounds — a pretty good size. Glad he didn't break loose."

The beleaguered fish gulped air, futilely searching for oxygen. Our eyes locked.

Suddenly, I wasn't having so much fun.

"Throw him back."

"What?" Ben frowned. "Why? This species is good eating. Or we could sell him at the fish market in Folly Beach."

The mackerel's jaw continued to work, opening and closing, but with less vigor now. A bubble formed at the tip of its mouth. Burst.

"Throw him back," I repeated, sharper this time. "Fish-face still has some living to do."

Ben scowled, but knew better than to argue. Over the past year the boys had come to accept my stubbornness, and the fact that I didn't lose too many arguments. Not when I dug in my heels. Just like my aunt Tempe.

You may have heard of her. Dr. Temperance Brennan, World-Famous Forensic Anthropologist. Some just call her the Bone Lady. She's my great-aunt, a wonderful fact I learned only after my mother's accident, when I moved in with my dad, Kit.

She's also my role model. My idol. Only everything I ever want to be. I might as well wear a What Would Tempe Do? necklace 24/7. My greatest ambition is to be as good a scientist as Tempe. To solve cases like she does. Leave my mark.

"Okay, pal." Ben gripped our captive at both ends. "Count your blessings that my friend here is a total softy."

He took one stride and tossed the mackerel back down to the sea. It hit the water and, with a flick of its tail fin, disappeared from sight.

"We caught him," I said. "*That's* the fun part." For us, at least. I doubt that fish would agree.

"Whatever." Ben began packing our gear. "Let's go find the others. Hi must've given up by now."

I secured hooks to poles, then scanned the ledge for trash. It'd been nice fishing alone with Ben. The two of us didn't spend much one-on-one time together, and he often went mute when Hi and Shelton were around. Probably because those two never let anyone get a word in edgewise.

Ben was already sixteen, the oldest of the Virals. He even had a driver's license. That should've made him our leader, but he preferred letting me make the decisions. Which was surprising, since I was fourteen and youngest, the only girl, and still learning about our home city of Charleston. But Ben usually let me have my way.

And he's a cutie, I had to admit, even though I only thought of him as a brother. Ben fascinated me, but he could be maddening, too. It was often impossible to read what was going on behind that intense gaze. I sometimes felt I understood him the least of my packmates.

After securing our tackle, we descended to the forest below. I'd barely touched boot to soil when a gray blur rocketed from the foliage.

"Coop, heel!" I wasn't anxious for a full-bodied lunge to my midsection. Mindful of his new training, the wolfdog checked his sprint and scampered to sit at my side.

"Good boy." Ear scratch. "Where's your family?"

Crackling leaves answered the question. I turned to see Whisper crouching by a large cedar at my back. The gray wolf regarded me quietly, then stepped aside for her mate, a German shepherd I'd named Polo. Beyond them, Coop's brother, Buster, alternated between chomping and shaking a stick.

"Release," I said.

Coop bounded back into the bushes, trailed by his fellow canines.

"Hanging around a wolf pack is nuts." Ben wiped his sweaty brow with a forearm, despite the mild temperature. "Whether it includes your mutt's mother or not."

"Don't be such a baby," I teased. "They're practically lapdogs."

"Lapdogs won't rip your face off. Or eat you."

"Hey, we're a wolf pack, too, remember?" I located the deer run we'd followed to Tern Point and started into the forest. "Why should we be scared of another one?"

Ben didn't answer. He still wasn't comfortable with the truth. Not like me.

Here's the deal. Last spring, my friends and I got zapped by a nasty supervirus. Me. Hiram. Shelton. Ben. And my wolfdog, Coop, of course.

The culprit was a designer pathogen created by Dr. Marcus Karsten, my father's former boss at the Loggerhead Island Research Institute. In a reckless attempt to strike it rich, Karsten combined DNA from two different types of parvovirus, accidentally creating a brand-new strain. A doozy.

Unfortunately for us, this vicious little germ was contagious to humans. We were infected while rescuing Coop, who'd been abducted by Karsten for use as a test subject.

First came the sickness. Headaches. Fevers. Blackouts. You name it.

The changes followed. We began to evolve. Or devolve.

Even now, I find it hard to describe. My mind twists and bends, sounding out new depths in my subconscious. My senses blast into hyperdrive, becoming more acute than humanly possible.

And sometimes I lose control, succumbing to primal instincts. Foreign impulses. Animal urges to hunt, or feed, or fight. It's the same with the others. Mostly.

The illness eventually passed, but not the changes. Our bodies had been transformed. The tiny viral invader had rewritten our genetic code, inserting canine DNA into human double helixes.

Shifting us. Hiding the wolf inside our cellular blueprint.

Welding us together as a pack.

Now we're Viral. To the core.

Scary thing is, we don't know if the sickness is truly finished. Or if the alterations are permanent. Could the effects grow more intense? Will they fade over time? No idea. With Karsten gone, so was our only link to the virus.

That's not to say we've given up. We don't have the answers, but we intend to find them. How? Still working on that.

Ben and I continued along the trail to a small clearing.

Beep! Beep!

Ben threw me a knowing glance. My eyes rolled in response. Obviously, Hi was still at it.

Beep! Beep! Beep!

Entering the meadow, I heard agitated voices.

"How much longer?" Shelton Devers pushed black-framed glasses up the bridge of his nose. "This stopped being interesting before it started."

Shelton is short and skinny, with dark chocolate skin and features common on the streets of Kyoto. Black father. Asian mother. You get the picture.

Shelton stood in the clearing's center, arms crossed, boredom etched on his face. He wore a yellow Pac-Man retro hoodie and oversized basketball shorts, which hung from his scrawny frame like clothes on a hanger.

"Why all the Haterade?" answered Hiram Stolowitski. "We found buried treasure once before, right?"

"A perfect reason to quit," Shelton said. "We've filled our lifetime quota."

"Not yet." Hi returned his attention to the device in his hands. "The geocache is supposed to be *right here*. Somewhere. I just have to find it."

"So far, all you've found are bottle caps, some pliers, and a Diet Coke."

"I re-jiggered the settings to ignore trash metal. No more false alarms."

"No more anything. It just beeps."

Hi wore a jarring arrangement: red Adidas headband, blue Hawaiian shirt, and white board shorts. In his hands was a Fisher Labs F2 metal detector, fresh from the package as of that morning. He'd been combing the clearing for thirty minutes, insisting something was buried there.

Chubby-faced and red-cheeked, Hi looked like he'd been running sprints rather than carefully walking a grid. No question he could be annoying at times, but we all respected his scientific curiosity. Hi loved experiments and gadgets, figuring things out. Usually I gave him the benefit of the doubt.

That day, not everyone was feeling as charitable.

"This is stupid." More a computer guy, Shelton preferred hacking websites to tramping through the woods. "Check the GPS again. We could be in the wrong place. And who'd bury something out here, anyway? It's private property."

Loggerhead Island is a private veterinary research preserve, complete with troops of free-ranging rhesus monkeys. The habitat is almost wholly undisturbed, with no permanent buildings outside the main LIRI complex.

We visited often. Loggerhead was one of the few places we could be totally alone.

"The geocaching website listed these coordinates," Hi repeated stubbornly. "This is the first cache ever posted for Loggerhead, and I intend to find it."

"When'd you adopt this wonderful new hobby?" Ben asked.

"When I ordered the detector. So last month, I guess. Now stop bugging me and let me finish scoping the clearing. The cache is within a hundred-foot radius."

Lazy Sunday. With no other plans, we'd selected our default option — messing around on Loggerhead. Our safe haven. We'd taken *Sewee*, as usual, then hiked over to explore the woods bordering Tern Point, a conical stone peak on the island's southeastern corner. Hi had insisted.

"Explain this again," I asked, not sure I fully understood the concept.

"I'm searching for a geocache." Hi, with infinite patience. "It's a game. Someone buries or hides a box with an object inside, then posts the coordinates online."

Shelton, skeptical. "How do you know a box is buried here?"

Hi continued at his deliberate pace, slowly sweeping the detector back and forth in front of him. "Because my iPhone says we're on the exact coordinates, and the clue told me to 'be sure to scratch the surface.'"

"All in all," Shelton said, "this is a tremendously dumb game."

"You're a dumb game," Hi shot back.

"Let me practice linking while Hi works," I suggested, knowing they wouldn't like the idea.

Three groans. As expected.

"We *have* to master our powers," I insisted. "What's the point of having special abilities if you can't control them?"

Hi grunted, eyes glued to the detector's LCD screen.

"It's creepy." Shelton shivered despite the warm October afternoon. "Invasive."

Ben nodded. "You should stay out of other people's minds."

Exposure to the supervirus had one major . . . side effect. Benefit? Curse?

We call it "flaring." When the changes come, our minds warp and snap, then the powers break free. Our senses shift to impossible clarity. Sight. Smell. Hearing. Taste. Even touch.

The wolf comes out, making us sharper and stronger.

Viral.

But evolution doesn't follow a single set of rules. The virus affected each of us differently. Perhaps the mutations were unique to our individual genetic sequences. Whatever the reason, our strengths vary. Hiram has eyes like an eagle with Lasik. Shelton can hear feathers flutter as a sparrow flaps its wings. Ben becomes strongest and fastest, like a bull on steroids. My nose gets so sensitive I can sniff out emotion, deception, and fear. And other things you'd rather not consider.

And, recently, our powers reached a whole new level.

For me, anyway.

The boys can't do it. Don't like it. But when our pack flares in close proximity, I can sometimes touch the other Virals' minds. Hear their thoughts, and pass on mine. This talent has come in handy more than a few times. Has saved our lives.

"Just one try, please." Firmly. "I need to gauge what Coop adds to the mix."

More dramatic moans, but the boys stopped what they were doing.

"Fine." Hi.

"Whatever." Shelton.

"One time." Ben held up a single finger. "One."

I nodded, then closed my eyes and stilled my mind. A deep breath, then I *reached* in a way I can't fully describe. My thoughts delved downward, backward, deep into the primordial center of my brain.

I visualized a single strand of DNA. The bedrock of my genetic being.

Honing my concentration, I imagined unzipping the double helix.

SNAP.

The flare burst through me like a river of molten lava. I gasped. Sweat exploded from my pores as the wolf came out.

Though I'd become better at summoning the power, that first wallop still challenged my defenses. Like a wild beast set loose in my nervous system. Control was tenuous and fragile. At best.

Focusing inward, I swam down into my subconscious. An image of each Viral appeared, sharpened. Hi first, then Shelton. Moments later Ben crystallized in my thoughts. I sensed Coop alert in the woods close by.

Flaming ropes connected the group. A golden nimbus surrounded each member.

Virals. Hear me.

My message smacked an invisible barrier. I tried again, concentrating harder.

VIRALS. HEAR ME.

This time I forced the message outward, driving it along the fiery cords. The boys flinched as if struck. Their glowing eyes widened in surprise.

I examined the mental barricade separating us. Probed for weaknesses. Suddenly, the roadblock weakened, then fragmented.

The other Virals' minds opened like a floodgate. Thoughts and feelings poured into me. Worries. Raw emotions. Random bits of foreign memories. The tide of information nearly scoured my brain clean.

I fought to hold against the onslaught, sensing danger to my sanity.

What shattered the barrier? How did I break through?

"What barrier?" Hi sputtered. "Why are you screaming?"

"Tory!" Shelton's hands flew to his head. "It hurts! Make it stop."

Ben stood rock still, grimacing, eyes focused on nothing. "Get out!" he sputtered.

My eyes darted, frantic, unable to comprehend. My mind gibbered, desperate to block the deluge of thoughts pouring into my brain.

I saw trees. Sky. The metal detector. Coop, edging into the clearing, eyes locked on to mine.

As if sensing my peril, Coop bowled into Shelton, who went down with a puff of surprise. The golden light abruptly vanished from his eyes.

The cerebral onslaught lessened.

Coop then bounded to Hi and barked full in his face. Startled, Hi backpedaled wildly, dropped the detector, and fell. His flare disappeared as he struck the ground.

Another wave winked out.

Suddenly on firmer ground, I stilled my mind and extinguished the flare.

SNUP.

The sensory bombardment ceased. I dropped to a knee and saw Ben do the same.

"Damn it, Tory!" Ben spat through gritted teeth. "You're playing with fire!"

"It's Coop," I panted, heart pounding. "When he's close, my ability skyrockets. But I couldn't control it."

"Then don't do it!" Shelton shirt-wiped his glasses with shaky hands. "You were yelling inside my head. I'm officially freaked out!"

Hi studied me with worried eyes. "You were in trouble, Tory, I could tell. You've got to be more careful. This mind stuff is dangerous."

"I will." *But I'm going to unlock this secret.*

I kept that to myself, though the thought wouldn't have surprised them.

Dangerous or not, I was determined to discover the full extent of our flare abilities. I needed to know what had happened to our bodies. What we were capable of. What could happen next.

Our mishmashed genetics gave us skills no one else possessed. Astonishing sensory abilities. But the changes went deeper than that. The cellular cross between man and beast had opened doors in our minds. I felt compelled to learn where they led.

Though, I had to admit, the idea of straight-up mind reading gave me the willies. I wouldn't want someone poking around in *my* head. Everyone has secrets, and the right to keep them. Finding the line between communication and mental invasion was proving to be tricky.

My hard drive finally came back online. Head clearing, I noticed a pulsating tone coming from Hi's metal detector, discarded in the grass.

Ding! Ding! Ding!

Hi collected his precious toy, then waved it over a rough patch of dirt close by.

DING DING DING!

"Bingo!" Hi shouted. "The bloody thing works!"

CHAPTER 2

Twenty minutes later, Hi's shovel thunked something solid.

"Finally!" Dropping to a knee, he used his fingers to trace an object at the bottom of the hole we'd dug. "Why bury it so freaking deep?"

"About time." Shelton tossed his spade aside. "How many of these —" his hand rose, "—*things* have you found, anyway?"

"They're called geocaches, and this is my third." Hi was carefully prying a grime-covered mass from the earth. "The other two weren't buried, just hidden. The first was on Morris, near the bridge. The second was jammed in a hedge next to the Folly Beach post office."

"The post office?" I peered over Hi's shoulder, trying to get a look. "That's so random. Why put something there?"

"That's how it works." Working methodically, Hi teased our find from the soil. "You hide a cache somewhere, anywhere, and post the GPS coordinates online. Then other players download the info and try to find it."

"This game is popular?" Ben was sitting on his tackle box in the shade of a large elm. "Sounds pretty nerdtastic to me."

"We can't all practice birdscalls like you." Hi brushed dirt from what appeared to be a plastic container. "There are millions of geocaches hidden worldwide, and dozens of websites listing where to find them. So, yeah, the game's kind of a hit."

"Back off, Blue." Shelton flashed a toothy grin. "Hi found more buried treasure. We're in business. I knew this was a good idea."

My eyes rolled at Shelton's abrupt one-eighty.

"The contents won't be valuable," Hi warned. "The point is the *finding*, not the getting. What's inside is usually trivial."

"That I can believe," Ben quipped. Shelton threw him a long-distance high five.

Ignoring their trash talk, I helped Hi wipe away the remaining grit. "Looks like some work went into this one."

The cache was roughly the size of a shoebox and carefully sealed with masking tape. The exterior was bright purple, and covered with dancing clown stickers. Wide grins stretched their contorted, cartoonish faces.

"Clowns," Shelton mumbled. "I hate those goofy bastards."

Hi nodded sagely. "I read *It* last summer. Stephen King. Never trust anything that paints on a smile."

"You guys are such dopes." Ben pulled a pocketknife from his cargoes and tossed it in Hi's direction. "Let's see what Bozo wanted you to find."

Hi made a fumbled catch, then flipped out the single blade. Four strokes cut the tape and freed the lid.

"More gold, perhaps?" Shelton winked. "There's a new X-Box due out this year."

"It won't be valuable," Hi repeated. "Just enjoy the sense of accomplishment."

"Right." Ben, straight-faced. "Accomplishment."

"Enough." I snapped my fingers. "Open sesame."

The container held two items: an envelope and a small, cloth-wrapped bundle.

Hi handed me the former and focused on the latter. "Here goes nothing."

The bundle contained a second rectangle composed of small, interlocking pieces of plum-colored metal. Cigar box–sized, the object had been hand painted with more leering, cavorting clowns.

But these clowns didn't smile. They scowled. Snarled.

The effect was eerie.

"Creepy." Hi rotated the box in his hands. "And no way to open it."

Coop nosed forward to sniff the box. I reached down to scratch his ears. Felt them flatten beneath my fingers.

A low growl rose from the wolfdog's throat.

"What's wrong, boy?" I tried to stroke his muzzle. "Something got you spooked?"

Coop whined, clearly agitated. His gaze flicked to Hi. To the box. Back to Hi.

"I don't like how Bow Wow is looking at me." Hi took a nervous step back. "I come in peace, soul brother."

"Coop, heel!" I ordered. "Be good."

The wolfdog yapped twice, eyes never leaving Hi. Then he circled to sit by my side.

"Read the letter," Shelton suggested. "It must explain the box."

My fingers rubbed the envelope. The stationery was thick, cream-colored, and obviously pricey. The flap was sealed with scarlet wax. The only marking was a majestic capital *G* penned in ornate calligraphy.

"*G*?" I glanced at Hi. "Does that mean anything?"

"For geocache, maybe?" Hi shrugged. "All I know is, whoever buried this went to *a lot* more effort than most players. It's gotta be a good cache."

"So open it," Shelton pressed.

Breaking the seal, I parted the envelope and removed two sheets of lilac-colored paper. High-grade bond. Excellent quality.

The first page was decorated with another elaborate, whirling *G* that ended with a single line running horizontally across the page.

"I guess that's the log sheet," Hi said.

I checked the back, but it was blank. "So we're the first to find this cache?"

Hi nodded. "There wasn't much info online. No clues, no past history, not even a record of who buried it. Just coordinates. It's the first cache ever listed for Loggerhead, so I'm not surprised it's never been logged before."

"And the other page?" Ben asked.

The second sheet contained a single phrase written in the same grandiose style: *Himitsu-Bako.*

"*Himitsu-Bako,*" I read aloud. "Anyone?"

"Chinese?" Hi mused. "Japanese? Burmese?"

Blank faces. No one knew.

"What now?" Shelton asked. "Sell it on eBay?"

Hi hefted the delicate box in one hand. Something rattled inside.

"I think this thing opens," Hi said. "We're supposed to figure out how."

"Then bag it." Ben yawned loudly. "This sideshow has been a snooze from the start."

"Philistine." Hi removed a wrinkled *Sports Illustrated* swimsuit issue from his backpack. "It's all I have to trade," he said with a shrug.

"Do we sign these or something?" I held up the first page from the envelope.

Hi considered. "Sign the *G* and put that sheet back, but keep the second one. The phrase is probably some kind of clue."

Pulling a pen from my pocket, I scribbled my name on the horizontal line and placed the paper inside the container next to the magazine. "Not exactly a fair trade, Hi."

"I know. Anyone have something to add?"

"Here." Shelton walked over and dropped in his battered green Timex. "This watch is low-rent. Plus I'm getting a new one for my birthday anyway. But you owe me, Stolowitski."

"Owe you what?" Hi said. "Who wears a wristwatch anymore? Cavemen?"

Satisfied with our swap, I closed the container and dropped it back into the hole. Ben and Shelton grabbed the shovels and quickly reburied it.

Hi was sticking the metal box in his bag when another growl caught his attention.

Cooper. Inches away. Teeth exposed.

"Yikes." Hi dropped the pack. "I thought we were bros!"

"No. Look." I pointed. Coop's attention was focused on the backpack.

Muscles tense, the wolfdog snuffled the bag, whined, sniffed again, and then began to growl.

"Must not be a geocache fan," Shelton cracked as he scooped up Hi's metal detector and switched off the power.

"The mutt's not alone," Ben mumbled.

"You guys are a riot," Hi said. "Laugh a minute. Now someone call off the attack dog."

I whistled for Coop's attention. "Here."

Reluctant, Coop gave Hi's bag one last pass, then trotted to my side.

"Coop really doesn't like that box." I knelt and rubbed the edgy wolfdog's snout. "It better not be stuffed with dead squirrels or something."

"Wouldn't surprise me at all," Ben grumbled, but he shot me a wink. He was just winding up Hi.

"It's not a rodent coffin!" Hi huffed. "This cache is legit. You'll see, haters."

"Okay, kids." I hoisted my fishing gear. "Let's call it a day. Kit wanted me back at LIRI a half hour ago."

"Can't upset the Big Boss Man," Shelton said. "Let's hustle."

One by one, we trooped from the clearing.

CHAPTER 3

LIRI's back gate rolled open with a soft whir.

"Come on if you're coming," Carl grumbled. A shade over five feet and weighing three hundred pounds, the ruddy-cheeked guard seemed winded by his short walk across the compound. "The magnets only release for thirty seconds."

"Thanks, Carl," I said cheerfully, familiar with his prickly demeanor. "Sorry to drag you out here. I wish Kit hadn't ordered these new auto-locks."

"Director Howard must've had his reasons." Carl's tone implied that we Virals might be primary among them.

As we passed through the reinforced perimeter fence, Carl punched numbers into a newly installed digital keypad. The gate closed behind us. Above, a pair of security cameras swiveled to track our movement.

"Can I assume you four won't be back out this way today?" Carl asked. "I'm getting tired of tramping across the courtyard."

"We're taking off," Hi said. "You can hit the gym early."

Carl gave Hi a level look, sky blue security uniform stretching precariously over his massive bulk.

"We'll be heading home shortly." I shoulder-barged Hi down the path. "I just need to see my father for a minute. Thanks again!"

Carl waddled in the direction of Building Four, muttering about the foolishness of youth.

"Making rounds of the vending machines," Shelton whispered. "They require constant security coverage."

"Moron." Ben had already started walking.

LIRI consists of a dozen glass-and-steel structures surrounded by an eight-foot-high chain-link fence. Aligned in two rows, the state-of-the-art buildings flank a well-tended central courtyard. Only two access points exist: a large front gate leading to the island's single dock, and the smaller portal at the rear. The complex contains nearly every permanent construction on Loggerhead.

Crossing the courtyard, I was struck again by the bustle of the place. A dozen white-coated scientists dotted the grounds, some hustling between labs, others clustered around benches discussing research, snacking, or just enjoying the afternoon sun.

Since Kit had assumed the directorship, LIRI buzzed with a new energy and sense of purpose. The staff had doubled; rare were the days you could cross the grounds without encountering a preoccupied veterinarian hurrying to update a project. With its funding permanently secured, LIRI was, once again, one of the premier wildlife research facilities on the planet.

"Do we have to go in?" Hi hand-shaded his eyes to peer at Building One. Four floors high, it was LIRI's biggest, housing the most sophisticated lab and the institute's administrative headquarters. "My dad's retooling the centrifuges, and won't be happy to see me inside."

Hi's father, Linus Stolowitski, was LIRI's chief laboratory technician, having been promoted by Kit the previous month. Since assuming the post, Mr. S had become more officious about Morris Island teens fiddling with facility equipment.

"Quit moaning," Shelton said. "*Both* my parents are in there."

Nelson Devers, Shelton's father, was LIRI's IT director. His office was on the ground floor. Shelton's mother, Lorelei, was a vet tech working in Lab One.

"It'll only take a sec," I said. "Lately Kit's so busy, I almost never see him."

It was true. In the two months since Kit had been named director he'd worked nonstop. Board meetings. Staff assemblies. Budget conferences. Though running himself ragged, Kit seemed happy. Ditto every worker at the institute.

On Loggerhead Island, Kit was practically a god.

When lack of funding had threatened to shut LIRI down, Kit's generosity had saved the day. At least, that's what everyone thought.

No one but Kit knew who'd really bankrolled the institute. That the boys and I had discovered and donated the she-pirate Anne Bonny's lost treasure to LIRI. That those underfoot teenagers had actually kept LIRI's doors open.

And the Virals were just fine with that.

The less scrutiny *we* received, the better.

"Wait here, boy." I attached Coop's rarely used leash and looped it around a railing beside the entrance. "No wolfdogs allowed."

Coop dropped to his belly, chin on paws, disapproval clear in his eyes. At seventy pounds and still growing, he was a sizeable animal. His half-wolf pedigree gave him a fearsome look, right up until he licked your face. I suspected he'd spook a few squints while he waited for us to return.

No big deal. A little something to spice up their day.

Passing through hermetically sealed doors, we approached the security kiosk. The other half of LIRI's frontline defense manned the desk. Sam was Carl's polar opposite, skeleton gaunt and completely bald.

Though older, and terminally sarcastic, he was usually the more congenial of the two.

"Ah, the vagrants return." Sam's lips twitched in a half smile. "Break anything expensive today?" He wasn't holding a shooting or hunting magazine, which could only mean one thing — his new boss was nearby.

On cue, a voice boomed from an office behind Sam's desk. "State your business."

Security Chief David Hudson emerged. Forty-something, graying, hair buzzed to his scalp, Hudson had the unyielding glare of a bird of prey. His uniform was neatly pressed, his shoes and name tag gleaming.

After recent events, Kit had decided to completely overhaul LIRI's security. New fences. New cameras. New locks. Updated protocols. Better equipment. And a hard-ass security supervisor to oversee it all. On the job less than a month, Hudson was proving to be Kit's least popular upgrade.

"I need to see my father, Mr. Hudson," I said politely. "Just a fast word."

"Wait." Hudson snatched a clipboard from the countertop. "Sign, please."

"I really won't be long," I said, beaming my most disarming smile. "I don't want to clutter your official records with a quick pop-in."

Finger tap. "Sign."

Locking my lips in the upright position, I scribbled my name. "Good?"

Hudson didn't smile. Never did. "No side trips."

Nodding obediently, we started toward the elevators.

"Halt!"

My eyes closed briefly before I turned. "Yes?"

"Just you." Hudson's gaze scanned Hi, Shelton, and Ben. "Unless these boys also have business?"

"Nope." Ben walked back outside.

"Mr. Hudson," I began, "we're just going to —"

"It's cool, Tory." Shelton headed after Ben, a head-shaking Hi at his heels. "We'll wait with Coop."

"Thanks, guys. Five minutes, tops." I raised my eyebrows at Hudson. He snapped off a curt nod.

I strode to the elevator, entered, and pressed the button for the fourth floor.

"No side trips!" Hudson barked again, as the doors slid shut.

"Jackass," I muttered, before remembering Hudson's cameras still tracked me.

The elevator stopped at the second floor, admitting two white-coated men. I knew the taller one by name.

"Hi, Anders." I tried not to blush.

"Tory. Off to see the Wizard?"

With pale green eyes and curly brown hair, Anders Sundberg was easily LIRI's most handsome employee. Just a shade past thirty, a former Olympic swimmer, he looked like a taller, buffer Justin Timberlake. In other words, pretty hot.

Anders had joined Kit's marine biology team the previous summer, adding a specialization in sea turtle habitats. Since Kit's promotion he'd been running the department on a provisional basis. His selection had ruffled some feathers among the senior PhDs, but, by all accounts, the guy was doing a good job. The position was his to lose.

"I'm assuming you mean Kit," I said, "so yeah."

"He's the one behind the curtain, pulling all the strings." Anders grinned. "The great and powerful Dr. Howard!"

The other man appeared a decade older than Anders. He had thinning black hair styled in a bad comb-over, close-set eyes, and a nose about an inch too long. His foot tapped impatiently as he waited for the doors to close.

"This barrel of laughs is Mike Iglehart." Anders elbowed his companion. "Say hello to Tory Brennan."

"Nice to meet you," Iglehart said blandly. "Is there a field trip on the island or something? I don't think you're supposed to leave the group."

He promptly lost interest, refocusing on Anders. "I need more bandwidth on the mainframe. The Triton program can only run half-time as it is. If we're going —"

"This is Director Howard's daughter, Mike. You might want to show a bit more courtesy."

"Kit's little girl, eh?" Iglehart really looked at me for the first time. "You must be thrilled about your father wrangling the director's office. It's too bad *I* didn't find a lost fortune."

My lips parted, but words didn't form. What was this guy's problem?

The elevator beeped our arrival on the third floor. The door opened, and Iglehart strode out without a backward glance.

"Don't mind him." Anders actually winked. "Mike came to LIRI about the same time as your dad, and hasn't exactly flown up the corporate ladder. Chalk the attitude up to sour grapes."

"No sweat." I tried for breezy, found myself standing straighter in response to Ander's undivided attention. "Have a good one."

"I'm dissecting a three-week-old turtle carcass," Anders said as the doors slowly closed. "How could I not?"

"*Have a good one,*" I repeated to the empty car. "You're such a dork, Brennan."

The elevator continued to the top floor. I exited into a short hallway leading to a pair of frosted-glass doors. The director's suite. Under Karsten, this whole area had been a ghost town. Abhorring distraction, he'd kept every office empty but his own.

Not so, Kit. The floor now hummed with activity, every workspace occupied or held open for guest researchers. Inside the director's suite, Kit had assembled LIRI's business-side officers. Fund-raising. Marketing. Public Relations. Trust Management.

I'd once asked Kit why he put up with so much distraction in his suite. "Better the pencil pushers are jammed in with me than bothering active scientists," he reasoned. "And I want these people out here on Loggerhead, not in cozy downtown high-rises. It'll help them remember what we're actually doing."

Passing through the doors, I encountered my last obstacle: Cordelia Hoke.

The Dragon.

Under Karsten, Hoke had been the only other employee stationed on the fourth floor. Though less than pleased by Kit's disruption of her once-private kingdom, she tried to keep it to herself. And usually failed.

Hoke as Kit's personal secretary? My guess, he was too chicken to let her go.

Kit had tried to stop Hoke's hourly puff break — LIRI was, and always had been, a smoke-free facility — but even *I* knew she still snuck a cig every chance she got. But that was less than under the previous regime.

The nicotine cutback hadn't improved the Dragon's temperament. She glared at me over the rims of her bifocals.

"May I help you, Tory?" Her tone suggested the opposite intent.

"I was hoping to snag Kit for a moment."

"Your father's very busy." Hoke shifted her impressive bulk, wiping cookie crumbs from the sleeves of her ragged cashmere sweater. She had one for each day of the week. Today was violet. "He can't come running every time you stub a toe."

Grrrr.

"I'd like to speak with him about his dinner plans."

Blank face. No response.

"So that I can make *my* dinner plans."

Nothing.

"Look, just tell my dad I'm here."

Hoke's face darkened. "Honey, in *my* day a young lady didn't speak to her elders like that. We were taught *manners.*"

I was about to further reduce her opinion of my upbringing when the shade to Kit's office rose. My father stood on the opposite side of the glass, phone to ear, a bored expression on his face. His charcoal suit and maroon tie were a far cry from the scuffed white lab coat that, until this year, he'd worn every working day of his life.

Kit made "can't talk now, I'm tied up, please feed yourself" motions with his hands. Nodding, I waved good-bye.

Kit shook his head ruefully, mouthed, "Sorry."

I gave him a thumbs-up, smiling to convey my understanding.

Hoke cleared her throat. "Will there be anything else?"

"Nope." I was already headed for the door.

CHAPTER 4

D r. Michael Iglehart strode the hall, ignoring his companion.

Dr. Sundberg prattled on about login issues and allocating server space, but Iglehart had checked out.

The Brennan girl rankled him. Now he had an errand to complete.

"I can only offer runtime after hours," Sundberg continued. "The backup is temporary — we'll have expansion packs in place by early next month. Dr. Howard has signed orders doubling our computing capacity."

"Wonderful." Choking back the bile in his throat.

Having to ask Anders Sundberg for permission was insult enough. Needing Kit Howard's authority was almost intolerable.

Life is never fair. Ever.

Iglehart had joined LIRI before either of these imbeciles. The three of them had nearly identical CVs. Now one ran his department, and the other headed the entire freaking institute!

And why? Because Kit Howard found a treasure in some sinkhole.

And what, pray, for Dr. Iglehart? Nothing. Zilch. Nada. The two frauds assumed he'd be *grateful* just to retain his position.

On that count, they'd miscalculated. Badly.

"Mike?"

Iglehart's attention snapped back to the present. He'd walked right past the conference room.

"Staff meetings still take place in here." Sundberg grinned, holding the door. "And don't worry about Triton, we'll get you squared away."

Iglehart forced a smile. "Sorry. I've forgotten a file I'll need. Won't be a moment."

"Sure." Sundberg waved a hand. "I can hold off for five. Take your time."

"Thanks." *Such graciousness from his lordship.* "Back in two shakes."

Iglehart hurried to his phone booth–sized office and pressed the space bar on his computer.

How he hated the cramped, windowless dungeon. Metal desk. Straight back chair. Soulless institutional bookshelves. Never enough space. To do any real research, he was forced to hunt for open conference rooms.

Which meant endless interruptions by the idiots working around him. Idiots with *bigger* offices. Galling.

So he'd taken steps. Howard and Sundberg thought him content to eat whatever scraps fell from their tables? Think again.

Howard had been director for two months, yet here Iglehart remained. Stuck in a broom closet with a second-rate Dell.

Not for long.

Agitated, he tapped the keyboard again. The institute's logo finally appeared on-screen. Entering the backdoor code he'd been given in secret, Iglehart accessed LIRI's mail server and deactivated the security protocols. Safely off the grid, he began to type.

The email was short and to the point. He knew what his contact wanted, even if the reasoning escaped him.

Iglehart pressed send, reset the protocols, and slapped his laptop shut.

You shouldn't have ignored me, Kit.

Wearing a satisfied smirk, Iglehart hurried to meet the coworkers he despised.

CHAPTER 5

I sensed trouble the moment I turned my key.

Coop shot inside and up the short flight of stairs to our townhome's small living room. Where he froze, tail erect and bristling.

Only one thing caused that reaction in my wolfdog: Kit's gal pal.

Blargh.

I trudged up the steps to see Whitney Dubois scootched to one end of my couch, eyeing Coop as she might an intruding ax murderer.

Mascaraed eyes darted in my direction. "Tory, control this creature!"

"Relax." I clicked my tongue. Coop glanced my way, padded to his doggie bed, circled three times, and sat. "He's just surprised to find you here. In our house. Alone. Unannounced."

"I came to *feed* you." Manicured hands poofed her salon-blonde hair. "Lord knows what you've been eating lately. Your daddy spends *far* too much time at work. And on the weekend, no less!"

"Kit's the director," I said flatly. "It's a demanding position."

"But that makes him the boss." Whitney's nose crinkled as her deep blue eyes filled with incomprehension. "Can't he leave whenever he wants?"

"That's not how it works." I suppressed a sigh. "To get LIRI back on its feet, Kit has a thousand details to square away. He's chairing board meetings, managing the expansion, all while still overseeing day-to-day operations. Plus, he has responsibilities to the trust. It's a huge job right now."

"He should delegate." Whitney's voice carried the conviction of someone with no idea what she's talking about. "Be more proactive."

"He can't." This time, the sigh escaped. "Kit will be very busy until LIRI is finally straightened out. That's going to be months, not weeks."

Kit had talked with me about this before accepting the post. At length. I'd given my full approval — Kit becoming LIRI's director meant no one had to move. That my friends' parents' jobs were safe, too. To keep everyone in Charleston, I'd have agreed to *much* worse than an overly busy father. Anything to preserve my pack.

Apparently Kit had failed to have the same conversation with Whitney.

"He needs to spend more time with his family," she said firmly.

That's me, not you.

"Whatever." Something else had snagged my attention.

Throw pillows littered the couch on which Whitney lounged with her half-eaten peach. Lime green ones, with swirling pink embroidery.

New. Frilly. *Definitely* not a Kit purchase.

I scanned the room, noted other troubling developments.

There, on the bookshelf: a black-and-white porcelain vase. And on the mantel: the picture of Kit's bowling team had been replaced by a framed shot of Kit and Whitney on the beach, wearing identical blue sweaters.

Other minor changes dotted the living room. A small ficus. Ceramic bookends. A wicker magazine caddy.

What the hell?

Kit and I share a townhouse on Morris, a four-square-mile island forming the south half of the entrance to Charleston Harbor. It's a skinny, four-story home that goes up more than out. On the ground floor is an office and single-car garage. Our kitchen, dining, and sitting areas make up the second level, while floor three consists of sleeping quarters. Upon my arrival Kit moved into the one in back, giving me the larger front bedroom overlooking the ocean.

Our top floor is Kit's man cave — an impressive media center that opens onto a spacious outdoor roof deck with a stunning view of the Atlantic. Every scrap of furniture was purchased from the good folks at Pottery Barn or IKEA. All in all, it's nice, so long as you can handle all the stairs.

Our entire neighborhood consists of ten identical units built inside a 430-foot concrete structure formerly known as Fort Wagner — a remnant of the island's days as a Civil War outpost. The community is so small that even most locals think Morris is uninhabited. Save for us, it is.

No other modern structures exist. There's only one road — an unpaved strip of asphalt winding south through the dunes before crossing to Folly Island. Our sole lifeline to civilization.

The Loggerhead Trust had recently purchased the whole landmass, and leased the units to scientists working on Loggerhead. The Stolowitskis occupied one, as did the Blues and the Devers family, making my crew some of the planet's most isolated teenagers.

The remoteness on Morris keeps visitors to a minimum. Yet here was Whitney, loafing on my sofa, making herself at home.

And practicing interior design.

I felt a hot flash of anger. The peroxide queen had overstepped — she had no right to redecorate my home without asking. She didn't live there. Wasn't my mother.

Whoa. There it was. As the emotional wave struck, I fought back tears.

Backstory. I'd come to live with Kit nine months earlier, after a drunk driver killed Mom. The pain of her loss still lingered just below the surface. Most of the time. Until some trigger caught me off guard.

Like unauthorized throw pillows on my couch.

I first met Kit a week after the accident. We got off to a rocky start, but lately had managed to find some common ground. That is, when I wasn't busy getting shot at, or being arrested.

Kit once said I terrified him. He meant it in a good way. I think. Pretty sure.

Though light-years from a normal father-daughter relationship, we weren't total strangers anymore. Progress. Baby steps.

As if I know what a normal father-daughter balance is, anyway.

But one thing became clear straight off. On the topic of Whitney, we did not agree.

I found the woman vapid, tactless, nosy, and overbearing. To Kit she was pure enchantment. Go figure. Bottom line, I had to endure her presence.

So far, I'd mostly succeeded. Barely. But here she went again.

Talk to Kit later. No point arguing now.

Movement in my periphery distracted me. Coop, scenting food, had slunk to the edge of the coffee table.

Whitney noticed at the same time. "Back! Back!" Swatting downward with a cloth napkin. "Get away, you mongrel!"

Whitney smacked Coop's snout while simultaneously pressing herself deeper into the couch. Coop fixed her with an unblinking ice-blue stare, gray-brown fur bristling along his spine.

"Tory!" Whitney squealed. "He's going to attack!"

"Maybe." I walked into the kitchen and snagged a Diet Coke from the fridge. "Try to protect your throat."

"Tory!!!"

"Oh, relax." Though enjoying Whitney's discomfort, I knew Kit wouldn't share my amusement. "Coop, heel!"

The wolfdog trotted to my side and sat. I couldn't prove it, but I swear he looked pleased with himself.

Whitney straightened her clothes, rolled her eyes skyward seeking patience, then rose and walked into the dining room.

"It's dinnertime." Placing flatware on the table. "I brought catfish po'boys, Cajun style. Black-eyed peas on the side."

I'll give Whitney one thing — she knows good food. I could usually tolerate her company if bribed with Lowcountry deliciousness.

I'd nearly finished my po'boy when she blew it again.

"I spoke to the Women's Committee today." Daintily wiping glossy red lipstick from her teeth. "It's just not practical to return you to next year's cohort. The invitations have been printed, and an official roster has gone to the paper. You'll be making your debut this season after all."

My head dropped. "What? I'm only fourteen! I'll be the youngest deb by almost two years!"

Despite my fervent wishes to the contrary, I was being forced to take part in the grand Southern tradition of a debutante ball. Whitney's idea, though Kit had thrown in his full support. Some nonsense about me needing "more refinement" and extra "girl time." Like it was *my* fault no teenage XX-chromosomes lived on Morris Island.

I'd been attending cotillion classes for the past six months, learning massively important skills such as formal dance, standing up straight, the proper use of silverware, and the etiquette of hosting a tea party. I hated all the pretension, but there was no escape. Whitney was determined to mold me into a proper young lady.

Okay, it wasn't *all* bad. I'd made a few friends, and was getting more comfortable around Bolton Prep's ruling elite. Dressing up was kind of fun. Plus, the organization had a charitable focus, and we spent lots of time doing good works in the community.

But, by age, I should've been a *junior* debutante, with my debut taking place the following season.

"You're a bit early to the party, I admit, but it's not like you're set-ting a record." Her Southern drawl became aggrieved. "I pulled *a lot* of strings to advance you when we thought you'd have to move away from Charleston. It's simply too much to untie that bow now."

My thoughts were already leaping ahead. "When is the ball?"

"Friday after next." Whitney giggled excitedly. "We'll need to hustle, and you have some important decisions to make."

Uh-oh. "Such as?"

Whitney gave me an indulgent look. "Your marshals and ushers, Tory. You'll need to select escorts to the ball."

Call it avoidance. Call it willful blindness. Call it whatever you like.

I can honestly say this hadn't crossed my mind until that moment.

"What? Who? How many?"

"One of each, usually, but you can include more if you want. But you *must* have a marshal for your debut."

I gaped. Who in the world could I drag to this disaster? Why would anyone want to go?

Whitney, as usual, misread me completely.

"I agree it's a very significant decision. So take some time to think. But I need your choices soon, sweetheart. The invitations will be late, as is, and the boys need to rent tuxedos if they don't already own them."

Whitney pushed from the table and began stacking dishes. I mum-bled thanks and retreated upstairs to my room. Flopping onto my bed, I couldn't shake that single, nagging question.

Who?

Whitney's delusions aside, I didn't view this as a prime dating oppor-tunity. I didn't even want to go. Like most cotillion events, I'd probably spend the ball avoiding crowds and trying not to embarrass myself. My goal was to *survive* these things, not make a love connection.

Small confession: I'd never had a quote-unquote boyfriend. Don't get me wrong, I wasn't a convent case or anything — I used to kiss

Sammy Branson behind the Dunkin' Donuts back in Westborough, even though Mom thought he was a total slacker. But I'd never dated anyone seriously. Or even officially.

When could I have? Mom and I had bounced around central Massachusetts for most of my childhood, never staying too long in one place. She'd been my only constant. I was only thirteen when the car accident happened, Mom died, and I was shipped down south to live with Kit.

My first year in Charleston hadn't been designed for romance. At Bolton Prep I'd been an outcast from day one — a geeky freshman transfer, on scholarship, a year younger than everyone else. How many strikes was that?

I'd had nothing in common with my classmates. My father wasn't a member of seven country clubs, or on the board of a local hospital. Most of the attention I'd received hadn't been the pleasant kind.

Outside of school, my world consisted of remote islands, Kit, and my packmates. No prospects there. While Hi, Shelton, and I were as close as friends can be, the idea of any brewing romance would've sent us into hysterics. Not gonna happen.

Ben, though. Ben was . . . different. I could admit it to myself, if not to anyone else. He was older, more worldly, and undeniably handsome. The only potential swimmer in Morris Island's microscopic dating pool. I'd even had a slight crush on him when I'd first moved down here.

But ever since the sickness, and the emergence of our abilities, we'd become a pack. To me, pack was family.

It was better that way. Cleaner. Safer.

"Blargh."

I stared at my notes, no closer to answering Whitney's question.

I needed a date.

But who?

CHAPTER 6

The locker beside mine banged shut.

"Why do we have calculus first thing?" Hi was fiddling with his tie. "Doesn't the faculty understand you have to ease into a school day?"

Monday morning. Bolton Preparatory Academy. 7:26 a.m.

First bell was minutes from sounding.

I was back in uniform: blue tartan-plaid tie with matching pleated skirt, white blouse, black knee socks, and simple black shoes. I wasn't a fan, but the uniform policy kept the richer girls from morphing Bolton's hallways into daily episodes of *Project Runway*. I was grateful for the trade-off.

"Better to get it done early." I shut my door and spun the combination lock. "Besides, I like math — there are no tricks, you just have to learn the rules."

"The rules *are* tricks." Ben sported the standard male uniform — navy blazer with griffin crest, white button-down shirt, maroon tie, tan slacks, and loafers. "When the problems dropped the equals sign, math stopped making any sense."

"There's Shelton," Hi said, blazer was in his trademark style: inside out, with the silk lining exposed. The teachers had given up trying to make him wear it properly. "He had enough time after all."

"Got it!" Shelton was puffing hard, a calculus book tucked under one arm, his uniform a disheveled mess. "Sprinting back to the docks takes longer than I thought. Next time I'll just borrow a text and get mine from your dad later."

"Told you," Ben said. His father, Tom Blue, shuttled us to and from downtown on school days. "You're lucky *Hugo* was still there. My dad's usually on his second run to Loggerhead by now."

As a perk for parents living way out where ours did, LIRI provided tuition for their children to attend Bolton Prep, Charleston's most prestigious private school. Shelton, Hi, and I were two months into our sophomore year, while Ben was beginning his junior campaign. Since driving to campus would take an hour each way, LIRI also provided daily boat service. Not a bad deal.

If we fit in. Which we didn't.

Most Bolton students were scions of the city's wealthiest families. My crew stuck out like hookers at church. We weren't part of their pampered, privileged world, and many of our classmates were quick to remind us of that fact. Taunting the "boat kids" was practically a varsity sport.

Thankfully, this year Shelton, Hi, and I had identical schedules, and Ben was in half our classes. We'd be able to watch each other's backs.

For a group of science geeks, Bolton was a minefield of potential disasters. Double that for me, since I was also the youngest in my class. Impressed by my lower-school brilliance, Mom had decided I should skip the sixth grade. Fast-forward four long years — I was Bolton's only fourteen-year-old sophomore.

The mocking had started from day one. And when my classmates discovered that "the little girl" was actually setting the academic bar, the sniping grew even nastier.

Freshman year had been rough. I'd hated it.

But lately, things were . . . different.

My first year, other students had openly sneered at me. Whispered behind their hands. Called me "loser," or "island refugee," even "peasant." High school bullies can be brutal, and I'd caught both barrels.

The constant ridicule had forced me to step lightly. Drop my guard, even for a nanosecond, and the local Mean Girls would pounce to "put me in my place."

But that was all before the summer.

Before I'd finally had enough, and decided to fight back.

Before I'd lost my cool.

As if cued by my thoughts, my nemeses appeared two doors down.

Madison Dunkle sauntered into the hall, flanked by her sycophant floozies. She practically glowed with well-groomed excess, from sculpted hair — brunette this semester, with smoky blonde tendrils — to stylish, five-figure jewelry.

Courtney Holt was on her left. Blonde, blue-eyed, and curvy, she radiated a cluelessness that was impossible to emulate. She'd been chosen as the captain of the cheerleader squad. I was amazed she'd avoided flunking out.

On Madison's opposite side strolled Ashley Bodford, a pit viper in her own right. Night to Courtney's day, Ashley had glossy black hair, mechanically tanned skin, and a cruel streak a mile long. Her favorite activity was preying on the insecurities of others with cutting, whispered digs.

The Tripod of Skank.

They hated me. I *loathed* them.

Last semester, the sight of these three would've filled me with dread. They'd made my freshman year a living hell.

That was over now.

Last August, at a cotillion event, I'd unloaded on the Tripod with all of Bolton's in-crowd watching. Flaring, I'd used my hypersenses to read their emotions. Sniff out their weaknesses. Then I'd struck without mercy.

Shocked speechless, the Tripod had retreated in angry tears.

The tell-off had been *epic.*

Since that outburst, the other "cool kids" had been slightly more respectful to me. Almost polite. Not out-and-out friendly or anything, but the open hostility was gone.

High school popularity is so fickle.

My classmates suddenly liked me more because I'd shown teeth. Because I'd savaged a few of their own. I could scream at the childishness of it all.

That day, I'd finally bested the Tripod. But then I made a mistake.

Unleashing the wolf had gotten my blood pumping. Flaring seemed to exacerbate my aggressive nature. Caught up in the rush, I'd done something incredibly foolish. Disastrous. I'd lifted my sunglasses and flashed my glowing eyes.

Courtney and Ashley had missed it, but Maddy had enjoyed a front-row seat. Terrified, she'd bolted. And had avoided me ever since.

Normally, I'd call that a win-win. The Tripod had fled and continued to stay away. The relentless harassment had stopped.

But I worried. What did Madison suspect? Who would she talk to?

If word of our powers got out, we'd be government lab rats by lunch the next day.

Thanks to my stupidity, Madison was a threat.

At that moment, the threat caught sight of me. Her face paled and she slowed.

Ashley and Courtney bumped into Madison from behind. Confused by their queen bee's hesitation, they followed her sight line.

Gripping her books tightly, Madison fired past me and ducked into a bathroom. Courtney and Ashley hurried on her heels, shooting uneasy glances my way.

"Man." Hi had noted the exchange. "You've got Madison spooked, that's for sure. Let's hope she's not sending letters to *Cosmo*."

I'd told the Virals about my blunder. They hadn't been pleased. At all.

I was about to respond to Hi's comment when Jason Taylor rounded the corner.

"Tory." Jason began fidgeting with his tie. "I hope you're, uh, doing well. Had a good weekend, all that."

Ben's lips formed a smirk. Eyes rolling, he turned and walked off. Hi and Shelton drifted a few feet down the hall.

Jason had the blue eyes and white-blond hair of a Nordic god. The physique too. Big and strong, he was a sick athlete, and captained Bolton's lacrosse team. A truly decent guy, he'd been an ally at Bolton from the outset.

An ally with a surprising interest in me.

I'd never known how to feel about Jason. Still didn't.

Jason was the only guy at Bolton who seemed to notice me. He was cute. Friendly. Funny. Super popular. Everything a girl could want in a boyfriend. At least, I thought so, having no real experience in the field.

And yet . . . nothing. For some reason, Jason just didn't do it for me. I'd never felt the same attraction. My palms didn't sweat. My pulse didn't race. It made no sense. I couldn't explain it, even to myself.

Which made the situation . . . awkward.

I shouldn't complain — for most girls, Jason's attention would've been all that mattered. And I treasured him as a friend. He looked out for me at school, keeping the nastier trust-fund brats off my back.

"Hi, Jason," I said awkwardly. "My weekend was fine. You?"

"Me? Oh, great. Took the boat out, played golf. Nice weather, um, right?"

"Definitely." I shifted, needlessly adjusting my book bag straps. "Sunny."

Uneasiness around Jason was collateral damage from my reckless display. Flustered by my blunder with Madison, I'd been totally unprepared when Jason offered to escort me to the debutante ball. Angry with myself, I'd lashed out at him, too.

We didn't speak again until school started, and even then we'd carefully avoided that topic. The eggshell dance was moving into its second month, with no end in sight.

It didn't help that Madison had eyes for Jason, and viewed *me* as a rival.

And Ben seriously disliked him.

Nothing is ever simple.

The bell spared us further discomfort.

"Gotta run," I said, thankful for the reprieve. "See you later!"

"Later." Jason tossed a head-nod to Shelton and Hi as he passed them. The Two Stooges clumsily returned the gesture.

Shelton drifted back to my side wearing a sly grin. "That was smooth, player."

"Shut it."

The awkward conversation had reminded me of Whitney's instructions. I needed guys for my stupid debut, and didn't have a plan.

Jason had volunteered, but that was months ago, and I'd rejected his offer. Rudely. Did it still stand? Choosing an A-lister might be a good move. Jason had always defended me when he could.

But I totally embarrassed him. Why would he say yes now?

Shelton tapped his watch. "Today, Brennan."

Just then, Hi scurried across the hallway in a rush. "Did you guys hear the news?"

"What news?" Shelton tugged his earlobe, a nervous habit. "I already know I'm not going to like it."

"It's all over Twitter. He's out! They released him last weekend."

"Who?" But I knew.

Had no doubt.

"Chance Claybourne." Hi shook his head in disbelief. "He's coming back to Bolton."

CHAPTER 7

Tiny droplets splashed my arms.

Tom Blue's shuttle, *Hugo,* was kicking spray up into a fine mist. I stood alone in the stern, watching downtown recede as we churned home across the harbor.

My thoughts were of Broad Street, and a pricey piece of real estate known as Claybourne Manor.

I bet he's alone in that gigantic mansion. Right now.

I'd been unable to concentrate in class.

Chance Claybourne.

Out of the hospital.

Returning to Bolton Prep.

Guilt shrouded me like a cold, wet blanket. The awful thing I'd done. How I'd played with Chance's mind to protect our secrets.

And now he's back.

Ben's voice floated from behind me. "It's not like you had a choice."

"I know." I sighed, turned. Ben often knew what I was thinking. "But messing with his head. Making him think he was crazy. I've felt terrible ever since."

If not *the* richest man in Charleston, Chance was certainly high on the list. Son of former state senator Hollis Claybourne, and heir to an enormous family fortune, Chance's mental breakdown had been the scandal of the decade.

Chance had suffered a total nervous collapse, with every salacious detail reported in the press. He'd been hospitalized for five months — leaving only once, to help us search for a lost pirate treasure.

Twice Chance had witnessed our flare powers unleashed. He'd seen our canine speed. Our strength. Our glowing eyes.

After the second incident, Chance had approached me, confused and vulnerable. Needing answers.

Instead of helping him, I'd twisted the knife. Betrayed his trust.

To protect the Virals, I'd convinced Chance that he'd imagined the whole thing. That the images he described were unreal. Figments of a distressed mind. Frightened, and in shock, he'd returned to the psych ward for further treatment.

Your revenge.

I sat up straight. Where had *that* thought come from?

A fresh wave of guilt crashed over me. My own hurt feelings hadn't factored into deceiving Chance . . . had they?

At Bolton, Chance had been a different story from Jason. I'd *definitely* had R-rated thoughts about Charleston's richest son. Chance was gorgeous, refined, and genteel. Sculpted like a gladiator, with the manner of a prince. Like every other girl in school, I'd dreamed of watching the sunrise while wrapped in his arms.

Fool. That was all out the window now.

At the end of freshman year Chance had manipulated me, using my crush against me in an attempt to hide his dark family secrets. It had almost worked, too.

I'd long since squashed any attraction I might've had for young Master Claybourne. I thought. Hoped.

"Hey, they let him out, right?" Hi plopped down on the bench beside me, tie askew, navy blazer folded across his knees. "So he must be cured. No harm, no foul."

"I guess." So why did I feel like a backstabber?

"He's a freaking millionaire." Ben waved a dismissive hand. "He'll be fine."

"We've got unfinished business with Chance," I said, "but not today. Let's hit the bunker. I want inside that stupid clown box."

○   ○   ○

Once home on Morris, I changed into a polo shirt and shorts, whistled for Coop, then hurried back down to the dock. The boys were already waiting aboard *Sewee*. Shelton and Hi pushed off, and Ben wound us through the sandbars leading to open sea.

As we rounded the island's northern point, Ben throttled down. After glancing around to be sure we were alone, he angled sharply back toward shore and nosed *Sewee* through a gap in the rocks barely wider than her hull.

Stone outcroppings rose on both sides, creating a circular cove with a white sand beach. Added bonus. The towering projections concealed the cozy anchorage from view by passing watercraft.

As secret places go, this one was killer.

Ben tied *Sewee* to a sunken post. Shelton dropped the anchor. Hi, Coop, and I hopped ashore and took a steep, narrow path up the sand hill overlooking the hidden bay. Nearing the crest we turned right and circled the hill. I dropped to my knees, and crawled through a person-sized hole cut into the hillside.

We'd reached our clubhouse.

Once a key to Charleston's harbor defenses, Morris Island is riddled with old military fortifications. The boys and I had discovered our bunker by accident, chasing an errant Frisbee. Practically invisible, it could double as a CIA safe house.

To our knowledge, only we knew of the bunker's existence.

We intended to keep it that way, though lately that'd been tough.

A soft buzzing greeted my arrival in the main chamber. The air smelled of ozone, dust, and packaging peanuts.

After worming in behind me, Shelton dropped into the ergonomic chair fronting our new computer workstation. Honest to God, the thing looked like something out of *Star Trek*.

Shelton's fingers tapped the keyboard, another piece of high-tech wireless wizardry.

"Run the fans when the system's powered," I reminded him. "We don't want the components overheating."

"I'll only be a sec." Shelton reached below the desk and flipped a switch. "I need to check some software I added to the hard drive. This stuff will blow your mind."

Over the previous weeks, we'd transformed the place.

Pirate gold goes a long way, if you spend wisely.

Indoor-outdoor carpet covered the floor. A retractable window secured the cannon slit facing the harbor. Sleek IKEA units had replaced the rickety wooden furniture. The old bench still ran along the wall beneath the window, but Ben had sanded, polished, and treated the wood with a dark cherry stain. Three lamps glowed with soft white light.

A mini-fridge occupied one corner. Hi had insisted.

The rear chamber had also been overhauled.

The mineshaft and cannon slit were sealed. Days of sweat there. Cables running from the main room snaked metal shelves stuffed with external hard drives, routers, Ethernet switches, AV components, and other hardware, along with a line of rechargeable batteries.

The far corner was now a doggie hotel for Coop: bed, chew toys, and automatic food and water dispensers. He padded over, curled up, and promptly fell asleep.

After weeks of online searching and ordering, secret deliveries, backbreaking transport, and maddening assembly, our clubhouse was as capable as an air traffic control tower. And there was still a decent balance in our checking account.

Thank you, Anne Bonny.

"Did you fix the WiFi?" Hi asked as he rooted through the fridge. "I couldn't capture an IP address yesterday."

Shelton nodded. "Loose cord. The router wasn't drawing power from the gennie. It's all good now."

Our prize addition was a solar-powered generator. Outside in the scrub brush, we'd hidden a four-panel array above the bunker's entrance to collect daylight. With a half-dozen batteries storing the juice, we had electricity 24/7.

I worried about the array constantly — it was easily our most expensive purchase. But so far the system had weathered two storms without a hitch. It was a pricy piece of equipment to leave exposed, unguarded, but what can you do? Solar panels need sunlight to work. Plus, no one else knew it was there.

"Testing new software?" Ben glanced at our workstation's massive twenty-seven-inch LED cinema display. "More like downloading *Crank Yankers.*"

"I'm multitasking," Shelton replied. "All work and no play makes me bored silly."

"Don't use up too much drive space," I warned, watching the screen from over his shoulder. "We bought this stuff to research parvovirus, not so you can watch 'Boom Goes the Dynamite' twenty times a day."

We'd agreed on a specific goal for our funds: learn everything possible about the invader twisting our DNA. Our powers were wild, mostly a mystery. And with Karsten gone, no one else knew the virus existed. Finding answers was on us.

"Who has the box from the geocache?" I was eager to have a look.

"That'd be me." Hi removed it from his bag and placed it in on the table. We each took a chair. Then, as one, the boys turned to look at me.

"Don't mind if I do." I lifted and rotated the odd purple object. There was no obvious top, bottom, or locking mechanism. The snarling clowns were evenly spaced and uniform in size. And in creepiness. When I shook the box, something rattled inside.

After a few minutes of fruitless tapping and tinkering, I handed the thing to Ben. He squeezed sides, pressed edges, and rubbed the surface before passing it on. Hi poked and prodded for what seemed like forever before sighing and giving the box to Shelton.

"That's your best shot?" Shelton frowned in mock disapproval. "Weak sauce."

"Think you can do better?" Ben, only half joking.

"Not think, dude. *Know.*" Toothy grin. "I'm the man with a plan."

CHAPTER 8

"*Himitsu-Bako.*"

Shelton flourished the sheet of paper we'd found inside the geocache.

"Himso Bucko?" Hi's face scrunched in confusion. "What the what?"

"*Himitsu-Bako,*" Shelton repeated. "It's Japanese, means 'personal secret box.' That's what this gadget must be."

"So there *is* something inside." I grabbed the page, embarrassed to have forgotten it. "And the phrase is a clue on how to gain access?"

"Exactly." Shelton rose and moved back to the workstation. "I've been googling. Puzzle boxes like this originated in nineteenth-century Japan. Hakone region. They're designed as games, and usually contain a good luck charm."

"Great work, Wikipedia," Hi deadpanned. "Now how do we open it?"

"It's not that simple." Shelton rejoined us at the table. "*Himitsu-Bako* only open through a specific series of manipulations. Some you just squeeze in the right place, but others require several movements at once. Each box is unique. The trick is figuring out the sequence."

My eyes fixed on the dancing, sneering clowns. They seemed to leer back at me.

"Are these things typically metal?" I asked.

"Nope," Shelton said. "Wood, usually. This puppy's a modern version."

"Fascinating." Ben sat back and crossed his arms. "So what next?"

"I've got some ideas." Shelton trained his thick lenses on Ben. "Unless you wanna take lead?"

Ben raised both arms. "Your show, maestro."

"Damn right."

As Shelton centered the box before him, the rest of us watched in silence.

"I'll start with an easy one," Shelton said. "Four corners." His fingers pressed the closest two, then the pair across. No effect. He flipped the box and tried again. Nada.

Shelton grunted. "Top and bottom."

Holding the box between his palms, Shelton squeezed, slid his hands forward and backward. Strike two.

"Side to side."

Nope.

"Rotating top."

Nyet.

"Bottom drop."

Nothing doing.

All attempts were futile. The box remained stubbornly sealed.

Frustrated, Hi rose and wandered to the computer. "I'm gonna check my email."

"I'm going to kill myself," Ben muttered.

Shelton ignored them. "Only three sides will move. This rectangle piece — which is either the top or bottom — and both short, vertical ends."

"Does knowing that help?" Hiding my impatience. "Maybe include that in a search string?"

"On it," Hi called.

Moments later the printer hummed. Hi snagged the page and handed it to Shelton.

Shelton scanned the instructions, shrugged. "Might work."

Spinning the box so it faced him longwise, Shelton gently pressed the left side. The metal slipped down a few millimeters, then stopped. Holding that position steady with one hand, Shelton pushed the top of the box toward the right with the other.

"Put your finger here." Motioning me to hold the cover in place, Shelton switched ends and pushed the right side down as he'd done with the left. Thumbing that in place, he pushed the top of the box back toward the left.

This time, the cover slid all the way off.

The box was open.

"Yes!" I fist-bumped Shelton. "And nice work, Hi."

"There's a ton online about these boxes." Hi was scanning the list of hits. "Man, how did people do *anything* before the Internet?"

"They actually had to think," Ben replied. "Cheating wasn't so easy."

Ignoring the banter, I reached into the box and withdrew another thick cream envelope. Like the one before, it was adorned with the now-familiar swooping *G*, dancing clowns, and a wax seal.

"Our host has a unique sense of style," Hi said. "And spares no expense."

Suddenly, Coop popped into the room. Drawing close, he froze and growled.

"Coop, no!" I tried to rub his muzzle, but he shied away, barked, then lunged at the envelope.

"Down, boy!" Sharp. His reaction was somewhat unnerving. "Bad dog!"

Coop growled again, then crossed to a corner and sat. Silent as ordered, but eyes glued to the envelope.

"Must hate clowns," Shelton said.

"Who can blame him?" Hi said.

"I've never seen him act like this." Shaking my head, I cracked the envelope's seal and withdrew two more sheets of bond paper.

The first contained a black semicircular drawing that looked like a serrated, gap-toothed smile. Centered below the smile at its lowest point was a large black square. Ten rectangles were spaced along the curve of the semicircle, five to each side. Nine of the rectangles faced inward, like teeth on a cartoonish lower jaw. But the last rectangle on the left faced outward, on the exterior side of the arc. A snaggletooth.

Below the strange image, a long string of numbers stretched across the page.

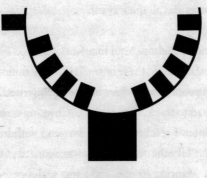

32 773645 -00 065437

"Wonderful," Hi said. "Another wacky clue."

The second page was styled as a letter, but the words were nonsense. The only legible portion was an elaborate signature at the bottom.

The Gamemaster

"Excuse me?" Shelton pulled his earlobe. "Who the hell is the Gamemaster?"

"A dork with *way* too much time on his hands," Ben answered.

I tapped my lip in thought. "The body of this letter is gibberish, but we're clearly supposed to read it."

"It's a code," Shelton said. "The message must be scrambled."

I flipped both pages over, checked the envelope, and rifled through the box. No other clues. "How are we supposed to decode this without a key?"

"Easy!" Shelton rubbed his palms theatrically. "We *break* that mug. And I know how to do it."

"Feeling pretty confident today, eh, tiger?" Hi leaned back in the astronaut chair. "Do tell."

"Using this." Shelton tapped a short string of characters just above the signature: Hrmxvivob.

"That's useful," Hi said. "Sounds like a sex position."

"Actually, that's the key." Shelton looked smug. "Look at where this word is. It stands alone, just above the sign-off, followed by a comma. Dead giveaway."

Nine characters, the first capitalized, followed by a comma.

Of course.

I stole Shelton's thunder. " 'Sincerely.' "

"It's gotta be, right?" Shelton tapped his temple. "And if we know a keyword, we can plug the whole thing into a cipher program for decoding."

"Internet, baby." Hi chuckled. "You make my heart sing."

"You're sure that will work?" Ben asked.

"No," Shelton said, "but I'm guessing it's a basic substitution cipher. My dad used to leave me coded notes like this when I was younger."

My mouth opened, closed. Hi grunted. Ben fixed Shelton with a squinty stare.

"Maybe you should explain a little more," I prodded.

"Look here." Shelton pointed to the keyword. "We all know how to spell 'sincerely,' right? The fifth and seventh letters are both *e*." He finger-jabbed the page. "In the scrambled keyword, the fifth and seventh letters are both *v*. So it looks like *v* and *e* are swapped in this cipher."

Okay. I could see that.

"In fact . . ." Shelton smiled wide. "I already cracked this sucker."

"BS." Ben, always the skeptic. "Prove it."

"Happy to." Shelton grabbed a blank sheet of paper and listed the alphabet. "I know *e* is the fifth letter in the alphabet. Guess where *v* is?"

"Twenty-second." My gray cells made the connection. "Fifth from last."

"Exactly. This is an inversion cipher. *A* and *z* flip-flop, so do *b* and *y*, *c* and *x*, and so on, working toward the middle. Check it out. The last letter in the keyword is *b*. That replaces *y*."

"All right," Ben said. "I'm officially impressed."

"Don't be, this formula's super easy." Shelton began scrawling letters, decoding the message. "Just give me a sec."

I leaned close to observe. Shelton's eyes rose to meet mine.

"A minute, Tor?" Finger-shoving his glasses back up his nose. "This is more difficult if you micromanage."

I stepped backed, mildly offended, but not wanting to slow the process. I crossed to Coop and rubbed his head. The wolfdog was still tense and agitated.

"It's okay, boy. Clowns are dumb, aren't they?"

Patting him one last time, I joined Hi at the computer for a game of Angry Birds.

Five minutes dragged by. Then five more.

"Done." Shelton's voice was tight, tense. "I won't lie, this message gives me the willies."

From deep in the corner, Cooper rumbled another low growl.

CHAPTER 9

The message was short.

Four sentences. Thirty-eight words. It took mere seconds to read.

> *Adventurous Souls,*
>
> *Congratulations! You've passed The Test, and have proven yourself worthy of The Game. My challenge is simple: Do you have what it takes to play? Follow the clues and unlock the ultimate surprise.*
>
> *Sincerely,*
> *The Gamemaster*

"Hmm." Hi scratched his chin. "Okay, that's not normal."

"What do you mean?" A scowl crimped Ben's features. "I thought you understood this geocaching nonsense."

"I do," Hi said primly. "And this isn't how it usually works."

"Explain." My arms folded across my chest.

"There are specific rules." Hi returned to the computer and began punching keys. "This is Geocaching.com, one of the main websites." A green and blue homepage appeared on-screen. "It lists the coordinates for all active caches, and any clues about how to find them."

"How many caches are out there?" Shelton asked.

Hi glanced at the monitor. "Currently, over 1.5 million. With five million players, worldwide."

"For real?" Shelton shook his head. "That's crazy!"

"*Soooo* many dorks," Ben muttered, his coal-black eyebrows forming a steep V. "A giant nerd army, digging up plastic boxes they hide for each other."

"Like everything *you* do is cool," Hi snorted. "Still have that ninja costume you wore to my twelfth birthday party?"

"Go back to what you said earlier," I insisted. Their trash-talking was wearing thin. "What isn't normal about this?"

"Let me show you." Hi spun back to the keyboard. "I'll record our discovery of the Loggerhead cache."

With varying degrees of enthusiasm, we crowded around the workstation.

"Enter a place-name, address, whatever, and the site compiles a list." Hi's fingers flew as he spoke. "Nearby caches are mapped. Last week I searched our zip code, and found a surprise."

A satellite image of Morris Island filled the screen. He pointed to a single red icon dotting the southwestern point.

"There. Someone planted a cache inside the Morris Lighthouse. I found it a few weeks ago, tucked under the spiral stairs."

"That's trespassing." Ben sat back down at the table and began examining the decoded message. "The lighthouse is off-limits to the public."

"Never stopped us," Shelton replied with a grin.

Hi shrugged. "Anyone can log a cache into the database. The site doesn't police where a box is hidden, or if a player has permission to be there."

"What led you to Loggerhead?" I asked. "It doesn't even *have* a zip code."

"I figured, why not check? Maybe some LIRI guys play among themselves."

Using the cursor, Hi dragged the edge of the map eastward into the Atlantic until an outline of Loggerhead Island appeared. As on Morris, a lone red marker glowed, positioned near the base of Tern Point.

"This Gamemaster didn't include much information." Hi double-clicked the icon. "There's no difficulty rating. No size info. Not even a user name, which I didn't think was possible. Just an exact set of GPS coordinates and a clue: 'Be sure to scratch the surface.' "

"Here's how it *should* look." Hi moved back to Morris Island and moused over the lighthouse box. "See? This one has complete info. 'Danger Mouse' buried his prize three months ago, and rated the difficulty, terrain, and cache size all as fours on a one-to-five scale. There's also a page-long clue. That's how it's supposed to work."

"What did Danger Mouse hide?" I was curious.

"Toy sailboat," Hi said. "He didn't want exchanges, so I signed the log and put the cache back where I found it. Later I logged on here, reported a successful find, and posted a comment."

"Why bother?" Ben quipped. But I could tell he was paying attention.

"The website tracks your stats. How many you've found, how many times a cache has been located, stuff like that. It's cool, noob. Get on board."

"Anyone find the Loggerhead box before us?" I asked. "This letter could be old news."

"Nobody," Hi said. "At least, no one's recorded it online, which almost every player does. It's a pride point when you crack a new geocache."

"So *you* had to find it." Shelton wasn't asking.

"Um, *yeah*. In fact . . ." Hi navigated back to the Loggerhead cache. "I'm claiming first blood right now."

"How'd you know the cache would be buried?" I asked.

"The clue." Hi grinned. "And I really just wanted to use my metal detector. The coordinates indicated that clearing, so it seemed likely the cache would be underground."

"Wait a second." Shelton's brow furrowed. "You need a GPS device for this, right? To check the coordinates, make sure you're on target?"

Hi nodded.

Ben leaned forward and gave Hi a hard look. "So when you're out playing hide-and-seek, you're being tracked the whole time. That program must know you're *here*, right now. In our secret, hidden clubhouse."

That got my attention. Bad memories tumbled through my mind. Hi's game risked revealing the bunker's location. The thought made me nervous.

"Not true," Hi replied. "I log out when I'm not playing, so the GPS isn't active. Don't worry, I'm careful."

"You'd better be," Ben warned. "We've got too much invested in this place."

Uncomfortable with the sudden tension in the room, I glanced at the other piece of paper lying on the table. The smile-like image remained a mystery, but the numbers running beneath it jumped out at me: 32.773645 -00.065437.

A synapse formed.

"Guys." I scooped up the sheet. "If the Gamemaster's into geocaching, wouldn't he leave more coordinates to follow?"

Hi shot from the astro-chair. "Of course! We can plug those numbers into the database." He made "gimme" hands. I complied.

Hi punched in the digits and hit search.

No hits.

"Shoot." Hi scratched his temple. "The numbers don't match a listed cache."

Hi blew out his lips, then clicked "display coordinates." A world map appeared, with a red flag pinpointing the exact location.

Northern Algeria.

"Err." Hi grimaced. "Geeh."

Ben snorted. "Should I track down my passport?"

"I'm not down with hiking the Sahara," Shelton said. "So unless you know a good place for camel-riding lessons, I think we can rule this out."

"But these *must* be coordinates." Hi knuckle-rapped the desk in frustration. "It's the correct number of digits for longitude and latitude. The second set is negative, for Pete's sake! That can't be a fluke."

"Agreed." I distrust coincidence. "We're obviously missing something."

"This Gamemaster's not even playing right," Hi grumbled. "You're supposed to list caches separately, not send players from one to the next. That's a completely different game, and even then you'd put the log in the *last* box, not the first."

"Dude's playing you," Shelton said. "It's a wild-goose chase."

"I doubt that." Hi's fingers shot through his hair, forming a mohawk. "I mean, why bother? Why put all this together for no reason? Leaving things to be found is the whole point of the game."

A second insight occurred to me.

"The Gamemaster's message was coded," I said. "Maybe the numbers are, too."

"It's possible," Shelton agreed. "I can test some numerical ciphers tonight."

"Wait." Ben glanced from face to face. "We're actually going to pursue this nonsense? We suddenly care what this fruitcake hid in a box somewhere?"

Ben's question caught me off guard. When *had* I decided to play?

From the moment you read the letter.

"I'm in," I said. "I'll admit it, I want to solve the puzzle."

"Me too," Hi said quickly. "Let's take Mr. Creepy Clowns down to Chinatown."

Shelton shrugged. "Could be fun. I like breaking codes."

Ben shook his head. "Whatever."

I looked again at the Gamemaster's challenge.

The numerical string. The mysterious picture.

So we'd passed The Test, and were invited to play The Game?

Like I could turn *that* down.

"Bring it on," I whispered.

CHAPTER 10

A buzz in my pocket startled me.

Text. Kit. Get my butt home for dinner.

"Gotta run, guys. Someone scan and email that image. I want to study it tonight." I looked pointedly at Hi. "And remember to secure the bunker door. We can't let the humidity get too high in here."

"One time," Hi mumbled, feeding paper into the printer. "I'll never live it down."

"Can you run me back?" I asked Ben, who nodded. Hi and Shelton would have to walk the mile and a half back to our complex.

"Don't sweat it, ya'll." Shelton flexed his scrawny biceps. "I'll have this nut cracked by morning."

"I have no doubt." Flashing an exaggerated thumbs-up.

Coop, Ben, and I crawled outside and descended to the cove. Fifteen minutes later we'd secured *Sewee* to the Morris Island dock.

"Later, Tor." Ben headed for the townhouse he shared with his father. "I'll take a look at those numbers, too. Shelton's not the only one with ideas. Stay logged on."

"Will do. Thanks for the ride."

Patting my side for Coop to follow, I walked to our front door. Paused.

"What do you think, boy?" I scratched his muzzle. "Will Kit inflict us with her company again tonight?"

Coop cocked his head. A soft, pink tongue dropped from his mouth.

"Unfortunately, I agree. Gotta go inside anyway."

Our canine instincts were dead-on. Whitney was swishing around the dining room in a yellow sundress, setting the table.

At least the food will be good.

"Whitney. Great to see you." I plopped onto the couch. Cooper curled at my feet. "It's been, what, twenty-four hours?"

Whitney smiled, her sarcasm detector broken as usual.

Kit hadn't missed it. "Tory, get cleaned up. Now."

Eyes rolling, I trudged upstairs. Stopped midway. Turned. Hanging on the wall beside me was a large white canvas depicting an oddly shaped blue dog.

"What is this?"

Whitney appeared at the bottom of the steps. "Oh! That, Sweetie, is my *favorite* painting. It's a Blue Dog, by Dan Kessler. Don't you just *adore* it?"

Actually, I did like it. But a single question was looping in my head.

What is it doing here? What is it doing here? What is it doing here?

I continued up in silence.

As I washed my face, unpleasant facts coalesced. A painting. The vase. Pink and green pillows. Whitney, alone in the townhouse, unannounced.

Like mold in a cellar, Kit's bimbo girlfriend was quietly invading my domain.

Do. Not. Like.

I stared into my bathroom mirror. My reflection stared back. Impasse.

"Tory!" Kit sounded annoyed. "We're waiting on you!"

"Blargh."

I reached the table just as Whitney unveiled her menu. Crab cakes, corn on the cob, collard greens, peach cobbler.

Freaking delicious.

The adults tried to draw me into conversation, but the sneaky buildup of Whitney's belongings had weirded me out. After scarfing my meal, I bolted for my bedroom and locked the door.

My Mac was awake, with a new message blinking on-screen. Ben. Requesting videoconference. I booted iFollow and found I was last to arrive.

Ben filled the top left quadrant of my monitor. As usual, he was lounging in sweats in his father's rec room, which was an actual wreck. Old magazines, boat parts, camping gear, and fishing tackle were stacked in precarious piles all around him.

Shelton's bespectacled face hung to Ben's right, framed by the two *Avatar* posters on his bedroom wall. Though barely six o'clock, he was already sporting PJs.

Hi occupied the frame below Shelton. He was sitting at his desk, wearing a "Wolfman's Got Nards!" T-shirt, and eating a bag of Nacho Cheese Doritos. My own image peered back from the final square.

"She's here." Shelton sounded impatient. "*Now* will you tell us what's up?"

"I wasn't going to repeat myself," Ben replied, but his dark eyes sparked with eagerness.

"Then talk," Hi said. "I'm missing *Man v. Food.*"

Ben got right to the point. "I solved the coordinates."

"Did not!" Shelton looked shocked, and a little jealous. "How?"

A thin smile stole across Ben's face. "For once, *I* had the flash of brilliance."

"Go on." Ben had my full attention.

"I was thinking about what Hi said earlier."

"Smart," Hi quipped.

"Not usually," Ben continued, "but in this case you were right. The numbers *have* to be coordinates. Problem is, they don't make sense."

"Not unless we go dune-surfing in Africa," Shelton joked.

Ben ignored him. "How much do you guys know about coordinate systems?"

"Not much," I admitted. "I know that a specific longitude and latitude cross at a single point on a map, but that's about it."

"That's right," Ben said. "Coordinates are just sets of numbers used to denote an exact location. The most commonly used system is longitude, latitude, and height."

"Latitude runs east-west," Hi contributed. "Longitude goes north-south, from pole to pole."

Ben nodded. "Now, for any system to work, there must be agreed-upon starting points. The reference planes defining latitude and longitude are the equator and the prime meridian."

"Everyone knows that." Shelton wiped and replaced his glasses. "The equator divides north from south. The prime meridian separates east and west."

"Doesn't the PM run through some observatory in England?" Hi asked.

"Greenwich," Ben agreed. "That's zero longitude. How far east or west a location is on a map is measured from that city."

"In degrees, right?" I ventured. "East is positive and west is negative."

"Gold star," Ben said. "That's how you calculate longitude — the number of degrees east or west of Greenwich."

"Latitude works the same way," Hi added. "North is positive, south is negative."

"But you have to understand —" Ben leaned forward toward his screen, "— choosing the prime meridian *wasn't* scientific. It's not like the equator, which must be equidistant from the poles, and therefore can only be in one place. For the prime meridian, cartographers simply agreed to use an old English telescope as the universal reference point."

"Really?" That surprised me. "When?"

"The 1880s." Hi mumbled through a mouthful of Doritos. Of *course* he knew. "The United States held a conference, and most countries voted for Greenwich. It's stuck ever since."

"The *point* is," Ben went on, "the choice was completely arbitrary. Before that conference, mapmakers had used dozens of other places as zero longitude. Rome. Paris. Rio. Mecca. Most countries just picked their own prime meridian."

"Is this going somewhere?" Shelton stifled a yawn. "We already tried the digits as coordinates. They pointed to the freakin' Sahara Desert, remember?"

"Say these *are* coordinates." Ben lifted his copy of the clue. "The first number would be latitude. 32.773645. The second would be longitude. -00.065437."

"And the closest town is —" Hi glanced down, face smeared with orange debris, "— Bou Semghoun. An oasis village in the Ghardaia region of southern Algeria. Think they get DirecTV?"

Ben's eyes twinkled. "Guess what *else* is at latitude 32.773645?"

"What?" I felt goose bumps prickle my skin.

"Downtown Charleston," Ben smacked his hands together. "Booyah!"

"Get out!" Hiram's eyes widened. "How'd you know that?"

"Fishing." Ben wore a smug grin. "If I find a good spot, I bookmark the location in *Sewee*'s GPS system. I've seen latitude 32.77 hundreds of times. I should've recognized it as soon as I saw the clue, but the rest of the string threw me."

"But we still need a longitude," Shelton pointed out. "We can't find anything without both numbers."

Ben's smile widened. "Got that, too."

"Spill it," I demanded.

"That's why I brought up the prime meridian," Ben said. "Zero degrees longitude *doesn't have to be fixed to Greenwich.* Not like zero latitude, which is always fixed to the equator and can't move."

I saw were Ben was going. "So this longitudinal coordinate could rely upon some other prime meridian. A totally different starting point!"

Ben leaned back, hands behind his head. "Bingo."

"But that could be anywhere," Shelton whined. "Literally any point on earth."

"Wait, wait!" In his excitement, Hi spilled nacho chips onto his keyboard. "This clue was hidden inside the geocache. On Loggerhead! And that's the only fixed location the Gamemaster gave us."

"Hi figured it out," Ben grumbled. "Sometimes I hate how smart you guys are."

Alone in his bedroom, Hi raised the roof.

"So we use the first number as a normal latitude." Dots were connecting for me. "Then we assume the second coordinate is for longitude, but with the Loggerhead cache location as the prime meridian."

Ben nodded. "That's our new zero longitude."

"Ben, that's brilliant!"

Suddenly, the boy was all blushes. "No big deal. Easy, really."

"So where does —" I scanned quickly, "— longitude -00.065437 lead now?"

"You've got mail." Ben tapped his mouse.

The message arrived almost instantly. I opened the lone attachment and loaded a JPEG onto my desktop.

And knew.

CHAPTER 11

"Castle Pinckney?" Shelton's voice was skeptical. "It's abandoned, has been for years."

"These coordinates are dead-on," Ben said firmly. "No way that's by accident."

"But there's nothing out there." Shelton frowned into his webcam. "Just a beat-up pile of old rocks."

"Part of the building still stands." Hi's gut filled a quarter of my screen as he searched above his desk. "I've got a book here, somewhere."

"Sounds like a good spot to hide something." I pulled up images as I spoke. "What do we know about the castle?"

"Hold on a sec," Hi called from off camera. "Must be in my closet."

My search results were not inviting.

Castle Pinckney was definitely deserted, and the neglect showed. A gnarly tumble of broken masonry and chest-high weeds, the dilapidated fort occupied a tiny atoll in the middle of Charleston Harbor.

The main building was circular, with a high curtain wall facing the harbor mouth. Scrub forest grew close, like a wild, tangled beard. Dark vines covered the crumbling gray stone, locking the fortress in a choking, shadowy embrace.

Though the isle sat a mere thousand feet from the downtown peninsula, the ruined battlements seemed lost in time. No one ever went there.

"At first, the British hanged pirates out there." Hi was back on camera, skimming some sort of military encyclopedia. "Then, in 1781, George Washington ordered the construction of a fort." Page flip. "The Confederate Army used Castle Pinckney as a POW camp. After that, the island became an artillery position, eventually a lighthouse."

"Now, mothballs." Shelton made a wipe-away gesture. "Ghost town."

"I've cruised by there dozens of times," Ben said. "Dumpsville."

"The perfect hiding place." Hi clicked his tongue. "Well played, Señor Gamemaster."

"Fine." Shelton sighed from the depths of his toes. "Put a visit on our to-do list."

My eyes drifted back to the images on my screen. Castle Pinckney had a brooding, ominous feel. Lonely. Foreboding.

I was hooked.

Watch check: six fifteen p.m. Plenty of daylight left.

"Meet me at the dock in ten," I said.

"Done!" Hi swiveled his chair, propped a foot, and started lacing his Adidas.

"Wait! What?" Shelton raised both hands. "Tonight? Why?"

"We've got over an hour before dark." I yanked my hair into a ponytail. "Let's show Mr. Gamemaster how quickly Virals solve puzzles."

Ben took a moment to consider, then shrugged. "I'll get *Sewee* ready."

"We've *got* to work on our decision-making process." Shelton was shaking his head. "Right now, we just follow Tory over every cliff."

"Oh, boohoo," I mocked. "Get moving."

"You're going *down,* clown!" Hi slapped his hands together. "Tory, don't forget the clue. We still don't know how that image factors."

"Got it."

Three faces winked out as I slapped my laptop shut.

○   ○   ○

"I'm taking Coop for a walk!"

Kit's head popped from the kitchen. "Now?"

I nodded, hoping he wouldn't ask more questions.

Kit didn't disappoint. "Okay, but be back before dark. It's a school night."

"Promise, bye!"

Coop and I shot down the front stairs and beelined to the dock. I heard another door open, turned to see Shelton hurrying from his unit.

"I'm serious, Brennan." Shelton had changed into white Nike gym shorts and a black *Walking Dead* hoodie. "My foot's coming down. No more last-minute hijacks of my evenings."

"Whatever you say."

"Believe that." He let the matter drop.

I didn't take Shelton too seriously. Though none of them would ever admit it, I think the boys secretly liked me bossing them around. Most of the time. Every snake needs a head.

Hi and Ben were already aboard. We cast off, rounded Morris Island, and entered Charleston Harbor.

The evening was pleasantly warm. Seagulls rode the thermals high above our heads, mirroring *Sewee*'s progress as we passed Fort Sumter and headed toward downtown.

A tiny islet materialized just short of the peninsula. Low and rocky, its shore consisted of a dismal stretch of sand running a few hundred yards before melting into the waves. A weathered stone structure occupied a stretch of high ground at the island's north end. Castle Pinckney.

What was left of it, anyway.

Loose stones littered the uneven ground. Whole trees grew from the crumbling mortar of the outer wall. Everything was soaked in pelican poop, and looked on the verge of collapse.

"What a dump," Ben grunted as he eased the runabout closer to shore.

"How come no one ever restored it?" I asked. "Aren't you Southerners crazy for preserving Civil War monuments?"

"I think you mean the War of Northern Aggression," Hi deadpanned in a prim Southern voice. "When ruthless Union troops invaded our sacred homeland to rob poor Dixie of her freedom. Being from Boston, it's mostly your people's fault."

My eyes rolled. "I lived in Westborough. All of New England isn't Boston, like everyone down here thinks."

"All Yankee towns are the same," Hi said with a wink. "Nothing but factories and coal mines."

I didn't return fire. Hi was just messing around, and I tried to avoid reminiscing in public. Thoughts of my former home inevitably led to thoughts of Mom, and that often led to waterworks. Best friends or not, I hated when the guys saw me cry.

"Fixing up Pinckney has been proposed a dozen times, but the money's never there." Shelton hopped into the surf and began helping Ben ease *Sewee* closer to dry land. "It gets overshadowed by Sumter and the outer forts, even though it's older."

Ben dropped anchor a few yards off the seaweed-strewn beach. We slipped off our sneakers and waded ashore, re-shoed, then crossed a short patch of grass to the base of the ruins. Sighting a flock of roosting seagulls, Coop gave chase. The birds scattered, cawing in irritation.

The castle's curtain wall was roughly twelve feet high and intermittently broken by rectangular openings that had once been windows. A single entry was cut into the center of the monolithic stone façade, which curved away to either side, totaling perhaps seventy feet in diameter.

We studied the ancient fortress. It glowered back.

Shelton spoke first. "I'm not setting foot inside that house of cards."

I pulled the Gamemaster's clue from my pocket, hoping for inspiration. No such luck. The smile-like image remained indecipherable.

"Think." A light breeze fluttered the page in my hand. "What are we missing?"

The wall loomed above us, empty windows spaced five yards apart like a row of black teeth. The castle seemed to scowl, like an evil, rotting jack-o'-lantern.

No, not scowling. The windows form a ghastly grin.

It hit me.

"Of course!" I waved the clue, used air quotes. "The 'teeth' in this picture match the windows!"

"Wow, you're right!" Hi said. "Which means the snaggletooth must be —"

"The cache location!" I finished. "Come on!"

Moving clockwise along the wall, I counted openings to the left of the archway. Stopped at number five.

"Here." I stood before a three-by-five gap. "This one corresponds with the outside rectangle in the sketch."

Air wafted from within the castle, cool and dry. The window was a yawning, black pit that the pre-dusk sunlight failed to penetrate. Even straining, I could see only a few feet ahead.

"This section seems less run-down," Hi observed.

"The stonework looks sturdier," Shelton conceded, "but that doesn't mean it's safe to go in. This castle's so old, the forest's grown *on top* of it."

Ben pushed the wall with both hands. Tugged the stones forming the windowsill. Kicked the fortification's base. Pushed again. "Seems pretty solid."

"Great work, Ben," Hi deadpanned. "That oughta do it."

"You have a better plan? Or should we run back home?"

"Actually, I do." Hi dropped his head. A beat, then shivers wracked his body. He snorted. Coughed. Spit.

When he straightened, his eyes burned with golden fire.

I nodded. "Good plan."

Eyes closed, I reached deep.

SNAP.

CHAPTER 12

Pressure. Pain.

A thousand needles danced on my flesh as fire coursed through my veins. Sweat burst from every pore. Shocks of energy burned through me, spiking the hairs on my limbs. My hands shook like leaves in a storm.

Seconds later, it was over. I flared.

I'd dropped to my knees, panting raggedly, waiting for the world to stop spinning. Suddenly, a large pink sea slug attacked my cheek.

"Blech." I shoved Coop's snout away. "Thanks, boy."

Inhaling deeply, I got to my feet. Wobbled. Tried to harness the adrenaline pooling in my extremities.

That was a bad one.

Beside me, Shelton had removed his glasses and was rubbing his forehead, eyes brimming with golden light. Ben's back was to me. His fists clenched as he struggled to tap his canine DNA. Hi had stepped to the window and was peering inside.

"Gotcha." Ben straightened and flexed his powerful shoulders. "Contact."

When Ben turned, his dark eyes danced with yellow light. Already handsome, flaring took his attractiveness to a whole new level. Ben's coppery skin practically glowed in the evening light. I turned quickly, surprised by the color rising to my cheeks.

Then I noticed a thrumming in my brain. A subtle shift, like gears slotting into place, connecting my consciousness to a larger system.

I closed my eyes. My perception billowed outward. I could feel the other Virals, could point to each without opening a lid. Even Coop.

Flaming ropes appeared, linking the five us.

My pack.

Concentrating hard, I *pushed* slightly, in a way I didn't understand, sweeping my awareness outward. My mind brushed the invisible boundary separating my thoughts from theirs. Hi. Coop. Shelton. Ben.

At first, a low buzzing. Then scattered feelings, too chaotic to follow.

I tried to pull back, mindful of invading the other Virals' headspace. I hadn't asked permission to attempt a link.

Abruptly, my perspective zoomed forward, like a comet being sucked into a black hole. I lost control. My mind seemed to untether from my body. Then my thoughts abruptly fired down the closest glowing cord.

Colors flashed. Red. Orange. Yellow. Black. Then a fuzzy image cut through the haze.

Me. Standing on the grass before Castle Pinckney. Eyes closed. Green-faced. Swaying.

"Stop it!" The voice was angry. Nervous. "Get out!"

The harsh words severed my fragile connection.

The universe snapped backward.

SNUP.

My eyes flew open. Ben's fingers were digging into the flesh of my shoulders. Strongest by far, with his power unleashed he could have broken my bones.

From the look on Ben's face, he was considering it.

"Stay out of my head," Ben said through gritted teeth. "You didn't even ask."

"Sorry," I squeaked. "I'm not sure what I did."

Coop nudged between us, eyes fixed on Ben.

Ben took a breath, seemed to realize how hard he was clutching me. His hands dropped as if burned. He backed away, cheeks flushed, sweat dampening his brow.

I placed a hand on Coop's head. The wolfdog sat, but his eyes tracked Ben's every move.

"It was an accident, Ben." I couldn't catch his eye. "I didn't mean to link, but somehow my mind was . . . *pulled* into it. I can't explain it very well."

Awkward silence.

"Hey, no sweat, Tor." Hi forced a laugh, anxious to defuse the tension. "Just throw us a warning next time, you know? We might confuse you with an alien abductor, or a CIA operative. Can't have that, right?"

"Everything's cool." Shelton worked his ear. "Whatever you did, we know it was an accident. Don't we, Ben?"

"Our minds aren't toys, Tory." Ben's voice was conciliatory, but he didn't meet my gaze. "You can't barge inside them without warning. Or permission."

He was right. I told him so.

"I screwed up. I swear I'll be more careful next time. No more mind games without explicit agreement. Promise."

"Okay then, that's done with!" Hi rapped the castle wall with his knuckles. "Daylight's wasting, so let's get back to the game."

"Do we have a play called?" Shelton asked.

"We go inside, genius." Hi's glance swept the group. "Everyone still flaring?"

Nods all around. Hi pointed into the gloom. "Then get crackin', soldiers."

"Why don't we look before we leap?" I suggested. "Literally."

"Good plan," Shelton agreed. "A little clichéd, but good."

Focusing my hypersenses, I noted minute cracks spiderwebbing the stone windowsill. My nose detected dank, earthy scents wafting from the darkness. Molding leaves. Moss. Stagnant water.

"We spend a *lot* of time in these places," Shelton observed. "Some might say, *too* much time."

"Builds character." Hi squatted down to examine the chamber's ceiling. "Makes you tough. Manly."

"Just what I'm looking for," I said absently, inspecting the gloom. "Manliness."

"You guys hear that?" Ben had moved beside me to get a look inside.

Shelton cocked one ear toward the opening. "Dripping water? No." His face scrunched in concentration. "Something tapping, maybe?"

Ben shook his head. "If you can't hear it, you know the rest of us can't."

Hi was squinting into the inky black. "It's a small room, with a doorway in back."

I waited, trusting Hi's superior flare vision.

"This first chamber seems empty," he said finally. "We'll have to go deeper."

"Great." Shelton kicked a rock. "Deeper."

"Come on, Shel-Dogg." Hi stuck out a fist. "After everything we've done, the dark shouldn't scare you anymore."

"And yet, it does." A moment passed, then Shelton reluctantly bumped Hi's fist. "I'm not going first, and that's a fact."

"Gimme a sec to grab lights from the boat." Ben hurried back the way we'd come.

Hi called into the black. *"Your cache is mine, clown! I'm coming to getcha! Uncle Hiram's got the scent!"* His words echoed in the darkness as he scrambled through the opening.

"Zip it!" Shelton hiss-whispered. "This building is struggling to hold your buck-sixty. Don't yodel the roof down on our heads."

"I'm light on my feet." Hi's response came from deep within. "Should've been a dancer."

For a moment, Shelton and I stood alone.

"Hey, Tor," he whispered, "what was that crap with Ben? Did something happen? He freaked pretty bad."

"I'm not sure. It was such a strange feeling. For a hot second I thought —"

Ben's reappearance cut me off. I didn't like talking behind his back, even if my comments weren't negative.

And I wasn't certain what I suspected. What *had* I seen? How had it happened? This latest telepathic experience had left me with more questions than ever. Could I really have seen my own image, through *Ben's* eyes?

I decided to keep quiet. I knew Ben wouldn't like it.

"Let's do this." Ben vaulted through the opening, then offered me a hand. Brushing it aside, I wiggled over on my stomach, then dropped to the floor. Shelton climbed in last.

Two paws appeared on the sill, followed by a whine.

"Stay outside, Coop." I patted one furry foot. "It's not safe."

Another whimper, then the paws withdrew.

"Now what?" Shelton whispered in the dark.

"Spread out." Hi grabbed a light from Ben, flicked it on. "Look for a box like the one we found on Loggerhead."

Having only two flashlights, we were forced to pair up. Hi and I went right, Ben and Shelton left. Minutes later we met at the back of the room.

"Anything?" I asked.

"Nope." Ben's voice was tense. Flaring, I could make out a tightness to his eyes.

Hi probed a rickety doorway straight ahead. "Let's try in there."

The second chamber was half as large as the first, about the size of a tennis court. It, too, was empty.

For several seconds, Hi worked his light horizontally across the room. Something winked in the pale white oval. Beside me, I felt Shelton flinch.

Hi slowly arced the beam back. Flaring, my eyes gathered enough radiance to see.

Another twinkle.

"There!" I said excitedly. "On the ground."

Ben added his light to Hi's. A dark metal box sat alone in the middle of the room.

"Buckeye." Hi's eyes gleamed golden as he hurried forward.

"Hold up!" Shelton's voice cracked. "The noise is stronger in here. Regular, like *tat-tat-tat*. It's coming from that box."

Undeterred, Hi scooped our find and began pawing at the lid. "Two for two!" he crowed. "Take that, Bozo."

"Hi, hold up." My sixth sense was on red alert.

"It's ticking!" Shelton yelped. "The package is ticking!"

"Ticking?" Hiram kept poking and prying. "Like a watch?"

My mouth opened to shout a warning. Too late. Hi popped the lid.

"It stopped." Shelton's voice trembled.

Inside the box something whirred, then clicked.

Beep! Beep! Beep!

Hi aimed his beam into the box and drew his face close. I actually heard him swallow. "That can't be good."

"What can't be good?" I hurried to his side.

The light was enough for my hypervision. I could see a purple plastic container sealed with black electrical tape. Affixed to its top was a digital watch with a tiny LCD.

As I watched, a message flashed on-screen: Failure to Open Properly. You Lose!

"What does that mean?" Shelton drew so close I could smell his sweat. "We didn't *have* instructions about opening it!"

"What the hell?" Ben spoke so softly I'd have missed it without my powers.

"Guys?"

"Yes?" I didn't like Hi's tone.

"This watch is at thirty seconds. Counting down."

My scalp began to tingle. "Down to what?"

"How should I know!?!"

"Turn it off!" Shelton yelped.

Beep! Beep! Beep!

"How?" I ran my fingers along the edge of the container. "We don't even know what this is!"

"Fifteen seconds." Sweat beaded Hi's brow.

"It's nothing," Ben grumbled. "A stupid trick to scare us."

"Ten."

Hi had barely said the word when the first message dissolved, and was replaced by a new pair of words: You're Dead!

"Oh no!" Shelton began backing away. "No no no no no!"

Beep! Beep! Beep!

"Run!" I yelled. "Hi, ditch it!"

Hi flung the cache into a corner and bolted for the door, hot on Shelton's heels. Ben and I were a step behind.

How much time left? I'd lost the count. Seven seconds? Three?

Something furry flew past me, arrowing straight for the beeping package.

I froze in horror.

"Cooper!"

How did he get inside!?

I whipped the beam his way. Coop had clamped the cache in his jaws and was shaking it like a giant bilge rat.

The box emitted a screeching tone that grew into a high-pitched whistle.

Coop went still, the package locked in his teeth.

Terrified, I lunged toward my wolfdog.

An arm circled my waist and dragged me to the ground.

"Get down!" Ben shouted.

"Coop!" I screamed, trying to claw free. "Cooper, no!"

Click.

BANG.

CHAPTER 13

A blinding light flashed in the inky blackness.

Once. Twice.

Coop yelped and dropped the cache, then scrambled a hasty retreat.

Flaring, I saw shards of color shoot outward from the container. Red. Blue. Yellow. Green. Fluttering scraps that twirled in and out of the flashlight beams. The chamber echoed with hoots, horns, and whistles that seemed impossibly loud.

"What the hell?" Hi gasped, spitting dust. "What happened? What's that noise?"

"Coop!" I grabbed a flashlight and rushed to my wolfdog. Coop had backed into a corner and slumped to the ground. "You okay, boy?"

He was panting, and blood trickled through the fur of his lower jaw. Heart pounding, I probed his body for wounds. Finding none, I cautiously grasped his snout. Coop tried to pull away, but I held him firmly.

"Everything's fine," I cooed, holding the flashlight in one hand and prying open his mouth with the other. "Just give me one look."

A red weal ran across Coop's tongue. The roof of his mouth was black with soot, and blood oozed from the base of a lower incisor. That seemed to be it. Thankfully, he wasn't badly hurt.

I exhaled, suddenly aware I'd been holding my breath.

"Confetti." Hi was crouching in the doorway, waving a flashlight. "It's raining freaking *confetti* in here!"

"And the box is playing carnival music." Shelton's shirt and face were caked with dust. "Fake bomb. This was a friggin' prank!"

I realized that no one was flaring.

"Not so fake." My fury rose as I stroked my wolfdog's head. "Coop's tongue is cut, and the roof of his mouth is burned."

"Shh!" Ben hissed.

The music had stopped. A low ringing filled the room.

"Great." Shelton backed toward the door. "Round two."

Furious, I stormed across the room and kicked the box. The boys flinched as it ricocheted off the wall and broke into pieces.

Something flat, black, and rectangular lay inside the wreckage.

"Are you insane!?!" Shelton shrieked. "It already exploded once!"

"That piece of crap injured my dog!" I nearly shook with rage. "When I find out who built it . . ."

"We won't get anywhere by breaking the thing," Hi said. "So how's 'bout getting a grip, huh?"

I nodded, blood still boiling.

Gamemaster, you've made an enemy.

"An iPad." Ben stood over the wreckage, light in hand. "*That's* what's ringing."

"Seriously?" Shelton inched toward Ben's side. "This guy left a freaking iPad? Is that normal?"

"Not even close." Hi joined the huddle, smacking dirt from his shorts. "An iPad's *way* too valuable to cache. The first to find it would steal it for sure."

Ben tapped the screen. A yellow background appeared, framing four words written in scrolling, purple calligraphy. Welcome to The Game.

Shelton groaned.

"The Game again?" I was reading over Ben's shoulder. "That's my *last* nerve."

A swipe bar appeared below the message.

"Should I unlock it?" Ben asked.

"No way," Shelton said. "Whatever game this is, I ain't playing."

"Do it." I wasn't making a suggestion. "We're tracking this wacko down."

"I'm with Tory," Hi said. "We need intel, and the iPad's our only lead."

"Here goes." Ben finger-swiped the screen.

A medieval scroll appeared, smoking purple letters affixed to its surface. A familiar signature flowed across the bottom of the page.

Valiant Players,

I'm disappointed. You failed at this task. Fortunately, the first round was mere practice. But now The Game has truly begun! From here forward the stakes increase, and there's no turning back.

To wit: I've hidden a bomb somewhere in Charleston. Unlike the first, this one is very real. To disarm the device, you must follow my clues and complete the tasks.

Fail at a task, the bomb goes off. Break a rule, the bomb goes off. Refuse to continue, the bomb goes off. Reveal The Game to anyone, the bomb goes off.

Accept my challenge and complete The Game, or innocents will die. Lives are in your hands. The clock is ticking!

Sincerely,
The Gamemaster

"When we find this assclown," I fumed, "I'm going to break his freaking —"

"It's a joke, right?" Shelton was tugging his lobe double-time. "A sick prank?"

"Of course." But Hi's face was uneasy. "Sorry I got us into this nonsense."

"A bomb?" Ben was shaking his head. "This doesn't make any sense."

"Look!" I pointed to the screen.

The scroll dissolved, replaced by a grainy, green-tinged image.

Four figures, huddled close inside an empty room.

"This is stupid." Shelton started toward the doorway. "Let's bounce. We can toss that iPad in the freaking harbor."

"Wait!" My heart skipped a beat. On-screen, one of the figures was moving to the right. "Shelton, walk back over here."

He grumbled, but rejoined the group. The figure on the iPad did the same.

Goose bumps. Boatloads.

"It's a video feed!" Hi spun, eyes darting to the ceiling.

I'd observed the screen as Hi moved. Sure enough, when he'd turned, so had one of the eerie green figures.

"It's live," Ben whispered. "The Gamemaster could be watching us, right now."

"There!" Hi aimed his flashlight at the far corner of the chamber. Where ceiling met wall, a tiny red light winked. "Sonofabitch!"

"It must be a night-vision lens," Shelton said. "That's why the image is so clear."

Ben handed me the iPad, scooped a rock, and fired. Coop yipped at the sound of impact.

The red light continued to wink. Ben grabbed a handful of stones and tossed them like buckshot. The rain of projectiles must've connected. I heard the tinkle of breaking glass, then the iPad went black.

"Can we please get out of here?" Shelton repeated. "This is way too weird."

Not waiting for comment, he ducked back into the first chamber. Hi hurried after, followed by Ben, Cooper, and me. We regrouped by the window through which we'd entered.

Dusky light poured through the opening. The salty harbor breeze was a welcome change from the fetid, musty air inside the castle.

"Ladies first," said Hi.

I was about to hoist myself onto the sill when I glanced at the iPad. "Crap."

"What?" Three voices.

A new image had filled the screen — a large red circle on a white field, dancing yellow letters inscribed on its face.

Two words. Press me.

Shelton was not interested. "Does the clown think we're idiots, or —"

Hi's finger darted forward and tapped the button.

"Hi!" I shouted. Things were happening too fast.

"You moron!" Shelton screeched.

"I couldn't help it." Hi shrugged. "How do you not press a button like that?"

Shelton's fingers found his temples. "We don't know —"

BOOM.

This blast was larger than the first, trembling the castle walls. Dirt and ancient mortar rained down on our heads. Behind us, a stone block fell to the floor.

"Out!" I yelled.

Ben tossed Coop through the window. We scrambled after, then booked it to the shoreline, getting as far from the building as possible.

There was a rumble, followed by a series of booms. I turned to see dust billowing from every window.

"Holy crap!" Shelton panted. "Did Hi blow up the castle?"

"No." Ben's voice was tight as he peered back at the fortress. "The walls are still standing. Something else must've happened."

"Good God." Hi's voice shook as he pointed the opposite direction. "Look."

My gaze followed Hi's finger. Across the harbor. *Downtown.*

A pillar of smoke was rising from Battery Park. Below it, trees were burning like torches soaked in pitch. As I stared in horror, sirens began to wail.

"You don't think . . ." Hi trailed off.

No one responded.

But I knew. My gaze dropped to the iPad, waiting.

In moments a new message appeared on-screen: Understand?

Two options took shape below the question: a white circle with gold writing, and a black square lettered in red.

The white circle read: Yes. Time to play The Game.

The black square read: No. I need another demonstration.

The image of a stopwatch formed. Began counting down from ten.

A hollow feeling welled in my gut.

Nine. Eight. Seven . . .

"Guys," I whispered, "I don't think this is a joke."

I held up the iPad.

Six. Five. Four . . .

Hi paled. Shelton swallowed. Ben clenched his fists.

The Gamemaster's warning flashed in my mind.

Accept my challenge and complete The Game, or innocents will die.

"We have no choice," I said quietly.

The boys nodded.

Three. Two . . .

Feeling helpless, I pressed the white button.

The display cycled through a series of colors before fading to white. Trumpets sounded. Then a snarling clown face filled the screen.

Black letters appeared in the now-familiar script: Clues to Follow!

I wanted to scream in frustration.

Whoever this Gamemaster was, he was toying with us. Shoving us around like his personal playthings.

The clown glared up at me. Sneering. Taunting.

We'd become pawns in a madman's game.

PART TWO:

CLUES

CHAPTER 14

I leaned against one of Bolton's granite lions.

Across the courtyard, a crowd of students lounged on wooden benches lining the central walk. The morning was sunny, a balmy sixty-five. No one was in a hurry to trudge inside.

The boys were bunched beside me, tapping their phones, searching for coverage of last night's explosion on The Battery.

I left the legwork to them. I just wanted answers.

"No one was hurt!" Relief was evident in Hi's voice. "But the wedding gazebo went up like a Roman candle."

"Lucky." Shelton pushed his glasses back into place. "Usually that thing is crawling with people. It's practically a landmark."

"Someone could've been killed," I said. "The Gamemaster clearly didn't care."

Ben frowned. "Do the police know what happened?"

"It was a bomb all right." Hi scrolled his iPhone. "This story calls the blast an act of terrorism."

Terrorism. Great. We're entangled with a freaking fanatic.

"So what now?" Hi glanced at his watch. First bell would ring any minute.

"Cops?" Shelton suggested.

I shook my head. "Against the rules, remember?"

"We care about that?" Shelton snorted. "Hi just blew up Battery Park."

"Accident!" Hi protested. "I didn't know what would happen! You see a button, you push it. That's practically a law of nature."

Level stares.

Hi waved away our skepticism. "The Gamemaster would've set it off anyway."

On *that* point, I agreed. "The bomb was a warning: Play the game or people die."

"Okay, no police," Ben said firmly. "And no talking to anyone else, either."

"Maybe." I'd been thinking about that. "Maybe not."

"The rules were clear," Ben argued.

"We can't go to the cops, reveal the clue, or talk about the game." Ticking fingers as I spoke. "But we don't have to be led around by our noses."

Shelton sighed. "Meaning what?"

"We turn the tables." I thumped my bag, which contained both the Gamemaster's iPad and what remained of the second cache.

Yesterday, watching the smoke rise, I'd made a decision. We needed a way to fight back. An edge our adversary didn't expect. That meant evidence.

Swift as thought, I'd slipped back inside Castle Pinckney. The boys hadn't been quick enough to stop me. A risky move, but worth it — I'd retrieved the scorched container and escaped unscathed. I'd even smiled through the berating they'd delivered back on the beach.

"The rules say we can't talk about—" I made air quotes, "—'The Game,' but they don't mention the Gamemaster himself. We'll use his own materials to track him down."

"How?" Ben's face was unreadable. "All we've got are the puzzle box, the two-page letter, and a blown-up cache."

"Don't forget the iPad." I pulled the tablet from my backpack. "Right now it only shows the clue that appeared last night, but we might eventually unlock more."

At midnight the night before, a pictogram had suddenly filled the iPad's screen. I'd spent an hour trying to make sense of it before giving up, snapping a pic, and forwarding it to the boys. Daylight wasn't providing additional inspiration.

"The image is incomprehensible." Hi examined the display with dubious eyes. "I stared at this all morning, and it's still nonsense. We'll never crack it in time."

Hi wasn't kidding. I couldn't even fathom a guess.

The picture was deceptively simple — the number 18, encircled by a long string of characters: CH3OHHBRCH3BRH2O. Surrounding that arrangement was a solid black circle, which, in turn, was surrounded by a larger blue one. A capital *K* crowned it all.

Beneath the image was a digital stopwatch. Sixty-four hours, counting down.

Shelton shuddered. "I don't like thinking about what happens at zero."

"Me either." I shoved the iPad back into my bag. "Which is why we have to find the Gamemaster first. We can work the clue and try to catch him at the same time."

"Sounds fantastic," Hi deadpanned, "but how do we do it?"

"Analyze everything. Every scrap of material we have. Hope the Gamemaster made a mistake."

First bell pealed. Students began filing into the building.

"Shall we?" I headed for the doors, the boys at my heels.

Classmates pressed close as we funneled through the entrance. Without warning, I found myself shoulder to shoulder with Madison.

Startled, I nodded and smiled, as if greeting her was the most natural thing in the world.

Madison's eyes widened. She rabbit-stepped backward, expensive jewelry rattling as she bumped the students behind her. Then she lowered her head and wormed through the mass of bodies with undignified haste. Casting one backward glance — red-faced, eyes nervous — her brunette curls disappeared into the river of identical Bolton Prep uniforms.

I suppressed a sigh. Maybe things were better this way.

"She's still not over that beat down," said a voice behind my ear.

This time, the sigh escaped. "Hi, Jason."

I turned left down the hallway. Jason hustled to walk beside me, bumping into Ben, who had moved to occupy the same space.

The boys glared like stray dogs squaring off in an alley. Shelton and Hi kept moving past us, oblivious, or choosing to avoid the awkward scene.

"Watch where you're going," Ben snapped.

"I am," Jason said dryly. "I'm going to chat with Tory."

Ben snorted. "I'm sure that'll make her day."

Jason's eyes flicked to me, momentarily uncertain.

"Enough, both of you." *What was it with these two? Oil and water.* "Jason, I need something from my locker before class. Talk later?"

"Sure, Tor. I just thought you'd want to know first."

That stopped me. "Know what?"

"That Chance will be back at school this week," Jason said. "Probably tomorrow morning."

"Oh." *Oh my.* "Thanks."

"No problem. See you later."

Jason straightened his tie, then turned and reached as if to fix Ben's. Ben flinched, then flushed scarlet, eyes growing hard.

Jason smirked as he headed off down the hall, ignoring Ben's icy look.

My legs resumed walking, but my mind wandered. Chance. Back tomorrow. A plan was needed.

Ben stomped at my side, his face a thunderhead. I knew that flinch was gnawing at him. He'd lost that round. *Meatheads.*

Shelton and Hi were waiting outside class.

"Everything cool?" Hi asked, eyeing Ben.

"Fine," I said. "But we have to make a stop after school."

Ben's head whipped my way. "You can't be serious."

Shelton frowned. "Serious about what?"

"Claybourne Manor." I ignored their protests. "It's past time we settled our debt."

"We'll have to hit the bank first." Hi sounded despondent. "Raid our deposit box."

"It's *his* share, guys. We'd never have done it without him. Plus, Chance saw way too much last summer. We need to feel him out. Find out how much he remembers."

No one bothered to protest. We'd had this out before.

"Who knows," I said hopefully, "maybe he can help ID the Gamemaster."

Three incredulous faces.

"Not *directly,* of course. But we need a forensic examination of the cache. Chance has serious connections. He might help."

To say the boys were unenthused is an understatement.

"Help screw us again?" Shelton snarked.

"Did you get hit in the head?" Hi asked.

"Dumb dumb dumb." Ben wagged his head slowly.

"Whatever," I snapped. "We're going, so man up."

The second bell sounded.

We trooped into class and found our desks. I dove into my calculus book, hoping to conceal my own uncertainty.

Last time, I'd barely escaped Claybourne Manor with my life.

Was I making a huge mistake?

CHAPTER 15

We met by the gates after last bell.

Though reluctant, the boys offered no further argument. They knew it was pointless once I'd made up my mind. Leaving our jackets in lockers, we headed east down Broad Street.

The guys sulked through our quick stop at the bank.

At Meeting Street we turned left. Claybourne Manor was a few blocks ahead, in Charleston's prestigious, hoity-toity quarter known as South of Broad. The neighborhood screamed of privilege, old money, and tradition. Ostentatious wealth. We couldn't have been more out of place.

Hi whistled, pointed to his right. "Look at *that* palace. Four stories, maybe five."

"These houses are insane." Shelton's head was swiveling nonstop. "My dad couldn't afford a parking space down here."

"He's better off." Ben's scowl was firmly in place. "The less time spent around blue-blooded jerks, the better."

Even among its elegant neighbors, Chance's ancestral home stands out. A registered historical landmark, Claybourne Manor is the largest private residence in South Carolina. Modeled after a nineteenth-century

Italian manse, the main building has forty rooms, twenty-four fireplaces, and sixty bathrooms, and occupies over two acres of prime downtown real estate. A home fit for royalty.

We halted outside a ten-foot, spike-topped wall split by an ornate iron gate. Twisting metalwork displayed the Claybourne family crest: a gray shield with three black foxes, encircled by black and red vines.

"My family needs a coat of arms," Hi mused. "Something that conveys what it means to be a Stolowitski."

Shelton chuckled. "What, like a stuffed-crust pizza?"

I held up a hand. "Everyone ready?"

No replies. At least they weren't complaining again.

Taking silence as assent, I rapped on a stout metal door beside the gate. Seconds passed, then a bolt slid sideways, and the portal swung inward.

"Yes?" The guard was lean, mid-forties, with salt-and-pepper hair and the demeanor of an ex-cop. No name tag. He didn't look happy to see us.

"Hello!" My brightest smile. "We're here to see Chance."

"Do you have an appointment?" Stern.

"No, but we're classmates from Bolton Academy." *Time to ham it up.* "We heard Chance is coming back to school, and wanted to give him a big Griffin welcome back!"

Hi snorted, then covered it with a fit of coughing. My grin stayed frozen in place.

"Master Claybourne isn't taking visitors." Boredom crept into the guard's voice. "Leave a name if you'd like, but you can't loiter on the street."

"But the four of us go way back with Chance," I said quickly. "Are you sure we can't —"

"Quite sure. Make an appointment."

Grrr. "Please tell Chance that Tory Brennan stopped by, along with Hi Stolowitski, Ben Blue, and Shelton Devers."

I hesitated. Should I say more? "Let Chance know we'd like to speak with him when it's convenient. We have something for him."

"Thank you." The door closed with a loud clank.

"You should've offered another Human Spirit Award," Hi quipped. "Worked last time."

"Shut it." I hate being thwarted. My mind raced, but came up empty. There was nothing to be done — the ball was now in Chance's court.

"Let's bail." Ben was already moving. "We should be working the Gamemaster's clue, not wasting time —"

The door abruptly reopened. The guard craned out, spied me, and breathed an audible sigh of relief.

"Terribly sorry, Miss Brennan!" Hustling out onto the sidewalk. "Name's Saltman. I'm a new hire, and haven't memorized the logs. *Of course* you may come inside. I'll let Master Claybourne know you've arrived."

Saltman nervously rotated his cap in his hands. "We don't need to mention this little mix-up, do we, miss? It was an honest mistake."

I covered my surprise with an airy wave. "Not at all."

But what was he talking about? I took a calculated risk. "I'm on the list?"

Saltman nodded like a bobblehead. "Oh, yes ma'am! The instructions are quite clear: no visitors except by appointment, but Miss Brennan is to be shown in at any time, day or night." He smiled ingratiatingly. "You must be very special to young Master Chance."

WTF?

Chance left *instructions* about me? Had assumed I'd come? Sometimes the world made no sense at all.

"Chance is home?" I asked, stalling for time.

"In his father's study." Saltman cringed as though slapped. "*His* study, I should say. If you'll wait in the reception, I'll have him summoned straight away." Then his gaze shifted to my companions. "The directive only mentions you, Miss Brennan. I'm not sure —"

"Chance will want to see everyone." I added steel to my voice. "Let's not waste more time gabbing in the driveway."

That was enough for Saltman. "Of course, right this way."

We traveled a short, flower-lined walk to the front entrance. Saltman pulled wide the massive oak door to reveal a cozy vestibule. The manor's signature room was just ahead — a fifty-foot grand entrance hall in antebellum style.

Memories flooded back. I pushed them away.

Keep your head straight. Chance is no one to trifle with.

Saltman led us to a smaller chamber on the right — a spacious wood-paneled parlor decorated with elaborate crown molding, painted friezes, a wooden mantel, and a giant crystal chandelier. In the center, six leather chairs surrounded a mahogany coffee table.

"Please have a seat." Saltman pressed a false panel to reveal an intercom system. "Inform Master Claybourne he has four guests in the reception. Tory Brennan and . . . some others."

When a liveried butler appeared, Saltman retreated the way he'd entered. After declining refreshments, we sat, waiting, taking in the rich appointments.

"I assume you've got a plan," Shelton whispered. "We're not just gonna toss this bag of loot at him, right?" He tapped a pocket containing two stacks of gold doubloons.

"We need to find out what he knows. If he suspects anything."

"How?" Ben asked quietly.

"Just follow my lead." Code for: I have no idea.

"Hey, check this weirdo out." Hi was inspecting a bust on the mantel.

"This face is ninety percent eyebrow. What do you wanna bet he owned slaves?"

Scowling to match the carving's expression, Hi spoke in a gravelly voice. *"In my day, we ate the poor people. We had a giant outdoor grill, and cooked up peasant steaks every Sunday."*

"That is General Clemmons Brutus Claybourne, you twit," a voice said dryly. "He commanded two companies during the Revolution, before dying at Yorktown. You might show a little respect."

Chance leaned in the doorway, one shoulder against its frame.

Whoa boy.

Chance was dusk made flesh. Dark skin, dark eyes, and dark humor. His thick black hair framed strong features and a Hollywood perfect chin. Tall, slender, and muscular without being bulky. In a word, he was gorgeous.

Last I'd seen Chance, he'd been tired and bedraggled, with purple crescents under his eyes and a nervous tic. Exhausted, haunted, and questioning his own sanity, soon thereafter he'd recommitted himself to a mental hospital.

That boy was gone.

"So. The gang's all here." Chance smiled as if enjoying a private joke. "Everyone have a nice end of summer?"

"Hello, Chance." Now that we'd come to it, my tongue was tied. "I hope you're doing well," I finished lamely.

"Do you now?"

Chance strolled into the room and gripped the back of the nearest chair, his fluid stride hinting of past athletic glories. The smirk remained on his face.

"Hey there, Chancy." Hi is impervious to awkward moments. This one was no exception. "When'd you get out of the nuthouse?"

I know I gasped. My eyes might've bugged.

Chance chuckled without humor. "Hiram, you never disappoint. Stop annoying Uncle Clemmons and join us."

As Hi flopped into a leather seat, Chance studied the group. "Nice uniforms."

"Heard you'll be sporting one again," Ben shot back. "Not enough credits, huh?"

Chance's grin slipped for a millisecond. "Good afternoon to you too, Ben. Yes, I'll be back for a few weeks. I missed a handful of exams last semester. But I'll be done with Bolton soon enough."

"You're eighteen now, right?" Shelton arced a hand, taking in the room. "That make all this yours?"

"Yes. I came into my inheritance last month. And with Father . . . away . . . I'm now *the* Claybourne of Claybourne Manor."

Chance winked at Hi. "That's when they discharged me. Funny thing. Turns out, I *do* own that hospital. Ironic, isn't it?"

Chance had no siblings, and his mother had died giving birth to him. His father was doing hard time. That made Chance perhaps the richest man in Charleston.

"So you bought your way free?" Ben scoffed.

"Nonsense. I'm cured." Chance's gaze found me. "I worked a few things out during my second stint. Reordered my mind. Got back onto firm ground. Plus, it was past time I assumed my position as head of the Claybourne empire."

"What about the criminal charges?" I hadn't forgotten. "They just let you walk?"

"The district attorney thought I'd suffered enough." Chance circled the chair and sat. "I agreed."

"That's crap!" I exploded. "You *attacked* us. Held us at gunpoint!"

"I wasn't in my right mind," Chance replied, all shocked innocence. "Ask my lawyers if you don't believe me."

His smugness infuriated me. "The court bought that crap?"

"It's nice having friends in high places." Chance flashed me his trademark wink. "Sympathetic ears."

I bit back a scathing reply. Though Chance hadn't been directly involved in the murder of Katherine Heaton, he'd done more than enough to deserve punishment. But arguing about it was pointless. He'd wriggled off the hook.

Chance seemed to be enjoying our visit. The old swagger was back, along with his former mock-stern levity.

But he's not exactly the same.

The drollness was there, but sharper now, more caustic, with a cynical, biting quality. Chance's eyes still twinkled, but without their former warmth.

He seemed harder. More jaded. We needed to be careful.

"Give him the bag and let's go." Ben shifted uncomfortably in his opulent chair. "I'm tired of this fake buddy-buddy garbage."

"Bag?" For the first time, Chance looked uncertain. "What bag?"

I signaled Shelton, who handed me the pouch. Unlacing its straps, I removed a handful of gold coins.

"You must know we found Anne Bonny's treasure. This is your share."

Chance looked momentarily stunned. "My share?"

I nodded. "We wouldn't have done it without your help. It's only fair."

"Fair." Chance's jaw tightened. "Fair," he repeated, dark eyes darkening. "And you'd never be unfair to me, would you, Tory?"

My heart threw in a few extra beats. "What do you mean? I'm giving you the coins right now." I held out the pouch.

Chance made no move to take it. He studied me, expression unreadable.

Abruptly, Chance stood. "Keep your trinkets. I'm a multimillionaire. I don't need a cut of your pathetic haul."

I shook my head. "Chance, this is yours. We owe you."

The wry smile returned. "Yes, you do. But I'd prefer different currency."

Chance crossed back to the doorway and turned. "If you'll excuse me, I have to prepare for tomorrow. A few weeks of high school, then I'm done with childish silliness forever."

"You won't take the coins?" I pressed.

"No. After all, I wasn't there to find them, was I?"

I didn't know what to think. Chance agreed we owed him, but refused a share of the spoils. Why?

"Instead of haggling over trifles, we will talk." Again Chance's eyes locked on to mine. "About many things. I have questions that need answering."

Butterflies fluttered in my gut.

Did Chance know I'd manipulated him? That I'd lied to protect our secrets? What things had he "worked out" in the hospital?

Suddenly, I didn't want to ask Chance about the Gamemaster, the fragmented cache, or anything else. I had a sinking feeling he was going to make my life much more difficult.

"Fine." I rose. The others did too. "I guess we'll see you at school tomorrow."

"Let me show you out."

Chance walked us to the door. We scurried out into the sunshine and headed for the gate.

"Wait."

I turned.

"I've changed my mind." Chance strode to my side. "I'd like one coin, please."

"Just one?" I scooped a doubloon and handed it over. "Why?"

"Gold reminds me of you, Tory." Ice-cold smile. "This coin will bring a twinkle to my eye."

Chance thumb-flipped the doubloon, caught it cleanly, then disappeared inside without a backward glance.

CHAPTER 16

"What now?" Shelton asked.

I had no answer. Chance's last words echoed in my head.

"We keep these coins for ourselves," Hi crowed. "*That's* what now."

We'd nearly reached the city marina. Ben texted his father, who was waiting to ferry us back to Morris Island. But I wasn't ready to call it a day.

"I'm going to Loggerhead," I said.

"Why?" Shelton frowned. "Something at LIRI?"

"We need to examine the second cache," I replied, "but don't have the equipment. Kit will lend me a lab if I make up a reasonable excuse."

I wasn't as sure as I sounded, but had no other ideas. Plus, investigating the scorched cache might take my mind off Chance.

Shelton spoiled the effort.

"We gonna talk about what Chance said?" he asked quietly. "That last crack about gold, and twinkling eyes . . . It hit a little too close to home."

I couldn't agree more. Chance's parting shot seemed like a challenge. A taunt. Or worse: a warning of things to come.

How much did he know? Suspect? What did he remember?

We descended to the waterfront. Tom Blue waited on the dock, *Hugo*'s motor already purring.

"Let's work one problem at a time," I said. "LIRI. The cache fragments."

"Not me," Ben said firmly. "I have a ton of homework, and can't follow a whim all the way to Loggerhead. Waste of time."

Thanks.

"How are we supposed to get there without *Sewee*?" Hi asked. "Swim?"

"My dad heads to LIRI right after Morris. Ride out with him, then take the evening shuttle back."

"I'm out too," Shelton said. "Mom's been on my case about cleaning my room lately. I've gotta knock that out before dinner."

I raised a hopeful brow at Hi. "Pretty please? We all know you're king of the lab."

Hi rubbed his chin, as if in deep thought. "Why do I feel like I'm being played?" Then he shrugged. "Sure. Why not? But I get to run the machines."

"Deal."

◇   ◇   ◇

Hi and I walked through the glass doors of Building One.

"Oh great," I muttered. Security Chief Hudson was manning the desk.

Deep creases appeared on Hudson's forehead. He rose, carefully straightening his immaculate powder-blue uniform.

"State your business."

"To see my father." A beat. "That's usually going to be my business, FYI."

Hudson didn't smile. "Is Director Howard expecting you?"

Annoyed with this routine, I gambled. "More than expecting. We're late."

Hudson's gaze slid to Hi. "Both of you?"

"Both," Hi said quickly. "He's our dodgeball coach, and we're working out some new defensive maneuvers."

Hudson's eyes narrowed. "Dodgeball?"

"District champs." Hi pounded his chest. "I'm a gunner. The key is to reach the balls first, and then throw with a *little* touch of spin, so that —"

"Should I log in?" Grabbing for the clipboard.

Hi couldn't resist, but he was dancing on thin ice. The *last* thing I needed was for Robocop to call upstairs.

Hudson gave us a hard look, perhaps concerned we were al Qaeda operatives in disguise. "Sign. No stops."

Minutes later we entered the fourth-floor director's suite. The Dragon was absent, no doubt sucking down a Marlboro behind a shed somewhere. I beelined to Kit's door and knocked.

"Come."

Kit sat behind a carved wooden desk, phone pressed to one ear. Surprised at our appearance, he waved for us to sit while he finished the call.

"But I don't *want* to cut the grant, Pete." Kit rubbed his eyes. "The institute has always cosponsored the aquarium's dolphin expert. I see no reason to change that." Pause. "Yes, I understand it costs money. What I'm telling you is that LIRI is going to spend it."

Kit covered the receiver. "One sec, guys. This bozo never stops talking."

The office hadn't changed much from Karsten's era. A coat rack occupied the corner, stuck between two overstuffed bookshelves. Behind the desk, a large bay window overlooked the Atlantic. A credenza and pair of wooden filing cabinets sat beneath.

Kit's main contribution had been a framed collection of antique veterinary diagrams on the walls. I had to admit, they looked pretty cool.

The desk was clear except for a laptop and two pictures. One was of Kit and me eating lunch on our roof deck. The other showed Kit and Whitney splitting an ice cream sundae.

"Holy crap." Hi nodded to the second photo. "Your dad's a huge dork, huh?"

I shrugged. "The evidence is fairly damning."

Kit hung up with a loud sigh. "These suits only think about money. Budgeting. Revenues versus costs. Don't they understand we're a *non-profit*? That the animals come first?"

I nodded sympathetically. "Keep fighting the good fight."

"Will do. And, happily, LIRI has the resources." Kit smiled. "Thanks again for that."

"No problem." Hiram and I, in unison.

"Now, what can I do for you two? Why are you here?"

Time to snow old dad. Again.

"School project," I said. "We're supposed to run some tests for AP chemistry. We were hoping you could spare a lab for a few hours."

Kit's expression grew wary. "School project, eh? Heard that one before."

"Seriously! We have to examine an object for trace evidence. It's totes legit. We just want to kick it up a notch."

Hi kept quiet, nodding with a plastic grin. I don't think it helped our cause.

"You can use Lab Two if it's open." Kit leaned forward. "But if you're up to something, know that I'm ready. The days of Kit the Clueless are over. I'm watching you guys, like a . . . like a . . . like a *really* good watcher of things." He cocked his head. "An owl, maybe?"

"'Up to something'?" I flapped a breezy hand. "*Pshh*. Relax."

○   ○   ○

"Kit's not so good with similes," I said, wiping down a steel counter. "I would've gone with a hawk, or maybe the Hubble telescope. I guess owl works."

We were setting up in Lab Two. Smallest in the main building, and tucked away on the third floor, the cozy workspace was perfect for avoiding attention. Thankfully, we had the room to ourselves.

"He tends to lose focus," Hi agreed. "It's more his delivery than anything."

"True."

As we spoke, Hi methodically set out the evidence: iPad. Puzzle box. Letter from Loggerhead. Scorched container from Castle Pinckney. Not much, but all we had. When finished, he clasped his hands together. "Now what?"

"I'm not sure," I admitted. "I wish Ben and Shelton had come."

Hi snorted. "Ben said this was a waste of time, remember?"

"How could I forget?" That was so unlike him. "Ben usually *loves* this kind of stuff. For all we know, this 'Game' is deadly serious, and some homicidal lunatic actually intends to *kill* people. So I don't get why —"

The sound of the door opening interrupted my response. I turned to see Anders Sundberg poke his head into the room.

"Hey you two." Anders ambled in wearing a white lab coat over medical scrubs. "What's going down? Anything I can help with?"

"No thanks." Trying not to smooth my hair. "I think we've got it covered."

Anders was too handsome for his own good. For anyone's good.

In my periphery, I saw Hi slip the Gamemaster's letter into a drawer. *Have to follow the rules.*

"We need a lab for a few hours," I said. "Kit thought this room was free?"

"Iglehart left for the day, so it's available." Anders grinned sheepishly. "And I'll level with you. Kit sent me in here to spy."

Did he now? Perhaps my act hadn't been as convincing as I'd thought. But maybe we could turn this to our advantage.

"Hate to disappoint," Hi said, "but it's only schoolwork."

Anders glanced at the assortment on the counter. "Interesting project."

"Kind of." *Here goes.* "We have to examine those objects for trace evidence."

"A forensic assignment?" Anders looked intrigued. "Sounds fun."

"You bet." Hi adapted smoothly. "Something has been planted on one of these articles. We're supposed to locate and identify it."

"I'm in." Sundberg removed a box of latex gloves from a cabinet. "The first rule of a forensic examination is to avoid contaminating the objects yourself. You don't want to introduce anything not already there."

I cringed. I'd been carrying this stuff loose in my backpack.

Oh well. Done was done.

"So what exactly should we look for?" Hi asked, snapping on gloves.

"Anything, really. Trace evidence is any material that transfers when two objects come into contact."

Anders moved to the counter. "Often the transfer is facilitated by heat, in a process we call contact friction. A fingerprint, for example." He carefully lifted the iPad. "This touch screen would be the perfect medium to capture one."

I glanced at Hi, who frowned sourly. We'd all handled the iPad. Whatever prints may have been present, that ship had sailed.

"I don't think that's it," I said. "We've used that as part of our assignment, so it must be covered with our own prints."

Sundberg shrugged and put it aside, then moved to the puzzle box. "What's this?"

"*Himitsu-Bako.*" Hi winked. "It's Japanese, yo."

"Does it open?"

"Hopefully." Grasping its sides, I tried to mimic Shelton's moves, but couldn't recall the sequence. After three tries I gave up. Hi had no better luck.

"We found some papers inside," I said, hiding my frustration. "But I guess further inspection will have to wait."

"When you get it open," Anders said, "look for things like hair, cosmetics, glass, or fibers." He glanced at the ceiling, thinking. "Also soils and botanical materials. Pollen. Maybe paint chips. You get the idea. And use tape to lift them."

"What about this?"

I tapped the cache from Castle Pinckney. Though scorched and smashed, the box was largely in one piece. I was pinning most of my hopes on it.

"Okay, *now* we're in business." Sundberg studied a singed area along the box's exterior. "An accelerant was used to make this burn. An oil perhaps, or some other fuel."

Hi edged in close. "How does that help?"

"Because accelerants don't burn completely clean. They leave a residue." Anders held up one hand. "Now, for chemistry sticklers, true accelerants are only compounds and gases that *promote* fuel burning — like an oxygen-bearing gas — and *not* the fuel itself. That would exclude gasoline, acetone, kerosene, and so on. But in forensics, any chemical fuel that causes a fire to burn hotter, spread quicker, or be harder to extinguish is considered an accelerant."

"Identifying the residue will reveal the accelerant." I'd caught on. "We'd know what caused the fire."

"And knowing *that* could lead to a suspect," Hi finished. "If a bomb was laced with butane, we could start frisking smokers."

"Exactly." Anders began pulling supplies from a drawer. "The best example is gunpowder residue. Even though it's invisible, it stains the shooter's trigger hand. Pretty useful when sorting out who shot whom."

"I hear ya, bro," said Hi. "So what's the next step?"

Anders brought his eyes close to the cache. "Let's have a go." Wielding a long swab, he carefully swiped the singed area, darkening the cotton tip with a greasy film.

"Bingo." Anders looked pleased with himself. "Whatever that gunk is, it fueled the blaze that charred this container. That's a trace evidence jackpot."

"Excellent." My spirits rose. Maybe this *would* work. "How can we identify the substance?"

"Run it through a mass spectrometer, or maybe a scanning electron microscope. Arson investigators might use a technique called headspace gas chromatography, which separates gas mixtures into their individual components. Or, if you had an idea what the accelerant was, you could try a chemical reaction test."

"Great!" I rubbed my hands together. "Which one first?"

Anders's eyebrows rose. "Tory, that's a hefty request. Those machines are extremely expensive. We rarely log time on them for side projects." He paused, lips pursed. "Your teacher couldn't have reasonably expected you to conduct a full microscopic analysis. How would you? I think you'll be okay with just the swab."

"Of course we will." Hi elbow-jabbed my side. "Tory's such a kidder. *Let's run the mass spectrometer.*" He flashed a "get a load of this guy" face at Anders while aiming a thumb back at me. "What a joker!"

"Yeah, you're right." I forced a laugh. "The residue sample should be plenty."

But how was I going to identify it?

I nearly growled in frustration. And worry. The Gamemaster's dire threats were looping inside my head. I couldn't let on to Anders, but we *needed* those tests.

Hi began repacking our evidence, talking the whole time. "I think we've made some real progress here. Dynamite stuff. First place in the . . . homework . . . contest should be ours for the taking. We'll get matching jackets, maybe with a sweet periodic table arm patch . . ."

I tuned him out.

Chemical analysis was a tall order. Only one idea sprang to mind.

Despite his über-wealthy background, as a young man Jason's father had bucked Taylor family tradition and chosen to protect and serve. After years working as a homicide detective, he'd eventually been promoted to head the violent crimes unit for the Charleston Police Department.

Should I try that angle? It didn't go so well last time, and what story would Jason believe? When it came to odd requests, my credibility had grown suspect. Even with my own father.

"Do you know who specializes in this type of analysis?" I asked casually.

"The police," Sundberg answered. "We've got better equipment, but they've got the expertise." A strange look crossed his face. "Why do you ask?"

"For the assignment. We're supposed to . . . we've got a list of forensic questions to answer. I think we're supposed to interview an expert."

"Oh, no problem." Anders tapped his chin, thinking. "There's a guy downtown at the CPD crime lab named Eric Marchant. Actually, Hudson knows him pretty well, if you can stomach talking to that guy. From what I've heard, Marchant is one of the city's go-to forensic experts. A ballistics ace."

Hmm. It's a start.

"Thanks so much for the help." Hi chucked Anders's shoulder, which seemed to startle him. "We'll be sure to acknowledge you when our paper wins the Nobel Prize for Awesome Research. We'll even drop you a footnote."

"You're too kind." Dryly. "Can I tell Kit that you've finished in here?"

"Yep." Hi swiveled to me. "Ready to rock, Tor?"

I nodded. "Thanks, Anders."

"Always a pleasure." He departed with a lazy wave.

"At least we found *something*, right?" Hi recovered the Gamemaster's letter and shoved it in his backpack. "Not a total waste."

"Not at all. Let's get home and tell the others."

Heading for the door, I had a bit more pep in my step. No answers yet, but we had a place to start. Progress.

For the first time since Coop was injured, I felt a measure of control. The humiliating feeling of being pushed around had lessened. It hadn't disappeared — we still had to dance to the Gamemaster's strings — but the bite wasn't quite as strong.

Watch your back, Gamemaster.

I almost smiled as we waited for the elevator.

You picked the wrong mark.

CHAPTER 17

Security Chief Hudson flipped on the lights.

Halogens flared overhead, bathing Lab Two in surreal brightness. The radiance gleamed off his polished name tag and wristwatch.

Hudson walked to the room's center. Rotated a slow three-sixty. Stopped. Rubbed his closely shaved chin.

This is pointless.

But his instructions had been clear. Watch the Brennan girl. Track her movements on the island. Discover if she was poking into things she shouldn't be.

So here he stood, inspecting an empty laboratory. Grasping at straws.

The girl doesn't leave a magic vapor trail to follow.

Hudson did a quick circuit, hoping for some clue to what Brennan and the fat kid had been doing. No luck. They'd cleaned up after themselves.

Hudson *had* learned a few things. Brennan was working with Dr. Sundberg. His ID locator hadn't budged from Lab Two while the girl was there.

What was *that* connection?

Hudson paced the room, idly running a finger along the metal counter bolted to the wall. Once more he scanned the cabinets, drawers, and jars, inspected the gadgets and machines. Looked for anything ajar, disturbed, used, or out of place.

Nothing. Like they'd never been there.

Perhaps the visit was harmless.

The kid was *always* out here, her and those boys. Underfoot, traipsing around the island like those blasted monkeys. Some whispered they'd befriended the pack of wild dogs! Hudson couldn't fathom why Director Howard allowed those animals to roam free.

Or his daughter, for that matter.

Hudson sighed. He'd simply report what he knew. Which, frankly, was zip. But a thin report was better than none. He couldn't botch this one.

One last glance, then Hudson slapped off the lights and headed out the door.

CHAPTER 18

The menu offered sloppy joes with a diced vegetable medley.

Even the best schools have terrible food days, and Bolton was no exception. Which is why I usually packed a lunch. That day, it was a cucumber-and-cream-cheese sandwich, SunChips, and Diet Coke. I never claimed to be a health nut.

"I'm telling you, we don't need him." Ben wouldn't let it go. "And he's not going to help anyway."

We sat in our usual corner. Around us, the cafeteria echoed with clattering trays, clinking silverware, and gossiping students. I barely noticed. My focus was on the three sets of skeptical eyes across the table.

"Jason's dad is a detective." Third time I'd repeated it. "We're trying to contact a police expert. Why *wouldn't* we use that connection?"

"The Gamemaster's rules." Ben leaned closer, dropped his voice. "We're not supposed to talk to anyone. People could get hurt."

Hi and Shelton flanked Ben. We'd arranged ourselves this way so Jason could sit next to me, but right now it felt like a firing squad.

"Ben could be right." Hi was shrugging off his inside-out jacket. "The rules don't specifically mention this, but I doubt the Gamemaster would see it that way."

"We just need an introduction." My patience was wearing thin. "Jason can get a message to this Marchant guy, and then we can give him the swab. Easy."

"What makes you think Marchant will help us?" Shelton asked. "We don't know him. And I thought those labs couldn't do side projects?"

"That's why we need Jason," I said, exasperated. "He's our in."

Hi glanced behind me. "He's coming now." Pause. "Ever notice how short Jason wears his ties? He looks like an insurance salesman. And learn a Windsor knot already."

Shelton snorted, covered it by shoveling vegetable medley into his mouth.

Jason slid into the chair beside me. "Something funny?"

Shelton expelled a few fake hacks. "Hiccups."

"Whatever." Jason seemed in good spirits. "Sorry I'm late. I didn't hit my locker until after third period, and just got your note. What's up?"

I smiled sweetly. I hoped. "We have a favor to ask."

"*She* has a favor to ask," Ben interjected.

Damn it, Ben! The last thing I needed.

Jason, to his credit, ignored Ben's clarification. "I live to serve. Name it."

"I need to reach someone at the CPD crime lab." Acting like my request was the most normal thing in the world. "A forensics expert named Eric Marchant."

"And you're hoping I can make that happen." Jason flashed a droll grin. "What'd you do this time? Shoot somebody?"

Ben sighed loudly. "Can you help Tory or not?"

Jason's cool slipped a notch. "If *you* don't need anything, why are you here?"

"I'm studying jerkoffs in the wild," Ben answered dryly. "This seemed like a good chance to observe one up close."

Jason leaned forward. "You want up close? We can step outside for a better look."

Hi and Shelton placed hands on Ben's shoulders.

"Enough!" I barked. "Ben, quit screwing around. Apologize."

Ben's gaze cut to me. Then he sat back and crossed his arms. "Sorry." His tone could not have been less sincere.

Jason gave Ben a level look. "Hey, no problem, pal. Misunderstandings happen."

Ben reddened, but held his tongue.

"I'm working on something for my father's birthday," I said quickly. "A scientist out at LIRI said I should speak to Marchant."

"What's the project?"

"I can't tell you." Coy. "It'd spoil the surprise."

Jason pulled a face. "But the surprise isn't for me."

The boys were right. This was a terrible cover story.

Unfortunately, hard as I'd tried, I hadn't come up with a single plausible reason why I'd need a CPD forensics expert. One that wouldn't lead to more questions. Questions I couldn't answer.

So I forged ahead, hoping I didn't sound as phony as I felt.

"My dad's way into history. Last week, I found this antique cash register in the old market that I knew he'd love."

Avoiding eye contact. *Antique cash register?*

"It's the bomb," Hi added. "Buttons everywhere. Really good at totaling prices."

"The problem is," I continued, "the gears need a specific type of oil to run properly. I don't know which one, but was told Marchant could identify things like that if given a sample."

Jason looked at me askance. "You need a police forensics expert to identify oil for an antique cash register?"

"Mmm-hmm." I tried not to squirm. *Sooo* ridiculous.

"You get into the weirdest things."

"You'll help me out?" Thousand-watt smile.

Jason shrugged. "Sure, why not. I can call over about Marchant."

"Thank you so much!" I removed the swab from my bag and handed it to Jason. "Here's the sample."

Jason raised the swab like a baton. "One condition."

"Anything."

"I get to see this amazing cash register."

Crap.

Shelton's brows climbed his forehead. Hi winced. Ben's attention snapped back to the table.

Jason didn't seem to notice. "You'll have to show me this machine, one-on-one."

"*'One-on-one,'*" Ben mimicked in a singsong voice. Then he got up and started for the door. "Jesus, this is painful to watch. I'm outta here."

Jason shot to his feet, nostrils flaring. Ben stopped dead.

The cafeteria went still. Everyone watched the boys square off.

"I'm not a violent person, Blue." Jason bit off the words. "But I've had enough of your mouth. I'll kick your ass right here."

Ben's jaw tightened. "You think so, rich boy?"

"You heard me." A vein was bulging in Jason's neck.

Ben's breathing quickened. The tiniest spark of gold flickered in his irises.

My stomach backflipped.

Oh my God! He's going to flare!

"Get him out of here!" I hissed at Shelton and Hi. "Hurry!"

Recognizing the danger, Hi jumped to his feet, planted both hands on Ben's chest and pushed him toward the door, whispering, "Use your head, use your head, use your head!"

Ben tried to hold his ground, but Shelton joined the effort. "Get it together! People are watching. Don't lose control!"

Slowly, the duo managed to back Ben away, but his glare never strayed from Jason. At the exit, Ben shrugged free and stalked down the hall alone.

I took my first breath since Jason stood.

Crisis averted, but barely.

Excited chatter filled the room. As classmates watched our table, hoping for more drama, Jason hastily retook his seat.

"That was . . ." I struggled for words. "Jason, I'm so sorry. I don't know why —"

"You really don't, do you?" Jason snapped. "Everyone else can figure it out."

"Figure out what?"

"Never mind. I'll get in touch with Marchant. It might take a few days for him to call you. That okay?"

"Yes." It would have to be. "And thank you again."

But his comment bothered me. "When you said everyone else —"

"I've got to get going." Rising quickly. "We'll talk again soon."

Jason strode through the doors, nodding to Shelton and Hi as they hurried back to the table. The three of us huddled close, our lunches forgotten.

"What in God's name was that?" Hi looked as alarmed as I felt.

"I saw your expression, Tor." Shelton's eyes darted, scanning for eavesdroppers. "Ben almost slipped, didn't he? Almost . . . changed?"

I nodded, not trusting myself to speak.

"Not good." Hi ran a hand down his face. "Not good at all."

"We've got to keep those two apart for a while." Shelton dodged my eye. "Let them cool down."

I rubbed my forehead, in a daze. "They've never been this bad before."

The look in Ben's eyes when Jason challenged him — it'd been dangerous. Borderline irrational. For him to get so angry he nearly *flared in public* . . . How could he allow such a loss of self-control? Would it happen again?

"Ben's always had a temper," I said, "but lately he's off the chain. Do you have any idea why?"

"Um. Huh." Hi wasn't looking at me. "I mean, look. I'm sure whatever it is, he'll get over it. Things happen. We should just give him some space."

"Space." Shelton was inspecting a thumbnail. "That's probably the best thing."

My eyes narrowed. Did these two know more than they were letting on?

I was about to probe further when Hi spoke. "Jason said we might not hear from Marchant for days. How much time do we have left?"

The Game. I'd almost forgotten.

I rooted inside my backpack, keeping the iPad hidden. Checked the timer.

"Thirty-six hours. Until tomorrow midnight."

"Then we can't wait," Shelton said. "We've got to solve the puzzle."

"You're right." I slapped the tabletop in frustration. "I'm tired of being jerked around like a yo-yo."

"I hate it too," Hi said. "But for now, we have to follow the script. No choice."

"We need an idea." Shelton tapped a finger. "Some plan of attack."

He was right.

But I didn't have one.

And we were running out of time.

Tick tick tick.

CHAPTER 19

"Tory! Get down here for dinner!"

Blargh.

I slipped the iPad into a drawer. No progress, though I'd scanned and uploaded the image. Shelton was combing the Internet for a match.

"Tory!" Kit's voice had reached level two.

"Coming!"

Gathering my hair with chopsticks, I hurried downstairs. Whitney was there, of course. I hadn't been informed she was dining with us. Of course.

Coop padded over and nuzzled my hand.

"Good boy." I pointed to his corner. "Place."

Coop yawned, then retreated to his doggie bed in the living room. Whitney eyed him, wary of a wolfdog sneak attack. Please.

Recently, I'd been working on Coop's begging. Kit had put his foot down — no four-leggers tableside during meals. No exceptions.

Coop obeyed me most of the time. When it suited him.

I didn't mind if Coop ruffled Whitney's feathers — she was a self-important, dog-hating whiner. But it put Kit in a tight spot. Best not to make waves.

Another accommodation for the bimbo.

Kit had come home early that night, surprising us both. Grocery bag pressed to his chest, he'd announced he'd be grilling. Whitney had practically squealed with delight.

The menu was a given. Kit cooked a mean cheeseburger, and that's about it.

I'd watched him hustle down to the communal grill, charcoal in tow. Mr. Devers had joined him with a trio of steaks, followed by Hi's father with marinated chicken breasts.

The temperature was a pleasant seventy-five degrees, one of those perfect October nights in the Lowcountry. The men had shared a few beers, waiting for the meat to cook.

I was happy Kit could still relax with the neighbors. He was their boss now, but it hadn't changed things back on Morris Island. They'd laughed and swapped stories, three dads hosting an impromptu barbeque, at ease in one another's company.

Kit makes that happen. He doesn't set himself apart, and they sense it.

"Dinner is served." Kit set three plates on the dining room table.

Whitney *ooh*ed and *aah*ed like a moron. I dug right in.

Kit cooked his burgers a true medium-rare. Pinker than Mom used to make, but I was coming around. Juice dribbled down my chin as I took large bites.

"Tory darling, have you made a decision?" Whitney sipped pinot grigio from a crystal-stemmed wineglass that she probably brought from home. "Who will be the lucky boys?"

"Do what now?"

"Your marshals, Tory." Whitney rolled her eyes. "This is only the *third* time I've asked you about it. The ball is next Friday."

Shoot. I'd managed to block that out.

In the last few days, I'd been to Loggerhead twice, accidentally detonated a bomb in Battery Park, stopped by Claybourne Manor, and watched Ben explode like an Indonesian volcano.

But Whitney wanted an update on my cotillion plans. FML.

"Still working on that." Chomping ground beef. "Lots of factors in play. Don't want to make a poor choice, right?"

"Don't speak with your mouth full, champ." Kit gave me a disapproving head shake. "Whitney needs those names ASAP. You know that."

"What about that nice Taylor boy, from Mount Pleasant?" Whitney tapped her lip with a cherry red fingernail. "James? No, Jason! The lacrosse player with the blond hair." She gave me a conspiratorial wink. "He's *cute*."

Gross.

Whitney discussing my friends was straight-up creepy.

Though he is cute. No denying that.

"I dunno, maybe."

"Would you like me to speak to his mother?" Whitney leaned close. "If you're uncomfortable inviting a boy, we could arrange for him to ask you."

I wanted to punch her face.

He already offered, you dolt. Everything's not as simple as you are.

"I can handle it." Crunching the last of my pickle. "May I be excused? Big chem test tomorrow."

Kit nodded. "Whitney needs an answer tomorrow night. No more delays. Deal?"

"Deal."

Slapping my leg for Coop to follow, I scurried upstairs and flopped onto my bed. Fought off an anxiety attack. I'd been avoiding this decision since learning I'd have to make it.

Whom to invite? Upon which gallant young men should I bestow the honor of walking me across a ballroom three times?

Such a hot ticket. I don't want to start a riot.

I decided to make a list. I like lists. They help me frame an issue. Plan a strategy. Sort the possible from impossible.

Grabbing paper and pen, I wrote Chance Claybourne. Immediately crossed it out.

Get real. My subconscious was an idiot.

First, Chance didn't like me after what I'd done. Second, he knew too much about the Virals, and suspected more. And third, I wanted to *avoid* the spotlight, not do the Dougie on center stage. Chance was the worst possible person I could ask.

And yet, that'd be pretty badass, right?

Moving on, I recorded my default trio. Hi. Shelton. And Ben.

I circled the third name, then drew a question mark beside it.

Lately Ben had been a live wire. I loved hanging out, but the *last* thing I needed was a scene at my debutante ball. These days, the slightest blip seemed to set Ben off. Could he control his temper?

I wrote Jason's name beneath Ben's. Totally unfair, but Whitney's approval was a huge strike against him. I racked my brain for other options, came up empty. Then I snorted at my own silliness.

What other options, exactly? This was always the complete list.

I knew the easy route — take the other Virals and hide in a corner all night. Whitney and Kit would be there, but they couldn't force me to branch out. A few hours killing time with my friends, then a quick spin down the runway. Boom. Over.

So why was this difficult?

Because Jason is the perfect choice.

Jason had attended debutante balls. Knew the drill. My crew would have to conduct research on YouTube. Jason was popular on the cotillion scene. My guys weren't even on the radar. Asking Jason would get Whitney off my back. Inviting only Morris Island boys might plummet her into a depression.

Jason *would* add credibility to the Tory Brennan Debutante Ball ticket. And *he'd* already asked *me* for the gig.

And he might be, you know, a real, actual date.

I sat up abruptly. Where had *that* thought come from?

My eyes returned to Ben's circled name.

On one count I had no illusions: Ben would be hurt if I choose Jason over him. He'd never show it, but I knew Ben Blue well enough to be certain.

Back to square one.

Frustrated, I fired up my Mac. I needed help from Google. A few searches later, I'd made my decision.

My list contained four names.

According to the Internet, four was an acceptable number.

"Jason and Ben as marshals." I jotted an *M* by each of their names. Older, they'd get the higher honor. "Mumbo and Jumbo as my stags."

I wanted Hi and Shelton there. As always, safety in numbers. I scribbled a big *S* beside those two.

Running the choices through my head, they appeared sound. Whitney would be so happy that I'd chosen "a boy from a fine Southern family" that she'd accept the Virals filling out my entourage. Everybody wins, right?

So why was I still as tense as a banjo string?

I wish Mom were here.

Tears spilled before I knew it. Sobs threatened to follow. Somehow I managed to hold the grief at arm's length.

It happened like that sometimes. The pain struck out of nowhere.

"Enough." I backhanded moisture from my cheeks.

Mom would've hated the frivolity of a deb ball, but she'd have loved helping me pick my dates. We'd have laughed about it. Together.

I probed the space in my heart where her love used to reside. Found only a void. And nearly went down again.

I miss you, Mommy. Every day.

Coop was on me like a Velcro Snuggie. Planting paws on my knees, he catapulted into my lap, nearly toppling my chair.

"Easy!" I rolled to the floor and wrapped him in a bear hug. "You'll kill us both."

Coop rested his head on my chest. I closed my eyes and stroked his muzzle.

"Thanks, dog breath. I needed that."

CHAPTER 20

The next morning I waited by my locker.

I hadn't taken the shuttle. Dentist appointment. Six a.m. Kit drove.

After forty excruciating minutes of scraping, poking, polishing, and flossing, I'd finally been paroled. My tongue kept probing my teeth, making sure all were still in their sockets.

I had a plan. Invite Jason first, just to make sure he'd still go. If he said yes, then I'd go down the line. Ben. Then Shelton and Hi.

If Jason said no, I'd die from embarrassment. After that, I'd ask Ben to be my only marshal. Perhaps that would make him feel better. But I didn't want to talk with Ben about Jason if I didn't need to.

Luck was with me. Jason appeared in the hallway before the others.

I waved awkwardly. "Got a sec?"

"Yeppers." Jason pivoted and sauntered my way.

"Yeppers?"

"I was trying it out." Jason leaned against the locker next to mine. He was wearing the standard Bolton uniform, but with one of the recently approved alternate ties: midnight blue, dotted with tiny white Griffins. "Wanted to see how it felt."

"I'd go in a different direction."

"Agreed."

My mouth opened, a prepared speech at the ready.

Jason spoke before I had the chance. "I want to apologize for how I acted in the cafeteria." His face grew serious. "I don't know what Ben has against me, but it's gone too far. We need to squash it. Fighting like this is pointless."

"You have nothing to apologize for. Ben was being a jerk."

"Yeah, but I took the bait."

"He set the hook." I sighed. "I'll talk to him. Ben's a good guy, I'm sure we can figure this out."

"Figure it out." Jason shook his head. "Right."

That look again. What?

Jason changed the subject. "I left that CPD guy a message and gave him your cell number. That okay?"

"Yes, that's perfect. Thanks so much."

"Like I said, it might be a few days." Jason glanced at his watch. "Bell coming. What did you need?"

Shoot! With Jason bouncing between topics, I'd had no opening.

I adjusted my backpack. Hid a deep breath. Unfortunately, my brain chose that moment to short circuit.

"Debutante ball," I blurted.

Nice job, genius!

"I know, right? It's so soon. Should be a blast." Jason's tone became oh-so-casual. "Who you taking? Anyone I know?"

No sir! You will not wrest control of this invite from me.

"I was hoping your offer still stood."

Jason blinked. His mouth dropped open. A beat, then, "Yeah. Yes, of course."

His reaction alarmed me. Did he still want to go?

Half the blood in my body flooded into my cheeks. Words tumbled out. "You don't have to. I mean, if you'd rather not, or if you're planning on escorting someone else, then —"

"No, no! I'm just . . . surprised. When I offered, you didn't seem too excited." He grinned like a chimp. "I'd be delighted."

Whew.

"Great! You'll be a marshal, of course. Ben will be the other, and Shelton and Hi will sing backup. My stags," I clarified lamely.

"Ben, huh." Jason's grin twisted at the corners. "Should be interesting."

"They're my best friends, Jason. I couldn't leave them out."

He nodded firmly. "Nor should you. We'll make it work. I promise."

"Thanks."

Jason's mature outlook reassured me. This would be okay. Right?

The bell rang our five-minute warning. Jason and I said good-bye and headed to our respective classes. I slid into my desk just as Shelton and Hi filled the two beside me.

Calculus dragged. Mr. Terenzoni's pinched, nasal voice droned on and on about an equation scrawled on the dry-erase board. Though I tried to pay attention, my mind wandered.

The Gamemaster's clue was still a mystery. No matter how I attacked it, the arrangement made no sense. Shelton was testing different coding systems, but so far had struck out. Hi was equally baffled, and Ben didn't seem to be trying.

The timer was counting down to midnight. For the first time, I began to doubt we'd actually solve the puzzle.

What would happen if we failed? Who would pay the price?

"Miss Brennan?"

My eyes shot to the front. Mr. Terenzoni was stroking his thin, black beard, irritation etched on his face. "We are waiting."

"Twelve?" Stock answer. I had no idea what the question was.

"No, Miss Brennan. The answer is not twelve. The answer is Green's theorem."

Snickers floated around me. Mr. Terenzoni wagged his head slowly.

Red-faced, I pushed aside my concerns and focused on not sounding like an idiot twice.

◇   ◇   ◇

I caught my next target just before lunch.

"Ben?" Pulling him aside. "I need to ask you something."

"Okay."

"My debutante ball is next Friday night."

No reaction. Ben sometimes made conversation difficult.

"I'm supposed to invite escorts. Marshals for the ceremony, and stags, too."

Still nothing.

"Would you like to be one?" I said. "A marshal, I mean. Escort me."

For a moment, Ben just stared.

"Don't strain yourself," I snapped. "You'll need a tux, and you'll have to behave around dozens of Bolton trust-funders. Can you handle that?"

Not the approach I'd planned, but his apathy got under my skin.

Ben remained quiet for another long moment. Then, "Sure."

"Okay, good." I nodded once, as if agreeing to a treaty. "That's settled then."

We began walking toward the cafeteria.

"Who else is going?"

"Shelton and Hi will be my stags. And Jason. He's co-marshal with you."

Ben stopped. "Jason?"

"Kit's girlfriend likes his family," I said swiftly. "She's the one making me debut. Plus, Jason knows the ropes, and he'd already asked if he could escort me, so —"

"Hold on." Ben's eyes were dark. "Jason asked if he could go? When?"

"At a cotillion thing this summer." What did that matter? "I never responded, but Whitney's pushing me hard, so I had to choose."

I threw my hands up, exasperated. "I don't even wanna go to this stupid thing!"

Ben's lips parted, but then he seemed to reconsider. Without a word, he strode off in the opposite direction.

"Ben, wait!"

He halted, but didn't turn.

"Will you be my marshal or not?"

"Yes."

Then I was alone outside the cafeteria doors.

"Juuuust great."

◇   ◇   ◇

"I need a tux?" Shelton's eyes widened behind their thick lenses. "What about dancing? I don't have to dance if I don't want to, right?"

We were at our usual table, secluded in the far corner by the emergency exit. The area closest to us was empty, which is just how we liked it. Hi and Shelton munched sandwiches while I ate a bowl of she-crab soup. Whitney had started preparing my lunches, an insult I couldn't bring myself to reject.

Curse her effective bribes! And me for taking them.

Ben was nowhere to be seen.

"Of course not," I said. "You two don't have any official functions. Basically, you just show up and hang out. And I'd *really* appreciate if you did."

"Yes, yes, a thousand times yes!" Hi wiped his mouth with a napkin before continuing. "Free food, free party. What's not to like? I can break out the robot." He gave a quick demonstration while sitting at the table.

"Very nice," I said. "I wasn't aware break dancing was back in style."

"Now you are." Hi tore open a bag of Bugles. "I also do a killer mime."

"So Ben and Jason are coming, too?" The wide eyes looked naked as Shelton removed and wiped his glasses. "That could get . . . messy."

"Jason seems cool, but Ben . . ." I trailed off. What more to say?

"We'll smooth him out," Hi said. "Plus, Ben would never embarrass you on the biggest, most special night of your life. Your one shot to marry well."

"You're a riot." I flung a carrot stick, but Hi dodged.

Shelton leaned forward. "How much time do we have left?"

Looking left, then right, I checked the iPad. T-minus twelve hours, and counting.

"If we don't solve this by midnight, we lose. Whatever *that* means."

"The Gamemaster *told* us what it means." Shelton hugged his body with both arms. "*Boom.* Somewhere. Could be anywhere. Innocent people are gonna get hurt."

His words chilled me. I'd lost focus on the danger. On what failure could mean.

We have to take this seriously. We have to win.

"Meet after school?" Hi suggested. "Unless you wanna ditch English and leave earlier. I'm fine with skipping old lady Mixon's dramatic interpretation of John Milton."

"It's not worth the risk." I bagged my trash and set the tray aside. "We don't want to draw any extra attention. We have all afternoon. That should be enough time."

"I don't know, Tor." Shelton eyed the iPad with apprehension. "I've tried a dozen ciphers. None worked, and I'm out of ideas. It might be time to tell the cops. If we can't break the code, shouldn't we give them a shot?"

Hi nodded reluctantly. "He's right. We can't just twiddle our thumbs while the clock runs out. What if the iPad *itself* is a bomb?"

"Agreed." I'd come to the same conclusion. "We'll give it one last shot at the bunker. If we strike out again, we'll call the police."

I glanced back down at the screen.

12:01:57. 12:01:56. 12:01:55 . . .

CHAPTER 21

"Give me your secrets, dammit!"

Hi slapped the iPad in disgust. Cooper's ears perked, then he returned to gnawing his Greenie bone.

Two hours had gotten us nowhere. Time was slipping away.

"We're done." Shelton sat across the table from Hi and me. "Let's bring in the law dogs before it's too late."

"We can't break the rules." Ben spun the computer chair to face us. "Talk, and the Gamemaster will detonate."

"Since when do you care so much about rules?" Shelton huffed. "And the bomb's going off anyway, if we can't crack the puzzle. This picture could be anything!"

I stared at the image: the figure 18, surrounded by letters and numbers, inside a black circle. All within a blue circle, and topped by a *K*.

What does it mean? What are we missing?

"We need to try something else." I stood and began to pace. "Another approach. Some new way of looking at the problem."

"I've tried everything," Shelton said. "There's no structure. How are we supposed to decode words without a pattern?"

Hi's gaze found the ceiling. "This is *killing* me."

Ben swiveled back to the computer and resumed surfing.

I stopped. "Maybe there *isn't* a pattern."

"No pattern?" Shelton sounded at a loss. "Then forget decoding the message."

I shook my head, unsure where I was going. "Maybe it's not a *message*. At least, not a straightforward one like last time."

Retaking my seat, I scribbled the letters and numbers on a blank sheet of paper: $CH_3OHHBRCH_3BRH_2O$. And got nothing. Inspiration failed to arrive. "We should've skipped class."

Hiram shot to his feet. "Chemistry!"

"Relax," Shelton said. "The paper isn't due till Monday."

"No! No!" Hi finger-jabbed my notepad. "Look at the last three characters. H_2O! What are we, idiots? That's the chemical formula for water!"

"You're right!" Shelton got it instantly. "It's not a message, it's a chemical equation!"

"Then let's solve it." Digging for my chemistry text. "This must be a list of different compounds. We need to identify them."

Ben joined us at the table. "Finally, some progress."

"Sixteen characters." I drew a line creating two groups of eight. "If you cut the sequence at its midpoint, both halves start with CH_3."

"Methyl," Hi said confidently. "But it's usually bonded with something else."

"O is oxygen, and H is hydrogen. Then another H." I bit my lower lip. "That must begin a new compound, or else it'd be H_2 instead."

I drew a second line through the first group, dividing CH_3OH and HBR.

"The equation has to balance." Hi was pointing to the second grouping: CH_3BRH_2O. "Nothing's lost in a chemical reaction."

"And we know the last part is water," Ben added. "H_2O."

Nodding, I drew a third line. "Then that's it. CH_3OH. HBR. CH_3BR. H_2O. The first two compounds must react to form the second two."

"Balanced," Hi agreed. "On paper, it works."

"First is CH3OH." I scanned the index of my textbook. *Bingo.* "Methanol. A simple alcohol — light, colorless, flammable. Used as an antifreeze, a solvent, and fuel."

Shelton took notes as I spoke. "Next?"

HBR. "Hmmm. Not listed."

"That's hydrogen and bromine." Hi ran a search on the computer. "Together they produce hydrogen bromide, a nonflammable gas. Forms hydrobromic acid in water. It's used to make lots of stuff."

"Methanol. Hydrogen bromide." I tapped the last two groups. "*These* chemicals must result from combining them."

"Exactly," Hi answered. "Otherwise the equation doesn't work."

"CH3BR and H2O." Shelton circled them both. "Same elements, just reorganized."

"Those two chemicals are the products," Ben said.

"H2O is easy," Shelton said. "We all know that stands for water."

"So the *third* compound must be the point of the reaction," Hi concluded. "It's what you're trying to make by adding methanol to hydrogen bromide, with water as a byproduct."

"CH3BR." I tapped the sheet with my index finger. "That's the answer."

"BR is still bromine, and I know CH3 stands for methane." Hi's forehead creased in thought. "Together, what? Methabromine? Bromethane?"

I rifled the index a second time. *Gotcha.* "Bromomethane."

"Nice." Hi started popping head nods. "Wassup, bromo. Sup, bromo."

I read aloud. "Bromomethane, known as methyl bromide, is a tetrahedral-shaped, odorless, colorless, nonflammable gas formerly used as a pesticide. Recognized as an ozone-depleting chemical, the widespread use of bromomethane was phased out in most First World countries by the early 2000s."

"Bugs? That's all it was used for?" Shelton asked.

"There's nothing more here." I bit my lower lip. "Check the interwebs."

"On it," Hi called.

Minutes passed, then Hi spoke slowly as he skimmed. "Bromomethane was used to sterilize soil, mainly for seed production ... and for things like strawberries and almonds." Quick glance our way. "Almonds are a crop? Man, I don't know anything about nuts."

I considered what we'd learned. "I'm not sure this helps. Anything else?"

Pause. Then, "For a while they used bromomethane in specialty fire extinguishers for electrical substations. On airplanes, too." Another pause. "That's all I can find."

"We're still missing something," Shelton said.

"Don't forget, this equation circles the number eighteen." Ben pointed to the maddening image on the iPad. "That has to factor somehow. And the K at the top, too."

I looked to Hi, at a loss.

"Nothing else here," he said glumly. "I'm stumped."

Shelton shook his head in frustration.

Then I had an idea.

O   O   O

"If you can spell the last name of the party you are trying to reach, please press one, otherwise, stay on the line and —"

Beep.

I began punching keys. *S. U. N. D. B.* Shoot. Was the next letter *E*, or *U*?

The voicemail system saved me from a guess. *"If you are trying to reach* 'Dr. Anders Sundberg' *—"* his voice interjected, *"— press one, now."*

Beep.

"One moment, please."

Ring-ring. Ring-ring.

"We're not allowed to ask for help," Ben argued. "It's against the rules."

"This is different," I insisted. "We aren't revealing anything about the game."

Shelton looked uneasy, but Hi nodded his agreement.

"I'm just going to ask about the chemical."

"What chemical would that be?" a voice inquired on the other end of the line.

I nearly squeaked. "Dr. Sundberg! I'm so glad I caught you in your office."

"A rarity, but you did just that." Pause. "This is . . . ?"

"Tory Brennan. Sorry."

"Tory?" Mild surprise. "What can I help you with?"

"Just a quick question. Regarding our school project." I wasn't handling this very smoothly. "Have you ever heard of a chemical known as bromomethane?"

"That's what we found?" The surprise turned to alarm. "Tory, methyl bromide is a highly toxic substance. You need to trash the swab, then wash *anything* that —"

"Oh no, sorry again! That wasn't the substance we pulled off the box. We're still working on identifying that."

"Well, thank goodness. Bromomethane is tough stuff. What's your interest?"

"A case study." Thinking on my feet. "We've been charged with figuring out the possible origin points of a localized contamination."

"Ah! I see. Interesting project. My high school never did cool stuff like this."

"Go Griffins," I said lamely. "So, any ideas?"

"Better. I think I know the answer." I heard a creak, as if Anders had leaned back in his chair. "Bromomethane was widely used in the Charleston area fifteen years ago, but almost solely for one purpose — golf course maintenance."

"Golf? Seriously?"

"You bet. It was very effective at controlling Bermuda grass. Especially on the greens. But the pesticide seeped into groundwater, creeks, rivers, and estuaries, resulting in some pretty severe ecological damage. Bromomethane is now banned — the side effects are just too dangerous."

A bell dinged somewhere deep in my brainpan. What was I missing?

"How do you know all this?" I asked.

"I'm a marine biologist, remember? In 1998, we traced a massive fish die-off to pollution by methyl bromide." Satisfaction coated Anders' voice. "Not to toot my own horn, but I helped get it banned."

I paused to digest this info. "Anything else you can think of?"

"Off the top of my head, no. But if that's your chemical, I'd be surprised if your assignment was pointing anywhere else."

I thanked Sundberg and hung up. Three faces beamed from across the table. Even Coop seemed to sense excitement. He rose and padded to my side.

"Locally, bromomethane was used to treat putting greens."

The boys had been listening. In fact, Hi looked pumped enough to wet himself.

His arms spread wide. "And how many holes make up a golf course?"

"Eighteen!" Shelton aimed two shooters at the iPad.

Of course. 18. The centerpiece of the Gamemaster's image.

Ben's fist struck the table. "We're getting close."

"Golf *must* be part of the answer!" Shelton insisted.

"Shhh!" I ordered. "Let me think."

The boys exchanged glances, but complied. I needed to do my thing.

Pesticide. The number eighteen. A golf course. Those parts fit together. Staring at the puzzle with a fresh outlook, I willed other pieces into place.

"The eighteen is within a circle." I traced it with one finger. "Black, like a hole."

"Golf again!" Hi interjected. "The eighteenth hole!"

I hand-shushed him. Hi rolled his eyes. Shelton rose and began dancing on the balls of his feet. Ben just watched me.

"The eighteenth hole of a golf course." My finger moved to the top of the image. "So what does this *K* mean?"

"A strikeout," Hi offered. "Or a symbol for the Ku Klux Klan — sorry, Shelton. Maybe a very 'special' breakfast cereal?"

Shelton squinted, thinking hard. I cycled the data in my brain, but came up blank. *K*? Alone? What could it mean?

"What about Kiawah," Ben offered quietly.

"Could be," Hi said. "Kiawah Island has incredible golf courses."

"Maybe." But I wasn't sure. Could it be that simple? "We need more to go on."

Shelton bumped his fists together in a rapid tattoo. "We're running out of time."

"Kiawah's Ocean Course is supposed to be dope," Hi commented. "It's hosting the PGA Championship soon. That tourney is extremely hard to get."

Something clicked.

My gaze dropped to the iPad screen. One element remained.

Surrounding the black circle. A larger, *blue* circle.

"Like the ocean," I breathed.

"What the what?" Shelton asked.

Ben smiled for the first time all afternoon. It was nice to see. When he deigned to flash his pearly whites, Ben went from sullen boy to charming young man. I *much* preferred the latter.

"Guys, we did it." My hands popped into a roof-raising celebration dance. Even Coop was impressed, and started spinning in little circles.

We'd broken the Gamemaster's clue. We could still win.

"Kiawah Island," I proclaimed. "And I know just where to look."

CHAPTER 22

*S*ewee knifed through the surf, tossing spray from her bow.

Ten p.m. We'd waited as long as possible.

We couldn't poke around the city's most famous golf course with people still out and about. But time was not on our side.

The clock expired in two hours. Whatever needed doing had to happen before then.

Everyone wore dark-colored athletic clothing. Nothing *too* sinister — the Ocean Course was famous, and even late at night we might be seen. No sense looking like criminals if we intended to commit a crime.

I sat in the bow, one arm looping Coop's neck. The wolfdog hadn't been on the guest list, but his whining had threatened my escape. Kit had continued snoring, but I'd decided not to risk more doggie noise.

Ben piloted, of course. He'd opted for the ocean route rather than risk the twisty, confusing Intracoastal Waterway after dark. Our target was close, a mere two islands to the south.

Hi and Shelton were huddled in the stern. No one spoke. Sneaking out early was trickier than our usual post-midnight jaunts, and the boys seemed on edge.

A crescent moon lit our path down the coast. The breeze was mild, but brisk. I wore a blue LIRI windbreaker, which I'd leave in the boat.

We'd cruised past Folly Beach and reached the Stono Inlet when a dark shadow appeared on the horizon just ahead.

Kiawah is a long, thin barrier island operated primarily as a high-end resort. Exclusive and private, with roughly a thousand permanent residents, the slender strip of land stays relatively quiet. Five world-class golf courses stretch from the densely wooded interior right up to the Atlantic.

The Ocean Course is the most famous of the lot.

Ben motored along the shoreline, passing a series of manicured holes. Minutes later we spied a large structure rising just beyond the first row of dunes.

"I'll pull as close as possible," Ben said in a low voice.

"Eighteen is right on the beach," Hi whispered. "Near the clubhouse. No one should be in there this late, so we shouldn't be spotted."

The three-story clubhouse was U-shaped, with massive, towering windows facing the ocean. Exterior lights burned, revealing a putting green at the base of the building. Between the halogens and the moon-light, visibility was excellent.

"We'd better *hope* nobody's home," Shelton said. "Anyone in there will have a front-row seat."

Ben cut the engine and dropped anchor. We slipped off our shoes and waded ashore, Coop splashing along beside me. Cresting a low sandbank, I was relieved to note an absence of residences close by. So long as the clubhouse was empty, we'd be okay.

The green was flat, oval, and groomed to perfection. A deep sand trap ran along its far side. A short hedge at its tip was all that screened it from the clubhouse.

Hi moved directly to the hole and reached inside.

"Nothing." He pounded his leg with a fist. "What a letdown."

I double-checked, hoping Hi was somehow mistaken. Ridiculous, but I was *sure* this was the place.

"Well, that didn't take long," said Shelton. "Let's bounce before security shows up." Hi nodded, but neither Ben nor I moved.

"It has to be here," I insisted. "The clue led directly to this spot."

"*If* we read it right," Shelton countered. "And who knows, maybe the whole game is a put-on. The Gamemaster might be full of crap."

He's not. And I'm not wrong. We're in the right place. I can feel it in my bones.

Something didn't add up. But what?

Ben was watching me. "What are you thinking?"

"The timer gave us seventy-two hours." The problem crystallized as I spoke. "But we could've solved the puzzle at any time. What if we'd cracked it earlier, and come during the day? The Gamemaster couldn't just leave something inside the hole. People golf here all day, every day."

"That's true." Hi pursed his lips. "So what are you thinking?"

"We're not wrong." I peered into the hole. "We just need to go a little deeper."

"Don't tell me you want to dig up this green!" Shelton stomped a foot. "Don't say it! I'm begging you."

"Whoa." Hi ran a hand over his scalp. "Tory, that's some pretty hefty vandalism. These greens take *years* to mature. They're worth tens of thousands of dollars."

Ben kept silent, face inscrutable. But his body was as taut as a snare drum.

"The clue points to the hole itself," I said. "That's all we need to excavate."

"Wait!" Hi's face lit up. "My metal detector is still in the boat!"

Ben snapped off a nod. "Grab it. We can scan the turf before doing any damage."

"Good idea," I agreed. "Go."

As Hi lumbered back over the dunes, Ben trotted to the clubhouse and peered inside. Coop ran beside him, quiet now, in stealth mode.

With nothing to do, Shelton and I sat on the green. For minutes I heard nothing but waves crashing on the beach and the whine of mosquitoes.

Shelton slapped his arm. Scratched. "If Hi doesn't find anything —"

"We leave it alone." I raised both palms. "Promise."

"I'll hold you to that. No sense trashing the place just because we're frustrated."

Ben and Coop reappeared first, and dropped down beside us.

"The coast seems clear." Ben rubbed Coop's ears. "The hound agrees. At least, he didn't act like anyone was inside."

Moments later Hi returned, device in tow.

"Scan the area around the hole," I instructed. "If that strikes out, we'll sweep the whole green." My eyes found Shelton's. "If *that* doesn't work, we call it a night."

"I like it." Hi fiddled with the dials, then positioned the wand. "If anything's down there, this baby should —"

Ding! Ding! Ding!

Everyone jumped. Coop barked once.

"That was easy." Hi took several steps back and the noise ceased.

I felt a surge of excitement. "Whatever's dinging is directly beneath the hole."

"Thanks, Captain Obvious." Hi powered off the detector.

Shelton exhaled the mother of all sighs. "So we're really going to dig?"

"Just inside the hole," I promised. "If we're careful, we won't cause any damage."

"Then let's *be* careful." Shelton's gaze swept the landscape. "Coop might've just triggered some unwanted attention."

"I'll get the trowels." Ben loped toward *Sewee*.

Coop moved to follow, but I called him back. Shelton was right — that yap hadn't helped our cause.

Ben returned moments later with my pack. I dug out a trowel, then slipped the bag on my back, ready for a quick getaway should the need arise.

"Avoid enlarging the circumference," Ben said. "If you can."

Prodding gently, I worried inside the hole until the cup came loose, exposing the earth beneath. Then I scratched with my trowel, hoping for something close to the surface. No such luck.

"The space is too tight to maneuver. I'll have to expand it the *tiniest* of bits."

Shelton groaned. Ben shifted his feet. Hi placed both hands on his head.

"There's no other way?" Shelton asked.

"None. But I know how to make this go smoother."

Eyes closed.

Mind clear.

I reached.

SNAP.

CHAPTER 23

The pain struck first.

Pins. Needles. Jets of fiery agony, sizzling beneath my skin.

Then came the power.

My vision sharpened to laser clarity. The island's marshy bouquet divided into an array of recognizable scents. I could hear wind swirling the manicured Bermuda grass. Could feel each individual grain of sand between my toes. I tasted the salt air, reveling in my hyperawareness.

Coop bounded close and licked my face. He always knew.

Hi eagerly grabbed for his flare, Shelton a tad less enthusiastically. Soon golden fires kindled in their eyes. Wordlessly, they surveyed the course, keeping watch.

Ben tensed. Squeezed his lids shut. Surprisingly, the transformation came quickly.

"Be careful," Ben warned, irises aflame. "The Gamemaster might be insane. His last cache exploded, and that was only a test."

"That's why I flared." Scooping up the trowel. "We need our edge."

"Work fast." Ben kept his eyes on the clubhouse. "If we're caught damaging this course, they'll burn us at the stake."

I inspected the ground. Found no defects. Whatever was down there hadn't been inserted recently. The grass looked uniform in color, height, density, and thickness. The soil at its roots appeared undisturbed.

How could someone bury a cache without leaving any sign?

Cringingly slightly, I dug a larger circle around the perimeter, doubling the size of the hole. The earth was soft and pliable, easy to move.

"Putting should be easier now," Hi quipped. "Maybe they'll thank us."

"Uh-huh," Shelton grunted. "Right after sentencing."

I teased off soil, millimeter by millimeter, widening and deepening the opening, the same questions running through my mind.

The Game.

What did it mean? Who was the Gamemaster? Why did he bother?

Elaborate caches. Intricate clues. The pieces were expensive — iPad, puzzle box, even night-vision video equipment.

Remote-controlled bomb. Don't forget that one.

Hours of planning had gone into this. What kind of person takes the time?

We'd stumbled into an elaborate trap. Become human toys.

Four high schoolers, out goofing around. Yet the Gamemaster clearly didn't care who'd swallowed his hook. That fact was most frightening of all.

As my thoughts wandered, a new awareness bloomed.

The four of us were huddled together, close enough to reach out and touch. But the nearness was more than just physical. I could *feel* the other Virals in a way I can't explain.

That had happened before. But now it was *five*, not four.

I could sense Coop as well. The wolfdog's presence tipped the balance.

"Ever notice how often we dig stuff up?" Hi's voice intruded. "We should form, like, an excavation company. Get matching hard hats. Blue ones."

"Be quiet," Shelton hissed. "We're exposed out here. There's too much light from those damn floods."

I kept digging. Physically. Mentally. My eyes lost focus as I probed the edges of my psyche, the deepening hole at my feet virtually forgotten.

The flaming cords appeared — twisting, fiery ropes that connected the minds of my pack to form a fragile mental network.

Even Coop. Yes! The wolfdog's proximity heightened the effect.

Tread carefully. Don't lose control.

I should've spoken up. Should've told the others what I was experiencing. But the connection was tenuous. Fragile as tissue paper. I knew speaking would severe the link.

Forgive me, boys.

Hands working robotically, I surrendered to my instincts and grasped a cord at random.

Lightning strobed inside my skull. My mind hurtled down the glowing cable.

Consciousness flickered. My perception split.

Two distinct images formed in my brain.

One showed my hands as they continued to shovel dirt.

The other watched a red-haired girl in dark clothes, digging with a trowel.

Me. I'm watching myself. And Coop is the only one at my back.

My breath caught. Sweat pumped from my pores.

I was seeing through Coop's eyes.

I felt the wolfdog's ears perk. Coop popped to his feet, momentarily uncertain and afraid. Then, recognizing me, he calmed, accepting my presence in his mind.

It's so easy for him. Why?

My hands continued their rhythmic tempo. I focused inward, anxious to preserve the connection.

As Coop resumed snuffling the putting surface, powerful odors flooded my brain. Spartina grass. Crickets. Salt. Dried mud.

And something . . . *else*. Harsh. Metallic. The inorganic scent seemed out of place.

Curious, I urged Coop toward the hedge bounding the green. I could sense his reluctance, but he complied.

Something was tucked in the foliage. I tried to drive Coop to investigate, but the wolfdog resisted my will. Suddenly, his attention snagged on a wisp of light rising from the base of the bushes.

The wolfdog was confused. But I wasn't.

Wire. Perhaps fishing line. Rising from the ground into the shrubs.

Clank.

My trowel struck something solid. The mental connection broke.

The wolfdog yipped as my full consciousness recoiled into my own skull. The dual perception shattered. My head spun, and my stomach nearly emptied.

The episode had lasted mere seconds. The boys hadn't noticed, their attention riveted on my trowel.

"That sounded like metal," Shelton squeaked. "Pull it out."

"Hold on a sec." Ben reached into the hole. "Whatever's down here won't come free. Like it's tethered somehow."

I tried to recapture the image from Coop's brain. We'd seen something important. But what? What was the significance?

My mind felt like mud. I couldn't shake my paralysis.

"Let me help." Hi moved beside Ben, his back to the hedge.

That seemed wrong.

"Okay." Ben cracked his knuckles. "Lift on three."

Wait. No. Stop.

"Ready?"

Hi nodded.

"Okay. One. Two. Thr —"

My brain finally rebooted.

I threw myself forward into Hi's chest. We toppled in a heap of elbows and knees. The move startled Ben, who slipped and fell backward.

CRACK! CRACK!

Smoke filled the air. I prayed I hadn't been too late.

Shelton was in a battle crouch. Ben was flat on his back. I lay atop Hi, panting like a sled dog.

"What the hell?" Hi wheezed. "Why did you jump me?"

"Trap. Wires." My scrambled wits could barely manage speech. "Anyone hurt?"

"Not me." Shelton said. "What happened?"

"A crazed female linebacker pummeled my chest," Hi grumbled. "She's still pinning me to the ground. And she isn't as light as she might think."

I rolled off Hi and got to my feet. "Ben?"

"I'm . . . I'm okay." He sounded shaken.

"Oh my God." Shelton pointed.

Coop was dragging a long black object from the bushes. Metal. Smoke spiraled upward from one end.

Ben raced to the wolfdog's side. "Gun!" He gingerly lifted the weapon. "I've never seen anything like this. Two barrels, both single shot, with two triggers."

A gray filament was tied to each trigger. Ben traced one with his fingers to where it disappeared into the bushes. "Wow."

My heart spiked. "Where's the cache?"

"I had it, but something knocked it from my grip." Ben swallowed. "A bullet, I think."

A plastic box lay beside the hole, a dime-sized gash in one side. The box was sealed with duct tape. Two lines ran from its base into the ground.

Shelton grabbed an ear. "Holy crap."

I slipped off my backpack and located my Swiss Army knife. Then, ever so cautiously, I snipped both lines. "We're taking the gun, too."

"Uh, Tory." Hi dropped to his knees by my side.

"Yes?"

Wordlessly, he lifted my pack and pointed to a small tear. The edges were seared, the fibers curled and black.

My stomach did a somersault.

Close. Inches.

Don't think about it. "Hi, check our time." *Don't think about the bullet.* "Ben, make sure that gun's empty." *Don't think about hot metal punching through your back.* "Shelton, grab Cooper. He's agitated. I don't want him barking."

"You guys aren't going to believe this." Hi had dug out the iPad. A smooth, round hole punctured its center.

Shelton's jaw dropped.

"Does it still work?" Ben asked.

"The timer does. We've got twenty minutes."

"We need to open the cache right now." I sliced the duct-tape seal. "Here goes nothing."

The contents were hardly what I'd expected. No drawing, image, or note. Only a heavy bronze figurine — a bearded man in a flowing robe, left arm outstretched as though reaching for the horizon. Chipped and scarred, the peculiar little statue was wrapped in black–and–white cloth.

Deformed metal fragments lay to one side.

Hi whistled. "How about that? Micro-man took the slug dead-on."

The iPad suddenly beeped. Hi nearly dropped it in fright.

The pictogram disappeared, leaving only the timer. Then a large purple circle appeared.

Text above it read: Task complete? Enter code and press the button.

"Code?" Ben growled. "What code?"

"Here!" Hi pointed to numbers printed on the cache's lid: 654321.

I hadn't noticed. "Good eye, Hiram."

"Don't press anything!" Shelton yelped. "We fell for that once already."

"We have to," I said. "A bomb might explode at zero."

But something troubled me. Why had the button appeared? How did the iPad know we'd found the cache?

Something cold crawled up my spine. Inside Castle Pinckney, a hidden camera had monitored the Gamemaster's cache. Were we being watched here as well?

"Tory's right," Ben said. "Press it."

Hi nodded. Shelton moaned, but waved me on.

Taking a deep breath, I input the numbers and tapped the circle.

The iPad went blank, then flashed brilliant white. Trumpets blared. Colored balls bounced across the wounded screen, each decorated by a snarling clown face.

"Wacko," Hi breathed.

Almost immediately, the bizarre display was replaced by a single large ball eerily centered over the bullet hole.

The timer reappeared: 48:00:00. Began counting down.

Words materialized above it: The Game continues! Complete your next task!

"Oh no." Shelton pressed fists to forehead. "It's not over."

Suddenly, high beams sliced through the darkness in the parking lot, followed by flashing red-and-blue lights.

"Frick! Cops!" Hi turned and sprinted for the beach. "Run!"

Ben and I scrambled to gather our things, then leaped across the dunes and splashed into the surf. Ahead, Hi and Shelton were hauling Coop aboard.

Radio static cut the stillness. Two flashlight beams bobbed toward the green.

"Go!" Shelton hissed as I dragged in the anchor.

Ben needed no prodding. Gunning the engine, he spun *Sewee* in a tight arc and fired through the waves.

CHAPTER 24

My phone vibrated and blared Coldplay.

Sighing, I put the figurine aside and glanced at the clock on my bedroom wall. Hours of examination, yet I was nowhere. And Friday was already half gone.

I glanced at the iPad, amazed it still functioned with a hole through its gut. The clock read 33:01:06. A quarter of our time gone, and still no leads.

Grabbing my iPhone, I frowned. The caller ID simply read "private." I debated letting it roll to voicemail, but yielded to curiosity.

"This is Tory."

"Tory Brennan?" A male voice.

"Yes." Cautious. I'd been pranked before, and had no intention of falling for more Bolton Prep immaturity.

"This is Eric Marchant at the CPD crime lab. Someone named —" papers shuffled in the background, "— Jason Taylor left me a message. I'm not sure how he got my office number, but it doesn't matter. He sent something for analysis."

"Mr. Marchant!" I stood and began to pace. "Thanks so much for calling."

"Not a problem, though I must admit the request was a bit odd. I received a cotton swab coated with an unknown substance. It was nothing more than diesel fuel."

Diesel fuel? Shoot, dead end. You could buy that anywhere.

Marchant's voice sounded tinny, probably coming from a speaker-phone. He had a clipped, precise way of speaking. I imagined a short, bookish man in a tweed jacket with a pocket protector.

"There was something about a cash register?" Marchant prompted.

Sudden thought.

This man was a ballistics expert. Last night, a contraption had fired at us. Someone could've been killed. Access to Marchant's expertise was incredibly fortunate.

A plan formed in my head.

"Jason must've been confused, sir. I have a serious issue." Adding a quaver to my voice. "Someone tried to kill my dog."

"My goodness." There was a soft click as Marchant lifted the receiver. "Have you filed an incident report?"

"I haven't told anyone." I opted for damsel in distress. "My neighborhood is very isolated, and the local cops hate coming out here. They don't care at all."

"Shameful." Irritation tinged Marchant's voice. "Though I can't say I'm surprised. Some of our more remote sheriffs wouldn't investigate a fire in their own station house. But why do you think someone wants to harm your pet?"

"My dog's half wolf, and a few weeks ago these rednecks threatened to shoot him." I invented details on the fly. "Last night, my friends and I found something buried in the dunes. A metal contraption, with two short barrels. We accidentally set it off, and I was nearly hit."

"The device *fired* at you?" Incredulous. "A projectile weapon?"

"Yes, sir. I think it's a gun, but I'm not sure."

"Of all the *irresponsible*—" I could almost see Marchant straighten in his chair. "Could you locate a bullet fired by the weapon?"

"Oh yessir! I have the weapon and two slugs."

"Excellent. Did you retrieve any shell casings?"

Why hadn't I thought of that? "No sir, but I could possibly look again."

"No need." Pages flapped. "I'm tied up today, but if you bring those items to me tomorrow, I'd be willing to take a look."

Jackpot. "Of course. Could you give me the crime lab's street address?"

"Certainly. Email emarchant@cpd.gov and I'll send directions. That way I'll have your contact info."

"Absolutely." I couldn't believe my luck. I'd just commandeered a ballistics expert to help fight the Gamemaster. Not too shabby. "Thank you so much!"

"Happy to help. I'd like to find whoever set this weapon. It's an incredibly stupid and dangerous thing to do."

I thanked him again, hung up, and sent the email.

Marchant replied a few minutes later: Mind is slipping. Lab closed on Saturdays. Could we meet at Twin Ponds Rifle Range? It's just north of Mount Pleasant on Highway 17. Close to where I live. 10:00 a.m.?

Hmmm. Trickier. We'd need a car. But I wasn't about to blow this opportunity.

Can do, I replied. See you there.

Then I shot a text message to the Virals.

We'd caught a break.

Now to take advantage.

○   ○   ○

My grand strategy lasted less than ten minutes.

I was hustling for the door when Kit stopped me cold. "We're having dinner with Whitney tonight. No exceptions."

Ugh. At least he'd warned me this time. "When?"

"Six o'clock." Kit's hazel eyes grew plaintive. He scratched the curly brown hair above his ear. "She's, uh, bringing a picnic and we're eating on the beach."

"The beach," I repeated. "With the sand. And the wind. And the bugs."

Kit adopted his long-suffering expression. "Come on Tor, be a sport. It'll be fun."

"Right. Fun!"

I headed back upstairs and sent another text. I'd be late to my own meeting.

The boys cracked a few jokes, but agreed to wait in the bunker. I'd get there as soon as I could.

At six sharp, Kit's voice boomed up the stairwell. "Let's go!"

Imploring various deities for strength, I trudged down and followed Kit out the door. Coop moved to join us, but I gently shoved him inside. Sadly, no dogs allowed.

A white canopy pavilion fluttered on the beach. Beneath it, fluffy cushions surrounded a sky blue tablecloth. Places were set for three.

The weather was smiling on Whitney — light breeze, sunset sky, temperature hovering at seventy. Some women had all the luck.

Our hostess was removing covered dishes from a cooler. She wore a snug tangerine sundress that accentuated her curves. Her hair was up, one of the few times I could recall it that way. She smiled at our approach.

"Best behavior." Kit spoke from the side of his mouth.

"This looks like an Usher video," I whispered back.

"Hello, hell-o!" Whitney waved a hand at the setup. "Do you like?"

"Wonderful!" Kit smiled ear to ear. Looked at me expectantly.

"How great." I feigned enthusiasm. "What a cute idea."

Whitney dropped a curtsy, seemingly destined to be a Real Housewife someday. I sat cross-legged on the cushion she indicated. The sun was low, and directly in my face. *Naturally.*

"Isn't this just a *hoot*?" Whitney began dishing out sides from various containers. Corn pudding. Okra. Green beans. Caprese salad. Her usual Lowcountry fare. *That,* at least, was fine by me.

We got all the way to the boiled shrimp before she pissed me off.

"Tory, sweetheart. Are you *sure* the boys you selected are right for the ball?"

The food had put me in an indulgent mood. "Yes, Whitney. They'll be fine."

"It's just—" dabbing her mouth with a blue gingham napkin, "— Jason's a *fine* choice, of course. But the other three." She spread her hands. "They aren't even part of cotillion."

I set down my fork. "They don't have to be. I can invite whoever I want."

"But don't you think you'd be better off with escorts who are familiar with the event? Boys who know the protocol. Or you could just take Jason, and that way—"

"Enough." I held Whitney's eyes. "Ben, Hi, and Shelton are my best friends. If I'm having a party, they're invited. Always. That's *my* choice. Understand?"

"Of course." Kit arm-wrapped the airhead, who seemed about to say more. "It's completely your decision, kiddo."

"Certainly." Whitney did her best to sound cheery. "I'm sure all will work out for the best."

Issue settled, we resumed our meal. The sun melted into the western horizon, throwing an artist's palette of reds and oranges across the harbor. I was forced to admit the picnic wasn't a horrible idea.

I was patting my own back for handling the matter so maturely when disaster struck.

"Tory."

Kit and Whitney had put down their utensils. He was holding her hand.

"Mmm-hmm?" Mouth stuffed with shrimp.

"We'd like to talk to you about something."

I nearly choked. *We?* Not good.

"Whitney and I have been discussing our future." Kit gave her shoulders a squeeze. "Last summer, when we considered leaving Charleston, Whitney made the difficult decision to go with us. Thankfully, we were all able to stay."

Deer in headlights.

Cornered suspect.

Mouse in the open, owls circling.

"That experience brought us all closer together."

Kit seemed unable to get to the point. I was very, very close to vomiting.

"We think it's time our relationship progressed to the next level. So, with your permission, I'd like to ask Whitney to —"

"Oh God."

"— move in with us," he finished in a rush.

First reaction — he didn't say get married! My chest unfroze a tick.

Second reaction — oh no. Oh please, no.

"Won't it be *so* much fun?!" Whitney clapped her hands like a preschooler. "We can finally spend real time together. Become closer. I know your mother isn't with us anymore, but I'd like to —"

Something snapped inside me.

"How *dare* you mention my mother?" Quiet. Cold. "What, do you think you can replace her? That it's an open position, like a McDonald's fry cook?"

Whitney's eyes widened. "Sweetheart, no! I only meant —"

"Meant what?" Anger made my voice shrill. "That you'd jump right in and fix me? Be my new best friend? Take care of me when I'm sick, or scared?"

Whitney stared, speechless. Part of me knew I was being unfair, even cruel, but I'd never been more furious. I couldn't stop the words.

"You're not my mother, and you never will be." I shot to my feet. "Next time try thinking before you speak."

"Tory!" Kit barked. "Watch your tone! Whitney wasn't implying she'd take anyone's place. You know that."

"Oh, spare me." My eyes burned. "At least you finally had the balls to say something. I figured I'd just keep finding Whitney's things in our house until one day, poof, she'd never leave!"

Kit flushed scarlet. Whitney burst into tears.

Escape. Now.

"I have to go." I stormed back down the beach.

"Tory, wait!" Whitney struggled to rise and follow me.

"Let her go." Kit looped a restraining arm around her waist. "It'll be okay."

I broke into a trot. Over the dunes, across the common, and up my front steps. My hands shook as I twisted the doorknob.

Coop trailed me up to my bedroom.

The door shut, then waterworks.

Head buried in my pillows, I let myself sob.

I'd never felt more alone.

CHAPTER 25

I'm not sure how long I lay there before my phone buzzed.

At first I ignored it. Then, remembering the meeting I'd scheduled but failed to attend, I snagged the thing, expecting an irritated Viral on the line.

Wrong. Jason Taylor. My finger pressed answer before I could stop it.

"Hello?"

"Hey, it's Jason. How are you?"

"Good." Wiping snot streaks from my face. "You?"

"Great. Listen, my parents drove to Hilton Head for the weekend, so I'm having a party. You have to come."

"Party?" Not what I'd expected. "When?"

"Tonight, princess." Jason's voice turned plaintive. "Don't say no. You *always* say no. It'll be fun, I promise. No drama."

My reflex was to decline. I hated cotillion enough. A Bolton Prep party? No thanks.

Then I thought of Kit and Whitney. The conversations I'd endure later that night.

Fine. Anywhere but home.

"One condition," I said.

"Name it." Eager.

"My friends are invited too. Hi, Shelton. And Ben."

Silence hummed across the line. Then, "Tory, be reasonable. The doofus twins can come, but Blue —"

"Those are my demands, sir. We've already made plans, so I won't just ditch them. Plus, Ben's boat is my only ride. It's all or nothing."

"Fine. Whatever. Just keep a lid on that guy, or I swear I'll toss him in the harbor. See you around eight?"

"See you then."

○   ○   ○

"It's that one, there." I pointed to a sturdy wooden walkway jutting into the Harbor. "Taylor is painted on the side."

"How very nice for his majesty."

"Ben, I swear to God, if you're going —"

"Relax." Ben eased *Sewee* toward the dock. He wore his usual black tee and jeans. "I'll be a good little boy. I promised, didn't I?"

"Yes, you did." But I was *not* reassured.

As we tied off and walked to the Taylors' backyard, I tried to still the butterflies. I wore a white tank and jeans, shooting for "sexy-casual." Hoping it wasn't "left farmhouse, got lost."

What are we even doing here?

We should be at the bunker, trying to ID the statue. Kiawah had proven the Gamemaster wasn't bluffing. And our time was almost gone. We should be using every second to crack his puzzle.

Except, I didn't want to. Not after the horror show on the beach. Right then, I needed an escape. From Kit. From the terrifying prospect of Whitney installing herself in my home.

Frankly, this party was a godsend. The perfect distraction.

Jason lived in the ritzy Mount Pleasant neighborhood of Old Village.

His house was three stories of molded stucco accented by gleaming white trim. The yard had a pool, hot tub, cabana, and a massive brick patio complete with a fireplace. Not too shabby.

A dozen classmates were scattered around the pool, drinking from red Solo cups. Others had clustered by the cabana, where Jason was flipping burgers and gripping a Bud Light.

Alcohol. Yikes.

I'm such a loser. It hadn't occurred to me that, this being an un-chaperoned affair, people would be boozing.

Don't be a wuss. You're a sophomore now, you can handle it.

"Those dudes are drinking," Shelton whispered. "Beer."

"No big deal," Ben said. "I got drunk a few times with my cousins this summer."

"What?" My eyes shot to Ben. That was news to me.

Ben shrugged. "It's not like it was regular thing."

Shelton tugged his earlobe. "Well, my parents would *skin* me if they knew I was at a keg party right now. Hi, your mom might have a heart attack. We can't even *drive* yet!"

"Just be cool." Hi was sporting an *Iron Man* hoodie and blue-and-yellow plaid shorts. "Remember: *It's Friday, Friday, gotta get down on Friday.* Right?"

"What are you talking about?" Shelton nervously tugged at his kha-kis and white polo shirt. "Tory, you still think this is a good idea?"

"Chill out." Sounding more confident than I felt. "Let's say hello to Jason."

"I'll pass." Ben strode toward an ice-filled trash can beside the hot tub.

I almost called him back, but Hi stopped me. "You really want those two face-to-face?"

Good point. Perhaps keeping Ben and Jason apart was the wisest course.

"Tory!" Jason was circling the pool to greet us. "Hey, Shelton. Hi."

I waved. "Hi, Jase."

"Hey." Shelton eyed Jason's beer can.

"Wassup, dog." Hi held out a fist. *Buffoon.*

" 'Sup dog' back at ya." With a friendly smile, Jason bumped knuckles. "Glad you guys could make it. Ben didn't come?"

"He's over there." I pointed to where Ben stood, pumping a keg, listening to some lacrosse guys I didn't know. As I watched, he took a long pull from a Solo cup.

"Should I get him?"

"He's doing fine on his own." Jason circled an arm around my shoulders. "Let's grab a drink first."

"Okay. Sure." *Not a problem.*

"Come along, you two." Jason waved for Hi and Shelton to follow. "Ever try Southern Comfort before?"

"No." Shelton reached for his earlobe.

"Maybe." Hi faked a yawn. "Not sure."

Liar. He'd never gotten drunk. None of us had.

Except Ben. Didn't know that.

"Well, you're in for a treat." Jason steered us toward the cabana, calling to his friends. "Jeff! Steve! Four So-Co and limes. The Morris Island crew needs a drink."

Things happened fast after that.

Shot glasses were lined up on the bar, filled with brown liquor, and topped with lime wedges. Jason lifted one and smiled encouragingly.

Other partygoers watched. Skeptical? Amused? No idea.

I'd never taken a shot. Had no interest in doing so then.

C'mon. What's the big deal?

The "big deal" was, I didn't want to drink. Then, or ever. Not after what happened to Mom.

I was about to decline when Hi stepped to the counter. "Thanks, man. Bottoms up." But I could see his anxiety.

Hi clinked glasses with Jason and downed it in one go. Then started coughing. "Wrong pipe," he wheezed.

Jason slapped his back. "Has a nice kick, huh?"

Some girl I didn't know shoved glasses at Shelton and me. I thanked her, playing it cool, but felt boxed in. Everyone was watching.

Shelton tensed, psyching himself up.

We lifted, clinked, and . . .

CHAPTER 26

Images flickered in my brain.

Twisted metal. Flashing lights. Broken glass.

A police officer standing in the doorway, unable to meet my eyes.

Mom.

As casually as possible, I placed my glass back on the counter, just as Shelton finished choking down his shot.

"Sorry, Jason." I hoped my voice didn't falter. "I don't drink. I hope that's okay."

Jason blinked. Then he sprang forward and swept the glass out of sight.

"Of course, no problem!" He laughed awkwardly. "More for the rest of us, right?"

I smiled, hoping my façade didn't crack. I desperately wanted to fit in, but wasn't going to bend on this point. I'd made a promise to myself. I intended to keep it.

Jason snagged my elbow and steered me away from the crowd. The rest of the partygoers had already forgotten me, getting back to their previous conversations. No one seemed to mind that I'd backed out.

"You play cards?" Jason asked. I could tell he wanted to change the subject.

"Hardly ever," I admitted.

His cocky grin appeared. "Well, I'm unbeatable. Stick with me."

○   ○   ○

"And I'm out!" I threw down three queens. "President again! Third term."

Good-natured groans erupted around the table.

Beginner's luck. I didn't know the rules, but was winning anyway. Beside me, Jason began cackling like a hyena.

I sipped a Diet Coke, keeping one eye on Shelton and Hi, who had somehow ended up at the beer pong table.

Shelton looked relaxed, no doubt a result of the booze. Hi was talking nonstop. Both were surprisingly good at hitting cups, and were riding a two-game winning streak.

Their Cinderella run had made Shelton and Hi popular with the older guys. The two were joking and talking trash, seemingly holding their own.

For some reason, this made me proud. *What an odd thought.*

"I'll be last out again," Jason muttered. "My cards are terrible." He slid an accusatory glance my way. "Why didn't you pass me that ace?"

"I have no idea what you're talking about. *You're* supposed to be coaching *me.*"

"And yet, she's crushing us," said a red-haired boy across the table. "Unreal."

I winked, happy to blend in. I'd finally started to unwind. Who knew parties could be fun?

Shelton and Hi had avoided more shots, but were holding beer-filled Solo cups. Holding had often led to sipping. I was toting my soft drink as cover. Somehow the three of us had been sucked into drinking games. Even me, although Jason was covering my losses as well as his own. The other players didn't care either way.

I hoped the boys were being as careful as I was.

From the looks of things, they weren't.

The hand ended, and Jason began gathering cards. "No more help for the genius. You've embarrassed us long enough."

My smile widened. "Oh, poor baby."

I checked for Ben, found him in the same spot by the keg. At that moment he was alone, staring into his cup.

Don't leave him by himself.

"I'm quitting while I'm ahead." Ignoring Jason's protests, I rose and walked across the patio.

"Hey," I said cheerfully.

Ben didn't look up. "Hey. Having fun assimilating?"

"Ben, come on. They aren't that bad. Even Shelton and Hi are having fun."

I glanced back at the beer pong table. Shelton and Hi had finally lost, and were chugging their opponent's remaining cups. Other players were cheering them on.

"Those two are going to be wasted." I tried not to judge. "We'll have to sneak them by their parents."

"They're acting like idiots." Ben was glassy-eyed, his voice surly.

I wondered how many beers he'd downed.

"You think those people really like us?" Ben blurted. "That we're all BFFs now? What a joke."

"Everyone's being nice. You could give them a chance."

"We're just tonight's special entertainment." He drained his cup and moved to refill it. "The flavor of the week."

I sighed, but kept quiet. Once in a funk, Ben stayed funked.

Then my breath caught.

Chance Claybourne was walking toward the cabana. And he wasn't alone.

Madison Dunkle clung to his arm.

Seeing them together jolted me. "I have to go."

"Whatever." Ben tipped back his cup, then wandered into the yard. "Go dance for the trust-fund babies."

The barb stung, but I ignored him. As casually as possible, I moved closer to Chance and Madison, alarm bells clanging in my brain.

Madison saw me first. She whispered to Chance, then scurried toward the cabana. I scanned for Courtney and Ashley, but didn't see them.

Had Madison and Chance come together?

I didn't like what that implied. These were the two people I absolutely did not want comparing notes. Here, or anywhere.

"Tory." Chance strolled to my side. "Fancy meeting you here."

He arced an arm at the party, which was becoming more rowdy. Shelton was doing a keg stand, skinny legs flapping in the air. Hi was counting off his time.

Those morons! What are they thinking?

Chance's voice pulled me back.

"Jason mentioned you needed help from the crime lab." Chance cocked his head. "More covert police work? What this time?"

My mouth went dry. Head spinning. He sounded offhand, but his questions were too pointed for comfort.

"It's nothing. Something for Kit."

Chance smiled, dropped his voice. "I don't believe you."

"Suit yourself."

"Oh, I intend to. And I'll be watching. Cheers."

With that, he joined the others in the cabana.

Enough for me. *Time to go.*

Just then I heard pounding feet, followed by a bellowing scream.

"CANNONBALL!!!!!"

I turned in time to see Hi launch himself skyward, tuck into a ball, and drop into the pool with an enormous splash.

Cups went flying as revelers attempted to dodge the spray.

Shelton was rolling on the grass, laughing hysterically. "He did it! Holy crap! I owe Hiram five bucks!"

Hi surfaced, spitting water. The party froze. Someone even killed the music.

"Come on, I nailed that!" Hi raised both fists. "Perfect ten."

A beat, then laughter swept the patio, followed by a round of applause.

A boy from the soccer team leaped into the pool, followed by two others carrying screaming girls. In moments, a dozen drunks were splashing and roughhousing in the water.

I spied Jason sneaking my way, a wicked glint in his eyes.

"No you don't!" I bolted. "I'm not going in!"

"Oh yes you are!" Jason hurdled deck furniture, chasing me around the pool. "My house, my rules, Brennan!"

Chance watched with distaste before withdrawing into the cabana.

We were on our second lap when Ben reappeared.

I whizzed by, just steps ahead of my pursuer. Startled, Ben grabbed Jason with both arms.

"What the hell are you doing?" Ben slurred, swaying slightly.

I stopped dead. "Ben, it's okay! We're just messing around."

"Out of the way, pal." Jason pushed Ben's chest with two hands. "You're my guest, remember."

Ben shoved back. "Don't touch me!"

Jason's eyes gleamed with too much booze and not enough caution.

Ben never saw the punch.

He went toppling, but was back up in heartbeat. Then he dove forward, slamming Jason to the bricks. Horrified, I watched them roll into the grass, grappling and punching, neither able to gain the advantage.

Time slowed.

Suddenly, Jason went flying.

Ben's head came up, irises flaming.

Nightmare.

Without thinking, I launched myself at Ben, catching him off guard. The weight of my body knocked him over backward. Never hesitating, I jumped on his chest and started slapping his face.

"Let it go!" I hissed. "Release your flare!"

Jason reached to pull me off, but Hi and Shelton got there first.

They boxed Jason away, grabbed Ben by the shoulders, and hauled him downslope into the yard. Ben tried to get past them, at Jason, but the fire was gone from his eyes. Abruptly he turned and stormed toward the dock.

"I'm going to kill him." Jason was red-cheeked and breathing heavily. "This is my house!"

"Jason, don't!" I moved to block his pursuit. "Ben's drunk and didn't know what was going on. Please just let it go. For me."

"Fine." Jason wiped his nose, checking for blood. "But that jackass isn't welcome around me anymore. You tell him that."

"I will. I have to go now."

As Jason stormed away, I fled the watching, whispering attention of the rest of his guests.

⬡　　⬡　　⬡

I pointed *Sewee* into Charleston Harbor, headed for home.

Ben had balked when I'd demanded the keys, but I'd given him no choice. The boys were wasted. I'd driven *Sewee* before, and knew the basics. And if I scratched her while docking, let that be a lesson.

We'd barely set off when Hi emptied his guts over the side. Shelton tried to clean his glasses, but kept dropping them. Ben was slouched in the copilot's chair, too dizzy to stand.

"He's no good for you," Ben said abruptly. "Doesn't deserve you."

"Just be quiet." Soft. "We're almost home."

Ben's eyes were slits. "That guy, he's . . ." His hand rose, fell. "Dime a dozen. Doesn't know anything. About you. The *real* you."

Mercifully, Ben trailed off. In moments he was snoring.

I tried not to ignore his words. Ben was drunk. Being super-overprotective. And he never missed a chance to put Jason down.

But he sounds . . . different. Almost jealous.

"It's the booze talking," I said to myself as I maneuvered *Sewee* into the harbor. "Doesn't mean a thing. Not one thing."

Then I barked a sour laugh.

A crazed lunatic was forcing us around the city.

My father wanted a bimbo to live in our home.

Chance was watching me, and consorting with Madison.

Canine DNA was hijacking my nervous system, and I had no idea how to stop it.

The last thing I needed was Ben's dating advice.

"Blargh."

I wished life could be simple again.

Knew it never would be.

So I motored toward Morris, eager to crawl into bed and fall blissfully asleep. Then I cringed. How would I sneak these dopes past their parents?

"Double blargh."

CHAPTER 27

Ben was behind the wheel of Kit's 4Runner.

We were fifteen minutes up Highway 17, heading north through the Francis Marion National Forest. Here, the road traversed a series of sultry, kudzu-draped swamps before reaching the towering woodlands of the park's interior.

Nine forty-five a.m. The mood was grim.

"I wanna die." Hi was slumped against a backseat window. "It's sixty-five in this car, but I'm still sweating my face off."

Shelton opened his eyes, seemed to consider replying. Didn't bother.

"Serves you right," I said from the front passenger seat. "*Cannonball!* You really made an impression."

"People loved that cannonball," Hi whispered. "You can't take that from me."

Shelton coughed, lowered his window, then hawked a loogie into space. Thankfully, his aim was true.

Given the shape the boys were in, I'd left Coop at home. The hungover trio looked a few jostles short of redecorating the car with their stomach linings.

Shelton rubbed his face. "Why get drunk if you feel like this afterward? It's like signing up for food poisoning."

"Carpe diem." Hi's pallor was a sickly green. "Or something. I dunno, kids like getting bombed. Kids are stupid."

"It's too dangerous for us." I made sure Ben was listening. "A Viral can't afford to lose control, not for a second. Not given our ... condition."

Ben kept his bloodshot eyes on the road. He wasn't about to apologize, and hated being scolded.

I didn't press. We all knew his mistake had been cataclysmic, but no one was anxious to discuss it then. Not with their heads pounding. Not with Ben scowling like an angry grizzly.

"We dodged a bullet," I said. "Let's just avoid any repeat performances."

"Not a problem," Shelton said. "My beer pong career was short."

"But epic." Hi raised a fist, which Shelton bumped weakly.

Miracle of miracles, no one had been caught. I still couldn't believe our luck.

After docking, it had taken some time to roust the boys into semi-presentable form. Then, slurring and stumbling, they'd headed for their doors. I'd held zero hope they'd pass muster.

But Shelton's parents had been out, and Tom Blue was asleep. Hi had snuck past his mother by faking a gastrointestinal illness. Gross.

Kit hadn't blinked when I'd beelined for my room. I don't think "coming home intoxicated" was on his radar yet. Which was reasonable, since I was fourteen, had never done anything like that, and hadn't been drinking anyway.

Up early the next morning, I'd made a round of calls. Incredibly, the guys hadn't backed out.

So there we were, me and three wildly hungover boys, riding in Kit's SUV.

I checked the iPad. Just over fourteen hours left.

Kit was at work, of course, even though it was Saturday. We hadn't asked to borrow the car. No need for daddy dearest to know I was meeting a stranger at a secluded firing range.

Ben turned right at Steed Creek and eased onto Willow Hall Road. Around us, the forest of longleaf pines grew denser.

"I don't remember anything," Ben said abruptly. "I blacked out."

"You took the whole world and drank it," Hi mumbled. "Then you tried to fight Jason. And *then* you —"

"Let's discuss last night another time," I said, hoping to avoid the subject. "Right now, we need to focus on finding the range."

Blacked out? I watched Ben from the corner of my eye. I'd never known him to lie, but I got the feeling he wasn't being completely honest either.

He remembers. But he's probably embarrassed about getting all sentimental.

I let the matter slide. "Blacked out" and forgotten worked fine for me.

"We're in the middle of nowhere." Hi, staring out his window. "There's nothing here but woodchucks."

It was true. The woods pressed close to the road, blocking the sun. I hadn't seen a building in miles.

Another half mile, then a wooden sign appeared: "Twin Ponds Rifle Range."

Ben pulled into a gravel lot. Only one other vehicle was present — a muddy Ford F-150, black, with oversized tires and a steel gun rack attached to its bed.

My sneakers hit the ground first. "Let's find our expert."

"Why does the Forest Service operate a shooting gallery?" Shelton leaned against the parked 4Runner, wheezing from the effort of getting out. "Seems weird."

"It's not much, just a designated area for firing weapons." Hi stretched, rubbed his lower back. "What better place to pop off some rounds than deep in the woods?"

A series of reports echoed from the trees ahead.

Hi cocked his ear. "Someone's popping caps as we speak."

I shouldered my backpack and we headed down a short trail toward a long, rectangular structure divided into stalls like an open-air market. Each section had its own bench, rack, and a firing platform facing the open field beyond.

Fifty yards out, a rough wooden beam crossed the field, designed for propping cans, bottles, and other small objects. Fifty yards beyond the beam was a thick earthen backstop suitable for pinning paper targets.

Debris littered the field — signs, old washing machines, TVs, and trash cans — all rusted and riddled with bullet holes.

The range felt neglected. Forgotten by the world. The surrounding forest was deathly quiet. Spooky.

I was very glad to have company.

"What a dump." Ben kicked a pile of casings at the building's edge.

"Rednecks like shooting things," Hi said. "But they don't like cleaning up."

More shots sounded in rapid sequence. I spied a man in military fatigues hunched over in the farthest stall, systematically firing a high-powered rifle. Bullets slammed a target at the edge of sight. There was no else on the property.

"Mr. Marchant?" I called.

No response. Of course not. The shooter was wearing earmuffs.

I waved an arm over my head. He noticed our presence, set down his rifle and headgear, and strode over to greet us.

The man was tall, with pale skin, hazel eyes, and light brown hair. Younger than I'd expected — no more than thirty-five — he had the wiry physique of a long-distance runner. He wore orange-tinted glasses and jackboots.

"Mr. Marchant?" I repeated.

"Call me Eric." He extended a hand. "You must be Tory. Hope you don't mind, but I thought I'd get in some practice this morning. I don't get out here too often."

Suddenly Ben stiffened. Without warning, he lurched sideways and puked noisily in the bushes.

The rest of us skittered back in surprise.

Damn it, Ben. Not now! This guy works for the police.

Ben wiped his mouth and retreated toward the parking lot. "Sorry. I'm not feeling —" He broke into a trot and disappeared into the woods.

My gaze whipped to Marchant.

"Your friend looks a little . . . worse for wear."

Shelton lowered his eyes. "I'll, uh, make sure he's okay. You coming, Hi?"

"Heck no." Hi pantomimed holding a machine gun. "I wanna see some firepower."

"Suit yourself." Shelton hurried after Ben.

"Please excuse them." I donned my most trustworthy face. "There's a bug going around school."

"A bug. Of course." Marchant let the matter drop. "Did you bring the firearm you found?"

"Yessir." Tapping the bag on my shoulder.

"Great." He gestured to where he'd been shooting. "Let's have a look."

Marchant wasn't what I'd expected. On the phone I'd imagined a bookish, squirrely type. This guy was clearly an outdoorsman.

Tucked inside Marchant's stall was a veritable arsenal. Three pistols. A shotgun. Two more hunting rifles. And some automatic bullet-spitter whose name I couldn't guess.

Hi's elbow jabbed my ribs. "On the end," he whispered. "That's an AK-47."

"You know your guns, young man."

Marchant looked at me expectantly. Taking the hint, I unzipped my bag and removed the golf course weapon and slugs.

Marchant's lips pooched out. "Now isn't *that* an odd piece."

"Do you recognize it?" I asked.

"I don't." Rotating the gun in his hands. "There are no manufacturer markings, and I don't see a serial number. This is a designer job, built by someone who knows what he's doing."

His gaze fixed on me. "Tell me what happened."

Stepping carefully around the truth, I explained how the gun was set, how it fired, and what we recovered. I only changed the location.

And never mentioned the Gamemaster, of course.

"A snare gun." Marchant grunted. "Rigged to fire when tripped in some fashion. The usual method is to string a wire from the trigger, or use a remote sensor."

"Sounds nasty." Hi was inspecting Marchant's stockpile.

"They are," Marchant agreed. "Snare guns are used to protect livestock from wild animals. They're also totally illegal, since they'll shoot anything that trips them. One like this wasn't purchased in a store."

My heart sank. "So it can't tell you anything?"

"Maybe not." Marchant set the weapon aside and picked up a slug. "But the bullet alone might tell the tale."

"All ears." I took a seat on the splintery wooden bench, careful not to jostle any of Marchant's weapons. The forest was silent. A line of cypress trees blocked all view of the parking lot, making the shooting stand feel like the most isolated place on earth.

"A bullet has four components — the primer, the casing, gunpowder, and the slug itself." Marchant handed me a loose round and lifted his Beretta 9mm. "When the trigger is pulled, a firing pin strikes the primer, exploding a powder charge beneath. This causes the larger charge of gunpowder to explode."

I turned the ammunition in my fingers. "And that fires the bullet?"

"Correct. That explosion propels the projectile down the barrel. The slug will then rotate inside the gun barrel, because of tiny grooves along its length. The shell casing remains in the chamber until removed."

"Unless it's a semi-auto," Hi chirped.

"True. Then the casing is automatically ejected when the bullet is fired." Marchant glanced at me. "You said you didn't collect any casings, right?"

I shook my head, frustrated. How could I have forgotten to look?

"No big deal. The grooves on the slug itself are more important."

"That's great you can match a bullet to a gun that way," Hi said, "but we already have the gun. You're holding it right now."

Marchant smiled. "Hopefully I can do more than that."

"How?" I asked.

"A bullet is marked with the unique signature of the weapon that fired it." Marchant waved at his collection. "Every barrel is different, even ones produced for the same type of gun, by the same company, in the same factory, on the same day. Each gun comes off the line with a distinct ballistic fingerprint."

"Why is that?" Hi asked.

"Tiny imperfections are produced during the manufacturing process. Microscopic slivers of metal are pressed into the barrel as it's being shaped. These flaws create a unique pattern of scrapes on a discharged bullet, called striations."

"So every bullet fired from the same gun will have the same unique striations." I followed that far. "And I assume these striations can be detected?"

He smiled. "Just like a fingerprint."

"Okay, but I still don't get the point." Hi pointed. "We *have* the gun. Why do we care about the signature?"

"Because we keep bullet signatures on file."

Marchant carefully placed the snare gun in a plastic bag. "When the police identify a weapon that might be linked to a crime, they send it to ballistics for analysis. That's me. First, I'll shoot air through the barrel to see what comes out. Sometimes tiny bits of matter like hair, skin, or fibers have been sucked in upon firing."

"DNA. Trace evidence." Hi nodded sagely. "Nice."

"Then I'll fire sample bullets into a trough or ballistics gel, and check the striations against our database. If the gun was used in any other crimes, I'll find a match."

"Match the gun, maybe find an owner." Made sense to me. "It's a shot, at least."

"I'll try our local files, then the South Carolina database. If that doesn't tell us anything, I can run it through the ATF's Ballistic Information Network."

"That's very generous," I said. "You're being incredibly helpful."

Marchant thumb-hooked his belt. "Snare guns are extremely dangerous. Anything or any*one* can walk into the field of fire. Whoever set that for your dog could just as easily have shot a child. They have to answer for that."

"So you think we have a chance at an ID?" Hi asked.

"I do." Marchant checked his watch. "A gun like this reeks of trouble. Give me a week and we'll know if it's reared its ugly head elsewhere."

"Sounds like a plan." Hi pointed to the AK. "So how's about me ripping off a banana clip with that bad boy?"

"There's zero chance of that happening." Marchant smiled, drawing the sting from his words. "But I'll let you know what I find."

Repeating our thanks, Hi and I headed for the lot. I hoped that Wimpy and the Vomitasaurus had gotten their acts together.

"We need one of those fully autos." Hi cracked his knuckles. "Maybe get one for the bunker, don't you think? Keep the rabbits in check."

"Hi, we're going to have a talk about pushing people's buttons."

"Hey, don't beat yourself up." He yawned huge. "I forgive you. Now, much more importantly — do you have any Advil?"

CHAPTER 28

The return trip began in silence.

Ben seemed flustered by his retching episode. He clutched the steering wheel in a two-handed death grip, driving faster than usual. Shelton just crawled in back to sleep.

I was happy we'd accomplished our goal, but still worried about The Game. Everything hinged on our solving the next puzzle. The pressure was starting to get to me.

Maybe Marchant would kick something loose. Fingers crossed.

Then Hi cleared his throat. "Time runs out at midnight. Any ideas?"

"We have to ID the figurine," I said. "It's our only clue."

Hi and I discussed a few ideas, planned a strategy for that afternoon. Shelton snored. Ben said nothing, eyes glued to the road.

He's embarrassed. Or worried he'll boot in Kit's ride.

Forty minutes later we arrived home on Morris. Ben pulled into my garage, tossed me the keys, and headed for his unit.

"Ben?" I called after. "Can you help this afternoon? We're almost out of time."

"Give me an hour." Then he hurried off.

"He's gonna spew." Shelton burped, grimaced. "Think I'll join him."

"But you're coming back too, right?"

Shelton raised a thumb. "Twenty minutes. Maybe thirty."

I turned to see Hi slinking away as well. "Food. Or else I'm done for. I'll come over when Shelton does."

And just like that, I was alone.

I entered through the garage and ascended the back stairs. Coop was waiting at the top.

"Hey, boy."

Coop's backward glance was my only warning.

"Tory?" Whitney was lurking within.

I took a deep, calming breath, then stepped into the living room.

Whitney was perched on the couch. "I'm so sorry about yesterday."

"It's okay," I said automatically, unsure of how I really felt but anxious to avoid the conversation. "Let's just forget it."

"I never meant to upset you." Placing one delicate hand to her chest. "Truly! Your father and I should *never* have sprung such news."

"Everything's fine." I decided there was no point being angry. "I overreacted."

"No." Whitney shook her head firmly. "This is *your* house, too."

"Look, if you and Kit want to live together —" my palms rose, pushed outward aimlessly, "— it's not my place to stand in your way."

Whitney was saying more, but I didn't hear. I'd noticed something . . . off.

I looked around. "Where's your stuff?"

The vase, picture, and other foreign articles were missing. I spun. The Blue Dog painting was no longer in the hallway.

"I took my things home. You were one hundred percent correct. It was presumptuous to move them in without your approval."

"No. Wait. I mean . . ."

A war raged inside me. On the one hand, this retreat was exactly what I'd wanted. Part of me felt like shouting "damn right!" and heading upstairs.

But Whitney was clearly trying to make good. Had gone to a lot of trouble.

For the first time I could recall, she actually seemed to get it.

But I really, really didn't want her living here.

Blargh.

Dilemma.

Be petulant, selfish, and happy? Or be generous . . . and miserable.

Then something grabbed my attention. I forgot all about the Whitney problem.

An object sat where Whitney's vase had been.

Small. Weathered. Metal.

The Gamemaster's figurine.

I bounded to the shelf. "Where'd you get this?"

"The statuette? I saw it on your desk, and thought Saint Benedict would look nice down here." Whitney's eyes widened. "Oh, dear. I've done it again, haven't I?"

My pulse quickened. "Say again?"

"Darling, I'm so sorry!" Whitney's face dropped to her hands. "I thought you'd *like* something of yours in place of my vase. I'm just terrible, aren't I?" She sounded on the verge of tears.

"Whitney, I'm not mad." I pointed at the figurine. "You said this is who?"

"Saint Benedict, of course." Whitney drew a fingertip under each watery eye. "I was raised Catholic, as you surely know. When I was a girl, his image hung in our family library. He's the patron of students."

I couldn't believe it. Hours of fruitless searches, and Whitney freaking Dubois just hands me the answer. Odds that long don't exist.

My mind raced. We had twelve hours to find the next cache.

I needed the boys ASAP.

"I prefer keeping this in my room." I snatched the figurine and bolted for the stairs. "But I do appreciate the thought."

"Forgive me." Whitney stood as I passed her. "I'll never touch your things again."

Impulsively, I turned and hugged her. "Not a problem."

Then I raced up the steps, leaving the stunned Barbie in my wake.

○   ○   ○

"Got it!" Hi kissed his laptop screen. "Come to Daddy."

I raised a brow. "Got what?" We'd been searching for thirty seconds.

We sat at my dining room table, waiting for Shelton and Ben. Whitney must've left soon after I'd gone upstairs.

I'd sent the boys a demanding text. So far, only Hi had surfaced.

"There's a Saint Benedict Catholic Church." He spun his computer for me to see. "In Mount Pleasant. How ya like *them* apples?"

"That's great." Could it be that easy?

I glanced at the black-and-white cloth that had covered the statue.

"What about the wrapping?" I tossed the fabric to Hi.

"Could be nothing." He turned it in his hands. "Did you notice this, though?"

"Notice what?"

Hi held the swatch by a corner, revealing a tiny piece of embroidery on its back.

"You've got to be kidding." I was getting sloppy. And at the wrong time.

I snatched the square back from Hi. The small and neat stitching formed a half circle with four squiggly lines rising from it.

"Looks like a sunrise," I said. "What could *that* mean?"

"Who knows? The fabric could just be protective packaging."

"Maybe." But something bothered me. "Don't you think this was too easy?"

Hi was already headed for my kitchen. "Too easy how?"

"Compared to the other tasks." I hugged my knees to my chest. "The other clues were hard. Intricate. They involved codes, puzzles, things like that."

Hi returned with a box of Wheat Thins. "Maybe we got lucky this time."

Perhaps. Probably.

No.

I didn't buy it.

"So far, the Gamemaster hasn't included *anything* in a clue that wasn't relevant." I tapped the fabric. "There's a shape here. And why is it black and white? This cloth has to factor somehow."

Hi sighed. "So you need my brilliance again."

"I do."

"Fine." Dropping the Wheat Thins on the table. "These are 'reduced fat' anyway. Blech."

We ran search after search. Shelton arrived and added his thoughts to the mix. Thirty minutes later we still had nothing.

"We're going in circles," Hi complained. "And where the heck is Ben?"

"AWOL." Shelton glanced at the clock. "He looked terrible this morning. I bet he lay down and passed out."

"Let's start over." I cleared the history and typed. "Saint Benedict. Charleston."

Familiar results. Every hit involved the Mount Pleasant church.

Was I overthinking this? I could be wasting precious time.

Trust your instincts. Keep looking.

"What if we remove that church from the results?" Shelton suggested.

"Do it." I yielded the keyboard.

Shelton's fingers danced as he adjusted search functions.

"Hell-o. What's this?"

I hunched over his shoulder. The screen contained a pleasant image of a country road lined with giant oaks. In the corner was a soft logo, white on black.

Mepkin Abbey.

"A monastery." Hi was leaning in close beside me. He did not smell tremendous.

"Monks?" Shelton snorted. "Seriously? In South Carolina?"

The website was organized and professional. A link at top read: "Who We Are."

"Click that."

Shelton did. The next page contained a mission statement and group portrait.

"These guys pray all day," Hi said. "And they don't talk."

Shelton chuckled. "You'd never make it."

"Weird." Hi was scanning text. "They also sell produce, tend gardens, and operate a modern library. And the grounds are open to visitors every day."

"Mepkin Abbey is a Trappist monastery," Shelton read aloud. "These guys follow something called the Rule of Saint Benedict. That's news to me, but it fits our search."

I ignored their banter, eyes glued to the photo. "Nice robes, don't you think?"

"Ah-ha!" Hi crowed.

Shelton nodded. "Nice catch, Tor."

The picture showed twenty monks in two rows, standing in a beautiful flower garden. All were smiling. The average age appeared to be north of sixty.

But that wasn't what had me grinning.

The men wore identical robes.

Identical *black-and-white* robes.

I kissed my index finger and pressed it to the screen.

"Gotcha."

CHAPTER 29

"Turn in . . . *here*."

I pointed to an odd marker beside the highway — a large white *M*, with a white cross rising from its center. The name *Mepkin Abbey* was carved into the stone pedestal.

"Took us long enough." Ben had been driving for over an hour. Add that to the ninety minutes we'd waited for Ben to reappear, and we'd burned off half the afternoon.

Shelton yawned, scratched the top of his head. "Talk about living in the boonies."

"They probably don't have cable," Hi quipped. "Or indoor plumbing."

We cruised down the tree-lined drive we'd seen on the abbey's website, massive live oaks flanking us on both sides. Sunlight and shadow danced on the windshield.

The setting was serene. Idyllic. Perfect for the contemplative life.

"Keep your eyes peeled during the tour," I reminded them. "The next cache must be hidden on these grounds."

I'd brought two trowels in my backpack, just in case. Only nine hours remained to crack the Gamemaster's clue.

"Monks live out here?" Shelton was peering out a backseat window. "In the middle of South Cack nowhere?"

"Since 1949." Hi began reading from his iPhone. "Founded by monks from the Abbey of Gethsemani, in Kentucky, the Mepkin brotherhood belongs to the Order of Cistercians of the Strict Observance."

"What does *that* mean?" Shelton asked.

"Don't ask me. But if you want to join, I'll put in a good word."

We parked in a guest lot, then followed a hedge-lined path to the welcome center. Inside was a shock — the interior was modern and well appointed. Exchanging astonished glances, we wandered into the gift shop.

And received a second surprise. The shop was airy and brightly lit. Tables and shelves overflowed with monastic artwork, carved bowls, knickknacks, knit scarves, blankets, and other handicrafts. Cookbooks and monastic texts shared space with vases and monk-made jams.

The store had an eclectic, arty feel, quite at odds with my expectation of dour monks living in stark, Spartan silence.

"Tory, look!" Hi pointed to a bookcase packed with idols and figurines. "Nice."

Excited, I scanned the assortment. *There!* On the middle shelf — a statue of Saint Benedict identical to the one in my bag.

I couldn't help but smile. "We're *definitely* in the right place."

Hi slapped me five. Ben nodded, looking pleased.

"Can you believe they sell beer?" Shelton was eyeing a tower of six-packs. "Do monks like to booze it up?"

"Our vows do not require abstention from alcohol."

We turned to see a small, clean-shaven man in his mid-forties. He had dirty blond hair fading to gray, sea green eyes, and soft, almost feminine features. He wore the black-and-white robes of a Mepkin brother.

"Indeed, the Order is somewhat famous for brewing," the monk said. "Mepkin offers some of the finer ales produced by Trappists worldwide."

"The shop is lovely." Random, but he'd caught me off guard. "I didn't expect so much . . . color. Variety."

"You're not the first to say so." The monk smiled. "Our store offers a wide range of items created in the monastic tradition, as well as works by local artisans. All reflect the beauty of God's creation."

"Do you make anything here?" Shelton asked.

"We do." The monk hefted a jar labeled Oyster Mushroom Powder. "Chapter forty-eight of the Rule of Saint Benedict states, 'For then are they monks in truth, if they live by the work of their hands.' We produce and sell goods to provide income for the monastery, and to honor the Lord through work. Our mushrooms are world famous, and our garden compost is top-notch. We also offer an array of honey products and a delightful fruit syrup."

"I thought you guys didn't talk." Hi wheezed as my elbow found his gut. "Took a vow of silence, I mean."

"A common misconception." The monk adopted a lecturing tone. "Saint Benedict described speech as disruptive to a disciple's duty for quietude and receptivity, and a temptation to exercise one's own will, instead of God's. As adherents, we respect his call for silence, but take no vow. That said, we only speak when necessary, and idle chatter is discouraged. We take our meals in contemplative peace, perhaps listening to a reading by a fellow brother."

"This isn't idle chatter right now?" Hi dodged my second jab.

"Of course not," the monk replied good-naturedly. "To instruct the inquisitive is to spread the joy of God. My name is Brother Patterson. I'm Guestmaster for today's tour. Were you planning to join us?"

"Tory Brennan," I replied. "And yes, that's why we're here."

"Wonderful." Patterson beamed. "We have so few younger visitors. Please follow me. Others have come today as well."

We exited into a tidy flower garden.

A wealthy-looking couple was gabbing loudly about the proper care of azaleas, while a trio of nuns glared in disapproval. Beside them, an elderly couple whispered quietly in what sounded like German.

"Welcome to Mepkin Abbey." Patterson addressed the group. "We are a Roman Catholic order of contemplative monks, more commonly known as Trappists. We live in silence and solitude, according to an ancient discipleship that focuses on seeking God through communal living. We praise our Lord through prayer, meditation, work, and hospitality. Again, welcome."

The female azalea freak dabbed on shiny lip gloss. "What's a Trappist?"

"The movement originated in Normandy in 1664, in reaction to relaxed practices in many Cistercian monasteries. In 1892, blessed by the Pope, the Trappists formed an independent order dedicated to closer adherence to the Rule of Saint Benedict."

Lip Gloss blinked. "Saint who?"

"Saint Benedict," Patterson answered patiently, "who wrote his Rule in the sixth century, describing the ideals and values of monastic life. The Trappist goal is to adhere to his three vows: stability, obedience, and fidelity to monastic life."

"Fidelity?" Lip Gloss's bald husband snorted. "What, you don't like broads?"

Again, the polite smile. "As Benedictine monks, we are sworn to God, but that doesn't mean we dislike women. In fact, each Cistercian order has a women's branch. Ours is known as the Trappistines."

"Are there a lot of Trappists?" Hi asked.

"Depends on your perspective." Patterson linked his hands and began moving into the garden, inviting the group to follow. "There are 170 Trappist monasteries around the world, home to approximately 2,100 monks and 1,800 nuns."

Hi nodded. "Not too many folks."

Patterson responded with a small smile. "Monastic life is not for everyone."

"Sounds good to me." Shelton walked alongside me as we passed rows of blue hydrangeas, white lilacs, and yellow jessamine. "Peace and quiet. Where do I sign?"

"First, we must see if you're a good fit." Patterson grinned, playing along. "Do you possess the physical, psychological, and spiritual vigor to live by our principles? Are you fully committed to a life of all-encompassing, continual prayer?"

One of Shelton's eyebrows rose. "Continual?"

"We wake at three for Vigils, followed by private meditation, then Lauds at five thirty before breakfast. The remainder of the day is divided between prayer, work, and private spiritual devotions. We retire at eight for the grand silence, lasting twelve hours."

Shelton cocked his head, as if considering. "Eh, probably not."

Patterson nodded. "You also need a diploma, work experience, and a Catholic background. Plus no debts or obligations to a wife, children, or parents."

"Then I'm out on all counts," Shelton said. "Maybe when I'm older."

"Who but the Lord knows?"

Brother Patterson led us to a courtyard fronting the monastery proper. In its center stood a fifty-foot tower housing four bells, stacked one atop the other.

"The Tower of the Seven Spirits," Patterson said. "Its bells announce each of our daily prayers." He pointed to a group of stucco buildings on our left. "Those are the cloisters, where our brothers reside."

Straight ahead was the church itself — a simple white stucco building topped by an iron cross. Warm yellow light spilled from within.

We crossed to the church and entered through carved wooden doors. The interior was bright and harmonious, with a tile floor and a yellow pine roof. A small nave offered seating for a few dozen. The altar was set at the transept crossing, with a massive organ just behind it. A round lantern window high above threw patterned sunlight across the stark white plaster walls.

"No adornments." I noted the absence of statues, paintings, or stained glass.

"Continual prayer requires strict discipline," Patterson explained. "External decorations, no matter how uplifting, would only be a distraction."

After allowing the group a few minutes to observe, Patterson led us back outside and down into a small ravine.

Hi drew close and whispered in my ear. "This place is huge. Way bigger than I thought."

"And modern, too. These monks are more than they seem."

He nodded. "It's gonna be tough to search."

We approached a five-story building set on massive concrete pilings. Colonial-brick arches fronted the lower levels, while limestone and pale stucco covered those above.

Patterson waited for the group to reassemble. "The library houses our theological collections, as well as religious art and many rare books. There are also meeting facilities, a conference center with state-of-the-art computer capability, and a high-definition theater."

Shelton whistled softly. "High tech."

"The tour has now ended." Patterson spread his arms wide. "Please feel free to wander the library or visit our many gardens. Stay as long as you like. We ask only that you avoid the cloisters, out of respect for the brothers' privacy, and the graveyards, to preserve the holiness of the interments."

With that, Patterson left, his robes swishing softly with every step. The German couple strolled down a garden path, while Lip Gloss and Baldy headed back toward the gift shop. The nuns entered the library.

"What now?" Hi asked.

I shrugged. "Any ideas?"

"I say we go left." Shelton was studying a free map he'd snagged in the gift shop. "There's a massive garden that overlooks the Cooper River."

"Sounds like a plan." I readjusted my backpack. "Remember, eyes peeled. For whatever."

We chose a trail skirting two natural ponds at the bottom of the ravine. It led by several small dwellings standing alone in the woods.

"Who lives in those?" Ben asked.

"Those are guest houses," I answered, recalling facts from my online investigation of Mepkin Abbey while we'd waited for Ben. "You can take a retreat here, and live like a monk for a weekend, a week, even longer if they let you. I guess that's one way to get right with God."

"Sounds relaxing," Shelton said. "I'd sleep the whole time."

"Not likely. You have to attend all the prayers, and work your butt off."

We navigated a maze garden, then crossed a meadow of native plants. The trail continued through a cluster of magnolias beside an ancient cemetery, then dropped down toward the riverbank.

Along the way we passed two wooden statues — one depicting the Crucifixion, the other the Holy Family's flight from Egypt. Interesting, but irrelevant to our clue.

"The main garden is down there." Shelton pointed to a lush, green area ahead.

"Stop." I looked from face to face. "We can't risk missing something."

All three took my meaning. I saw their bodies tense, their eyes close.

SNAP.

Like that, everyone's flare was burning. I could sense their thoughts, though not as strongly with Coop absent.

I didn't attempt contact. Didn't want a mutiny on my hands.

"Follow me."

We entered the heart of the Mepkin Abbey gardens. Ancient trees shaded a series of terraced fields dotted with gates and vine-covered statues. Azaleas, camellias, and other flowering shrubs sloped down to the river below.

The place was gorgeous, yet secretive, filled with hidden nooks and crannies tucked into the verdant foliage. Hushed. Mysterious.

We cast out our super-senses, examining every sculpture, niche, and gravestone.

Nothing clicked. We discovered no hint of the Gamemaster's cache.

"We're in the wrong place." My voice radiated frustration. "But I don't know where else to look."

"There's one more possibility." Hi had commandeered the map and was pointing to the woods at our backs. "The abbey's oldest cemetery is beyond that ridge. It's the most remote point on the grounds."

"Why didn't you say so?" I was already moving.

"Off-limits," Shelton muttered. I chose not to hear.

We entered the woods and continued to the base of a narrow plank bridge. Towering pines and thick understory blocked our view of the garden and river.

"We have to cross?" Shelton asked.

"Come on, you wuss." Ben fired across.

The rest of us followed.

After climbing a staircase on the opposite embankment, we spotted our objective. Fifty yards square, and bounded by a shoulder-high brick wall, the ancient graveyard was crammed with headstones and monuments. A rusty iron gate blocked entry.

No birds chirped. No crickets hummed. The air was heavy with moisture and deathly still.

"We can't enter a burial ground," Shelton insisted. "Patterson was clear on that."

"Guys, look!" My hypervision had already zeroed in.

A small mausoleum sat dead center in the cemetery.

Adorning its roof was a marble sphere.

Carved into its surface was a familiar pattern.

An inverted semicircle with radiating spikes.

A rising sun.

CHAPTER 30

"We're going in."

I rattled the gate, hoping to spring it free. No such luck. A thick steel padlock held the barrier in place.

"Cemeteries are out of bounds!" Shelton's whine was a personal best. "We can't disrespect the dead."

"The sun symbol matches." I waved the black-and-white cloth. "The cache *must* be hidden in that tomb, and we've got less than eight hours on the clock. Or did you want to come back after dark?"

"No, sir!" Shelton shivered. Literally. "I'm not down for midnight tomb raiding."

"Tory's right." Hi was peering back toward the bridge. "We're alone, and already flaring. A quick in and out, and nobody knows the difference."

"Nobody but *God*!" Shelton squeaked. "That's holy ground!"

"Enough." Ben gripped the wall and vaulted over with ease. "Come on if you're coming."

"A little help," I requested.

Hi intertwined his fingers. I stepped up, swung a leg over the wall, and dropped inside. Hi scrambled over next, losing his balance and tumbling in a heap. Ben grabbed Shelton's outstretched arms and pulled him across.

I tossed a guilty glance over one shoulder, eyes and ears on full alert. No one in sight. No sound of alarm.

We mean no disrespect.

The mausoleum's marble walls formed a square structure no larger than a minivan. Three steps led up to a door flanked by stone columns and sealed by an iron grate. Faded Latin phrases decorated the sides.

Shelton sighed. "We're really going in?"

I pointed to the rising sun adorning the roof. "Seems pretty clear."

"Stop wasting time." Ben motioned Shelton forward. "Open sesame."

"Since you asked so nicely." Shelton stepped to the grate, lock pick set in hand, head shaking in disapproval. "You're lucky. I almost didn't bring these with me."

"The coast is still clear." Hi was keeping watch on the trail. "But I feel like a grave robber."

"We won't disturb anything." I meant it. "The dead will understand."

"Hope so." Hi wiped sweaty palms on his blue checkerboard shorts. "I can't be haunted this semester. I've got a full schedule."

A rusty screech signaled that Shelton had beaten the first barrier. I cringed, but no one appeared. Shelton moved to the stone door.

"We've got to be careful inside." Ben's voice was tight. "The last cache was dangerous. This one might be, too."

"Got it!" Shelton straightened. "Somebody tell the brothers these locks are a joke."

"Let's move." Ben swung the door inward, revealing a steep staircase descending into darkness.

"Oh *come on*!" Shelton's hands flew to his head. "Underground? You can't be serious!"

"It's a short flight," I said, trying to soothe Shelton's nerves as I peered down into the gloom. "I have flashlights in my pack."

"Shh!" Shelton froze. "I heard something."

Hi inhaled sharply. "Someone's crossing the bridge!"

"Inside!" I hissed. "Ben, close us in!"

"Hide in the dead man's house!?" Shelton looked frantic. "*That's* your plan?"

"Move!" I pushed Hi and Shelton toward the steps. "We can check for the cache while the person passes."

We scurried inside. The hinges squeaked again as Ben pulled the door shut.

"What about the outer grate?" I asked. "Did you close it, too?"

Ben shook his head. "Too much noise. The door alone might've given us away."

"Lights, please?" Shelton's voice cracked.

Fumbling in the darkness, I handed one flashlight to Ben and powered the other. Slowly, we crept down the stone stairs.

Ten steps, then we entered a dusty chamber three times the size of the monument above. A sarcophagus sat at center stage. I swung my beam, scrutinizing the room with my flare vision. Crumbling stone markers adorned the walls, each engraved with a name and date.

"The boss man must be in here." Hi rapped the sarcophagus with a fist. "Whoever that is. And his family is probably stashed in the walls."

"Look!" Ben's light was trained on the sarcophagus lid. A rising sun was chiseled into the rock.

Then Ben's beam caught a splash of color. Scarlet.

I added my light to his. An object was resting beside the symbol.

A single rose, tied with a purple ribbon. Flaring, I could make out every delicate petal, could tease the components of its fragrance from the stale air.

The ribbon was stamped with a row of leering clown faces.

There could be no mistake.

"Wait." Hi cleared his throat. "Does that mean . . . Are we supposed to . . . ?"

"Open the coffin?" Shelton backpedaled fast. "No chance!"

"But the Game," I countered weakly. "The bomb. It'll explode if we don't . . ."

My voice trailed off. Necessary or not, like Shelton I had serious issues with disturbing someone's final resting place.

"We have no choice!" Ben's lips tightened as his neck flushed red. "If we don't find the cache, everyone loses."

"He's right." Steeling myself. "Let's just get this over with."

"Be careful," Ben warned again. "Keep an eye out for traps. Or hidden cameras."

We crept forward, flare senses humming, listening for the slightest click, snap, or scrape. My eyes were everywhere at once.

A gigantic marble slab sealed the sarcophagus.

"Maybe the Gamemaster thinks we can't open it?" Hi said. "It looks wicked heavy."

Ben grasped a corner and strained to shove the lid aside. It didn't budge.

"A little help," he panted.

Shelton moved beside Ben and they pushed as one.

The slab inched backward.

"We shouldn't slide the monster all the way off," Ben wheezed. "The marble will fracture. Plus, we'd never be able to lift it back into place."

Hiram and I moved to the other end, across from Ben and Shelton, and pushed in the opposite direction. Centimeter by exhausting centimeter, the lid rotated clockwise, until it rested sideways across the center.

The head of the sarcophagus lay exposed.

"An envelope!" Hi was closest, and reached inside. "Tory, shine the light!"

At that moment, my nose caught something pungent. Oily. Foreign.

A warning blared from my primordial brain stem. *Danger! Urgent!*

My hand shot out, caught Hi's arm, and jerked it backward.

Something flashed where his fingers had been. A hiss filled the room.

"Whaaa!" Hi tumbled to the ground.

I leaped aside as a black silhouette darted in my direction. "Look out!"

A dark, sinuous cord slithered from the vault.

"Snake!" Shelton bolted for the staircase. "*Snake snake snake!*"

The reptile rose, fangs outstretched, exposing the white lining of its jaws.

"Cottonmouth," Ben said hoarsely. "Aggressive. Very poisonous."

We packed into the opening at the foot of the stairwell.

For a few beats, the cottonmouth watched us with cold, unblinking eyes. Then it slithered over the edge of the sarcophagus, dropped to the floor, zigzagged to the far corner, and disappeared.

Ben aimed his light after it, exposing a jagged crack in the floor. The snake was nowhere in sight.

"Gone," Ben said. "It found a bolt-hole."

"Are you sure?" Shelton moaned. "How can you know?"

"That's a four-foot pit viper," Ben responded dryly. "I'm pretty sure we'd notice if it was still around."

Hi stared at his hand, as if imagining the bite. "I could kiss you, Tory."

"Some other time." To Ben: "Could that thing have gotten in there on its own?"

"Maybe, but I doubt it. Cottonmouths are water snakes, and we're at least a hundred yards above the river. Plus the lid was intact when we moved it."

"Then we know who left it for us," I said grimly.

"This has gotten out of control." Ben seemed to speak to no one in particular.

"Let's grab the envelope and bail," Hi said. "I've had enough for one day."

"I'll do it." Ben crept to the coffin, pointed his beam inside, and leaped back. Waited. Repeated the process.

Satisfied nothing else lurked within, he waved us close. "There *is* an envelope."

"Of course there is!" Hi grumbled. "I'm dumb, not stupid."

Ben reached in to claim it.

Froze. Even in the gloom, I saw him pale.

"Oh my God."

Ben's golden eyes found mine. In them I saw naked horror.

I moved to his side and added my light to his.

The envelope was there, plum-colored, decorated with the now-familiar ghastly clowns. That barely registered.

My eyes were glued to what lay beneath.

Oh no.

CHAPTER 31

The body was curled in a fetal position.

The part of my brain not frozen in horror did a quick anthropological profile.

Male. Mid-forties. Smallish. Short-cropped red hair.

The man's beard was neatly trimmed. He wore a dress shirt, jeans, and loafers. A pair of tortoiseshell glasses stuck from his breast pocket.

He was pale. And very clearly dead.

The shock hit me like a kick to the abdomen.

Ben began to hyperventilate. Shelton shuffled in reverse until his back was flat against the crypt wall. Hi kept clenching and unclenching his hands, muttering, "It can't be real, it can't be real."

But it was. We'd solved the clue. But now that seemed meaningless.

A man was dead. This was no game.

Not dead. Murdered. The Gamemaster killed this man and placed him here.

Something beeped inside my backpack. The boys jumped, but I knew instantly.

Removing the iPad, I wasn't surprised to see a new message.

A single line crossed the screen: Please enter code. A cursor blinked, ready for input.

"Sick bastard," I whispered.

"We have to call the cops!" Hi sputtered. "No excuses!"

Shelton nodded vigorously. "We're in way over our heads."

I was about to agree when a disturbing thought struck me.

"He knows we're in here." I stared at the iPad. "The message changed without us doing anything."

"The guy on the bridge!" Shelton gasped. "Was it the Gamemaster?! We could be trapped! I bet he's watching us right now!"

Eyes wide, Shelton began frantically searching for cameras. He squatted to investigate the far corner, running his hands along the ground. Then he jerked his fingers back, no doubt abruptly remembering that a poisonous reptile was still at large.

"How'd that wacko get a body into this coffin?" Hi began pacing. "All the way out here, in the woods? Past the monks, through all those gardens? That's incredibly far to carry so much dead weight. And how'd he move the lid?"

Ben opened his mouth, but nothing came out. He seemed dazed.

I had a second terrible notion.

Though awful to contemplate, I *had* to be sure.

Moving to the sarcophagus, I aimed my flashlight at the poor soul crumpled within. Then, gathering my courage, I reached down and began rolling up one of his sleeves.

"What are you doing?" Shelton was close to hysterical. "Tory, stop it!"

I met Shelton's eye. "It's important. I promise."

"Then please, please be careful. We shouldn't tamper with the scene."

Moving deliberately, I pressed two fingers against the man's exposed forearm. Was the skin still warm? I couldn't be sure, but it definitely wasn't cold. After a three count, I removed the pressure and examined the contacted area.

The spot I'd pressed was now bone white. As I watched, color flooded back, as blood refilled the subsurface capillaries. In seconds the white spot was gone.

I nearly fainted.

My flare withered and died.

Ben must've read my expression. "What is it?"

"Blanching," I whispered.

"What?"

"Blanching." I cleared my throat, unable to process my finding. "I was checking to see if blood would return to the soft tissue where skin is pressed and released. It did."

Hi looked confused. "So?"

"The phenomenon only occurs for a short period after death." I wiped shaky hands on my jeans. "Within *thirty minutes,* Hiram."

"Oh Lord." The yellow glow died in Shelton's eyes. "So this man was alive —"

"A half hour ago," I blurted. "Maybe less."

Ben whirled, slammed both fists against the wall. He swore. Punched again and again until his knuckles ran bloody. His flare died. I'd never seen him so shaken.

"The Gamemaster probably *walked* this poor bastard here!" Hi's voice rose in panic. "Made him push open his own grave!"

I nodded, unable to speak.

This killer wasn't merely heartless and cruel.

The Gamemaster was a thrill seeker. A risk taker.

"He murdered this man while we *toured the grounds.*" I had to say it out loud.

Shelton shuddered. "Unthinkable. Insane!"

"The message," Hi said. "Should we open it?"

I retrieved the envelope, careful not to further disturb the victim inside the coffin. Using my flashlight, I examined its exterior.

Printed on the flap was a string of numbers: 123456.

The code.

I handed the letter to Hi.

No one protested as I input the digits. Everyone seemed numb.

The screen turned white. Bells pealed from the iPad's speakers.

Orange letters appeared on a field of green:

Task complete!

Now it's time for the <u>Final Challenge</u>.
Combine what you've learned to uncover The
Danger. But don't dally! Fail this time, and
you lose The Game for good.

You have until Friday at 9:00 p.m. Tell no
one, ever, or suffer The Consequences.

Good luck!
The Gamemaster

"Screw you!" Chest heaving, Shelton slammed the iPad to the ground. "The police can deal with this psychopath now!"

Hi drew in a short, quick breath. His knees wobbled and he nearly collapsed.

I grabbed his arm. "You okay?"

"No cops." Hi was shaking uncontrollably. "Not now."

"What are you talking about?" Shelton demanded. "Why not?"

Hi had opened the envelope. He handed it to me.

Bold letters adorned the outside flap: The Consequences.

Heart hammering, I pulled a stack of papers from inside.

One look, and my knees wobbled, too.

I may have gasped.

The envelope was stuffed with pictures. Ben and I walking to the dock. Shelton and Hi exiting Bolton's front gates. The four of us preparing *Sewee* for a cruise.

And those weren't the worst.

There were photos of Kit and Whitney in a Folly Beach café. Of Ruth Stolowitski taking out the trash. One showed Ben's mother reading on her porch in Mount Pleasant. Another caught Nelson Devers sneaking a cig behind his garage.

The pictures were of excellent quality. Many from close range. There were shots of our front doors, our parents' cars, even one of Coop, bounding through the dunes.

The message was crystal clear: I know where you live. I know your families. I can get to them at anytime.

Play The Game, or your loved ones will suffer.

Hi was right. We couldn't talk. Had no choice but to keep going.

Once again, the Gamemaster was a step ahead.

I'd never been more afraid.

PART THREE:
COTILLION

CHAPTER 32

"This is serious, Tory."

I shrugged, staring into my cereal bowl.

"I'm not kidding," Kit flipped a page of the *Post and Courier*. "We're smack in the danger zone."

"Uh-huh."

His words barely registered. A sleepless night had done nothing for my nerves.

Or my guilty conscience.

"The projected path has Morris taking a direct hit." Kit set the newspaper aside. "Let's pray they're wrong and the storm tracks out to sea."

"Yeah."

Sunday morning. Kitchen. Oatmeal. The normalcy jarred my brain.

Yesterday we'd broken into a crypt, dodged a venomous snake, and discovered a fresh corpse. A madman was threatening the city, and our families were smack in his crosshairs.

Yet I couldn't tell a soul.

We'd left the body inside the sarcophagus. Even muscled the lid back into place. Sneaking from the tomb, we'd found ourselves alone in the cemetery. Unobserved. We'd stumbled to the parking lot and simply driven away.

What else could we do?

The Gamemaster was in control. If we didn't follow the rules and finish his sick game, everyone we loved was at risk. The stakes had skyrocketed.

So we'd hidden the hideous crime and fled.

Shame burned inside me, so powerful I actually shuddered.

"You okay?" Kit was eyeing me with concern. "You look a little peaked."

"Fine."

"Don't stress." He misread things, as usual. "Category Four is a major hurricane, no question, but it'll probably miss like all the rest. If ol' Katelyn actually decides to visit lovely Charleston, we'll evacuate well ahead of her."

Robotic nod. "I'm just worried about the animals on Loggerhead."

"My first order of business." Kit carried his bowl to the sink. "I'll remove the barriers blocking those caverns south of Dead Cat Beach. Along with the old mines, that should give the monkeys plenty of shelter. And the wolf pack can hole up in their cave under Tern Point."

I felt a pang for Whisper and her brood, but pushed it away.

I had more pressing concerns.

Kit grabbed his keys and slipped on his jacket. "You sure everything's good?"

"Never better." Forced smile. "See you tonight."

I was texting before the door clicked shut. My phone soon buzzed with replies. Three affirmatives. I threw on jeans and a LIRI sweatshirt, whistled to Coop, and headed for the driveway.

Drizzle was falling from a slate-gray sky, slicking the blacktop behind our complex. The gusting winds made ocean travel dicey, so we'd pedal to the bunker instead of taking *Sewee*.

Two Virals were already mounted and waiting: Shelton on his black

BMX and Hi on his trusty Schwinn ten-speed. I rolled my Trek from the garage and joined them.

Ben appeared, jumped on his beat-up mountain bike, and took off without a word. We followed, far enough behind to avoid his tire spray. Coop loped beside us for a stretch before disappearing into the dunes.

"I see Ben's still a ray of sunshine." Hi's poncho hood was cinched tightly around his face. "Should be great company."

"The stiff freaked him out." Droplets beaded on Shelton's glasses. "I've never seen Ben so spooked. Can't say I blame him."

Coop burst from behind a sand hill and cut across our path, forcing me to brake.

"Watch it, dog face!"

We finished our ride in silence.

At the bunker's entrance I quickly checked our precious solar array. Despite the foul weather everything seemed in order.

If the hurricane strikes, we'll have to shelter this somehow. Ugh.

Inside, I found Shelton manning the computer and Hi pawing through the mini-fridge. Ben sat staring out the window, silent and brooding.

Coop bumped my legs as he trotted into the back room. I pictured the sodden dog shaking himself dry beside our expensive network components. Mental note: relocate doggie apartment.

I reached behind me into the crawl, shut the portal, then crossed and took a seat at the table. "We need a plan."

Hi joined me, popping string cheese into his mouth. "Does the iPad still work?"

"It's toast." I set the hateful thing in front of me.

Shelton swiveled, tapped his chest. "My bad. All pumped up and flaring, I kinda freaked out."

Back in the crypt, Shelton had spiked the iPad in anger. Moments later smoke had begun oozing from its sides. There'd been a burst of static before the screen went dark. Charging had failed to revive a signal. I had a feeling the tablet was dead for good.

"Do we need it anymore?" Shelton took a chair and placed the Gamemaster's most recent letter before him. "This note doesn't mention another clue. Only that we're supposed to —" he read aloud, "—'combine what you've learned to unlock The Danger.' Whatever that means."

I had no answer.

Was the iPad's demise irrelevant? Or had it fizzled before revealing our last hint?

Too late to worry about that now.

"We'll proceed as if there are no more clues," I said. "That leaves this message."

"Okay." Hi placed the surveillance photos next to the iPad. Just thinking of them gave me chills. "So let's combine what we've learned."

"How?" Shelton gestured at the items on the tabletop. "Where do we even start?"

My gaze flicked to Ben in the corner. "Will you join us?"

After a long pause, he shoved to his feet, slouched over, and dropped into the last empty chair.

"Let's examine our finds, cache by cache." I grabbed a notebook and began a list. "First was the Loggerhead box. Inside was a coded letter and the disguised image of Castle Pinckney."

"Our first direct message from the Gamemaster." Hi retrieved the pages from our workstation and added them to the collection.

"Weak-ass code." Shelton brushed imaginary dust from his shoulder. "Cracked it in no time."

"Don't forget," Hi said, "it was all locked in that Japanese puzzle doohickey."

"*Himitsu-Bako,*" Shelton corrected. "It's called *Himitsu-Bako.*"

"Whatever." Hi rummaged the desk until he located the box. "We solved it."

Shelton elbowed me, then mock-whispered, "*I* solved it."

He winked. I rolled my eyes.

"The altered coordinates," Ben added quietly. "*That's* what led us to Pinckney."

"Right." I wrote "puzzle box" and "Castle Pinckney" on the next two lines. "At Pinckney we found the iPad. The first clue it displayed was the eighteenth-hole pictogram." I added my copy of the image to the assemblage.

"The Pinckney cache freaking exploded." Hi shrugged. "Might be relevant, might not."

"Good." I recorded the details. "The accelerant used was diesel fuel."

Ben looked startled. "What?"

"That's what Dr. Sundberg swabbed from the scorch marks on the container. Marchant said so."

"You never mentioned *anything* about diesel." Ben looked at me oddly.

I realized Ben was right. After Kit and Whitney's beach blanket ambush, the swab results had slipped my mind. We'd gone straight to Jason's party instead.

"Sorry. Does it mean anything to you?"

"What? No." Ben looked annoyed. "Why would it? I just don't like being left out of the loop."

"Ben, I'm sorry."

"No big deal," Hi interjected smoothly. "Next, we found Saint Benedict."

Shelton retrieved the statue and positioned him in line. The black-and-white cloth was still draped across his holy shoulders.

"On Kiawah." Shelton helped Hi get us back on track. "Ocean Course, hole eighteen, guarded by a wicked snare gun. The chemical equation in the pictogram was the key to finding it."

"Bromomethane." I scribbled. "The cloth resembled a monk's robe, and was embroidered with a rising sun. That led us to Mepkin Abbey, the cemetery, and . . . what we found last."

"The dead body," Ben spat. "And the pit viper. And the envelope full of threats."

I nodded. Wrote it all down.

"That's it?" Hi grabbed my notebook and read out loud. "Castle Pinckney. Diesel fuel. Bromomethane. Kiawah Island. Saint Benedict. Mepkin Abbey. Not exactly hot leads."

"Worthless." Ben slumped back, arms across his chest. "Random useless facts."

I sighed. Was he right?

Coop emerged from the back and padded to his corner. One more set of eyes watching me.

A very long moment passed.

Hi broke the silence. "Anyone think it's odd that the final deadline is so specific?"

"What do you mean?" Shelton asked. "The timer was pretty specific, too."

"But that just counted down." Hi scooped up the Gamemaster's most recent letter. "This message states a precise day and time — Friday at nine. Why the change in format?"

I wasn't sure I saw Hi's point. "We need to examine everything we know about the Gamemaster. Look for patterns, or common threads. Dots that we can connect."

"No, we *need* to ID the corpse." Shelton raised both palms. "That's why you took the photo, right?"

"Of course."

Just before bolting the crypt, I'd had an idea. It was a long shot, but a Hail Mary beats no play at all. Reaching into the sarcophagus, I'd turned the dead man and taken a picture of his face.

"We'll do both," I said. "Connect the dots, *and* find out who the victim is."

"Both?" Hi looked skeptical. "How do we accomplish either?"

Though stumped on the first issue, I had a plan for the second. "There might be a way to figure out who's in that coffin."

The boys waited.

"Time for another trip to Loggerhead."

CHAPTER 33

"Why can't we just ask permission?" Shelton complained.

"Because there's no good excuse." I led the Virals along the trail from the dock to the LIRI compound. "Plus, I think Kit's suspicious. Last time he sent Sundberg to spy on us. We can't risk it."

"We need full network access," Hi pointed out. "Lab Six has a dedicated terminal, but without a valid password we can't tap into the mainframe."

I glanced at Shelton, who dodged my eye.

Just as I thought.

"Hi, you're forgetting!" I clamped a hand on Shelton's shoulder. "Our hacker friend here happens to be the son of LIRI's IT guru. I bet he knows a backdoor code or two."

"He does." Ben's voice came from behind me. "We've done it before."

Shelton groaned. "Even so, our session will be logged. I can't prevent that."

"Security doesn't checks those reports," I assured him. "Not without a reason. We'll be careful not to give them one."

"They didn't *used* to check," Shelton countered. "We don't know what Hudson does now."

Good point.

I brushed it off. My plan was all we had.

Approaching the front gate, I got down to business. "Once inside, head straight for Lab Six. If anyone's watching we walk right by, hit the annex vending machines, then double back."

Our luck was good: the courtyard was empty. We beelined to our target and slipped through the doors. Inside the building, the lobby was dark. Even LIRI scientists hate working Sundays.

As I flipped the light switch, memories flooded back. Rusty dog tags. A whirring sonicator. A thick metal door.

Coop, locked in a cage, tubes running from his paw.

From their faces, I could tell the boys were thinking the same.

We'd contracted the supervirus, here, in this building. Our break-in six months earlier had started it all. Had triggered our evolution into something unique. Had made us Virals.

Goose bumps. So much had changed since that day.

Ben yanked on the doors leading to Lab Six. They didn't budge.

"Locked?" I hadn't planned for that.

"I didn't bring my picks." Shelton looked almost relieved.

"Another building?" Hi suggested. "Maybe try to wrangle Lab Two again?"

"Maybe." We needed a quiet terminal, one that wouldn't be observed. I was racking my brain for a likely spot when Shelton surprised me.

He pointed to the staircase. "What about up there?"

"Karsten's lab?" That hadn't occurred to me. "You think it's still functional?"

"The secret, diabolical torture chamber that nearly caused a major scandal?" Hi looked dubious. "Pretty unlikely Kit would keep it running."

Shelton shrugged. "It had a computer. I remember that much."

"Worth a look." Ben was already moving.

We followed him up the steps and down a dark hallway, retracing the path we took on that fateful May afternoon. Every stride triggered memories. Being soaked by the thunderstorm. Chasing the echo of a dog bark.

Déjà vu.

We reached the end of the hall.

My spirits plummeted.

The lab had been gutted.

The hulking security door was propped open and deactivated. The racks of medical supplies and scientific equipment were gone. All that remained were two file cabinets, a half-dozen folding chairs, and a battered wooden desk.

With a desktop computer centered on its surface.

"Hell-o, beautiful!" Shelton quickly assessed the wiring. "Extension cord. Check. Ethernet cable. Check. Let's see if this baby still puts out."

Shelton booted the PC while Hiram and I arranged chairs. After the hard drive sputtered to life, the monitor displayed LIRI's intranet homepage.

"We're live." Shelton input a series of commands I didn't follow. A new portal appeared. "I'll log in under system maintenance and override the tracking protocols, but I can't erase our session altogether."

"That's fine." I scooted closer. "We only need the one application. Should I email the photo?"

"Give me a sec. Gotta open Gmail to receive."

"Explain what we're doing again." Ben was standing behind me. "Some program scans the picture?"

"It's called Spotter — Kit went on and on about it once." I tried to remember his exact words. "The software uses facial recognition technology to match uploaded images to pictures on the Internet. The idea is simple, but Spotter's techniques are cutting edge. Expensive too. Kit said most clients are security organizations, law enforcement, or part of the gaming industry."

"So why would LIRI buy it?" Hi asked.

"Kit learned that the technology works just as effectively with primates. He wants to track the Loggerhead monkeys without tags or tattoos, and hopes facial recognition is the answer. It's brilliant, actually. He's going to hire professional wildlife photographers to build the database."

"But today," Shelton said, "we'll use Spotter as its developers intended."

Hi gave a thumbs-up. "To stalk people online!"

Ignoring him, Shelton tapped the screen. "Send the pic to this address, Tor."

Pulling up the image killed any good vibes I'd been feeling. Reality crashed back. I was forwarding the image of a corpse.

My email blipped on-screen. Shelton dragged it to the desktop, then searched for Spotter on LIRI's network. An imposing black-and-white start page welcomed us to the program.

"Seems simple." Shelton's lips moved as he read. "We upload the pic, select full Internet search, and click run. Then we wait."

"This has to be a scam," Ben said. "How can a program search the entire web?"

"It's legit, noob." Shelton dragged my image to the search window. "The software measures facial features and dimensions, converts them to data form, then cross-checks thousands of databases in a blink. It's bawse."

"Which features?" Hi pointed to his own face. "A manly schnozz?"

"Not only that." I'd done some research myself. "Every face has landmarks — various peaks and valleys that compose our appearance.

Spotter identifies seventy of them as focal points. Things like the distance between your eyes, the length of your jawline, the structure of your cheekbone, or the shape of your eye sockets. Those points are translated into a numeric code called a faceprint. Once calculated, the program searches the net for a match."

"I'll believe it when I see it," Ben scoffed. "These programs never work."

"Watch and learn, punk." Shelton clicked the mouse.

An hourglass appeared, rotated, was replaced by an estimated time to completion.

Shelton ripped off his glasses. "Seventy-four hours!?"

Ben smirked. "Told you. What do you wanna bet it comes back with nothing?"

"Can we narrow the parameters?" Hi asked. "Search smaller, somehow?"

Tempting, but I didn't want to miss anything. "Will this keep running if we exit the program?"

Shelton nodded. "We can check back later, but we have to use a LIRI terminal."

"Then we should let it work. We need to be as thorough as possible."

"Seventy-four freaking hours," Shelton muttered as he logged out. "I could buy a handgun in less time."

"I'll shut this down." Ben nudged Shelton from the seat before the terminal and took his place.

"You know how this system works?" Shelton asked skeptically. "It takes a while to exit all these programs."

Ben nodded. "You guys check the lobby. We don't want any surprises."

"Yes, sir!" Hi gave a mock salute, but headed for the door. Shelton and I followed on his heels.

The three of us snuck downstairs to the ground floor. The coast remained clear.

Minutes later Ben appeared and we slipped from the building, heading for the front gate. We were halfway across the courtyard when I spotted trouble.

"Crap. It's Hudson."

The security chief made straight for us from Building One. Unable to avoid him, we halted by a pair of wooden benches.

"Act natural."

"Right," Hi whispered. "That always works."

"State your business." Sunlight glinted off Hudson's silver shades.

"Good afternoon, Mr. Hudson." I didn't bother with fake smiles. "We came to look for conchs on Turtle Beach, but Ben just remembered we have choir practice. We're leaving now."

"You failed to sign in at the security desk."

"I know. We forgot. We're very sorry."

"You must sign in each and every time you visit Loggerhead Island."

"Understood. It was an oversight."

"There are no exceptions to this rule. Not even for family."

"Won't happen again." I edged around his looming figure. "We're out of here, so don't worry about us. Have a good one."

Hudson pivoted slowly as we moved past him toward the gate.

"Conch shells? Do you think I'm stupid, Miss Brennan?"

The question startled me. "Of course not, sir."

Hudson peered in the direction of Lab Six. "Conch shells, huh?"

"Right." My sweat glands kicked into gear. "But we didn't get a chance. We have to go home."

"Well then, Miss Brennan." The reflective lenses hid Hudson's eyes, making him impossible to read. "By all means, be on your way."

Uneasy, I turned and herded the boys toward the front entrance. Hudson stood statue still, watching our departure.

"That guy has it in for us," Hi swore as we hustled down the trail.

"He's like that second Terminator, the liquid metal one. I bet his arms turn into knives."

"'Choir practice'?" Ben rolled his eyes. "Perhaps your worst cover story ever."

"Not my best," I admitted. "Feel free to step up next time."

Casting nervous backward glances, we hurried for the dock.

CHAPTER 34

"It has to mean something!"

Hi slapped a knee in frustration. Shelton glanced up from his iPhone, but when Hi didn't elaborate he resumed surfing.

Ben had *Sewee* aimed toward home. The open ocean between Morris and Loggerhead can be unnerving. At the midpoint, both islands disappear from view, and for a short span one seems adrift in the endless Atlantic. It's my least favorite part of the voyage.

"Care to elaborate?" I was sitting between Hi and Shelton in the stern. "Or was that a yoga move I don't know?"

"The hard deadline still bugs me. Friday at nine p.m. Why so specific?"

"I've been thinking about that." Shelton leaned closer so Hi and I could hear over the wind. "Everything the Gamemaster has set up seems meticulously planned. Agreed?"

"Absolutely," Hi said. "Some of his toys are expensive, too."

"I think your instincts are dead-on, Hi." Shelton shifted to face us. "Here's my theory. The Gamemaster began setting this game up a long time ago. Did serious planning. I'm talking weeks, maybe months."

"Or even years," I said. "How'd he run those wires beneath the eighteenth green?"

Shelton nodded rapidly. "I've been meaning to check when Kiawah's Ocean Course was last resurfaced. But you get my point."

"Yes. But not where you're going."

"We found that first cache — the Loggerhead one — right after it was registered online." Shelton pointed to Hi. "You said it'd been on the geo-cache site less than a week."

"Okay." Hi wasn't following either.

"Then we were forced into a series of tasks with varying time limits — Castle Pinckney was untimed, we had forty-eight hours to locate Kiawah, and then seventy-two to find Mepkin."

"And now we have a specific deadline — Friday at nine." I tried to calculate the total hours, but gave up. "More than five whole days. It makes no sense."

"*Unless,*" Shelton said, "the endgame was *always* going to be Friday at nine."

Deep in my brainpan, a faint bell began jingling. "Keep going."

"Maybe, for some reason, the game *has* to end then." Shelton made a chopping motion. "*Right* then. No matter how much time the earlier legs might've taken us."

"Because the early legs were variable." I felt a rush of insight. "We could've taken much longer to find Pinckney, since it didn't have a time limit. And though we came down to the wire that night on the golf course, we still had hours remaining at the abbey when we found the . . . last clue."

Corpse. Why couldn't I say it?

"Exactly." Shelton slid from the bench to crouch before Hi and me. "So the upshot is this — the Gamemaster couldn't know how long it would take us to reach this particular point. He had to allow enough flexibility in his sick schedule for his pawns to complete all the tasks."

"Assuming we didn't get killed along the way," Hi grumbled.

"So he *couldn't* use a timer." It all made sense. "Not if the final task requires a specific hour and date. Because he couldn't know when we'd actually get to the crypt."

"That's why the last note is different. The Gamemaster just needed us to have reached the crypt before Friday at nine, when he obviously has something planned. If that left seven days, five days, or two days, so what? We'd still be on pace for his timetable."

Hi grabbed Shelton by the cheeks. "You, sir, are a genius." He leaned forward to kiss each one.

"I try." Shelton flailed as Hi planted his first sloppy smacker. "Man, get off me!"

I ignored the doofuses.

This changed everything. If the Gamemaster's finale *had* to take place Friday at nine, we might be able to determine what it involved.

The jingling in my head morphed to gonging. *What?*

"Combine what we've learned," I said, wheels spinning. "Add this deadline to the mix."

Shelton moved back to the bench. "It's definitely going to be a problem."

"Problem? Why?"

Hi looked at me strangely. "We're a little busy Friday night."

"Busy? Doing what?"

The boys exchanged a look. Hi snorted.

"I don't know about you," Shelton said, "but I'm escorting my friend Victoria to her debutante ball."

"Oh. Right." How could I forget?

Willful blindness.

"We'll all be stuck at The Citadel," Shelton went on. "No boat, no ride. No way to sneak away with your dad there. Plus, don't you have to walk the runway?"

"Sometime after eight," I said glumly. "I'm not sure where I'll be in the order."

"Aim for back of the line," Hi said. "Those with swag should strut the castle last."

Thunderbolt.

Facts coalesced in my mind.

Friday. Nine. Smack in the middle of my debutante ball.

Combine what you know.

The Citadel.

Combine what you know.

Castle Pinckney. The answer to the Gamemaster's first clue.

Combine what you know.

"The Citadel is a castle," I breathed. "That's what 'citadel' means."

"Say what now?" Shelton didn't get it.

"So?" Neither did Hi.

The Gamemaster knew things about us: where we lived, who our families were, even the activities we liked. Could he know our schedule, too?

A chill spread through me.

He always seems to be watching.

The debutante ball was the perfect target for a madman.

"I don't think we'll have to sneak away on Friday." Pulse racing, I gazed out across the open sea.

"I think we'll already be in the right place."

CHAPTER 35

The next morning, I couldn't focus.

Up by the whiteboard, Mr. Terenzoni was explaining something about derivative functions and linear operations, but I didn't catch a word. My brain remained on tilt from the day before.

Castle Pinckney. The Citadel. Two famous Charleston fortresses.

Were they really linked?

Was my freaking debutante ball the Gamemaster's ultimate target?

My eyes wandered the room. How many classmates would be there on Friday? The guest list topped three hundred. If my intuition was correct, every single one of them was at risk.

What to do? The situation seemed unreal. But I didn't doubt the Gamemaster's willingness to kill innocent people. One dead body was proof enough.

The boys weren't being much help. Shelton was openly skeptical of my theory, while Hi admitted to being uncertain. Only Ben thought my idea made a twisted kind of sense.

The "castle" connection was tenuous — even *I* admitted that. But I felt so sure. Trusted my gut. And that meant hundreds of lives could be at stake.

We need hard evidence. Something tangible.

But what? How could we find a lead with no clues to follow?

The bell startled me back to reality. Gathering my things, I followed Hi and Shelton out into the hallway.

The busy mass of Bolton blazers and plaid skirts brought home the danger.

We had to do something. We couldn't let these people walk blindly into a trap.

After a quick locker stop, I hurried for second period. Conversational Spanish. The boys hadn't waited. A stickler for punctuality, Señor Messi had a firm lockout policy.

Rounding a corner, I barreled straight into the Tripod.

Frick.

Madison stopped short, eyes darting for an escape route. Ashley didn't miss a beat.

"Boat girl!" Eyes gleaming, she flipped her glossy black hair. "Heard you crashed Jason's party. Did he really beat up all your friends?"

"They were stealing." Courtney was jammed into a cheerleading uniform three sizes too small. "Then the fat one almost drowned, or something."

Madison wouldn't meet my eye.

Six months earlier I'd have cowered before these bitches, but those days were over. "Jason invited us," I said coldly. "So you can stop spreading rumors."

"I'm sure you're right." Ashley flashed her shark smile. "But that's what *everyone* is saying. You know how cruel gossip can be."

I tried to hide my uncertainty. Were people really saying that?

Ben's drunken rant replayed in my head. *We're just tonight's entertainment.*

Taking heart from Ashley's attack, Madison grinned slyly. "That's how *I* remember it."

Their words bothered me. Which, in turn, surprised me.

After the misery of freshman year, I'd thought myself immune from caring what the A-list thought. This garbage was nothing new. What was one more hatchet job among all the rest?

You thought it was over. That people liked you now.

There it was.

Somehow, I'd let down my guard. Had started thinking things could be different. Hell, I'd been *enjoying* myself at Jason's party, before the roof caved in.

Reality was facing me in that hallway. The Tripod had no intention of playing nice. *So be it.*

"Funny." I stepped very close to Madison. "What *I* remember is you hiding in the cabana until I left."

Madison's mouth opened, but no sound came out.

I raised a brow in challenge. She looked away.

"That's what I thought."

Courtney and Ashley exchanged exasperated looks.

"Say something, Maddy!" Courtney hissed. "She's making fun of you."

"Don't let Brennan talk to you like that!" Ashley glared at her friend. "She's nobody. A charity-case toddler from the sticks." Then she whispered in Madison's ear. "What's *with* you? People are starting to notice."

Madison's gaze skittered left, then right. "I, uh . . . have things to do." She bolted around the corner and was gone.

Ashley and Courtney watched in disbelief.

"I don't get it." Courtney spoke as if I wasn't there. "Did Brennan, like, hypnotize her or something?"

Ashley was more direct. "I don't know what you did to her, Boat Girl, but it doesn't matter. *I'll* make sure everyone remembers you're a loser. And I don't scare so easily."

I calmly held her gaze.

Ashley looked away first. "Come on, Courtney. Let's find people our own age." The two stalked off, one baffled, the other furious.

I stood in place a few beats, processing the encounter and assessing potential damage. I'd always considered Madison the most dangerous leg of the Tripod, but Ashley's cruel streak was legendary. Was she the brains of the operation?

A sigh escaped. Nothing is ever easy.

A familiar voice snapped me back. "I never expected to see *that*. She runs from you like a field mouse."

I whipped around. Chance was leaning against a locker a few yards away. I hadn't noticed him, but apparently he'd been watching.

"It's nothing." *Damn him!* The boy moved like an alley cat.

"Hardly." Chance ambled over, black hair expertly tousled, Griffin uniform molded to his frame as if specifically designed with him in mind. "When we first met, you'd have crawled into a sewer to avoid Madison Dunkle. Now you're staring her down in public."

"Your advice, remember? No fear?"

Instantly regretted. I didn't want Chance thinking about last summer.

"Oh, I recall." Chance smiled thinly. "I haven't crashed on your floor so many times that I'd forget. But showing a little backbone doesn't explain why Madison turns to jelly at the mention of your name."

I shrugged, not knowing what to say.

"I wonder if it's something else." Chance idly tapped a locker. "Maybe she saw something surprising in you. A unique quality, one others don't possess."

My pulse quickened. Color rose to my pale cheeks. Was Chance flirting, or threatening me? I wasn't sure which I'd prefer.

"I have no idea what you're talking about." Careful not to meet his eye.

"You don't think you're special? I do."

"What I *think* is that I'm going to be late for class." I hoisted my pack and started past him. "Excuse me."

"Save me a dance on Friday."

That stopped me. I glanced over my shoulder.

"You're going to the debutante ball?"

Chance executed a small bow. "Madison asked me to be her escort. I think it's just the two of us. But I hear you're bringing the whole entourage."

"That's right." Anxiety fueled my temper. "The four of us look out for each other. So if some rich douchebag tries to start trouble, we'll have each other's backs."

"Good for you, then." Smug smile. "Tell the Morris boys they're invited as well. Though Ben must promise to behave himself."

"Invited where?" I didn't follow.

"To my after party, of course. At Claybourne Manor."

"After party? Claybourne Manor?" I knew I was gibbering, but couldn't stop.

"I'll drop the invitation in your locker." He snapped a wink. "It should be quite an event." Then he turned and strode away.

"Wait!"

But Chance entered a classroom and shut the door behind him.

"I'm not going to your freaking party!" I shouted at the closed door. "In *that* house? No way!"

The few students hurrying by shot me odd glances.

I barely noticed. Things were spinning out of control.

Special? Unique quality? What was Chance hinting at?

A cold pit opened in my stomach. He could only mean one thing — Chance had seen our flare abilities on more than one occasion.

So why would he invite me and my friends to a party?

I was still rooted in place when the bell pealed.

"Crap balls!"

I sprinted for class. Was halted outside the room by a gray-haired man in a bad guayabera shirt.

"*Qué lástima, Señorita Brennan!*" Señor Messi intoned sadly. "*Estás tardía. Frente a la detención, por favor.*"

"*Sí, Señor Messi.*" I sighed. "*Lo siento mucho.*"

The door clicked shut, leaving me alone in the hallway.

"*Ay de mi.*"

CHAPTER 36

Lockout dragged.

Barring tardy students from class made no sense to me. I got that we're supposed to be on time, but how did missing a full lesson improve the situation? Didn't an absence just make the problem worse?

I sighed. At the front table, Mr. Warnock glanced up briefly, then returned to his John Grisham novel. He looked as thrilled to be there as I was.

Two boys shared the cafeteria with me. One was sleeping, the other was doodling. I'd never met either.

After reading the next unit in my Spanish text, I slumped in my seat, bored and frustrated.

Watch check: thirty minutes to go.

This is nuts.

The other Virals would be wondering where I was. Skipping class wasn't a hobby of mine.

I should do something productive.

But what? I'd finished my homework, and didn't know what the next assignments would be. Plus my other books were still in my locker.

Forget about school. We've got bigger issues to deal with.

Número uno being the Gamemaster.

I thought of Marchant. The snare gun. We'd never heard back about ballistics. I could follow up on that.

But how? Technology was forbidden in lockout, or else kids might skip class just to surf and text their friends. Warnock would confiscate my iPhone on sight.

I watched the apathetic gym teacher slouching at the front table. Devised a plan.

"Mr. Warnock?"

My jailer looked up, surprised at the break in silence.

"If you need something, Miss Brennan, come to the front so I don't have to yell."

Shouldering my bag, I approached. "Could I dash to my locker? I don't have my world history book, and I'd like to read ahead."

Warnock frowned. "You know the rules. Though I can't say I've seen you in here before. No one can leave until the next bell."

"I know. It's just, I have *nothing* to do, and it makes more sense to study than to stare at the wall."

"I couldn't agree more." Warnock set his book aside. "I've taught at Bolton for over two decades, and have never understood this policy. We *all* could be making better use of our time. But rules are rules."

"My locker's just down the hall." Hopeful look. "I won't tell if you won't?"

Warnock regarded me for a moment. "You're the one who wrote that letter to the school paper, aren't you?" He nodded to the empty kitchen behind him. "The op-ed about childhood obesity, criticizing the nutritional value of our lunch menus?"

"Yes, sir." Hesitant smile.

"For that fine piece of work, you get a hall pass. I've been complaining for years about ketchup counting as a vegetable. Glad someone agrees."

"Thanks. I promise I won't be long."

"See that you aren't." He handed me a pass. "Though why I'm sup-posed to imprison one of our brightest students I'll never understand. Hurry now."

Speeding from the cafeteria, I ducked into the closest ladies' room, locked myself in a stall, and dialed Marchant's number.

Four rings. Then a robotic voice asked me to leave a message.

Damn.

"Good morning, Mr. Marchant. This is Tory Brennan, calling about the issue we discussed last weekend. If you could get back to me, I'd love an update. And thanks again for your help. Bye-bye."

I hung up, regretting the childish "bye-bye," but unable to take it back. I slipped back into the hall and hurried for my locker.

Something dropped as I opened the door.

A thick white envelope, my name in calligraphy on its face.

Chance's invitation.

"Nope nope nope." Yet I jammed the envelope into my bag.

I was almost back to the cafeteria when my phone buzzed. No caller ID. Pumping a fist, I ducked back into the restroom and answered.

"Sorry I missed you," Marchant said, "department meetings seem to eat up all of my time."

"Oh no, don't worry." Backing into a stall, sitting, and locking the door. "I appreciate you returning my call so quickly."

"I found something interesting," Marchant continued. "Are you free to meet? I'm headed out for a caffeine fix in thirty minutes."

Um, what? Did this guy not understand I was fourteen? Bolton wasn't big on students popping out for midday lattes.

But the Gamemaster was my top priority. The Roman Empire could sit tight until tomorrow.

"Sure. Where?"

Marchant gave me an address and the line went dead.

Uncertain what I'd gotten myself into, I returned to the cafeteria, cracked my text, and killed the last fifteen minutes reading about Caligula. Dude was a wacko.

After the bell, I slipped out a side door and through the front gates. Hustling down Broad Street, I crossed my fingers that I hadn't been observed.

I felt guilty not telling the other Virals about the meeting. They'd probably worry after back-to-back missed classes. But I wasn't calling the shots. I'd fill them in at lunch.

City Lights Coffee is a relaxed, hipster café on Market Street, in the heart of the tourist district. An easy ten-minute walk. Marchant was sitting at a window table, sipping from an oversized mug.

He waved as I entered. "Glad you could make it. Would you like something?"

"No, thank you. I can only stay a few minutes."

"Of course." Marchant noted my uniform with obvious embarrassment. "You're in school today. What was I thinking?"

"I'm on my lunch break," I lied. "It's okay, we're allowed to leave."

"Regardless, that was incredibly stupid of me." Shaking his head, Marchant slid a file across the table. "But I think you'll find this interesting."

I opened the file. "Were you able to ID the gun's owner?"

"Yes and no. The weapon is registered to a business entity, not an individual."

My eyes rose to meet his. "A business? Which one?"

Marchant reached over and flipped to the file's last page.

I stared in disbelief.

Four words had been typed on the line marked, "Registrant's Name."

Loggerhead Island Research Institute.

"What the hell?"

"That was my reaction as well," Marchant said. "Apparently, it's an extremely high-tech facility based on an island just off the coast. A non-profit, focused on veterinary medicine. Someone in its security department submitted the snare gun for a permit exception."

"But I thought these guns were totally illegal?"

"So did I." Marchant stirred his cappuccino. "I wasn't aware an exception existed, and I work for the police."

"Why would . . . this place need this type of weapon?" For some reason, I was hesitant to reveal my connection to LIRI.

"The application states that snare guns are necessary to protect bird-nesting areas from predators. Since the whole island is private property, with no human inhabitants, the request was approved. The institute applied for *two* such permits."

"Crazy." I couldn't wrap my head around what I was hearing.

Snare guns? On Loggerhead? I wondered if Kit had approved the requisition. And why would *security* apply for weapons intended to protect birds? None of it made sense.

First alarming thought: *Whisper and her family.*

These guns fire indiscriminately, at anything. If there was another on Loggerhead, the pack was in danger.

Second alarming thought: *The Gamemaster's gun was registered to LIRI.*

And the first cache had been buried on Loggerhead.

My blood pressure spiked.

Did the Gamemaster work at the institute?

"Are you okay?" Marchant's face was crimped in concern.

"I'm fine." Calm as I could manage. "I just don't get what this crazy zoo has to do with me. My dog, I mean."

"I dug a bit further. Turns out, this institute is bigger than just the one island." Marchant retrieved his file. "My guess? Some worker swiped the weapon to make a buck. A snare gun is pretty unique — they might've thought it was worth a bundle if they pawned it, or sold it at a local gun show. Anyone could've bought it off the books."

Was it that simple? Was it coincidence that connected the Gamemaster to LIRI?

Not on your life.

Marchant ran a hand across the file. "Sorry I couldn't score a name."

"You can't find what isn't there." I checked my watch. "Yikes! I've got to get going. Thanks again."

Marchant nodded. "I'll keep looking. You've piqued my curiosity."

Leaving the café we headed in different directions.

I ran all the way back to Bolton.

◇   ◇   ◇

"You shouldn't sneak off to meet strangers without telling one of us," Hi admonished between bites of his Philly cheesesteak. "Don't you watch *Dateline*?"

"Marchant's a cop." I tried not to sound defensive. "Almost, anyway."

Hi wasn't swayed. "Bad policy is still *bad* policy."

We were sitting at our usual table in the cafeteria. The boys were expressing their disapproval of my solo day trip.

Ben was even more blunt.

"Meeting that guy alone was freaking crazy." He glared at me until I dropped my eyes. "You don't know *anything* about him."

Ben seemed about to say more, but couldn't find the words. Finally, "No more risks like that, Tory. Promise me. No more secret meetings without another Viral there to watch your back."

The scolding touched a nerve. "I'm a big girl, Ben. I think I can talk to a *police official* without masculine backup." My hand shot up to forestall his angry reply. "Fine! I won't go anywhere else alone. Ever again. Scout's honor."

"You're not a Scout," Hi pointed out. "No loopholes, Miss Brennan."

I nearly ground my teeth. "On my honor as lady, Hiram."

"Excellent! I accept." Hi glanced at Ben, who nodded reluctantly.

"Things are tying back to Loggerhead." Shelton pushed his sandwich aside, untouched. "I don't like that at all."

"You think the Gamemaster works at LIRI?" Ben scoffed. "That's ridiculous."

"Why?" His dismissive response surprised me.

"Because it is."

"From day one," I countered, "we've assumed our involvement in this game was random. Pure bad luck, us finding the Gamemaster's first cache before anybody else. But what if there was nothing random about it?"

Shelton's forehead hit the table, barely missing his ham and cheese. "You think we were handpicked." More statement than question.

"I don't know. But if we were somehow . . . *chosen* to be the players, then targeting the debutante ball makes perfect sense!"

"You're nuts," Ben insisted. "Jumping to wild conclusions just to fit your theory. We don't know *jack squat* right now. Targeted? How?" He raised both hands. "How could someone know we'd go dig up that first cache? *We* didn't even know until that day! And the gun was probably stolen and sold, like Marchant said."

"We still need something concrete," Hi said quietly. "Hard evidence."

On that point, I agreed. "We have to ID the body."

"Spotter will finish its face recognition search by tomorrow," Shelton said.

"So we go back to LIRI then." I tapped my temple. "And we keep our eyes open."

"Where is the ballistics report?" Hi began pawing at my bag.

"Marchant kept it." I made a mental note to call and ask for a copy.

Hi lifted the heavy cream envelope penned with my name. "What's this?"

"Oh, *that*." Could anything matter less right now? "You guys are gonna love it."

I passed along our invitation to Claybourne Manor.

Their groans drew every eye in the room.

CHAPTER 37

3:27 p.m. Tuesday afternoon.

Sewee bounced across the surf, her bow rising and falling with loud smacking sounds. I rode in the passenger seat as Ben steered toward Loggerhead.

Hi and Shelton had bailed, claiming family obligations. I'd had to endure thirty minutes of instructions before Shelton was satisfied I could handle Spotter.

"Sneaking around will be trickier," I said. "Today's a workday."

"We'll just blend in with the staff," Ben answered. "Plus, I doubt anyone uses that upstairs terminal."

"True, but we have to avoid Hudson this time. I don't need Kit finding out."

"You could practice catwalk turns in the courtyard." Ben's voice dripped sarcasm. "Or waltz your way upstairs."

"Are you done?" It was his third crack since we'd left the Morris dock.

He didn't reply, but suddenly I'd had enough.

"Ben, stop the boat."

He looked at me funny. "We're in the middle of the ocean, Victoria."

"Stop the damn boat!"

Ben rolled eyes, but eased off the throttle. *Sewee* decelerated until we just bobbed along with the current.

"Did you want to jump in?" Ben asked dryly. "Water's pretty cold in October."

"I want to know why you've been such a jerk lately."

My anger caught him off guard. "I have not."

"Ben, enough! We *never* used to fight. But now it's like a storm cloud follows you twenty-four/seven." My voice softened. "What is it? Tell me."

I saw a flicker of something in his brown-black eyes. For a moment he seemed almost . . . stricken. Panicked, even. Then he looked away.

Seconds ticked by. Ben seemed about to speak. Instead, his features hardened.

"I hate that douchebag Jason, all right?" With a jerk of his wrist, Ben restarted the engine. "He's a classic silver-spoon asshat, yet you can't get enough of him. It's pathetic."

Sudden flashback. Ben's drunken rant after the pool party. I knew that lately his problem with Jason had reached a boiling point.

But for some reason, I was certain Ben had been about to say something else. I didn't know what, exactly, but I felt it in my bones.

One last effort.

"Jason's my friend," I said quietly, "but he's not a Viral. He's not part of my pack. He'll never mean as much to me as you do."

Ben's eyes snapped to meet mine. He stared intently. I felt my cheeks burn.

"And Hi and Shelton, of course," I added quickly.

"Of course." Ben goosed the throttle and we lurched forward.

Whatever opening might've existed was gone. The stone mask was back in place.

The trip proceeded in silence, leaving me alone with my thoughts. Uncomfortable ones.

How did *I* feel about what Ben said that night? His slurred declarations about Jason and me. I'd never answered that question. Like I was hiding the issue from myself.

Am I any less confused than he is?

○   ○   ○

"I'm in." I searched for Spotter on the LIRI network. "Shelton said the program was buried in a subfolder."

"There." Ben tapped an icon halfway down the list of applications. "Capital *S*."

There'd been no more talk of feelings. Thankfully, focusing on our task dispelled the lingering tension. We had a job to do. We needed to work together.

Our entrance had been trouble free. We'd strolled through the gate and over to Building Six. Finding the lobby empty, we'd scurried upstairs. Alone in the stripped-down lab, we'd exchanged an awkward high five.

Best buds, right?

I opened Spotter and clicked "prior searches." A sparrow with giant binoculars informed us that our query was complete.

"Here we go." I tapped the link.

A stop sign flashed on-screen. The cartoon sparrow frowned: No Matches.

"Damn!" My disappointment was incalculable.

"Told you." Ben shook his head. "These programs never work."

I clicked "More Information." A text box stated that the sample image was of insufficient quality to find a match.

"My pic was bad?" I slammed a fist on the desktop. "Why didn't the program say that *before* running a three-day search!?"

Ben straightened. "Did you hear that?"

"Hear what?" My attention was fixed on hating the developers of Spotter.

"Something rattled, or fell, when you . . . I think you knocked something loose."

"Whatever." Sulky. Couldn't help it.

Muttering four-letter words, I moved to my second task — tracking the permit Marchant had mentioned. There had to be a record somewhere.

Ben was opening and closing desk drawers. Loudly.

"What are you doing?" I snapped, still irked by our failure.

"I swear I heard something. These drawers were empty when I checked three days ago." Ben paused. "Why not ask your dad about the guns?"

"My interest might be a little hard to explain, don't you think?"

"True."

My second query was another dead end. I checked dozens of LIRI folders. Procurement. Supplies. Acquisitions. Inventory. Even a subfolder entitled "Weaponry," which listed several animal control devices but no snare guns.

I tried to open the security subfolder. Access was denied.

Hudson. Registered weapons must fall under his jurisdiction.

Ben interrupted my thoughts. "Check it out!"

The lining of the left-hand drawer had dislodged, revealing empty space beneath.

"A false bottom." Ben wedged a key into the newly exposed gap. "I *knew* I heard something."

Ben levered upward, then used his fingers to remove the panel. A single object lay in the shallow compartment beneath. A red flash drive.

Tiny words were printed on its side: "Property of Dr. Marcus Karsten. Private and Confidential." The drive was stamped with a bright yellow *C*.

"Oh my God." I could hardly breathe. "This belonged to Karsten."

"Concealed in a hidden compartment, in his private desk, in his secret lab." Ben's eyes were Frisbees. "What did we just find, Tor?"

My pulse thumped. I'd thought all hope of learning more about our affliction had died with Karsten. Yet because I'd pounded a stupid desk, we might've stumbled onto . . . everything.

Another realization struck. "The logo! That *C* is a trademark of Candela Pharmaceuticals!"

Ben whistled. "The company that underwrote Karsten's secret parvo experiments. Chance Claybourne's company," he added unnecessarily.

"This is huge." All thoughts of the Gamemaster had been blasted from my mind. "This drive might hold the key to understanding our condition. Our prognosis. If there's any chance of cure!"

"Plug it in!" For once, Ben sounded as wired as I was.

Hands shaking, I inserted the drive into a USB port and clicked it open. A single folder appeared: MK.

A text box demanded a password.

"Frick." I chewed my thumb in agitation. "Any ideas?"

Ben gave me a flat look. "How would I know Karsten's private password?"

Footfalls sounded in the hall. My heart went hummingbird. I yanked and pocketed the drive an instant before the door banged open.

"What are you two doing in here?" Mike Iglehart wore an eye-blistering white lab coat and a surly expression. "This isn't some teenage make-out room."

My face flushed scarlet. "Excuse me?"

"We were using the computer!" Ben barked. "That's it."

Iglehart smirked. "I'm sure. Which reminds me this terminal needs to be removed. We can't waste bandwidth so you kids can play Angry Birds."

I rose, furious, intending to storm out.

"Does your father know you're here?" Iglehart's brows formed a V above his nose.

"He said we could use a lab."

Half true. Kit's prior approval hadn't been date specific.

"Yes, I heard you were grubbing up *my* workspace a few days ago." Iglehart spread his arms to encompass the room. "But this is clearly not a lab. I'll be sure to inform Kit you've been sneaking into empty spaces unchaperoned. I'll brief Hudson as well."

My cheeks burned, but I kept my mouth shut. There was nothing to be gained by arguing. Ben just stared at the floor.

We weren't doing anything wrong, Ben. Not like he's implying.

Yet Ben looked like a kid caught stealing.

Iglehart escorted us down to the lobby, where Dr. Sundberg was waiting impatiently.

"We need to hurry, Mike." Anders nodded my way. "Hi, Tory. Hope the project is going well."

"I doubt these two were studying." Iglehart's expression was close to a sneer. "They were locked away in that . . . room we found. It was *awfully* quiet before I opened the door."

That did it. I'd stomach Iglehart's private taunts, but no way was he going to defame me to others. "We needed to use a computer. That's it."

"Whatever you say. It's your father's problem, not mine. Thank God *I* don't have a teenage daughter."

"Leave off, Mike," Sundberg said wearily. "We've got work to do. I'm sure Tory and her friend can look after themselves."

Sundberg tossed me a sympathetic glance as he and Iglehart exited the building.

"Who the hell was that jerk?" Ben asked. "Will he really tell your dad?"

"And Hudson," I confirmed. "Mike Iglehart doesn't seem to like me much."

"Then let's jet before anyone finds us." Ben said. "We need to get that drive to the bunker."

I couldn't have agreed more.

CHAPTER 38

"Let's see what we've got."

Shelton double-clicked the flash drive icon.

"Is there any way around the password?" I was watching over Shelton's shoulder. Hi was beside me. Ben was slouching in his usual spot on the bunker's window bench.

"Doubtful." Shelton glanced at me. "You don't happen to know it, do you?"

"Oh sure." I leaned back against the table behind me. "Karsten emailed it to me right after we stole Cooper. I have his ATM code too, if that'd be helpful."

"Just asking." Shelton popped the collar of his navy polo. "Because this is gonna be a tough nut to crack."

"Ideas?" Hi rubbed his chin. "We're incredibly smart. Maybe we know enough to figure it out."

I thought back to the day we discovered Karsten's secret lab. The pouring rain. Shelton picking locks. The shock of finding Karsten's ghastly experiment.

So much security. So much effort to keep the project hidden.

Could we crack his password?

"Try 'Candela,' " Hi suggested. "Or '3-3-3-3.' That was the door code."

Shelton did. "Nope. And . . . nope."

"What about 'parvovirus'?" Ben offered. "Or maybe Karsten used his name."

Shelton entered the possibilities. None worked. "This is getting old, fast."

"Wait." I was thinking out loud. "It wasn't regular parvovirus. Karsten mixed canine parvo with the harmless form that's contagious to humans."

"That's right!" Hi said excitedly. "The human strain is Parvovirus B19. Try that."

"No." Suddenly I had it. "Karsten created an experimental strain. That was the point."

"Shoot!" Shelton pressed his fists to his temples. "I can't remember. And Karsten said he destroyed all the records."

"Except *this* drive," Ben said. "We have to access it somehow."

I tried to visualize the lab as it had been that day. Desk. Computer. Quarantine chamber. Clipboard hanging next to Coop's cage.

What had I read? What had Karsten told us that night in the bunker?

I smiled as it came to me. "Parvovirus XPB-19. The experimental form of B19."

Shelton was already typing. His fists rose in triumph. "We're in!"

Then his hands found his cranium once more. "Oh no!"

The words on-screen were pure gibberish.

"What is it?" I said.

"The individual files are encrypted." Shelton clicked one at random. A new password box appeared. "And this level uses a code key. Meaning it's synced to a device that changes the password every few minutes."

"So the answer won't be Karsten's favorite color." Hi shook his head. "Bummer."

"To get past this mother, we'll need professional help," Shelton said. "Even then we might strike out."

"Blargh." Computers were conspiring to thwart me. "We're nowhere on identifying the body either. Spotter won't work without a better pic of the victim's face."

"Oh no." Shelton's chin dropped to his chest. "No no no."

"What's your problem?" Ben said. "We'll figure something out."

"You think she doesn't already have a plan? Can't you guess what it is?"

Hi paled. Ben looked from face to face, clearly still confused.

Shelton groaned. "I'm not going at night. Period."

"Tomorrow afternoon." I gave his shoulder a squeeze. "Broad daylight."

"Okay, people." Ben crossed his arms. "Care to share?"

"No big deal." Shelton's tone was nonchalant. "Just a quick stop at Mepkin Abbey to get a new headshot of Mr. Dead Guy."

"Oh." Ben's expression soured. "That."

Shelton turned from Ben to look at me. "Did I guess right, Tor?"

"We have to give Spotter another try." Firm, to hide my own misgivings. "We need to know who's inside that crypt."

I glanced at the items lined up on the table. We'd examined every scrap connected to the Gamemaster. Gotten nowhere.

"We have no other cards to play."

◇   ◇   ◇

The guest lot was nearly empty. We entered the abbey's welcome center in silence. Though our cover story was solid, the mood was grim. No one wanted to revisit the crypt.

Brother Patterson was behind the gift shop register. His face lit up. "Welcome back!" His black-and-white robes swished as he swept around the counter. "What a pleasure to see you again so soon."

"We really enjoyed our visit." I conspicuously hitched the backpack on my shoulders. "So much, in fact, that we decided to make Mepkin Abbey the subject of our local cultural report."

"Wonderful! The store offers several volumes of Mepkin Abbey history, or you can review our texts and original documents in the conference facility at no cost."

Perfect.

"We'll visit the library, if that's okay. We're supposed to use primary sources."

"Be our guest." Patterson gestured to the rear door. "Do you remember the way, or shall I escort you?"

"We remember," I said quickly. "Thanks so much."

○   ○   ○

Ben was last over the cemetery wall.

Hi stood on tiptoes, peering back the way we'd come. "The path is clear. No one followed."

Our luck was good. We hadn't encountered a soul as we snuck past the library, through the gardens, and over the wooden bridge leading to the graveyard. I was feeling confident we'd pull off this mission.

But I didn't want to think about what came next.

Shelton worked the lock on the iron grate, then proceeded to the crypt door. Finally, "God help us, but we're in." Despite the mild temperature, beads of sweat dotted his brow.

I made a decision. "There's no need for everyone to go inside. Shelton, you keep watch out here."

Relieved, he hurried to the fence.

"You'll need me to move the lid," Ben said. "Doughboy, too."

Hi grimaced. "Let's just get this done, then get the hell out of here."

"Agreed." I handed out flashlights, drew a calming breath, then started down the steps.

Ben snagged my elbow and squeezed past. "Me first."

Fine by me, snake bait.

I followed Ben down the narrow flight, with Hi right on my heels. I nearly jarred a tooth loose when the staircase ended sooner than expected. A reminder that we hadn't unleashed our inner wolves.

"Guys," I whispered. "Should we flare? It's hard to see down here."

"Don't bother." Ben's response echoed in the crypt, conveying anger and shock. "No one's home."

"What?" I rushed to the sarcophagus and added my light to Ben's.

The coffin was open. The corpse was gone.

I leaned inside the sarcophagus and shined my beam down its length. The only thing present was a withered set of bones.

The original tenant.

I pounded the lid in frustration. "The Gamemaster covered his tracks. He's *toying* with us!"

Ben moved to the other side of the coffin. "Hi, help me push this back into place."

"Why bother?" Hi whined. "Skeletor won't care."

"This is still a grave. Show some respect."

Hi huffed, but joined Ben. Together they muscled the stone slab back into place.

"That wasn't worth it," Hi wheezed.

"Yeah, it was." Ben was barely breathing hard. "Your good deed for today."

Hi arched a brow. "Does it cancel out tomb raiding in the first place?"

Without bothering to answer, Ben picked up his flashlight and headed for the staircase. Hi hurried after.

I made no move to follow.

"Tory?" Hi had one foot on the steps, anxious to be gone. "What's wrong?"

At first I didn't answer. Couldn't. But then my fury bubbled out.

"We're always one step behind. Running straight in whatever direction the Gamemaster points. He's *owning* us right now. Scripting our every freaking move!"

Abruptly Ben was beside me, his hand finding mine. "Later, Tor. Right now we need to get out of this poor sap's final resting place."

He's right. Maintain focus.

Forcing myself calm, I bottled my rage for a later date.

Then Shelton's voice echoed from above. "Someone's coming down the path!"

"What should we do?" Hi hissed. "We can't hide down here."

"It's a monk!" Shelton squeaked. "He just crossed the bridge!"

"Plan?" Ben was watching me intently.

My mind raced, came up empty. This trip was a full-fledged debacle.

I sighed. "We take our medicine. Pray for leniency."

"Guys, come on up." Shelton called in a tight voice. "It's Brother Patterson. He's at the gate, and he's . . . he's not happy. At all."

That was a massive understatement.

Turns out, a monk can be livid. I saw it firsthand after stepping into the sunlight.

"Of all the disrespectful, *reprehensible* acts!" Patterson herded us out of the cemetery at a near trot. "I don't know what kind of juvenile pranks you had planned, but you are *never* to set foot on these grounds again! The entire order will be given your names and descriptions."

We took the haranguing in silence. What was there to say?

"To think I'd gone to the library to *help* you!" A vein bulged on Patterson's forehead. "The brother there had no idea what I was talking about. Of course not, since you never entered the building! I almost didn't check up here, since I'd specifically told you the cemetery was off-limits."

I couldn't meet his eye. "We're very sorry."

"Don't apologize to me, young lady. You violated holy ground. It's to God you owe penance. Count yourself lucky I'm not taking the time to track down your parents."

The walk to the welcome center was endless.

Once there, the boys scurried to Kit's 4Runner like rats. Patterson stood in the parking lot, intent on actually watching us drive away.

Before climbing into the passenger seat, I made one last effort. "I'm deeply sorry, Brother Patterson. I don't expect you to believe me, but we truly meant no disrespect. Thank you for showing us your wonderful abbey."

Patterson's eyes softened ever so slightly. "I've no idea why you would do a thing like this, young lady. Disturbing a grave! You seem like a nice girl, so I hope the shame of this day stays with you, and helps you make better choices in the future."

Having gutted me with guilt, Patterson turned and walked back to the building.

O   O   O

"Options?" Ben asked as he pulled out onto the highway.

"I think some charitable work might be in order," Hi said. "I'm not a Jesus man, but I'm pretty sure getting ripped a new one by a monk is bad karma in any religion."

Ben snorted. "I meant about The Game."

"What do you think, Tor?" Shelton was methodically wiping his glasses. "Lately it seems like everything we try blows up in our faces."

"We've reached a dead end." Admitting failure burned, but facts were facts. "We can't trace the snare gun without access to LIRI's security files, and we can't ID the Gamemaster's victim without a new picture. And since the body just vanished, we can't even report a crime."

"So our hunt for the Gamemaster is over?" Hi asked.

It'll never be over. Not for me. I know Aunt Tempe wouldn't quit.

"Temporarily," I said. "Right now, we have to focus on winning The Game. We have to nail down the final location, and stop whatever horror this psychopath has planned."

"Two days." Hi was staring out the window. "That's not much time."

No. It's not.

CHAPTER 39

The next day, Bolton's halls buzzed with talk of Hurricane Katelyn.

"The projections have all jogged to the northeast." Hi was reading weather.com on his iPhone. "Winds are down to Cat Three, with possible landfalls now including most of North Carolina."

"So long as it's *North* Cack." Shelton shut his locker. "Don't forget where we live, bro. A good storm surge could put Morris Island completely underwater."

"The good news is —" Hi placed a faux-comforting hand on my shoulder, "— the hurricane won't strike until the weekend, at the earliest. The deb ball is safe."

"Wonderful." I rolled my eyes. "I'd hate to have my execution stayed."

I was twirling my combination lock when Ben appeared.

"Anything new?" He stepped close to avoid being overheard. "About The Game, I mean. The deadline's tomorrow night."

"The castle connection is all I've got," I said. "But it feels right. It can't be coincidence that zero hour falls at the exact time of the ball."

"Why not?" Shelton argued. "If we've just randomly fallen into some wackjob's trap, the timing might have nothing to do with our social calendar."

"Even if we weren't targeted originally," I countered, "the Gamemaster certainly knows about us now. The photos, remember? It's not a stretch to think he learned our schedules."

"The very first cache sent us to Pinckney," Hi pointed out. "So the Gamemaster picked that destination *before* we started playing. That means one of three things." He raised a finger for each possibility. "We were selected from the beginning. The bomb location changed to The Citadel *after* he started following us. Or Tory's castle theory simply doesn't fly."

I paused to assess Hi's reasoning. "Or the debutante ball was always the final objective, and our attendance is a fluke."

"So now coincidence is back in play?" Ben derided. "Make up your mind."

Ben's jaw was tense. It seemed like the pressure was getting to him.

He wasn't the only one. Every minute that slipped by amped my anxiety level. What if we weren't up to the Gamemaster's challenge? If we failed, it could cost the lives of people walking this very hallway. The stakes were staggering.

Shelton spoke softly. "There's nothing solid pointing to The Citadel."

He was right. But every fiber of my being was screaming that my hunch was correct. Which meant, logically, that we were *chosen* to play The Game.

The notion filled me with dread.

"Let's talk at lunch." I started down the hall. "We'll figure it out, once and for all."

The morning came and went. Most Bolton students were attending the ball in some capacity, and gossip was everywhere. I overheard dozens of whispered conversations about escort selections and rumored dress prices. When lunch finally arrived, I headed outside to meet the other Virals.

As if to deny the possibility of an onrushing tempest, the weather was a crisp, cloudless sixty-five. I circled to the rear of the grounds, expecting the area near the pond to be empty.

I was wrong.

Madison and Chance were seated on a bench with their backs to the building. She was speaking animatedly, hands fluttering to emphasize her points. Chance contributed the occasional nod.

I would've given my life savings to eavesdrop.

Then do it. You know you can.

My pulse quickened. Should I? A quick three-sixty confirmed that no one else was close by. What's the point of superpowers if you never use them?

I slipped behind a tree.

SNAP.

The flare came easily, boosting my senses into hyperspace.

A thousand scents flooded my nostrils. Sticky, pitchy pine. Algae-coated pond water. A slight hint of peanut butter. My eyes tracked fruit flies swarming in the branches overhead, dancing among bright arrows of sunlight. I tasted a tang on the breeze, loamy dust mixed with sweet hydrangea. Felt the wind caress individual hairs on my arms.

Most importantly, I heard two voices arguing quietly.

Peering around the tree, I studied my quarry. Madison's shoulders were tense and her back was rigid. A ring-decked hand kept worrying her hair.

Nice rocks. Keep talking.

"You're not taking me seriously!" Frustration sharpened Madison's words.

"Of course I am." Chance said calmly, eyes never leaving the pond. "I don't share everything with you, but I haven't been idle."

"Do you really think —" Madison's voice dropped to a shrill whisper.

I inched forward, straining to overhear.

"Don't you think there's something *freaky* about her? Like, *for real*?

That she's not normal?" Madison's delicate features contorted into a grimace. "Other than being a total loser, I mean."

Chance took a long time to answer. "Enough with the petty insults. You saw what you saw. I have my own suspicions. But neither of us has any proof."

"Tory's *possessed*." Madison shook with the vehemence of her words. "Or, like, a witch or something. I saw evil in her eyes. It wasn't natural, I just know it!"

A tremor ran through me.

My worst fears, confirmed.

Madison had seen the flare in my eyes. Chance had witnessed much more than that. And here they were, together, discussing me. Making plans.

Nightmare.

What did Chance mean, that he hadn't been idle? I *had* to know more.

In the corner of my eye, I saw Hi and Shelton stroll from the building. They angled for a bench beyond the trees screening me from Chance and Madison. A moment later Ben joined them. Facing the opposite direction, the trio pulled sandwiches from their lunch bags.

Neither group was looking my way.

I felt a tingle in my brainpan. My pack was close, though not complete.

No. Crazy.

The idea scared me, but I acted before reconsidering.

Closing my eyes, I sought the empty space in my mind. Visualized the flaming cords connecting me to the other Virals. And there they were. Fiery lines, faint, weakened by distance and the fact that the boys were not flaring. Coop was no more than a blur in the ether.

You're not at full strength. This might be a bad idea.

Ignoring my own good advice, I tried something I'd never done.

I opened my eyes. Narrowed my focus to the couple on the bench by the pond.

Chance and Madison. Madison and Chance.

Projecting my consciousness in their direction, I searched for *their* minds.

Heat surged through me. Shards of glass pierced my skull and raked across my cerebral cortex. Ignoring the pain, I forced my thoughts forward, *outward,* untethered from my body.

The world grew hazy. Grainy. My head swam. I shut my eyes again.

Two bubbles appeared in the subliminal void.

I forced my mind toward them. Contacted one.

A deafening buzz. Then Madison's voice exploded inside my head. Thunderous. Words too garbled to understand.

It's working! I can hear her thoughts!

Someone shrieked.

SNUP.

My eyes flew open.

I wasn't sure if the scream came from outside or within.

Madison slapped at herself as if covered in spiders. Her head whipped wildly, like a hunted animal.

I clung to the tree, shaking, thankful it hid me from the duo by the pond. Glancing over one shoulder, I saw the other Virals staring at me in shock.

My consciousness recoiled like a broken rubber band.

I tumbled into darkness.

CHAPTER 40

Voices intruded from far away.

"Oh man, she really did it this time!"

"Should we call the nurse?" Panicky. "An ambulance?"

"And say what, exactly?" hissed a third. "That our friend passed out after some bad telepathy?"

The words were distant. Thin. Like radio transmissions from an old submarine. I tried to block them, to stay wrapped in murky oblivion.

The voices wouldn't let me.

"What was she thinking?" Angry. Disturbing my blissful drift.

Ben. Why's he so upset?

"She went too far!" Fretful. *Shelton?* "What if she couldn't get back?"

Against my will, one eye cracked open. Three silhouettes hovered over me, backlit by brilliant white light. For a crazy moment I thought of heaven.

That notion jarred me awake.

I moaned weakly.

"She's coming around!" The roundest shape coalesced into Hi. "Tor? You okay? If you've gone vegetable, blink at me."

"Real nice," I wheezed. The effort nearly put me back under.

"Help her sit." Shelton still sounded anxious. "Ben, get some water."

As Ben ran off, Hi and Shelton pulled me to a seated position. My head pounded. I was very close to puking in my own lap.

Gingerly, I surveyed my surroundings. Bolton Prep. Outside. East lawn, just off the main entrance.

I licked my lips. "Time?"

"Lunch is almost over." Hi was scanning for observers. "You've been out two full minutes."

Unsure how to help, Shelton nervously patted my arm. "What happened?"

"Flared. Tried to read minds." I was too shell-shocked to lie.

"Chance and Madison?" Shelton grabbed both earlobes. "Are you crazy!?"

"Maybe." I leaned to the side, hawked, spat. "Didn't work."

"So *that's* why Madison wigged out." Shelton began pacing. "She jetted inside a second after you dropped."

Hi was rubbing his forehead. "Tell me they didn't catch you."

"Not sure." I staggered upright. Wiped spittle from my cheek. "Don't think so."

I replayed the moment my consciousness touched the bubble. I'd known it was Madison, not Chance. Was certain. For a nanosecond I'd recognized her thoughts, though I hadn't understood them.

Had Madison felt something on her end? Did she sense it was *me* poking around?

How could I be so stupid?

"How could you be so stupid?"

Ben unsealed a bottled water and held it to my lips. I gulped, swished a mouthful, then spat on the grass.

I agreed with Ben, but would never admit it now.

"They were saying things. About me." My brain was still slightly derailed. "They suspect. I was trying to find out what they know."

"Not cool." Surprisingly, it was Hi who said it. "Breaking into their minds? That's going way too far."

"Didn't work." Though my pride wouldn't let me simply agree, I was ashamed of my impulsive decision. The intensity of the last few days was warping my judgment.

The bell rang. The trio examined me, appraising my condition.

"I'm fine." No way they'd decide what was best for me. "Just help me to class."

My eyes wouldn't focus. Golf balls rattled inside my skull. My stomach writhed like a shaken Coke. But I was determined to avoid more attention.

You did this to yourself. Take your punishment.

Wobbly, I allowed the boys to shepherd me through the front doors.

It was going to be a long afternoon.

○   ○   ○

Trudging up my front steps, I thanked every deity I could name. I'd survived. My bed was mere seconds away.

I hadn't fully processed the incident with Madison. Keeping upright in class had required all my energy. But standing outside my home, fumbling for keys, I finally reflected on what happened.

Why had my telepathy failed? Because I'd reached outside the pack? Because the boys hadn't been flaring? Because Coop wasn't there?

My splitting headache proved the experiment had been dangerous.

Had I learned my lesson? Probably not.

If anything, I was even more curious about what my powers could do.

Flashbulb images strobed in my head. Darkness on the golf course. A thin, gleaming wire. Myself, seen through Coop's eyes.

Was that what I'd been hoping for? To sneak inside my enemies' minds?

A sour feeling clenched my gut. So blatantly wrong.

But I *had* touched Madison's thoughts, if only for a moment. It *was* possible.

Then some force had repelled my probing, KO'ing me in the process. Since I didn't understand how I'd made contact, how could I guess why things went sideways?

Problems for another time.

Right then, a nap topped my agenda.

Which made Whitney's presence so incredibly cruel.

"There you are, sugar!" Practically dancing across the carpet in her lavender ballet flats. "You'll never guess what I have!"

"What?" Choking back tears. It was sleepy time. I glared at Cooper snoozing in his doggie bed. *Thanks for the warning, mutt.*

Whitney swept a hand toward a long white box on the dining room table.

"Your gown is *finally* ready." As if its status was of national importance. "At long last. I can't wait to see it on!"

Blargh.

I'd forgotten about the damn dress.

Whitney had nattered on about it for weeks, casually reminding Kit and me that it was expensive, trendy, and very hard to find. Her boutique BFF had resisted the idea of alterations — the dress being a loaner — but Whitney had insisted. The woman is a world-class insister.

So there it was.

And I couldn't have cared less.

"Let's try it on later." I opted for manipulation over defiance. "I'm exhausted from school, and won't do the dress justice. After dinner we can make a show of it."

Whitney's smile nearly dislocated her jaw. "What a fabulous idea!"

○   ○   ○

Banging. Loud.

"Tory!" Kit yelled through my door. "It's past seven. Time to eat."

"Wha happa cha?" My thoughts were scrambled by dark dreams of snapping jaws and watching eyes.

"Dinner. Whitney says you two have a surprise planned?"

The lingering nightmare was replaced by a waking one.

I had zero interest in parading for my father's girlfriend.

FML. "Coming."

I trudged to the bathroom, scrubbed my teeth, then plodded downstairs. Whitney and Kit were at the table, spooning salad into bowls.

"There's our princess!" Whitney virtually bounced in her chair. "Are you excited? Think you'll sleep tonight? I didn't get a *wink* for two days before my debut!"

"Hope so." Diplomatic. I might not sleep later, but not because of any stupid ball. "Where's Coop?"

"Enjoying a rawhide thingy in the guest room," Whitney said. "He'll be fine there until after the fashion show."

Kit aimed his fork at me. "Hudson stopped by my office this morning."

"Oh?"

"Something about you and Ben, sneaking around in Building Six?"

Whitney adopted a posture of extreme disapproval.

"There was nothing funny going on —" I shot a look at Whitney, who dropped her eyes, "— so don't even ask. We were using a computer terminal when that creep Iglehart busted through the door and started chewing us out."

"So I heard." Was Kit suppressing a smile? No. Of course not. "Why didn't you sign in with security like you're supposed to? Or ask *me* for

network access? And, while we're at it, why'd you need a LIRI workstation in the first place?"

"Same project." I was mildly disturbed at how easily the lies came.
"We needed to search a few online journals, and you know LIRI has free
access to a kajillion of them. Check the logs if you don't believe me."

Please don't. Please please don't.

"Fine, fine." Kit began spooning green beans onto his plate. "But
you have to sign the log, if only to spare me from more meetings with
Hudson."

"Will do. Sorry." I was relieved Kit hadn't probed further, or thought
to ask *how* we gained access to the system. "Hudson's the main reason
we don't bother."

"A young lady shouldn't place herself alone with a boy." Whitney
put a hand to her breast. "Innocent though it may be, such behavior can
lead to unseemly rumors."

Having dodged a sticky issue, I chose not to engage.

I felt guilty about lying. After all, LIRI was Kit's domain. He might
even know who'd registered the snare guns. But I couldn't see a way to
bring it up without revealing our struggle against the Gamemaster.

Too much was at stake. There might be people at LIRI we couldn't
trust. For all I knew, the Gamemaster worked there. Until we knew
more, it was best to play it safe.

Plus, being honest, Kit isn't great with secrets. He's the trusting sort,
while I'm far from it. Bottom line: I trust *my* instincts over his.

"Time for the main course." Whitney doled out thick slices of lasa-
gna to herself and Kit. My portion was noticeably smaller. "Can't have
you overfilling your gown." She actually winked.

I considered running away. Joining a traveling circus. I had a savings
account, and a tiny trust fund courtesy of Aunt Tempe. I could probably
get as far as Singapore before anyone noticed. I'm very resourceful.

But then the Gamemaster would win, and the price of failure might be too terrible to contemplate. My own family had been threatened.

I had no choice but to keep playing. Hope my instincts were correct.

Hope I could locate the threat in time.

Hope I didn't humiliate myself in the process. Or murder Whitney.

Suppressing a sigh, I shoved my plate aside. "All right. Let's try this thing on."

Whitney's squeal grated like a skinned knee.

CHAPTER 41

The next twenty-four hours zoomed by in a flash.

Sleep. Wake. School. Home. Shower. Dinner. Deodorant. Dress. More deodorant. Avoid Whitney's hair and makeup assaults. Then we were off — six bodies packed into a 4Runner.

I'd obsessed over The Game all day. The boys and I had met for lunch, then once more after school. Neither gathering had yielded a breakthrough. The boys were still dubious of my castle theory.

But one thing *was* certain: Tonight was the night. We had to beat the Gamemaster or live with the consequences. The thought left me a jangling ball of nerves.

Kit and Whitney rode up front. Ben and Hi sandwiched me in the backseat. Shelton, being smallest, had been relegated to the rear. He didn't seem to mind.

The boys looked good. Uncomfortable, but good.

Ben and Shelton sported the classic "James Bond" look — straight-cut black tuxedos with black bow ties and cummerbunds. Ben looked particularly handsome — despite his obvious discomfort, the formal wear complemented his copper skin, black hair, and dark eyes. One hand drummed his leg as we rode side by side in the car.

Hi, naturally, had opted for flair. His tux was crushed purple velvet with tails, accented by all white silk — tie, vest, gloves, and suspenders. He completed the outfit with a freaking top hat and cane. Whitney had nearly fainted on seeing him.

The trip to The Citadel took thirty minutes. Kit entered through Hagood Gate and eased onto the Avenue of Remembrance. A row of imposing stone halls appeared on our right, forming one side of a rectangle that boxed in the expansive marshaling ground at the center of campus.

"Where's Jason meeting us?" Kit asked.

"Outside Mark Clark Hall," I replied. "Near visitor parking."

"This might be the place for me." Hi was peering at the stark three-story barracks lining the field's opposite side. "I like uniforms. And marching."

Shelton chuckled. "Man, this school would eat you alive. These folks are all about hard-core discipline. Toeing the line. You wouldn't last five minutes."

"Nonsense." Hi wrist-tugged a velvet sleeve. "Honor. Duty. Respect. Those are classic Stolowitski values. I could be a leader here."

"My dear boy." Whitney turned in her seat as Kit searched for parking. "The Citadel is the *finest* military academy in the South. The Corps of Cadets is nothing to mock. Those who enlist complete a rigorous program combining academics, physical fitness, and military discipline. It's a fabulous honor to be allowed to hold the debutante ball on these grounds."

"So — book learning, push-ups, and war games." Hi ticked off fingers as he spoke. "Check, check, and check. Plus gray is my sexy color."

Kit snickered. Whitney puffed her lips in annoyance.

Kit pulled into a spot fronting Summerall Chapel and killed the engine. One by one we exited the clown car.

"This *is* a good school." Ben's first words all night. "The Citadel's

been a part of Charleston since 1842. Enrolling here is just like joining the military. There's physical training every morning and afternoon,
drills, courses on leadership and weaponry, and regular college classes,
too. Even meals are structured like the armed forces."

"Are you interested in The Citadel?" I asked.

Ben's speech surprised me — he rarely uttered so much at once. And
I'd never heard him voice an interest in the military. It occurred to me
that I didn't know what Ben wanted to do after high school.

Ben shrugged. "I'm just saying it's a good college."

"It's perfect." Hi adjusted the lean of his top hat. "Shaved heads.
Flags. Parading. Demerits. Everything a young man needs to express his
individuality."

Ben glared, but held his tongue. Support came from an unlikely
source.

"Benjamin is quite right." Whitney nodded at him with approval.
"The pillars of South Carolina have matriculated here. You could do *far*
worse for yourself."

A figure approached from the shadows. "Everyone ready to present
Victoria to society?"

Hi clapped loudly. "Bring on the first debutante! I'm bidding fifty
bucks!"

Ben slapped him on the back of the head.

Jason's tuxedo was identical to Kit's — black vest paired with a long
black tie. With his Nordic features and white-blond hair, he presented
the opposite effect as Ben, but was no less attractive. I could get used to
these tuxedos.

Jason turned and bowed, motioning toward the illuminated building behind him. "Your debut awaits!"

The lantern-lined walk led to a three-story hall posing as a castle.
Inside, directly across the lobby, a grand central staircase climbed to

ornate double doors on the second floor. Beyond them was a marble-floored ballroom.

Shelton whistled as we peeked inside. "Nice digs."

The space was lavishly decorated. Silk streamers draped the walls, while towering floral arrangements centered each table. Golden candles flickered inside delicate hurricane lanterns. A massive crystal chandelier overhung everything, cleverly illuminated from within to cast prisms of light across the room. To say the setup was extravagant would be like saying Taylor Swift sold a few albums.

Rows of chairs filled the back half of the room, bisected by a runway wide enough for three to walk side by side. Beyond the chairs, a parquet dance floor ran to a raised stage set against the far wall, where a ten-piece band was playing "Take Me to the River." The parquet was already half-full.

Corner food stations offered an array of delicacies. Sliced fruit. Goat cheese croquets. Shrimp cocktail. Thai chicken skewers. A gaggle of partygoers circled each one.

I'd attended a dozen fancy cotillion events. This bash left them all in the dust. The ballroom was infused with a royal-wedding level of extravagance. And waste. The kids I'd grown up with in Massachusetts would've been floored.

I sucked in my gut and tugged my dress into place.

Whitney had really outdone herself with this one.

I wore a strapless silk gown by Tadashi Shoji, whose name I'd never heard until the night before. To be fair, on a good day I could name maybe two designers, tops.

The floor-length number featured tiered white chiffon and a sweet-heart neckline. Whitney had accessorized me with pearls, diamond stud earrings, elbow-length satin gloves, and sparkly silver sandals.

My hair was up, with loosely-curled tendrils framing my face.

I had to admit — I looked pretty damn good.

Whitney's dress seemed intentionally chosen to counter mine — deep scarlet, low cut, and not-at-all floor-length. She drew many eyes as she scanned the party, relishing the attention while pretending not to notice.

From the doorway I spotted dozens of classmates and familiar faces. Several older men wore formal military dress, no doubt Citadel graduates. The women wore everything from satin to velour, in all colors of the rainbow.

Not so, the debutantes.

Wherever they clustered was a blaze of blinding white.

I stood a moment watching Charleston's richest mingle, tiny plates in hand, basking in the indulgent glow of spent money.

Beside me, Ben frowned. Shelton fidgeted with his tie.

They felt it, too. How out of place we were. Intruders in a foreign land.

Only Hi seemed at ease, spinning his cane like the Mad Hatter.

Watch check — seven fifteen. Less than two hours remained in The Game.

My hope of answers jumping out at me was fading away. Inside their satin gloves, my hands began to sweat.

"Come on, sweetheart." Whitney tugged Kit toward French doors on the left-hand side of the ballroom. "We shouldn't crowd the debutante on her big night. Let's adjourn to the parents' lounge." With an annoying wink, she sashayed Kit out of sight.

I took a calming breath. Tried to focus.

There was a bomb in the building. This ball was the target.

Nothing else mattered.

I turned to rally the other Virals, but had to hold back.

Jason was standing right beside me. Worse, he and Ben had locked eyes.

"Stop it." I planted myself between them. "Not here. Not tonight. You two are *going* to get along."

I gave Ben my "get your head right" look. "It's *very important* we work together. That we focus on our goal."

Ben reddened, then nodded tightly. To the surprise of everyone, he turned and stuck out his hand. After a moment's hesitation, Jason grasped and shook it. Shelton and Hi expelled sighs of relief.

"Absolutely." Jason was oblivious. "Neither of us would spoil your debut. You've got nothing to worry about."

"Good. Now let's do a lap before we commit to a location."

Debs had gathered into bunches to compare dresses and swap gossip. Everyone was talking about the hurricane. While Katelyn *was* expected to miss Charleston, the margins were pretty fine.

Many classmates greeted us as we passed. I even received a few compliments on my dress. I was starting to feel a bit of swagger before remembering that Jason was with me. Insanely popular, he was likely the reason for the warm reception.

Shelton paced nervously at my side. Beside him, Hi strutted, tipping his top hat to anyone who looked his way. Though a few rolled their eyes, most chuckled and returned the gesture. Hi grinned either way.

We were halfway around the room when I spotted two prongs of the Tripod. Ashley and Courtney were holding court at a corner table, looking stunning, surrounded by a crowd of escorts. Spotting me, Ashley covered her mouth and whispered. The group exploded in laughter.

My ears burned. My cheeks.

Yes. These skanks could still sting me.

Ben shot a scowl, but I caught his elbow. "It doesn't matter. We have more pressing issues."

"Ignore them." Jason nodded to a table across the room. "Let's set up camp there. It's time to stuff our faces."

Working through a Vera Wang–Dior bottleneck, I found myself

shoulder to shoulder with Madison, so deeply tanned she looked like a photo negative in her snow-white frock. Her shimmering diamond necklace out-valued my college fund. Times ten.

Not again.

If my presence had spooked Madison before, it now clearly petrified her.

Eyes bulging, she backpedaled into Chance, slipped sideways around him, and rabbited out the main doors.

Her flight did not go unnoticed.

Hushed conversations spread. About the Boat Girl. The brainiac grade-skipper who blew up at the yacht club. The sophomore with some weird hold over Madison.

Classmates watched. Some amused, some confused. Some angry.

"Can we keep moving?" Shelton spoke out the side of his mouth. "My social anxiety disorder is kicking in big time."

"Just smile and wave, like you're prom queen." Hi took his own advice as he and Shelton crossed to join Jason at the open table.

As I moved to follow, Chance blocked my path. "A moment?"

I nodded toward Crab Cake Corner. Ben regarded us a moment before following the others.

"You always make an entrance." Chance had forgone a tuxedo in favor of a sharp black suit. He looked like a movie star, dark and handsome.

I shrugged, tried to play it cool. "I can't help if Madison freaks every time she sees me."

"True. She thinks you're a witch or something."

My mouth opened.

"I know, I know." Chance's hand rose to cut me off. "But she's convinced you tried to possess her at school the other day. During lunch, which is bizarre, since we were alone at the time. Madison told me you're trying to steal her soul."

I went stone still.

Madison felt me! I really did make contact!

Chance was watching me from the corner of his eye. Hoping for a reaction?

Careful.

"That's completely insane," I said, forcing a laugh.

He shrugged. "As her marshal, I should probably have kept that to myself."

"Well *I'm* not going to spread it around."

"Good idea." Chance changed the subject. "Are you coming to my post-ball soiree? It's going to be epic. A-list only."

My head tilted. "I don't think so." *Not on your life.*

"Pity. You'll be missed."

Suddenly, the conversation felt surreal.

A psychopath was jerking me around. I was supposed to be hunting a freaking bomb. We could all be dead in minutes if my friends and I didn't win The Game.

Yet there I was, chatting with Chance Claybourne.

Why? Was Chance putting me at ease for reasons of his own? Reasons I wouldn't like?

Remember. He suspects.

Chance covered a yawn. "These events are such a drag. Be thankful you're leading off. You won't have to wait in that tedious line."

"What?" Mild panic. "Why? Because I'm youngest?"

"No, Miss Brennan." Chance was adjusting his black silk tie. "In this case the alphabet was the culprit. Ashley begged off going first for some reason."

Great. I'd never seen this absurdity done before, yet had to open the show. My luck is consistent, I'll say that much. And I was instantly suspicious of why Ashley changed spots.

I was about to pepper Chance with a million questions — I should've paid more attention in cotillion — when something caught my eye.

My breath caught.

My heart almost stopped.

Above the ballroom's main entrance was a simple decoration formed of white and yellow streamers. The silk swatches were twisted and tied to form a yard-square tableau hanging high up over the end of the catwalk. I'd never have noticed it without turning around.

A sunburst.

The one embroidered on the cloth wrapping the Saint Benedict statue.

The one chiseled onto the Mepkin Abbey crypt.

"Paging Miss Brennan." Chance waved a hand before my eyes. "You okay?"

No.

"Yes. I'm just . . . surprised I'll be first."

"I'm sure you'll dazzle. Until then." Chance strolled off after Madison, leaving me alone.

I stared at the sunburst.

The Gamemaster's symbol. Here. On this night. At this time.

No way it was coincidence.

My heart hammered so loudly I feared others might hear it.

We *were* in the right place.

Which meant everyone present was in terrible danger.

I raced to find the Virals. We had to move fast. A deadly clock was ticking.

At zero, we all die.

CHAPTER 42

Outside the would-be castle, the air was still.

Thick. Tepid. As if the night held its breath. A full moon rode high in the sky, illuminating the lawn and sending shadows across the stately old campus.

Faint sounds floated from within the stone hall, worrying crows roosting in a nearby oak. Music. Laughter. Clinking dishes.

The door swept open. Closed with a thump.

A hooded figure emerged, body cloaked by a long brown robe.

The figure paused. Drank deeply of the evening breeze.

The board was set.

Each piece was present.

Everything was unfolding according to plan.

The Game was nearing its climax. Would the players pass?

A rueful grin twisted the moonlit face. *No.*

Pale hands emerged from the coarse brown sleeves, rubbed together in anticipation. The figure spun in childish delight.

The crows flapped and hopped in agitation.

An eerie, high-pitched giggle leaked from beneath the dark hood.

Warbling and off-key, it keened on for long moments before mercifully fading to silence.

The crows took wing and scattered into the night.

The twirling abruptly stopped. The figure bowed as if in prayer, or deep in thought. Seconds ticked by.

The hood slowly nodded. Once. Twice. Then the figure hurried down to street level two steps at a time. Rotating a three-sixty, it wagged a finger at the lively hall.

"Time's almost up!"

The figure hurried around the building, melted into the gloom, and was gone.

CHAPTER 43

I needed the Virals alone. ASAP.

But Jason was lounging at our table, shoveling hors d'oeuvres like a starving man.

With no time to plan, and slightly freaked, I kept it simple.

"Can you give us a sec, Jase?" My smile felt more like a grimace. "I need a quick Morris Island moment."

"Okay. Sure." Jason gave me an odd look, but didn't press. "There are some folks I should say hi to anyway. I'll swing back in a few."

"Thanks so much." As soon as Jason was out of earshot, I hissed, "The bomb is definitely here!"

"Seriously?" Hi's knuckles whitened on his cane. "How can you be sure?"

I pointed to the sunburst above the entrance.

"Oh." Shelton went rigid. "Damn."

"It's identical," Hi said miserably.

Ben shook his head slowly. "I don't believe it."

"Believe it. The bomb is somewhere in *this building*."

"How do we find it?" Shelton was nervously scanning the room. "We don't have a clue to follow, or even a guess!"

I snapped my fingers at Hi. "Notes."

He pulled the rumpled pages from his jacket pocket. "We keep beating these to death, but never get anywhere."

We huddled close while Hi read my list aloud. Places we'd been. Facts we'd learned. Hurdles we'd cleared.

The Gamemaster's final message claimed the answers were there, somewhere in that tangle of information.

But, as before, nothing added up.

"New plan." Ben removed and draped his jacket over a chair. "We search the building, top to bottom. Everyone takes an area."

"Yes. Good!" Doing anything was an improvement over nothing.

I was about to say more when Kit and Whitney joined us.

"Tory, *darling*," Whitney cooed, "you must come and meet the ladies from the Women's Committee. Your father has already charmed them."

Kit blushed. "Doubtful. My reputation usually results in disappointment. I'm hardly the Indiana Jones people envision."

"*Pssh.*" Whitney flapped a hand. "Modest."

"I'd like to meet them, Whitney," I began, "but the boys and I were just—"

"These women pulled strings for you, Tory." Whitney's tone became a little less honeyed. "We need to express our gratitude."

I was about to refuse — what could possibly matter less — when Hi jumped in. "You go ahead, Tory. We can inspect the buffet tables alone." Then he whispered under his breath. "We got this. Go. Sneak away when you can."

Reluctantly, I followed Kit and Whitney to the adults' parlor for rounds of hand-shaking and banal conversation. Precious time slipped by. Too distracted to focus, I responded to questions like a trained parrot.

My anxiety increased with each passing minute.

This was nuts. Everyone there was in mortal danger, yet only I knew it.

Was that fair? Should I be screaming warnings? Sounding the alarm? Rallying a massive search of the premises?

Break the rules and innocents will suffer.

The Gamemaster's warning. I knew he wasn't bluffing.

He'd already killed once. I had zero doubt he'd do it again. And his eye seemed to be everywhere.

The Gamemaster could be in this room, right now.

We had to beat The Game by honoring his rules. But how?

Soon I could stand it no longer. I had to help the other Virals.

When Kit and Whitney turned their backs, I scurried into the ballroom. Failing to spot the boys, I sped down the catwalk and out the main entrance.

I halted on the landing, frozen by indecision.

Sensing eyes on my back. I spun. Chance was a few steps behind me.

"Thinking of running?" he asked softly.

"What? No." Why was Chance following me?

"I'd understand. It could be a wild night."

Something in his half smile made me . . . uncomfortable.

Glancing back into the ballroom, I spotted Shelton back at our table. Our eyes met. He motioned to the right and slipped through a door.

"I have to go."

I retraced my steps down the catwalk, drawing more snarky giggles from the Tripod's table. Ignoring them, I ducked out after Shelton.

Please have good news.

Shelton dashed my hopes immediately.

"Zilch." Anxiously cracking his knuckles. "Hi checked the rooms on this floor, and I covered the one above. Wasn't hard, since none of the doors have locks."

"Where's Ben?"

"Right here." Ben hurried down the hallway to join us. "I checked the lobby and first floor. Nothing out of the ordinary, no obvious clues."

"The bomb could be in a duct somewhere," I said. "Or lodged behind a ceiling tile."

"Possibly." Hi didn't sound convinced.

"Spill," I demanded.

"It's just . . ." Having ditched the top hat, Hi's hair formed a wild brown tangle above his brow. "The previous caches were all placed where they could be found. Clues pointed directly to their locations. So why would the final one be different? To me, it doesn't fit the Gamemaster's style to hide something where we couldn't reasonably be expected to track it down."

Hi was right. The Gamemaster had said so. We already held the key to locating The Danger. I thought furiously. What had we overlooked?

I was concentrating so hard, I didn't hear Jason approach.

"Hey, crew!" He swung a lazy arm around my shoulder. "Ready to break it down with Charleston's finest?"

Ben shoved Jason before I could react. "Get lost, jackass! Bigger things are happening than this stupid ball!"

Jason stepped nose to nose with Ben. "We had an agreement, Blue. Don't make me embarrass you in front of your friends."

"Stop it, both of you! I can't have you acting like idiots. Not now!"

Things could not have gotten worse. But they did.

Whitney swooped in like a Predator drone.

"There you are!" Annoyance pinched her painted features. "Let me know next time you're planning to slip away. We're supposed to be in position already!"

I shook my head, failing to comprehend.

"It's time, kiddo." Kit was straightening his bow tie. "Let's go turn some heads."

"Now?" I was light-years from ready.

"Of course, *now*." Whitney tapped her diamond wristwatch. "It's showtime!"

"I . . . but . . ."

Microphone feedback screeched through the door. A woman's voice welcomed all present to the "evening of a lifetime."

It was really happening. I froze like a deer scenting coyotes.

"We're not in position!" Whitney sounded horrified as she peeked through the door. "Everyone's seated!"

"This hallway leads to the landing," Kit said. "We don't have to cut through."

"Then move!" Using two hands, Whitney propelled me down the corridor and around a corner to the main landing.

The other debutantes were already lined up like a procession of swans, flanked by fathers and escorts. The mass flowed like a flouncy, jittery stream down the grand staircase.

A thick curtain had been stretched across the doorway, blocking the ballroom from view. I spotted Ashley up front, Madison and Courtney farther back in the line. No help there.

A frantic-looking woman spotted me, nearly threw out her back waving my party to the head of the queue. Inside, the speaker paused for a round of applause.

"Now, remember the routine." Whitney was grooming me like a cat, wiping away smudges and spit-stamping stray hairs. "Walk straight down the catwalk at a leisurely pace, then turn and do your curtsy. Then your father will come to meet you, and pace you up and back."

Like a show pony. Then her words breached my skull.

"Curtsy? Say again?"

Whitney's eyebrows nearly shot off her head. "Surely they taught you the Saint James Bow in cotillion? We're not talking the Texas Dip here!"

"Saint James what? Who?" I began to hyperventilate.

Whitney turned horror-filled eyes on Jason. Behind me, I heard Ashley snicker.

"We never covered it." Jason looked stricken. "They assumed we all knew it already, *which I thought everyone did.*"

Whitney's eyes squeezed shut.

Beyond the curtain, the crowd stirred as another woman took the mic.

"Guys!" Hi had poked his head through the curtains. "Botox Lady is up. I think you're on."

Shelton danced on the balls of his feet. Ben looked at me helplessly.

I knew there was a bomb in the building. I knew the ball was meaningless in the face of that danger. But at that moment, I was more terrified of making a public fool of myself than anything the Gamemaster had contrived.

Whitney's eyes snapped open.

She grabbed my shoulders. "Pay attention!" Then she scooted backward, took a deep breath, and adopted a wide pageant smile. "Like so."

Dipping her chin demurely, Whitney bent her knees and swept one foot behind the other, fanning an imaginary skirt with one hand. Her head dropped gracefully and she held a beat, then rose, smile never shifting an inch all the way.

Quite a feat in her tourniquet dress. Marshals grinned in appreciation.

"Got it?" Whitney hissed, wringing her hands.

"Can you show me again?"

More applause from inside. Then the scrape of shifting chairs.

"No time." Whitney nodded to Ben and Jason. "Which marshal escorts you off?"

"Do what now?" It was all getting to be too much.

Whitney physically repressed a scream. "One of them must take your hand from Kit, and then walk you the hell out of the room. *Which. One?*"

"I don't . . . I haven't . . ."

My blood pressure spiked. I wobbled. Spots peppered the edge of my vision.

Ben lurched forward to catch my elbow. "Jason will escort her."

Unable to speak, I thanked him with my eyes.

"You'll do great," Ben whispered, patting my hand. "Just picture them all in their underwear." I gave a decidedly unladylike snort.

Ben turned to Jason. "You know the drill. Get it done."

Jason nodded and moved into position beside me.

I stole one glance at the Swan Lake parade behind me. Ashley flashed her vicious predatory smile, all but confirming why she'd skipped back and made me walk first. She was hoping I'd humiliate myself.

For some reason, that realization brought back my composure.

"Walk down, turn, curtsy, wait for Kit." I straightened my shoulders as the curtain parted. "Up and back, then Jason comes and walks me out. Right?"

"Yes!" Whitney crushed me with a bear hug. "You'll be great!"

A third female voice boomed from the loudspeakers.

I rolled my shoulders, bounced twice on my toes.

"Let's do this."

My hand shot out, found Whitney's. Gave it a quick squeeze.

Then, body tingling, I started down the aisle.

CHAPTER 44

"Ladies and gentlemen, please allow me to present: Miss Victoria Grace Brennan."

Applause.

Behind me, Ashley leaned close to whisper in my ear. "Don't choke, Boat Girl."

I almost laughed. "Step off, bitch."

I didn't think, didn't pause to reflect. I began pacing the catwalk with all the poise I could muster, thankful the floor-length gown concealed my shaking legs.

Back straight. Smile plastered. Arms slightly bent and held out to the sides to accentuate the lines of my dress. I counted off steps in my head, determined to neither run nor lag. Then I spotted a small X taped to the center of the dance floor.

The curtsy spot.

I visualized Whitney's move. Seemed simple enough. Why not a test drive with all of Charleston watching?

Shoving that thought aside, I reached the mark.

Halted.

Turned.

You can do this.

As gracefully as I could manage, I sank into the bow. Time slowed. My head dropped gently until I was staring at the parquet. Pulse racing, I waited two full beats as Whitney had done.

Cameras flashed. Someone coughed.

Silence. Had I done it right? Or was everyone embarrassed for me and choking back laughter?

Precariously balanced, eyes glued to the floor, I had no idea.

Who cares? There's a freaking bomb in the building, and I don't know where.

Then, as I gazed at the hardwood, the answer hit home.

Where did the Gamemaster's clues always lead?

Down. Underground.

Deep, dark places.

The bowels of Castle Pinckney. An earthen hole. An ancient, subterranean crypt.

We hadn't searched below the first floor. That's where The Danger must be!

The bomb is right beneath my feet. Ticking away.

I straightened, outwardly calm by force of will alone. Every eye in the room was on me. Gauging. Judging. Determining if I belonged.

One of them might be the Gamemaster.

Then Kit was striding toward me, pride beaming from his face.

Offering an arm, he squired me up the catwalk and back to the curtsy spot. Then he leaned over and kissed my cheek. For a second I forgot the danger, reveling in a rare moment of closeness with my dad.

Then Jason was there, taking my hand. "Perfect," he whispered. Smiling, he turned with a flourish and accompanied me on my final glide down the aisle.

Applause broke out. I saw approval on many faces as my handsome blond champion escorted me through the crowd. Comments floated to my ears.

"Gorgeous. Such regal bearing."

"A flawless curtsy. Which family is she?"

"Those two make a *fine* match."

"She's come a long way, that one. What a beauty!"

They like me. These people like me.

I have to admit, I lapped up their praise. It felt good to fit in. To be judged and found worthy. Lord knows I'd felt the opposite enough times.

A part of me was disgusted. Why should I care what these high society snobs thought? But I basked in their acceptance nonetheless.

As we neared the end of the catwalk I spotted Whitney in the final row, waving maniacally, dabbing her eyes with a lavender hankie.

A sharp reminder of how silly this was.

Jason and I exited the ballroom.

It was over. The whole thing had taken less than two minutes.

"Nailed it!" Hi crowed as the curtains closed behind us. "A princess for the new generation. Totally Kate. Eh, maybe Pippa."

"Good job, Tor." Shelton wheezed a throaty chuckle. "I think I was more nervous than you."

The waiting debs and escorts made a path. Ashley was standing by the curtain, listening for her name to be called.

She shot me a nasty look. I raised a brow, stared back.

Ashley laughed. Then, rolling her eyes, she nodded in grudging approval.

Surprised, I returned the gesture.

It's true what they say about bullies.

I noticed Ben watching and quickly disengaged from Jason.

"You did great," Ben said awkwardly. "I was half-afraid you'd fall down."

I snorted. "Thanks for the vote of confidence."

Reality slammed back.

I motioned the Virals down the hall to a spot where we could talk.

"We have to search the basement!" I blurted. "Think about it — the Gamemaster's clues all led below the surface. That's the thread we missed! The final cache must be underground, too!"

"Uh, Tory." Shelton tapped his nose and nodded sharply to my left.

At Jason. My non-Viral escort, right beside me.

"Gamemaster?" Jason looked confused. "Search the basement? What are you talking about?"

"Oh, we're, um, playing a pretty fierce game of Dungeons and Dragons," Hi stammered. "I'm, like, the head . . . unicorn master, and Tory has to find my magic . . . beans. Seeds."

Ben glanced at his watch. "Eight fifty. Ten minutes left."

"There's no time." I grabbed Jason by the shoulders. "Real talk — we're in some serious trouble right now. There's a bomb in the building set to explode at nine. We have to find it!"

"Bomb? Here?" Jason took a step backward. "Are you serious?"

"Dead serious," Hi said. "As in, 'we'll all be dead if we don't find it' serious."

Ben and Shelton nodded grimly.

"Oh my God." Jason's eyes shot to the mass of kids clogging the staircase. "We have to tell everyone! Warn them!"

I shook my head. "The Gamemaster will trigger the bomb early if we tell anyone. We have to find it ourselves, now, and win The Game."

"What game?" Jason's eyes narrowed. "Have you guys been drinking? Because you're not very good at it, believe me, and I don't think —"

"She's telling the truth." Ben fist-slammed his palm several times. "Bomb. Here. Now. So either help us search or piss off."

"I'm with you." Jason's voice broke. "My kid sister's in that ballroom."

"Then let's move!" I dashed for the stairs, skirting the mass of debs and escorts waiting for their moment in the spotlight. Most barely noticed. A few shook their heads — the Island Refugees, acting weird as always.

In the first-floor lobby I spun in a circle, looking for some kind of basement access.

"There!" Hi raced to a steel door hidden in the back right-hand corner. "Emergency stairwell. Going down."

We descended twenty steps to a single door labeled "Electrical."

Hand-painted below the lettering was a simple yellow image — a rising sun.

"Bingo!" Hi slapped the drawing with his palm.

"A sunrise?" Jason moved closer for a better look. "What does it mean?"

"It means I was right. This is real. Our enemy was here." I closed my eyes and took a single deep breath. "Time check?"

"Eight fifty-five." Ben's voice was tight. "We should hurry."

Like those upstairs, this door had no lock. Ben went first. Then me. The others brought up the rear.

We entered a long, dark room packed with humming machinery. The air was hot and stale, and smelled of thousand-year dust. Tiny lights flickered on control panels, adding to the weak yellow glow oozing from the ancient halogens overhead.

The chamber had an oppressive, claustrophobic feel.

I knew we were in the right place.

I scanned my immediate area, but saw nothing sinister. "Any ideas?"

Jason was peering ahead into the gloom. "There's an archway at the far end."

"That must be the way."

With Jason leading, we squeezed through a maze of equipment. My eyes were darting everywhere. I was acutely aware of the Gamemaster's love for traps. This was the final cache location. It was sure to be protected.

In seconds we reached the archway. Beyond it was a short passage, which ended at another filthy door. Metallic shavings littered the floor beneath the jamb.

"Rust flakes." I brushed an orange hinge with one finger. "This door was opened recently."

Jason was reaching for the knob when Ben caught his forearm.

"Let me. This psychopath likes nasty surprises."

Jason stepped aside.

Ben grasped the brass knob. It turned without resistance.

The door creaked open, revealing a dim chamber beyond. Bunched tightly together, we tiptoed inside.

I heard Hi hand-strafe the wall. Seconds later overhead bulbs flickered to life.

"Wow." Shelton pointed.

This room was smaller than the first, dominated by two massive HVAC units locked inside a chain-link corral. A labyrinth of air ducts and pipes snaked across the ceiling before disappearing upward to the floors above. The only access was the door through which we'd entered.

But none of that had caught Shelton's attention.

Hanging from a wire in the room's center was a single red balloon.

CHAPTER 45

"**D**on't touch it!"

Every Viral shouted at once.

"Okay!" Jason raised both palms. "But how can a balloon be dangerous?"

"In this game, *everything* is dangerous!" Shelton had dropped into a judo stance.

Though fully inflated, the balloon dangled from the ceiling. My every instinct screamed in warning.

"Nobody move." I tried to order my thoughts. "Where are we?"

"That's AC equipment." Ben pointed to the riot of metalwork above our heads. "We're in some kind of ventilation room."

The first inkling of suspicion formed in my mind. "Is the AC on tonight?"

Hi shook his head. "If those suckers were running, you'd know it. HVAC units roar like jet engines."

Shelton jabbed another finger. "What's *that*?"

A steel box sat to the left of the corral. Shiny and dirt free, the modern-looking cube stood out from the rest of the grimy machinery. I craned my neck for a better look.

The box was constructed of sheer metal sheets bolted together along the edges. Its exterior was smooth and unmarked, except for the top, which had two rectangular niches cut into its surface. The first niche held a built-in LCD touchscreen covered by a clear Plexiglas shield. The second was empty. Its thick plastic cover allowed a view into the guts of the device.

Curious, I took a step toward the box and rose up on my tiptoes, thankful that Whitney had chosen dressy sandals for my outfit and not murderous high heels.

My neck hairs went vertical.

Above the LCD screen, stamped into the metal, was a single leering clown face.

"This is it!" Adrenaline shot through me. "We found the bomb!"

"How do we turn it off?" Jason started forward before I could stop him. On his third step, I heard a soft snap.

"Get down!" I screamed.

Everyone but Jason reacted instantly.

The balloon dropped from its wire.

Behind me, I heard the screech of metal on metal.

THUMP!

The lights flickered, recovered, then resumed their electric buzz.

I cringed, face pressed to the dirty floor, eyes squeezed in fearful anticipation.

Nothing happened.

I cracked one eyelid. The other. Glanced around.

Jason had frozen in a half-crouch. Ben was lying flat on his stomach, eyes darting. Hi had assumed the airplane crash position, while Shelton was curled into a ball.

"Everyone okay?" I checked myself for wounds, found none. But streaks of brownish grit ran the length of my white silk gown.

"Yeah." Ben dusted himself off.

"I think so," Jason said, still rooted in place.

"I'm tired of this garbage!" Shelton whined. "But fine."

"Ah, guys?" Hi had un-turtled and was staring back the way we'd entered.

The light from the passage had dimmed.

Ben dashed through the door, then cursed loudly. Metal rattled in the corridor.

I lurched to my feet, recalling the room-shaking thump. "What is it?"

"Some sort of . . . grate." More harsh clanking. "It dropped from the ceiling and is blocking the entrance."

"No no no!" Shelton streaked to Ben's side. "Lift it up!"

I hurried to investigate. Down the passage, Ben was shaking a steel grill similar to those used to secure stores in shopping malls. It had fallen directly between the electrical room and us.

"Won't budge." Ben's arms bulged as he strained to raise the grate. "It's set on runners. Should lift easily. Something's jamming the tracks." Face flushed, he abandoned his efforts. "We're stuck."

"Always trapped!" Shelton actually stamped a foot. "Always underground! If we get out of here, I'm moving to a high-rise on a mountaintop. Penthouse! And ya'll ain't invited!"

Keep calm.

Stepping back into the ventilation room, I saw Jason kneel, pinch his fingers, and lift a broken wire. "Oops. My bad."

The balloon was now resting on the floor tiles. I watched it nervously. Was there more to this trap?

"I bet he's watching us *right now,*" Shelton whispered. His gaze rose to the tangle of pipes bolted to the ceiling. "A dozen cameras could be hidden up there."

Something about the whole setup bothered me.

If the debutante ball was the target, why put a bomb down here?

This building was a fortress, literally, and these rooms were deep underground. The party was two full floors above us.

The Gamemaster was ruthless. I suspected he'd want the highest body count possible. Burying explosives in the basement didn't fit the bill.

"Why'd the Gamemaster want us down here?" I asked. "In this room?"

"To kill us!" Shelton was close to panic. "We can't get out!"

My mind raced, trying to fit the pieces. "But we almost didn't find this location. What if we hadn't?"

Hi started chewing his thumb. "Keep going."

"According to The Rules, if we fail, *innocents* will die." My eyes scanned the room. "An explosion down here might kill the five of us, sure, but only if we'd guessed correctly, and were in the right place."

Shelton threw up both hands. "Does it matter now?"

"Could an explosion centered here level the building?" Jason asked.

"Not likely," Ben said. "The Citadel was built to last. It'd take an enormous blast to collapse this whole structure."

"I'm with Tory." Hi began pacing. "The Gamemaster plans to hurt a lot of people if we don't succeed. The deb ball is the obvious target."

"But he also wanted *us* trapped in *this* room." I pinched my forehead, trying to force my thoughts into logical order. "It all has to connect somehow."

No one had an answer.

Jason kicked the balloon in frustration.

Pop!

A lime green mist oozed from the torn red plastic. Jason grabbed his throat and began coughing madly. Cheeks flushing scarlet, he stumbled backward, trying to cover his face.

Noxious vapors spread through the room. My eyes watered and burned.

Tumblers fell in my head.

A key turned. Terrible insight followed.

Combine what you've learned to uncover The Danger.

"Oh no."

Hi grabbed Jason and yanked him toward the door. Shelton stripped off his jacket and fanned the vapors. Shielding his nose and mouth, Ben raced forward, scooped the balloon, and tossed it into a corner.

Frantic seconds later, the air seemed to clear.

The sound of Jason's hacking filled the room. "That . . . was . . . *cough, cough* . . . pretty dumb, huh?" he rasped.

"Just take it easy." Hi thumped his back. "And yes, you're a dumbass."

I remained rooted, a sick feeling roiling my gut.

Combine what you've learned.

Heart pounding, I raced to the Gamemaster's box, certain I'd identified The Danger. And found what I'd feared most: clear plastic tubing, connecting the rear of the device to the pipes overhead.

As if on cue, the massive HVACs grumbled to life.

My head whipped to Hi. "Time?"

"Oh crap!" Hi swallowed. "It's nine o'clock!"

"Can we turn these units off?" I asked.

Ben shook his head. "The corral is triple-padlocked. We'll never get inside."

Almost out of time.

My eyes shot to the top panel of the box. Through the second niche I could see the inner workings of the sinister device.

Another jolt. I knew why the window was there.

The Gamemaster wants me to see. Now that it's too late. Now that he's won.

I saw two silver objects inside the machine. Guessed their evil function.

A cry of alarm escaped me.

Jason grabbed my arm. "Tory, what is it?"

"This isn't a bomb." My voice trembled. "At least, not the kind that explodes."

I pointed to twin silver canisters visible through the glass.

The labels were easy to see.

Jason squinted, then read aloud. "*Bromo . . . bromometh.*"

"Bromomethane." My voice was numb. "A toxic pesticide. The balloon must've contained a weak dose. A sample for us to enjoy."

Hiram's eyes widened. "We're standing in the freaking ventilation room."

Ben winced. Shelton covered his face and moaned.

"So it's flammable?" Jason didn't understand. "Explosive?"

"It's a poisonous gas." I had to shout over the rumbling AC units.

Jason shook his head in confusion.

"The pipes, Jason!" I pointed at the ceiling. "This device is hooked into the air-conditioning system."

"The HVACs will pump the gas into the ballroom." Ben shook the chain-link barrier in frustration. "The debs are still being introduced. Everyone up there is a sitting duck!"

"Poison gas?" Jason took a few steps backward. "That's crazy!"

Hi grabbed Jason by his lapels. "Exactly! We're dealing with a lunatic. Got it?"

I thought of the people above us. Kit. Whitney. My classmates. A large swath of Charleston's wealthiest one percent. All crammed into that ballroom.

With so many bodies in such close quarters, the temperature would've risen.

The tightly packed crowd, decked out in stifling formal wear, would welcome the influx of cool air.

Until it started killing them.

"We have to shut this thing down!" Jason shoved Hi aside and started banging the metal box with both hands. "There must be a way to kill the power."

I caught one of his sleeves. "Let me look."

The others crowded behind me while I studied the mechanism.

"The outer shell consists of five metal plates bolted at the seams." Thinking analytically calmed me down. "Each side is riveted to the floor. I see no way to access the canisters inside."

Shelton smacked a side panel. "Building this took *mad* effort. The Gamemaster must've spent hours holed up in this dungeon."

"Agreed," I said. "The exterior must've been assembled on-site."

"We rip it open." Ben gestured with his hands. "Get inside before the canisters discharge. Simple."

"How?" Hi ran his fingers along one edge. "This box is fastened tight. We'd need power tools to get under its skirt."

"There *must* be a way." But I couldn't see it. My panic meter was rising again.

"The Plexiglas." Shelton smacked his hand on the little window. "Bash it open."

"No good." My gut warned against tampering with the box's construction. "The plastic won't break easily, and the opening's too small anyway."

Shelton reached for his earlobe. "We have to do something!"

I waved a hand in annoyance. "Let me think."

There must *be a way to gain entry. A way to win The Game.*

Beneath its plastic cover, the touchscreen suddenly flared to life. Cartoon clowns danced and rolled as a familiar script flashed on-screen, red words burning against a black background.

Ready to play?

"This is it." Trying to still my shaking hands. "We have no choice."

Hi nodded. Shelton groaned. Jason had locked up, eyes wide, unable to speak.

"There's no other way?" Ben glared at the screen in anger.

I shook my head. "We play or they die."

A look of despair twisted Ben's features, then vanished so swiftly I questioned having seen it. "Do it," was all he said.

"Here we go."

Bracing myself, I tapped the Plexiglas with my index finger. The shield didn't move or open.

"How do I accept? I can't reach the screen."

Before anyone could answer, I heard the scrape of a footfall.

All heads whipped to the door at our backs.

Hi ran to investigate. Froze at the threshold. "What are *you* doing here?"

"Hi?" I couldn't see past him into the corridor. "Is someone there?"

"Yes."

His tone chilled my spine. I sprang to Hiram's side and peered into the passage.

Locked eyes with the last person I expected to see.

CHAPTER 46

C hance smiled coldly from the other side of the grate.

"Trapped in a cage, are we? Seems to be a specialty of yours."

Ice ran through my veins as I hurried through the passage. The others followed at my back.

Chance Claybourne.

Down here in the bowels of the building, where he had no business being.

Where only the Gamemaster knew we'd be.

How could I have been so dense?

"You!" Shelton shouted. "You're a monster. Let us out!"

Hi covered his face with his hands. "Man, I did *not* see that coming."

"What's going on?" Jason called from behind me. "Claybourne, bust us loose!"

"Chance, why?" I could barely form the words. "All those people!"

His face pinched. "What people?"

I pressed close to grate. "You have to disarm the device!"

"Device?" Chance squinted. "Victoria, I have no idea what you're talking about. How'd you lock yourself in there?"

"Stop lying, you turd!" Shelton's voice crackled with fury and fear. "Murderer! Lunatic!"

"A former mental patient, too," Hi said bitterly. "God, why didn't I see it? We *knew* the Gamemaster was no-joke crazy. Plus Chance hates us, and has all that money." He smacked his forehead. "I'm such an idiot!"

"That's the *last* time I'll be called a 'murderer' by you freaks," Chance snapped. "Or 'crazy.' Now what the hell is this? What's a Gamemaster? Why are you down here?"

Doubt crept in. Chance sounded genuinely confused.

"Why are *you* down here?" I shot back.

"I followed you. Your exit wasn't exactly subtle, stampeding past everyone on the stairs. And now I see Jason's involved too. I want to know what's going on."

"Wait." Shelton pointed with both hands. "You're *not* the Gamemaster?"

"Enough, you moron! What absurd game are you playing? Tonight of all nights."

I believed him. Chance really was clueless. He wasn't the Gamemaster.

But he might just save our asses.

"Listen up!" I said. "There's a machine in this room that will poison everyone upstairs. We're trying to shut it down. *You* have to free us."

"Poison people?" Chance's gaze bounced from face to face. "Like, kill them? Is this some kind of nerd joke?"

"No, you jackass!" Ben elbowed forward and slammed the grate with both hands. "Everyone upstairs could *die* in the next few minutes. Just do what she says!"

"It's true," Jason added. "Get this thing open as fast as you can."

Chance's lips parted, but I cut off whatever he planned to say.

"Please. Trust me. I'll explain everything later."

I saw a thousand questions burning in Chance's eyes.

"Please!" I slapped the sides of my stained white dress.

"Fine!" Chance stepped back and examined the barrier from his side. "This is some type of sliding door, like in a garage." Pause. "Two clamps are locking the runners in place. I'll have to release them."

"Just do it!" I ran back into the ventilation room, the boys on my heels.

Under the Plexiglas, a timer was counting down.

15 . . . 14 . . . 13 . . .

I stared at the screen I couldn't touch. "What do we do?"

Hi wiped sweat from his brow. "I guess we wait."

A loud clanging kicked up behind us.

Hurry, Chance!

The five of us stared at the device, hoping we weren't too late.

The HVAC units continued to roar.

I looked at Shelton. He was tracking the clear tubes exiting the rear of the Gamemaster's box. "Those feed into the duct for the unit marked 'second floor.' The gas will shoot straight up to the ballroom."

"We bust the tubes," Ben said. "Problem solved."

"And have the poison discharge in here?" Hi looked incredulous. "You got some kind of a death wish? Chance has to clear the doorway first."

Shelton's voice cracked. "So it's either us or them?"

The prospect of such a choice shocked everyone to silence.

Jason finally spoke. "We can't let the gas into the AC. No matter what."

Horrific images strobed in my mind. Debutantes collapsing. Panicked guests scrambling for doors. Kit and Whitney, gasping, choking, struggling to breathe. Bodies littering the gleaming parquet.

"We won't," I swore. "We're going to win this sick game."

The HVACs shifted to a low humming. Red lights blinked on both units.

Hi paled. "Oh crap. Are we out of time?"

My eyes shot to the tubes. "I don't think the gas released."

Ben pressed close to the chain-link and peered inside the corral. "The HVACs have switched to standby. AC isn't blowing right now."

My eyes flicked from the tubes to the timer.

3 . . . 2 . . . 1 . . .

Horns blared from speakers inside the box. The sound morphed into a whimsical, circus-like tune.

The question dissolved from the screen. A new message took its place.

Type the Magic Word to disarm the device!

A touchscreen keyboard appeared at the bottom of the display.

Above it, a cursor blinked.

The timer reset to five minutes and began counting down.

A cacophony of beeps and shrieks replaced the music.

My eyes flew back to the tubes. Still clear.

On the screen, a second line scrolled below the first.

Don't be wrong, or pay The Price!

Jason looked at me, eyes hopeful. "You know the magic word, right?"

"No. Yes. I mean . . . we must already know the answer, but have to figure out what it is. That's how The Game works."

Jason locked his hands on his head. "This isn't a game, Tory!"

"How do we enter *anything*?" Shelton pushed against the plastic barrier sealing off the niche. "We can't reach the screen."

I ignored him, tried to block out the piercing racket blasting from the device.

Combine what you've learned to uncover The Danger.

"What led us here?" I asked.

"Your castle theory," Hi said. "Along with the specific date and time."

"No, I mean tonight." I answered my own question. "We found the sunburst symbol upstairs, and again on the electrical room door."

"That led us to the red balloon." Shelton slapped the clown face stamped onto the box. "And this nightmare."

Combine what you've learned.

My brain formed a synapse. "He's using elements from earlier clues."

Hi yanked my list from his pocket. "So what's left?"

"Several of these factors are already in play." I read aloud. "Castle. Sunburst. Bromomethane."

"This box wants a magic word," Ben said. "Like a code. The Gamemaster's *first* letter — the one on Loggerhead — was encrypted. Maybe that's a connection."

"But there's no message to decipher!" Shelton wailed. "Nothing to decode."

My mind scrambled for links, but the clanging in the passage, combined with the grating static, kept breaking my concentration. "I can't hear myself think!"

"The noise!" Shelton squealed.

"It's a distraction," Hi said. "And we're down to three minutes."

"No, listen! The volume is going up as the clock runs down. Maybe the sounds aren't random."

"Listen for a pattern." But all I heard was an atonal mess.

"Dots and dashes!" Shelton cried. "The audio *is* the message!"

"Can you crack it?" Hi asked. "Because that'd be really useful right now."

Shelton's eyes closed. His lips moved silently as he listened. "It's Morse code. First one my dad taught me. I got this."

"I can help," Ben said eagerly. "I know some, too."

Shelton froze, head cocked to one side. Sweat beaded his temples.

I watched the timer.

Ten seconds passed. Twenty. Thirty.

Come on, Devers. You own stuff like this.

"Two words," Shelton said finally. "Repeating every few seconds. The first letter is definitely *H*."

Ben nodded. "I have *H* and then *I*, but can't get the next one."

Shelton scratched his cheek nervously. "This might take a bit."

"Two and a half minutes," Hi mumbled.

"There's no signal down here." Jason was waving his cell. "I can't get online."

"Quiet!" Shelton ordered.

Everyone shut up. For long moments the only sounds were the shrill static pumping from the device, the humming of the HVACs, and the metallic hammering reverberating down the passage.

"Third is an *M*." Shelton jammed his glasses back into place. "Then another *I*, but after that I'm stuck. I haven't done this in years. I don't remember what a single dot means!"

H. I. M. I.

I rifled my vocabulary. Couldn't find a single fit.

"I have a dictionary app!" Hi typed frantically on his iPhone. "Nothing starts with *himi*—"

Another synapse. My head nearly exploded.

"The puzzle box! What was its Japanese name?"

Shelton began dancing on the balls of his feet. "Um . . . um . . ."

"Himcho-Taco?" Hi guessed. "Hiro-Bono?"

"*Himitsu-Bako.*" Shelton beamed. "That's it!"

"Hurry!" Ben said. "Type it in!"

My fingertips smacked the Plexiglas shield. "I still can't reach the keyboard!"

"Two minutes," Hi reported hoarsely. "There has to be a way to open the glass."

My fingers curled into fists.

Think!

More gray cells linked hands in my brain.

"That's not the magic word!" I squawked. "*Himitsu-Bako* is two words, anyway. But it must be a clue to opening the shield."

"*Move.*" Shelton leaned over the box, flexed his fingers, then pressed down on the edges of the plastic barrier. "We got into the puzzle box by pushing each side, then easing the top section —"

The Plexiglas slid back.

Everyone shouted in triumph.

"But what's the answer?" Ben said. "What's the magic word?"

"We've got one shot." Hi jerked free his bow tie and loosened his collar. "Anyone have a guess?"

All eyes shifted to me.

"Can I see my notes?" I tried to keep my voice from shaking.

Hi passed them to me. "Ninety seconds, Tor."

I shut out the world. Reviewed every task the Gamemaster had given us. Tried to create order from chaos.

Where had the Gamemaster sent us? What were the keys?

Castle Pinckney — we'd opened a puzzle box and cracked a coded message.

The Ocean Course — we'd solved a chemical equation and deciphered the picture.

Mepkin Abbey — we'd identified a statue and the symbol on its shroud.

"Only one minute left." Hi was deathly pale. "Time to give something a shot."

I ignored him. Kept sorting data.

Combine what you've learned to uncover The Danger.

What have we used?

The sunburst. Morse code. *Himitsu-Bako.* Bromomethane.

Symbol. Code. Puzzle. Equation.

What did that leave?

"Thirty seconds."

"Tory, we have to try something!" Ben stepped up to the panel. "Now!"

Combine what you've learned to uncover The Danger.

We never used the equation.

"Bromomethane." I was sure. "It's the missing piece."

No one moved. Enter the wrong thing, and we doomed the people upstairs.

The situation felt like a bad joke: five teenagers, dressed in formal wear, locked in a basement, trying to defuse a poison gas machine.

Yet it was very real. Lives depended on getting this right.

And we were finally, totally, and completely out of time.

"Fifteen seconds." Hi swallowed audibly.

"I'll do it." Ben reached for the screen. "Tell me how to spell it."

Hi called out the letters. Shelton covered his face, unable to watch. Jason closed his eyes and mumbled a prayer.

As I watched Ben's fingers, my universe narrowed to the blinking cursor skipping across the screen.

Something was wrong.

What?

13 . . . 12 . . . 11 . . .

What?

10 . . . 9 . . . 8 . . .

We never used the equation.

"Here goes nothing." Ben crossed himself. Reached for the keyboard.

A voice screamed inside my head.

The equation!

"STOP!"

Ben's finger froze.

I shoved him aside.

6 . . . 5 . . . 4 . . .

Hammering backspace, I wiped out Ben's entry and tapped a new sequence as fast as my fingers could fly. Pressed enter.

3 . . . 2 . . .

Beep! Beep! Beep!

The deafening static ceased.

The timer flickered, went blank.

Accepted.

Everyone gasped with relief.

"What did you type?" Shelton demanded.

"CH_3BR. The *formula* led us to Kiawah, not the chemical name."

Within the box, metal scraped metal. I heard a series of clicks.

The HVACs shut down.

The screen filled with bouncing red balloons. The horns returned. Fiery letters spelled out a single word.

CONGRATULATIONS!

"We did it!" Shelton pumped his fists, then gave Hi a flying chest-bump.

Jason and Ben high-fived like crazy. Then they froze, realizing exactly what they were doing. A beat passed, then the two boys nodded and shook hands. Hi and Shelton stared in disbelief.

I closed my eyes, too relieved to celebrate.

"What's happening?" Chance's voice carried from the passage. "These freaking clamps won't come loose."

I was about to explain when a new message lit the screen.

My elation gave way to dread. "Guys."

The others followed my sight line. All celebrations died.

Well done, Players!

 Through quick wits and skillful perfor-mance you have won The Game and suc-cessfully averted The Danger. However, you broke The Rules, and therefore must pay The Penalty. Make your choice.

Sincerely,
The Gamemaster

More clicks. Whirs. Inside the box, a canister rotated.

The HVACs blasted back to life.

"We didn't break any rules!" Shelton shrieked. "We followed every-thing exactly!"

"Oh holy hell." Hi was staring at Jason.

Oh no.

Jason. Chance.

We'd told others about The Game.

We'd sought outside help, which was strictly forbidden.

We *had* broken The Rules.

And the Gamemaster intended to exact punishment.

I heard a rattle by my feet. Looked down. A small hole had opened at the base of the front panel.

Adrenaline shot through me. Every hair on my body stood on end.

I knew what was coming.

Sweet mother of God.

We'd saved the people at the debutante ball.

Now the gas was for us.

CHAPTER 47

"We have to get out of here!"

My hands shook. My heart banged my ribs. I saw nothing but the small round hole that might soon spew my death.

Hi's cheeks flushed as dark as his purple tuxedo. "Is that what I think it is?"

"We didn't cheat!" Shelton verged on tears. "We beat The Game without help!"

Ben charged into the passage and shoulder-slammed the grate.

Chance hopped backward in surprise. "What are you doing, man?"

"Get us out!" Ben bellowed.

"It won't budge." Chance sounded exhausted. "These clamps must be made of freaking Kevlar. I can't hammer them off."

"Find a way!" Ben shouted. "We're about to *die* in here, Claybourne!"

The banging resumed, more frenzied than before.

Inside the device, one deadly canister spun. As I watched, it slotted forward into a narrow chute. On-screen, the Gamemaster's final message winked out.

The second Plexiglas cover abruptly slid sideways.

A metal handle emerged to fill the empty space.

"What the frick?" Jason said.

I stared at the strange mechanism. It looked like the grip of a shovel. Arrows on its surface pointed both clockwise and counterclockwise.

"It must turn," I said, vaguely aware that Ben had rejoined us.

"Like a valve?" Hi said. "But what does it do?"

I was considering that very question when my ears detected a low hiss.

"Move away!" I screamed.

Everyone backpedaled but me. We were out of options.

Gripping the handle, I turned it as far clockwise as it would go.

"You did it!" Jason kicked the base of the device. "The hole closed!"

"But look at the pipes!" Shelton pointed to the tubes exiting the Gamemaster's box. Dark green vapor was misting into them and trickling upward toward the air ducts.

The sickening truth crashed home.

We faced a devil's choice.

"The gas is releasing." My voice was flat. "But we choose where it goes."

"Choose how?" Shelton asked in hushed voice.

"The handle. Turn it right and the gas will flow into the tubes, hit the AC, and dump into the ballroom. Turn it left, and it will release in here."

Shelton's eyes bugged. "In here?"

"The Gamemaster wants his kill one way or another." Hi understood the ghastly decision we faced. "But now it's *our* call who dies."

Ben's fists clenched in helpless rage. "I'll kill him."

"So it's really us or them?" Shelton was close to panic. "We have to pick?!"

Jason's eyes met my mine. "We can't gas all those people. We just can't."

I nodded. "Not a chance."

We still have a card left to play.

The Gamemaster thought he'd covered every angle. Painted us into a corner. Planned for every possibility.

But he didn't know what I could do.

What the Virals could do.

This time I didn't hesitate. Using all my strength I heaved left and spun the handle counterclockwise.

Inside the tubes, the green vapor thinned, then vanished entirely.

The hole at the base of the box snapped open.

"Back!" Hi dragged a paralyzed Shelton toward the door. "Come on, Tory! Ben!"

I froze. Watched in horror as a thick stream of green fog flowed from the opening and began pooling on the floor. Heavier than air, the sickly cloud swirled into a low corner before creeping back toward the door.

We had minutes. At most.

Move!

"Into the passageway!" I barked.

The boys needed no urging. I raced through the door behind them and slammed it shut, closing off the ventilation room.

"I need a jacket!" I ordered.

Hi ripped off his velvet monstrosity and shoved it into the crack. The makeshift wedge wouldn't stop the poison, but it might buy us precious seconds.

I pressed close to the grate. "Chance, we're out of time. Can you free us?"

Chance was dripping sweat, his suit a dirty mess. Blood dripped from his fingers as he swung a rusty crowbar.

Clang!

He glanced at me with pain-filled eyes. "I'm sorry. The clamps won't budge. I don't know what else to try."

"Look around! Maybe there's a key."

"There isn't. I checked."

"Search the stairwell. It could be hidden there. Hurry!"

Chance nodded, then stumbled out of sight.

One down.

A noxious odor began fouling the air. Hi and Shelton started coughing.

I saw Ben watching me. He understood my plan, and, judging by his sideways glance, the remainder of the problem.

"Hiram, kill the lights," Ben said.

"What?" Hi was hacking and spitting. "Why would —"

Ben flicked his eyes to Jason.

Hi started. "But how . . . he'll still notice . . ."

The ghost of a smile appeared on Ben's lips. "Have faith."

Hi nodded, then whispered in Shelton's ear.

"Yes!" Shelton practically dove for the switch.

"What the hell?" Jason spun to yell at Shelton. "We need the light! We have to call for —"

Whack!

Ben's elbow connected with Jason's temple.

I caught Jason as he dropped.

"*That* was your plan?" Hi screeched. "Knock him unconscious?"

"It worked," said Ben.

"Little help!" I grunted.

The boys grabbed Jason and lowered him to the floor.

There were no more prying eyes.

Throat burning. Eyes stinging. Light-headed. Black patches floating across my vision. I peered as far as I could into the electrical room. Chance was nowhere in sight.

"Ready?"

"Ready." Three voices as one.

I gripped the bottom of the barrier with both hands.

Hi stepped to my right. Ben and Shelton lined up on my left.

My lids slid shut.

SNAP.

The flare burned like a thousand suns, electrifying my senses.

My nose magnified the caustic stench, nearly overwhelming me. My eyeballs cut through the gloom. My ears amplified the hiss of poison gas leaking around Hi's jacket.

Ignoring the sensory bombardment, I sought something else.

Reached deep within. Tapped the *power* of the wolf.

The pack followed where I led. Glowing cords scorched across our minds, smoldering with superhuman force.

I fired a single command into their minds.

NOW.

As one, we strained. The gate refused to yield.

Muscles cording, I poured everything into the effort. Could feel the boys doing the same. The barrier quivered, but remained locked in place.

The noxious reek grew stronger, causing me to gag. I felt despair infest the other Virals' minds. Linked as we were, their stray thoughts struck me like shards of glass.

. . . going to fail . . .

. . . don't want to die in here . . .

We can't . . .

We lost . . .

. . . all my fault . . .

NO!

Pushing my own terror aside, I embraced what lurked beneath.

Boiling. Snarling. Storming. All consuming.

Rage.

I would *not* let the Gamemaster kill us.

This would *not* be the end.

Neurons fired. Scalding heat infused my extremities.

I forced the energy outward, down the fiery links connecting my pack.

The boys screamed.

It took several seconds to realize that I was screaming, too.

Naked power surged into my chest. My muscles. My whole being.

Far too much. I had to free it. Had to drive the energy *away*.

AGAIN.

We pulled as one.

The grate shuddered. Rose an inch. Stuck fast.

No! I WILL NOT LOSE!

I focused. Pushed more and more energy down the flaming cords.

Something popped. My arms ripped upward.

I heard the screech of twisting metal.

My eyes opened. I stared in shock.

The bottom third of the grate was bent inward, its steel bars twisted like overstretched Play-Doh. The track had ripped free of the wall.

"Go! Go! Go!" I shouted.

Shelton and Hi crawled under the grate, then reached back and grabbed Jason's arms. With Ben and me pushing, we forced his unconscious body beneath the barrier. Then Ben and I scrambled to freedom.

Lurching to our feet, we dragged Jason across the electrical room. Once safely beyond the toxic odor, we collapsed, gasping for breath.

I looked up as Chance emerged from the direction of the stairwell. He stiffened, staring at the mangled grate, naked shock on his face.

I shut my eyes and sent a message to the other Virals: *Snuff your flares!*

SNUP.

The connection broke. Strength drained from my limbs.

"I'll sound the alarm." Chance turned to run.

"No."

All eyes whipped to me.

I coughed and spat, trying to clear my throat. "The Consequences, remember? We can't tell anyone."

"What consequences?" Chance demanded. "What are you talking about?"

"The bastard who did this threatened to hurt our families if we talk." My voice was a dull rasp. "*Ever.* I don't think he was bluffing."

"But we have to warn people!" Shelton aimed a finger toward the ventilation room. "The gas could escape the basement."

I shook my head. "Bromomethane is heavier than air. It won't rise."

"You all need medical treatment." Chance knelt beside his former lacrosse teammate. "Jason's *unconscious,* for God's sake! The poison might be killing him."

"That wasn't the gas." Ben avoided Chance's eye. "He . . . tripped. Hard."

"Help me up." I was still woozy from the loss of my flare. "I have a plan."

Chance gave me an odd look, but extended a hand.

I stumbled toward the stairs. "Follow."

The boys trailed me up the steps, Chance and Ben lugging Jason's dead weight. On the landing beside the lobby door, I spotted my target. Without hesitating, I pulled the fire alarm.

Sirens screamed. Blue lights flickered inside the emergency stairwell.

"This will get them outside," I shouted. "A fire scare should give us some cover for how we look. But no one says a word about what happened down there."

"That's crazy!" Shelton wailed. "We should call the police right now!"

"*We're* gonna catch the psycho who did this." The words gave me strength. "The Gamemaster is still loose. Probably thinks we're dead. I bet he's celebrating his victory right now. Let's show him he chose the wrong pawns for his amusement."

That said, I bent over and vomited on the concrete.

Out in the lobby, feet began pounding down the grand staircase. The foyer soon filled with nervous guests hurrying for the front door.

I tried to smooth my rumpled gown. Gave up. I was reasonably sure we'd have to pay for it. Whitney was going to flip out. The thought made me feel a little better.

The boys looked equally bad. Lost jackets. Ripped pants. Stained cuffs. Everything drenched in panic-sweat. I hoped it was dark outside.

"Now." Clasping my hands in front of me. "Let's close this night-mare, shall we? Don't forget — I have gifts for all my escorts."

Hi and Shelton chortled. Ben snorted as he helped Jason to his feet.

"Wha?" Jason asked groggily.

"Take it easy, tiger." Ben patted Jason's back. "You ran into a pole."

Chance never smiled. Never took his eyes off me.

I remembered his expression upon seeing the twisted metal. The shattered grate he'd pounded with a crowbar without success.

Later.

Hi cracked the door. "Ladies first."

"Why, thank you, sir."

For the hell of it, I dropped into another formal curtsy.

The boys snickered. Then, straightening their soiled garments as best they could, they gave me a polite round of applause.

"Off we go then." I winked. "There's still cake and dancing on the program."

Joining the stream of anxious partygoers, we slipped out into the night.

PART FOUR:
CONFRONTATION

CHAPTER 48

"How do you get into these messes?"

Jason's words jarred me back to full wakefulness. There'd been a lull in conversation, and Chance's overstuffed chair was far too comfortable for my level of fatigue.

"You heard the story," Shelton grumbled. "It's not *our* fault some wackjob likes playing insane games."

"We won." Ben's eyes didn't open. "No one got hurt. That's all that matters."

"I assume there's no antique cash register in need of special oil?" Jason said.

No one bothered to answer.

Eleven forty-five p.m. Claybourne Manor. The six of us were gathered in Chance's study, ignoring the revelry one floor below.

My tired eyes wandered the room. I had bad memories of this place.

Little had changed since the days Hollis Claybourne ruled the cavernous chamber. Floor-to-ceiling windows and bookcases. Scarlet drapes. Mahogany desk the size of a tank.

My gaze tracked the wrought-iron catwalk circling high overhead. I thought of the day Chance had caught me up there. Our confrontation.

Definitely *bad* memories.

Not now. Focus.

Cedar logs crackled, the orange and yellow flames casting long shadows across the chamber. Shelton, Ben, and I sat facing the huge stone fireplace. Chance was leaning back against his desk. Jason was slumped on the floor, back to the coffee table, an ice pack strapped to his head. Hi lay flat on his back on the Persian rug.

I'd briefed Jason and Chance on the events of the last two weeks. Our find on Loggerhead. The string of caches. The Game. Our wild trips around the Lowcountry. The Gamemaster's folder of threats. I withheld only the secrets we could never share.

An avalanche of questions followed. I'd answered as best I could.

"So we aren't calling the cops?" Shelton removed his glasses and pinched the bridge of his nose. "Am I the only one who thinks that *they're* supposed to handle murders and bomb threats?"

"We can't risk it," I said firmly. "The Gamemaster might believe his rules still apply."

"Captain Psychopath knows about our parents, our homes, even Tory's dog." Hi's fingers were interlaced on his chest, his eyes glued to the oak rafters stretching above us. "If we talk, who knows what he'll do? The guy's into *clowns,* for God's sake."

I took a deep breath. "We can catch this chump ourselves."

"How are we going to do that?" Shelton squawked.

"I'll think of something." *I will.*

"You're positive the gas won't escape?" Jason asked for the third time.

"Yes," I said. "I double-checked on my phone. Bromomethane is heavier than air, and should simply pool in the electrical room. And if someone goes down to the basement, they'll smell the fumes and book it out of there. A slight delay in reporting the danger shouldn't pose a risk."

I hoped.

The Gamemaster belonged to me now. I wanted blood.

A wave of music and laughter carried from below. Everyone ignored it. There was a crash of breaking glass. Chance didn't flinch.

Two hours earlier, my impromptu fire drill had caused a mild panic. Flustered debs stumbling across the grass in ankle-breaking heels. Escorts struggling to locate their dates. Parents and siblings searching for one another. Chance had slipped away to find Madison, leaving the rest of us mercifully alone. Shelton had pulled a bleary Jason aside and brought him up to speed.

Whitney went apoplectic upon seeing me. Mussed hair. Stained gown. Jacketless entourage. Kit demanded an explanation.

Thank God for Hiram.

He launched into an improvised tale of woe and misfortune. We'd found ourselves in the dark. Flustered and disoriented, we'd blundered through an emergency exit. Then we'd tumbled down a staircase in a complicated domino sequence that incorporated each one of us.

The story was bizarre, confusing, and wildly improbable.

They'd bought it without hesitation.

Working like a field surgeon, Whitney had blotted and fluffed my dress, then repaired my makeup using cosmetics from her purse. When I'd casually asked permission to attend Chance's after party, Kit had been quick to agree.

After the fire marshal declared a false alarm, everyone scurried back inside. The remaining debs were presented in full splendor, averting heart attacks and dousing a few temper tantrums.

Dancing followed. I endured three formal numbers — Kit twice, then an awkward turn with Jason — solely for appearances' sake. The rest of my crew sat in chairs along the wall. I kept one eye on Chance as he twirled Madison across the hardwood.

Finally, mercifully, the ball ended. I handed my boys their

monogrammed cuff links and Kit drove us to Claybourne Manor. Chance's bash was supposed to run late — he'd even chartered a car service to take guests home.

Kit told me to enjoy myself. He'd inform the other parents.

Chance had demanded answers as soon as we arrived. He marched my group upstairs, leaving a butler to see to his guests.

So there we were, an hour later.

A wild celebration raged downstairs. Half the school was in attendance.

Partying was the furthest thing from our minds.

Chance stirred. "How did you destroy the grate?"

"Adrenaline." Hi sat up. Flexed. "The human body is capable of amazing things."

"There were four of us." Shelton was inspecting his shoes. "That probably made the difference."

"Four." Jason's gaze shifted to Ben. "Because *I* was unconscious. Having run into a pole. Which I don't remember."

Ben shrugged. "Not my fault you're clumsy."

Jason turned dubious eyes to me. "That's how it happened, Tor?"

"Yes," I lied. "You were doubled over coughing up a lung and lost your bearings. The passage was narrow and dim. Too many people, too much chaos."

"Makes sense, I guess." Jason tested his jaw by easing it left, then right. Then his mouth formed a lopsided grin. "That's the second function where I've gotten knocked silly. You're dangerous to my brain, Miss Brennan."

Chance crossed to the hearth, crouched, and began stoking the fire. He spoke without turning.

"I pounded those clamps with a crowbar for a good ten minutes. Each was solid iron, and bigger than a fist. I didn't make a dent."

Chance rose and turned to face us. "Yet you four ripped the grate from its tracks. Then you ripped the *tracks from the wall,* bending the metal bars like they were drinking straws. How? How is that possible?"

"I read once where this guy in Ulan Bator powerlifted a Chinese tank after —"

"Can it, Stolowitski. Let Tory explain."

I sat up straight. Kept my voice steady. "What more is there to say?"

"So that's your story? A massive surge of adrenaline? Hormones to the rescue?"

"What else could it be?"

Chance pointed without looking, eyes on me. "And poor Jason *ran into a pole,* conveniently missing this dramatic feat?"

I nodded. Met him stare for stare.

"Nor was *I* there," Chance went on. "Because you suggested I search the stairwell for a key. That seemed unlikely at the time, but I was exhausted and out of ideas. Thankfully, *you* had the presence of mind to send me . . . off."

"What's your point?" Jason was unwinding his ice pack. "We escaped. Be happy."

"My point, Jason, is that this story is a pack of lies." Chance's face went hard. "A new entry in a long list of deceptions. And not a very good one."

"Watch it," Ben warned from the chair beside mine. "I don't like your tone."

Chance ignored him, focused entirely on me. "I want the truth, Tory. The *real* story. An explanation of what we both know has been going on for months."

"It happened like I said." Holding his gaze. "Jason hit a post. The rest of us worked together and managed to knock out the gate. Believe me, or don't believe me, but you won't get a different version. From anyone."

Our eyes remained locked for what seemed an eternity.

Then his smirk returned.

"So be it."

Chance spun and walked out the door.

CHAPTER 49

Hi was first to deliver the news.

Kit and I were eating Saturday breakfast when he pounded on our door.

Coop bounded over to investigate. Spotting Hi through the glass, he returned to his doggie bed and settled down to nap.

"Hurricane Katelyn took a hard left," Hi said breathlessly. "She's now on a collision course with Charleston."

Kit began searching for the TV remote. "What are local officials saying?"

"There's an evacuation order for downtown and the barrier islands, including Morris. Pretty much the whole Lowcountry."

"Blargh." A thousand things ran through my mind. "How soon?"

"We have to be gone by tomorrow noon." As Hi snagged half my English muffin, he gave me a meaningful look. Our time was suddenly very short. "I've gotta run. My mother has me sounding the alarm." Hi rubbed Coop's head, then fired back outside.

Kit was frowning at CNN. "Katelyn picked up strength overnight. She's now a Category Four, with sustained winds over 131 miles per hour."

"Ouch."

"Tell me about it. A Cat Four hasn't hit South Carolina since Hugo in '89. Before that, you'd have to go all the way back to Hazel in '54. This is bad."

I powered my laptop and scanned the National Weather Service homepage, then checked Weather Underground. "This state hasn't been hit by *any* hurricane for almost a decade. Guess we're due."

"They're saying the storm surge shouldn't be like Katrina." Kit was surfing the 24-hour news channels, bouncing between overcaffeinated meteorologists analyzing the coming tempest. "Because of how she's spinning or something. No more than ten feet. But her wind speeds are fierce."

I felt a stab of worry. "Is Loggerhead ready?"

Kit grunted. "As much as it can be. We prepared for this possibility. The monkeys have shelter available, and they're smart enough to use it. Same with Coop's family. LIRI buildings were designed to withstand winds over 150 miles per hour, but we'll see. We'll be needing a new fence for sure."

Kit went upstairs to make calls. I stayed at the table to stew.

Hurricane Katelyn was ruining my plans.

My gut said we had a narrow window to catch the Gamemaster. A forced evacuation would destroy our chance.

What chance? We have no leads, no evidence. Nothing.

"Arrgh!"

I cleared the table, then walked out to the front steps and sat.

The breeze was light, the sky gray. I smelled the brackish odor of the salt marsh just down the road. The honeysuckle crawling along the Stolowitskis' trellis.

The Atlantic appeared unnaturally calm. But I knew that somewhere over the horizon, a maelstrom was barreling toward my little island home.

Morris sits at the mouth of Charleston Harbor. Beyond it lies nothing but open sea.

I examined the construction of our row of townhouses. Sun-baked brick walls. Wooden trim. Stone foundation. My lips whispered a quiet prayer for the old fort. It was about to get smacked.

Kit stuck his head out the door. "I'm heading down to Folly. Nelson Devers bought a load of plywood, but needs help hauling it back. Then we're all going to pitch in boarding up the units."

"I'll be here."

"If anyone from LIRI calls, give them my mobile number."

"Will do."

Kit left. I lingered on the stoop, stuck in a funk.

We'd foiled the attack at The Citadel, but that didn't feel like enough. As things stood the Gamemaster would escape unpunished. The thought made me sick.

And I worried.

Everything about The Game pointed to obsession. The planning. The expense. All those crafty twists. The fanatical attention to detail.

It added up to a pair of inescapable conclusions: The Gamemaster had done this before. Perhaps many times. And if he'd done it before, he'd do it again.

My anger built. The lunatic could already be plotting his next game. Building deadly traps. Designing lavish clues.

How many geocaches had he buried? How many lives had he ruined?

He'd never stop.

Unless *we* shut him down.

I thought of the body in the crypt. The poor soul whose life had ended mere minutes before we found him. We'd never even learned his name.

The Gamemaster was a psychopath. A merciless, narcissistic predator. Maybe even a serial killer.

We couldn't let him escape. Couldn't let him hurt more people.

I'm not letting this go.

"You look ready to chew nails." Shelton grinned at me from his own stoop.

"There's a certain murderer I'd like to chat with."

"Not me." Shelton descended to the sidewalk. "I wanna bust the lunatic, not spend time with him. Who knows? Crazy might be catching."

I joined Shelton and we ambled toward the docks.

"Heard your dad scored some primo storm supplies," I said.

"Had to go three places. Katelyn's another cat I'd prefer to avoid." Shelton gestured toward the horizon. "It's creepy. You can't even tell she's out there."

"We need to lock down the bunker."

"I know. Think everything will fit in the back room?"

I nodded. "If we seal both windows, plug the crawl, and nail the interior door shut, things should be okay. The real pain will be getting the solar array inside."

"I hope you're right. We don't have the cash to replace everything if the equipment gets soaked."

"The bunker's way up the hill," I said hopefully. "No surge can reach that high."

"Careful what you say. We've tempted fate enough this week."

At the dock we looked for *Sewee,* but the runabout wasn't in her berth. We turned and started back up the hill.

"Have you seen Ben?" I asked.

"Not since last night. I think he's still mad we went to Claybourne Manor after the ball."

I shook my head in exasperation. "Did he think we could just go home, without explaining things? Jason and Chance were in that basement. They had a right to know."

Shelton raised both palms. "No argument here."

"If you see Ben first, tell him the bunker needs attention. We have to sneak out there sometime today and lock it down."

"Sounds like a fun couple of days." Shelton glanced around, then lowered his voice. "You got anything on the Gamemaster? I racked my brain, but can't think of a single angle to pursue."

"Working on it." I wasn't ready to admit the same. Not yet.

"You'll think of something. You always do." Shelton yawned. "I'm gonna take a nap before my Pops gets back and turns this block into *Extreme Home Makeover: Hurricane Edition.*"

"Adios."

Coop blitzed me at the front door, upset that I'd gone strolling without him.

"Ya snooze ya lose, dog face."

CHAPTER 50

I cursed and dropped my hammer.

"Owie owie owie!" Waving the thumb didn't help, so I stuck it in my mouth.

"Construction is not your forte," Hi said from the base of the ladder.

I shot him a look. "My nails are straighter than yours."

"True. But I haven't bashed my hand. You're like a cartoon character."

We were securing a plywood sheet over the Stolowitskis' bay window. Neighbors worked all around us, everyone pitching in to fortify the ten lonely townhouses perched on the neck of Morris Island.

The mood was cooperative, but with an undercurrent of tension. Katelyn was a monster. Morris was exposed and sitting smack in her path. No one really knew if our homes — built on the remnants of a Civil War outpost — could withstand a Category Four beat down.

Like it or not, we'd soon find out.

"You okay, Tor?" Shelton had a sandbag on one shoulder, hauled up from the beach. "We don't have time for an ER run."

"We could amputate," Hi suggested. "Shelton, get the whiskey."

"Comedians, the both of you." I descended the rungs and hopped onto the ground.

I glanced at my unit. Coop's nose pressed against our bay window. He yapped, scratching at the glass with his paws.

Sorry, boy. You've gotta hang inside today.

"That's the last one," Hi said. "Does Kit still need us to stow the grill?"

"Your dad took care of it," Shelton replied. "I think we're almost done."

"Thank God." Hi plopped down on his front steps. "My body's not designed for manual labor."

I resisted the opening. But he was right. It had been a long afternoon.

We'd had a neighborhood meeting to coordinate weatherproofing efforts, and to make sure everyone had transportation off the island. Then the boys and I had snuck out to the bunker. It took three sweaty hours, but our clubhouse was sealed tight. We hoped.

Back at the compound, dozens of tasks needed doing. Boarding windows. Securing garage doors. Moving deck furniture inside. Ben and his dad were running boats to the leeward side of Isle of Palms. Only their two vessels, *Hugo* and *Sewee,* were still docked at our pier.

Having chosen her target, Hurricane Katelyn was picking up speed. Each new report confirmed a direct hit on Charleston.

Our parents worked quickly, trying to hide their anxiety. Departure was first thing the following morning. Kit had been forced to ride out a hurricane before, and had no wish to repeat the experience.

My conscience ate at me all day long. Every hour we'd wasted hammering plywood should've been spent hunting the Gamemaster. But the tasks had to be done. It had been impossible to get away.

Threats or no threats, I was starting to feel very guilty about not calling the police. If the Gamemaster escaped, was it *our* fault?

I was icing my hand when two figures rounded the corner of our building. The surprise made me forget my throbbing thumb.

"What are *they* doing here?" Hi hissed.

"Not good." Shelton reached for his earlobe. "Whatever they want, I'm not going to like it."

Spotting me, Jason hurried over. Chance followed at a leisurely pace.

I didn't waste time on pleasantries. "What's going on?"

"I'm not sure," Jason replied. "But we thought you should know right away."

"Know what?" My eyes flicked to Chance, but his face revealed nothing.

"I slept at Chance's place last night. My phone died, and I didn't recharge it until I got home this morning. That's when I noticed a message from Greg Kirkham, the guy I called last week about the swab you wanted analyzed."

"Okay." But I didn't see why Kirkham mattered. Eric Marchant had already contacted me and determined the accelerant was diesel fuel.

"Kirkham works in the crime lab with Marchant." Jason's forehead crinkled. "Get this — he'd called to apologize for not getting back to me about the swab. He said Marchant hadn't been to work for a week."

"That doesn't make sense. I spoke to Marchant on Monday. Met him, actually."

Hi squinted at me. "When did Marchant first contact you?"

"Last Friday, the day of Jason's party. He called and told me the swab from the Castle Pinckney cache was coated with diesel fuel. Then we went to the firing range the next morning and gave him the snare gun and bullet fragments."

I turned back to Jason. "I called Marchant's office on Monday, but he didn't answer so I left a message. But he called right back, and I met him at the coffee shop."

Jason looked uneasy. "Kirkham said Marchant hadn't been at the lab all this week. Said he isn't returning calls or emails. Yesterday someone went by his apartment where he lives alone. He wasn't home and his mailbox was overflowing."

At that moment, Ben came striding up the hill from the dock. Frowning at Jason and Chance, he tugged Shelton's elbow and drew him aside. I ignored their whispered conference, perplexed by Jason's report.

"Why would Marchant skip work?" I asked. "I *personally* saw him on Monday, and he didn't say anything about taking time off or leaving town."

Hi began to fidget. "How'd he analyze our swab without using the crime lab?"

Good point. Something wasn't right.

Glancing at Chance, I saw a frown that mirrored my own.

"I asked Kirkham that," Jason answered. "He said there's no record of any analysis. He said normally that wouldn't raise eyebrows, since the test is inexpensive and the project was off the books. But Kirkham claimed that Marchant *always* logs his machine time."

"So he took a shortcut," Shelton said.

Jason shook his head. "I guessed that, too, but Kirkham doesn't think so. He said Marchant is very particular and only uses certain equipment. Around the lab they call him the OCD Chuck Norris."

"Chuck Norris?" I didn't get it.

"Because of the red hair and beard," Jason explained. "Kirkham said Marchant's a nice guy, but kind of a finicky little shrimp. Definitely not the type to miss a week's work without calling in."

The world shrank around me.

My blood pressure spiked.

I pictured City Light Coffee. The man sipping an oversized cappuccino across the table from me.

"Red hair?" I clutched Jason's arm. "Beard?"

"Those were his words." Jason glanced at the fingers tight around his wrist.

"The man we met was tall, clean-shaven, and had light brown hair." Hi forcefully ticked off fingers. "No beard, not a ginger, and definitely not a shrimp."

Chance's eyebrows rose.

Jason glanced from face to face. "What are you saying?"

I tried to organize my thoughts.

Fact: The man I'd had coffee with wasn't Eric Marchant.

Question: Then who was he?

The answer stared me in the face.

Oh my God.

My steady voice surprised me. "It seems we've met the Gamemaster after all."

Hi sucked in his breath. Shelton wore a puzzled look. Ben turned abruptly, walked several steps toward the green, and rubbed the back of his neck.

"He was impersonating Marchant." Hi's head wagged slowly from side to side. "Holy crap balls."

Jason's eyes widened. Shelton nearly choked. Ben's shoulders tensed, but with his back to me I couldn't see his face.

"Why would this lunatic pretend to be a lab geek?" Chance asked.

"To get near us." The insight terrified and disgusted me. "To study his playthings up close and personal."

"But why Marchant?" Chance glanced at Jason, who shrugged helplessly. "How would the Gamemaster know to assume *that* identity?"

"He's been watching us from the beginning." I was suddenly sure. "Tracking our movements. Our communications. He's freaking *taunting* us!"

"Jesus." Shelton's hand flew to his mouth. "Red hair! Tory, that means —"

"Yes." I backhanded an angry tear from my cheek.

My mind cycled through another series of images. A murky crypt. A stone sarcophagus. Deathly pale features below a shock of ruddy hair.

This time, I couldn't keep the tremor from my voice. "We know who was inside that coffin."

I mouthed a silent prayer for the soul of Eric Marchant.

CHAPTER 51

We had no time to ponder the implications.

Kit appeared with a new set of storm-proofing tasks. Nodding to our visitors, he voiced surprise they were so far from home with Katelyn bearing down. Hi theatrically thanked Chance and Jason for bringing over his tuxedo jacket. The two left, promising to meet with us again after the storm.

I followed Kit's instructions like a zombie. Pack the car. Clean Coop's cage. Fill a cooler with bottled water.

My mind reeled. I shivered again and again, shaken by how close I'd been to a cold-blooded murderer.

Two hours slipped by in a haze. Finally, Kit signaled that I was done.

I fired a text to the other Virals. Coop and I met them by the dock.

"We have to examine every interaction with the killer," Hi said. "See if we missed anything. Find the dots, then connect them."

"He drove a Ford F-150," Shelton said. "Black, with oversized tires."

"Complete with a redneck gun rack," Hi added. "The Gamemaster had an arsenal in his shooting stand. Rifles. Pistols. A shotgun. An AK-47." He paled slightly while rattling off the firepower.

"What else?" I glanced at Ben, who was sitting with his legs hanging off the edge of the pier. He looked far away, lost in thought.

Coop's interest fizzled and he began snuffling down the beach. I let him wander — it'd be a while before he could roam the island again.

The sun was dropping in the west. The air was heavy and still, as if the sky held its breath. Rarely had the Atlantic been so flat and glassy. The deceptive calm seemed like a tease by Mother Nature: *Come out to sea. Everything's fine. Pay no attention to the maelstrom behind the curtain.*

"We're wasting our time." Ben began coiling a line tied to the first berth. "The Gamemaster always covers his tracks."

"It's not a waste," I shot back. "We might have missed something."

"You think?" Ben snorted. "You had a tea party with that wacko."

My cheeks burned, but I held my tongue. *Why is he being so moody?*

Then I remembered. Ben had puked on his shoes that morning at the rifle range. Massively hungover, both he and Shelton had waited by the 4Runner.

Not exactly his One Shining Moment. Ben was probably still embarrassed.

"He's a skilled marksman." Hi leaned back against one of the wooden pilings. "I saw his practice targets. All bull's-eyes. And he knew a *ton* about ballistics. Whoever we met, he definitely knows his weapons."

I replayed that first meeting in my mind. Nothing seemed out of order.

The imposter at the range had been friendly. Eager to help. For the zillionth time I wondered how the Gamemaster knew we'd contacted Marchant.

"On the very first call," Shelton asked me, "who do you think it was? Marchant or the Gamemaster?"

"The real Marchant." I'd considered this point, and felt sure. "When we met at the range, I remember being surprised at his appearance. He wasn't at all what I'd pictured. But I didn't give it a second thought. That happens all the time."

A chill passed through me as another domino fell.

"My email."

"What about it?" Hi asked.

"I'd almost forgotten. During the first call Marchant and I originally agreed to meet at his lab. I emailed his work account so he could send directions. A few minutes later I got a reply — Marchant wanted to switch locations to the shooting range."

"So you spoke to Marchant and then emailed his work account." Hi was thinking out loud. "But *the Gamemaster* wrote you back."

"He was intercepting your communications." Shelton tugged his earlobe. "Damn. That phone call may have signed Marchant's death warrant."

No one spoke for a while.

"At the gun range, you two stayed in the parking lot," Hi said to Shelton and Ben. "Do you remember anything about the truck? Like maybe the license plate number?"

Shelton frowned. "I wasn't my best that day. Sorry."

We waited. Finally, my patience wore thin. "Ben?"

More seconds passed. Then, "There was a G. On the rear window. Purple."

"What, for Gamemaster?" Shelton pulled a face. "Talk about ego. But that doesn't help us. Anything else?"

Ben shook his head.

Shelton turned to me. "What about your chat at the coffee shop?"

"I called Marchant's office and left a message. Less than a minute later my cell rang and March —" I gritted my teeth, "—*the Gamemaster* asked me to meet him at City Lights Coffee. So I did."

"So dumb," Hi muttered. "And it really *was* a murderer."

Shelton ignored him. "So he was monitoring Marchant's voicemail after he . . . got rid of him. Email too."

I pictured hazel eyes across a coffee shop table. "We can't trust anything he told us about the snare gun."

Shelton's eyebrows rose. "So the snare gun might not be from LIRI at all."

"The Gamemaster knows things about us," I said. "He might've been looking for a reaction. More mind games for his sick enjoyment."

"We can't say anything about the gun either way." Hi ran agitated fingers through his hair, which left it standing on end. "This is so frustrating! We have nothing to investigate."

"Maybe we should let it go." Ben had abandoned the rope to stare out over the water. "For once. We're not going to catch him. The police have a better shot."

"Are you suffering short-term memory loss?" Shelton tapped a temple. "Did you forget the surveillance photographs?"

Hi nodded in vigorous agreement. "That didn't feel like a bluff."

Ben shrugged, eyes glued to the horizon.

"We can't talk. Not yet." I spun, whistled for Coop, and headed back up to the townhouses. "I'll think of something."

◇   ◇   ◇

That night, sleep wouldn't come. When I finally dozed off, my dreams were dark and worrisome.

I was alone in the woods at night. Somewhere unfamiliar.

No sounds. Not the slightest chirp of a cricket.

Crack! Crack!

Shots in the darkness. I turned. Marchant — the man I'd *thought* to be Marchant — was crouched in the shadows, grinning through a mask of peeling clown paint.

I stared down the barrel of his AK-47.

Marchant pulled the trigger. Bullets peppered the dirt at my feet.

I screamed. Ran.

Longleaf pines towered above me, blocking the moonlight. Tangled undergrowth tore at my legs. I stumbled blindly, never looking back.

I heard footsteps giving chase. Maniacal laughter. Every few yards there was a burst of gunfire. Bullets shredded the branches and trunks around me.

I reached a parking lot. Recognized my location. *The firing range.*

The Gamemaster's F-150 was parked on my left. I saw the gun rack, the oversized tires, and a glowing purple *G* on the rear window. *Ben was right.*

No other cars. No Virals. No 4Runner.

A twig snapped behind me.

I whirled. The Gamemaster was less than a yard away. His hazel eyes burned in the darkness, narrow and unblinking.

Dropping the gun, he pulled a twelve-inch carving knife from his belt. Congealed blood coated its razor-sharp edge.

I couldn't move. Couldn't call out.

The Gamemaster stepped close. Ran the blade down my cheek.

"Game over, Victoria," he whispered.

I screamed. Woke.

Drenched in sweat, I sat up, tried to regain control of my heartbeat. The nightmare felt so real. So personal. I rubbed the goose bumps from my arms.

The first morning rays were slanting through my window.

Coop was scratching at my door, in tune with my distress.

I had one foot on the floor when the epiphany hit.

I lunged for my phone.

○   ○   ○

"The *G* on the Gamemaster's truck!" I paced, too wired to stand still. "It must be a parking permit for downtown. They assign a separate letter to each residential zone!"

"And you know this how?" Shelton was still in his Dark Knight PJs.

The boys weren't excited about a seven a.m. meeting. We huddled on Shelton's front steps, trying not to shiver in the misty morning air. It was still dark. The sun was struggling to rise through a purple bruise spanning the eastern horizon.

"I dreamed it."

"Aha! You dreamed it." Hi yawned and rubbed his eyes. "I think it's time we get you medicated."

"I already checked," ignoring Hi's barb, "and *G* permits cover only a four-block area on the western side of the downtown peninsula." When this failed to elicit the proper reaction, I held up a printout. "The *G* stickers are purple this year."

"She could be right." Ben snatched the page from my hand and studied it closely. "This matches the picture in my head."

"Fine," Shelton said. "When we get back in town, we'll check that district for the Gamemaster's truck."

I stared as if he was crazy. "We can't wait! If we evacuate, we'll lose two or three days. The Gamemaster will be long gone." I stepped closer and dropped my voice. "But if we go *right now,* we can catch him off guard!"

This didn't play well.

Shelton hooted. "There's a hurricane coming, Tory!"

"Katelyn is moving way faster than projected," Hi confirmed. "It's like she decided to sprint for the coast. The news said landfall is now expected before noon, and maybe much earlier. My dad said we're all jetting in sixty minutes."

"Why would the Gamemaster be at home?" Ben asked sharply. "He'll evacuate too, right?"

"No, he won't. He's a thrill seeker. I'm positive he'll stay for the big show. That's how he rolls. And that's how we can nab him!"

"You're suggesting the impossible," Shelton argued. "The roads are shutting down. All traffic is going one way — out of town. And our parents expect us in seat belts in an hour."

"The police are busy clearing tourists," Hi added. "They won't bother with our story about a psychopathic gun master with more weapons than Syria. They'll just lock us into a storm shelter."

"We don't even know where he lives!" Shelton finished.

I countered their rant with my own.

"The Gamemaster is a murderer. Maybe a serial killer. But *we* know how to find him, and *we* have the skills to catch him." I glared at Shelton. "If we leave with our parents, we're gone for days. You *know* that. The Gamemaster will slip away before we get back! And if he does, how many others might die? Can you live with that?"

I turned on Ben and Hi. "What about you two? Ready to bail? There's a deranged psycho out there who knows what your mothers eat for breakfast. That cool with you?"

Shelton dropped to the stoop and sighed. "How would you do it?"

"We leave a note. Take *Sewee* to the city marina, then do a quick sweep of zone G. If we don't spot the truck, we head to police headquarters and tell them about the Gamemaster. Take our punishment."

My voice went steely. "But if we *do* find him, we take him out ourselves."

Hi swallowed. "Take him out?"

I didn't flinch. *This man committed murder for sport.* "Whatever it takes."

"My boat." Ben looked stricken. "I was going to moor her in the cove by the bunker. *Sewee* will get torn to pieces at the marina."

I smiled hopefully. "All the other boats will be gone, so you can pick your berth."

"We're considering this?" Shelton's forehead dropped to his knuckles. "For real?"

"Our parents will lose it," Hi said. "I'm serious. They might all stroke out."

"Whatever happens, we'll tell them everything," I said. "Afterward."

"You want to capture a gun-crazed murderer during a Category Four hurricane." Shelton's gaze rose to the heavens. "Any idea how dangerous that sounds?"

"Good thing we're Virals," Ben said.

Our eyes met. He actually smiled.

"I'm with Tory," Ben said firmly. "To the end."

"Thank you." I felt a rush of affection.

When it really matters, I can always count on Ben.

My gaze bored into Hi and Shelton.

"Ben and I are going either way." I crossed my arms. "In or out?"

◇   ◇   ◇

"Hurry!" I whispered-shouted at Hi as he jumped aboard.

Shelton crouched in the stern while Ben untied *Sewee*'s lines. Even while docked the runabout was rolling and pitching in the quickly rising chop. The ocean had gone from placid to rough in the forty minutes we'd wasted getting ready.

Hurricane Katelyn was closing in. Everyone could feel it.

"I'm dead," Hi moaned as he slid onto the stern bench. "So, so dead. My parents will fillet me. You guys, too."

Sorry, Kit. This one is my bad.

I waved to Ben. "Go!"

"Wait!" Shelton pointed. Coop was bounding down the dock.

"No, boy!" I shooed him with my hands. "Go back!"

Ignoring my command, Coop hopped from the pier and settled in the bow.

I froze, undecided.

"Movement on the hill!" Hi warned.

Ben glanced at me. I nodded.

He fired the engine and we motored from the dock.

CHAPTER 52

The Gamemaster stoked the flames until they licked the roof of his fireplace.

Luminous tendrils danced before his eyes.

Satisfied, he began feeding the blaze. Driver's license. Credit card. Lease. Auto registration. Strands of an identity no longer of use.

Outside, the wind tickled the yellow jessamine climbing the chipped wood siding. A stop sign waggled in the quickening breeze.

The Gamemaster smiled. Giggled shrilly as he donned his coarse brown cloak.

It had been a *wonderful* game. Exquisitely orchestrated.

He shrugged off the sense of loss that assailed him each time a Game ended. Soon he'd write a new script, more elaborate than the last. He always did. Always would.

And this time, God had sent a gift. A mighty Tempest to commemorate his finale.

A small part of him felt uneasy. He was usually gone by this point, enjoying media reports of his triumph while settling into his next life.

His new cover was ready. Documents secured. Job in place. All that remained was the selection of players and a final target. The Game would soon recommence.

But nature's wrath was too delicious a lure.

He wanted to witness the fury firsthand — a grinding crescendo of wind and rain that would acclaim his genius. His victory. Then he'd vanish, never to return.

Task complete, the Gamemaster straightened and walked to the kitchen, passing a half-dozen empty duffel bags piled in the hallway. He'd need to pack his beloved collection soon, before the storm arrived in force.

The Gamemaster thought of his snare gun. Smiled. He'd regretted almost losing the clever weapon, uncertain he'd ever find another quite like it. But his fondness for the device hadn't stopped him — tools were meant to be used.

Then he giggled, remembering his hardly contained joy when the kids had handed the gun right back to him! Now *that* was a stroke of luck. Delightful!

Humming softly, the Gamemaster began washing dishes stacked in the sink.

Outside, fat drops began ticking the window.

This Game had been special. His players had been young, but incredibly resourceful. So many Games never reached the final stage, yet these four adolescents had somehow conquered every challenge. Remarkable!

They'd failed in the end, of course. And died, of course.

He'd never before come so close to losing. The little scamps even averted The Danger. No one had accomplished that in years. Extraordinary!

A shocking realization froze his hands.

He had *liked* this Tory Brennan. Respected her. Been wary of her.

He thought back to their coffee shop meeting. Bright. Resourceful.

Up for the challenge. Brennan had been the rarest of treasures — a worthy opponent. It was a pity she and her friends had cheated.

He tsked. *You mustn't break The Rules.*

He'd been very clear. The kids had earned The Punishment.

All in all, a very satisfying Game indeed.

Only one detail troubled him — there'd been no reports on their deaths. Odd. The press usually went berserk when children were killed.

Relax. He shut off the tap and dried his hands, chuckling at his impatience.

The Game ended only yesterday. The hurricane was no doubt disrupting everything. The police would withhold details from the media until they'd notified the families. Perhaps the bodies hadn't been discovered.

Be patient. The trophies will come.

The Gamemaster did have one regret.

Never again would he work with a partner.

Too many variables. Too little control.

The thrill of added danger wasn't worth the headache.

Whistling off-tune, the Gamemaster returned to his living room and powered his laptop. Slowly, he scrolled through images.

Soon his collection would expand.

Smiling, the Gamemaster settled in to enjoy the storm.

CHAPTER 53

The sky was the color of dried blood.

A massive, towering inkblot covered the eastern horizon.

Hurricane Katelyn was coming. *Fast.*

Gusts snapped my windbreaker as *Sewee* bucked across the white-caps. Overhead, gulls streamed inland, flapping ahead of the strengthening gale.

Boating at that moment felt like suicide.

As *Sewee* rounded Morris, passed Fort Sumter, and muscled across Charleston Harbor, I saw no other vessels on the water. I was in the bow, with Coop's snout buried in my lap. The wolfdog had no fondness for boats.

What am I supposed to do with him?

"Does this bucket move any faster?" Shelton was staring back out to sea, transfixed by the approaching vortex. "If that mess catches us on the water, it's all over."

"Relax." Ben had the engine running full throttle. "We'll make it."

I tried to focus on our mission, but guilt was eating me alive.

The note I'd left was vague, and would provide no comfort. I could imagine Kit at that moment, terrified, pacing our boarded-up kitchen, unable to comprehend my decision.

> *Dear Kit,*
>
> *The boys and I have to do something <u>right now</u>. It's extremely important. We're taking SEWEE into the city and will shelter at a police station. PLEASE DON'T FOLLOW!!! I'll explain everything in a few hours. Promise. Don't worry, we're being very, very careful.*
>
> *Love, Tory*
>
> *PS—Don't hate me. I swear to God this is important. Please trust me.*
> *PPS—Don't follow!*

I'd scrawled a second message in my notebook and tossed it on the dock: "I have Coop!"

Best I could do.

I knew it was terrible. What parent could read those words and not panic? We'd set sail for an evacuated city, on an open sixteen-foot boat, with a Cat Four hurricane breathing down our necks. A bad action movie, starring his daughter.

I'll make it up to you, Kit. Somehow.

Despite the early hour, the sky was darkening fast. The gusts were growing wetter, stronger, heavier, and more frequent. As if sensing landfall, Katelyn thundered and hissed. Tense minutes passed before the marina finally hove into view.

Ben cut our speed and we glided up to a row of quays. He chose a berth well away from the handful of other boats still at dock. Then we wasted twenty precious minutes tying *Sewee* down with every available rope in the Lowcountry.

Finally satisfied, Ben led us up to the street. Coop's tail wagged in happiness at being back on dry land. That went for everyone.

No more distractions. We had a psycho to bag.

Walking quickly, we crossed Lockwood to Calhoun, turned left onto Courtenay Drive, and headed north through the medical district. The streets and sidewalks were empty. Houses and businesses were boarded with plywood, or protected by metal storm shutters. Few lights burned in the gloom. The city had a creepy, abandoned feeling, like a war zone or a postapocalyptic future.

A blast of sodden wind slammed me from behind and nearly sent me sprawling. An early taste of the nightmare to come.

Katelyn must be entering the harbor. We don't have much time.

As we reached Spring Street, rain began falling in bands. Fat droplets smacked my forehead, face, and cheeks. I leaned forward for balance as a series of gusts ripped down the sidewalk. Head lowered, I scrunched my hood tight.

"This is the southern boundary of zone *G*." Hi was shouting to be heard. "It's small, like Tory said. If the Gamemaster lives here, his F-150 should be parked on one of the next three blocks."

"Unless he's got a garage," Shelton griped. "Or left town with the sane people."

"If he has a garage, why buy a street permit?" Hi countered.

"This is pointless," Ben yelled. "Let's go look."

"We'll walk up Norman," I said, "then cut back and forth, working a grid until we locate the truck."

"Should we split up?" Ben gestured left, then right. "Spread out to cover more ground?"

Before I could answer the sky opened up, drenching us in a salty deluge. Visibility shrank to a few dozen yards. Coop whined and shook furiously.

"Let's stick together." I scratched the wolfdog's ears. "The Gamemaster is armed and dangerous. We shouldn't separate the pack for any reason."

"Should we light 'em up?" Hi glanced at the angry sky. "We might need our flare strength sooner than you think."

"Not yet." Though I was tempted. "We can't risk burning too soon. We'll need our powers when we corner this snake."

"Any plan for that bit?" Shelton asked dully. "You keep glossing over how we're actually gonna make the citizen's arrest."

"Of course." I chucked his shoulder. "We'll improvise."

"Great. Well thought out." Shelton pulled his hoodie tighter around his face.

A burst of wind barreled up Spring Street, fluttering streetlights and rocking stop signs. Rain blew horizontally, needling my skin and stinging my eyes. This time the velocity held steady, refusing to die back down.

Hurricane Katelyn had arrived.

Hi circled a finger above his head. "Move out."

With Ben leading, we hurried up the block and turned left onto Ashton. Pacing down a line of row houses and modest residences, we checked every driveway, carport, and curb. No black truck.

At block's end we turned right, advanced a street, and worked our way back. Coop trotted at my side, alert but uncertain, pausing now and again to shake rain from his coat.

Cheap duplex apartments lined the left side of the road. A small grocery store sat midway up on the right.

I slogged to the store and stepped under the awning. Gusts tore at my windbreaker, forcing the hood back and filling it with rainwater. I gave up trying to keep the sodden thing on my head. Hand-shielding my eyes, I squinted down the block.

And saw it.

My heart began thumping triple time.

"What now?" Hi shouted.

"*Now* we break in."

I pointed at a wooden row house a dozen yards from where we stood.

At the black F-150, parked in its backyard.

CHAPTER 54

"Ben, you and Shelton slip around back. Get a look through that window."

I gathered my sopping hair into a ponytail. The wind and rain had doubled in intensity. Trash and bits of debris were cartwheeling down the street, rising and spiraling, then dropping only to lift back up again. Bottles and bags began shooting along the gutters.

Our grace period was over. We were caught in a full-blown hurricane.

Huddled beside the grocery, we formed a game plan. Coop's eyes were white and round with fear. I held his collar so he couldn't dart away.

"Why do *I* have to scout?" Shelton whined. "I suck at sneaking up on people!"

Ben backhanded rain from his face. "I thought you said no splitting up?" His thick black hair was pasted to his scalp.

"Just this once, and only for a few seconds. We can't let the Gamemaster spot us all together. We'd lose any element of surprise."

"Can we flare?" Hi was red-faced and breathing hard. "We need to be ready."

I hesitated. What if the Gamemaster wasn't home?

Then this whole adventure was pointless.

"We need to be sure he's in there," Ben said. "We only get one shot."

I nodded. "No flares yet. You two go first. Head for the truck. Hi and I will count to thirty, then buzz the front of the house. If you spot the Gamemaster, whistle twice. Otherwise we'll reconnect in the backyard."

"You won't hear a whistle in this." Ben gestured to the chaos swirling around us. "Or anything else."

"Then just sit tight wherever you are. If we don't see you in the driveway, we'll keep circling the house and link up by the truck."

"What about Coop?" Hi kept his gaze on our target.

"He stays with me." I grabbed the wolfdog's snout and looked him in the eye. "You hear that, dog breath? By my side."

Coop licked my hand.

Impossibly, the gusting kicked up a notch, making it difficult to even stand up straight. I braced myself against the store's wall and prayed for a lull.

Time was up. We'd need to seek shelter in minutes.

After what seemed like an eon, the wind's force dropped a fraction. Everyone struggled to their feet.

I gave Shelton a reassuring hug. "Good luck."

"Stupidest thing I've ever done." Shelton blinked through water-blurred lenses. "At least if the Gamemaster kills me, my parents won't have the chance."

"Stay close." Ben squeezed Shelton's shoulder. "Nothing's gonna happen to you."

Bending into the wind, they disappeared behind the rear of the store.

A powerful blast stripped a Miller Lite sign from the wall above my head. I watched the metal square careen across the street, slam into a car, then spin sideways and vanish into the gloom.

Hi and I silently counted. At thirty, we worked our way around the front of the store. At the corner of the building, we stopped to survey our objective.

The one-story row house was small and decrepit, its faded blue paint cracked and peeling. The exterior was a neglected eyesore of warped wooden slats, loose shingles, and dirty windows.

Not boarded up. Katelyn's going to smash that place.

A fractured concrete walk connected the front door to the street. The lawn to either side was patchy and overgrown with weeds. No shrubs. No shade trees.

I pointed to a pair of windows flanking the entrance. "I'll go left, you go right."

Hi nodded. We sloshed forward, Coop by my side. At the window I dropped to a crouch beneath the sill.

Cautiously wiping grime from the unscreened glass, I examined what lay on the other side. Couch. Coffee table. Two armchairs. TV stand. Bare walls.

The room was dark. No one was in it.

I stepped back and signaled Hi. Sticking close to the building, we stole around to a gravel driveway on its opposite side. Sensing our need for stealth, Coop loped silently at my knee.

A chain-link fence bounded the property, running along the far edge of the gravel. A single window overlooked the drive from the house's rear corner.

We crept forward, heads lowered, muscles tense.

I can't see anything in this downpour. I could stumble right into him.

At the window, Hi boosted me with his hands. I peeked into a tiny chamber containing a bare mattress and a large black trunk. Lights off. Vacant.

When I stepped down, Hi cupped his hands over my ear. "What now?"

I pointed to the yard. "Truck."

We found Ben and Shelton hunkered behind the Ford's rear bumper. Glancing into the backyard, I saw a wheelbarrow, a stack of bricks, and a dilapidated storage shed in the near corner. Then I peered over the empty truck bed at the row house.

We were facing a screened-in porch, its wooden door banging in the shifting gale.

Ben pointed to three tiny windows lined up to the left of the porch. "Kitchen," he yelled as we ducked back down. "No lights on, nothing moving."

"Same for the living room and bedroom," Hi shouted.

"So nobody's home." Shelton couldn't hide his relief.

Coop chose that moment to shake vigorously, spraying us with doggie castoff.

Ben glared at the wolfdog, then nodded back the way he and Shelton had come. "I think there's another room on that side. No windows."

"Then we have to go in." Sounding braver than I felt. "Make absolutely sure."

Ben nodded, face tense. He started to rise but I snagged his elbow.

"Wait. It's time."

"Thank God," Shelton breathed. "Now?"

"Now."

SNAP.

The transformation came easily. No struggle. No battle for concentration.

The power flowed as though I'd flipped a switch.

Heat seared through my blood vessels. My irises ignited with golden fire.

Every sense blasted into hyperdrive. Sight. Smell. Hearing. Taste. Touch.

The surrounding maelstrom took on a thousand new dimensions. My brain could detect the tiniest details with laser precision. I was no longer blinded by the storm, wasn't overwhelmed by nature's savage fury.

I glanced at Coop, found him staring back at me.

He knew I'd unleashed the wolf inside me. That his pack was now fully alive.

With Coop so close the sensations were stronger, every faculty more supercharged. My flare power felt sharper than ever before.

Full strength. This is how it feels.

The boys looked at me with blazing yellow eyes. I felt their amazement.

"Whoa." Hi blinked. "It's like flaring on crack."

Shelton removed his glasses and stuck them in his pocket. "Intense."

Ben cracked his knuckles.

We were ready.

I'm coming for you, Gamemaster.

"Now," I whispered, no longer needing to shout.

I bounded onto the porch, reached the door, and quietly turned the knob. Slipping inside the kitchen, I sidestepped along the wall so the others could follow.

Every sense was on high alert.

No movement. No sound of alarm.

Moving silently, Ben crept through a door on the left, Coop on his heels. A second later they were back, Ben shaking his head.

Anxious to retain the advantage of surprise, I tiptoed down a short hallway leading to the front. My pack followed in a noiseless line.

Bedroom. Bathroom. Living room.

All unoccupied. The five of us were alone in the house.

But a small blaze crackled in the fireplace.

"What should we do?" Hi whispered. "There's a fire. The Gamemaster's truck's still here. He must be coming back."

"Where would he go?" Shelton cracked open a door. Closet. Empty. "The city's a ghost town. It's not like he could pop out for a Whopper."

"Guys, look!" Hi pointed to a Dell laptop lying on the couch.

I set the computer on the coffee table and booted. The boys sat beside me. Lacking tech skills, Coop began a nasal inspection of the drapes.

"*Please* have something we can use." Shelton was dry-washing his hands.

A background image appeared — the man I'd met as Eric Marchant, shirtless, loading a giant marlin into his truck.

The Gamemaster.

I wanted to punch his smirking face.

The desktop held a single folder. Double-clicking the icon launched a slideshow.

Images began scrolling. Crime scene photos. Scanned newspaper clippings. Pictures of flipped cars and fire-gutted buildings. Obituaries. Autopsy reports.

Each item related to an accident or crime.

I paused the slideshow to scan several articles. Detected the theme.

Every crime was unsolved. Every accident was freakish and unexplained.

Many incidents had numerous victims. Some were grisly. All were terrible.

One after another the entries flashed on-screen. A few settings were identifiable. Seattle. New York City. Las Vegas. The majority were unrecognizable.

Shelton turned to me. "So what, he's into police reports? Disaster stories?"

"They're *his* work." My stomach churned with revulsion. "Everything on here. This must be the Gamemaster's private archive. A diary of his twisted games."

"Trophies." Hi's voice was hushed. "His collection. Every serial killer has one."

Ben's fist slammed the coffee table. "I'll kill this sick freak!"

Suddenly the screen went blank. There were sounds like a video-game, then a new program opened.

The Gamemaster's face appeared.

"Hello, Tory." He smiled. "Welcome to my humble home."

CHAPTER 55

Hazel eyes. Strong chin. Features I'd encountered twice before.

"It's a shame I can't see you, but the audio functions both ways, so we can chat. Frankly, I'm stunned you're all still alive."

The Gamemaster was indoors, out of the storm. He wore an odd brown robe, and his thin brown hair lay dry and flat against his scalp. His body filled the screen, making it impossible to guess his location. I had the impression he was transmitting from a smart phone.

"Monster," I hissed, flare powers roiling in response to my anger.

Shelton and Hi were beside me on the couch, staring at the screen, their glowing eyes round with shock. Ben's face paled, then he popped to his feet and began pacing the room. Sensing the tension, Coop trotted to my side and dropped to his haunches.

"Not so," the Gamemaster replied calmly. "I'm an artist."

"Artist?" Hi spat. "We've seen your repulsive slideshow. You're a terrorist!"

The bastard laughed. "*Hardly.* I create violent masterpieces. Conduct symphonies of destruction. Your game was simply my latest triumph."

"Toying with lives is not a game!" I snapped. "You're psychotic!"

"*Everything* is a game." He spoke patiently, as if instructing a child. "I merely design fantastic examples. It's a shame you'll never understand."

"We beat you," Hi taunted. "We're here, *alive*. The debutante ball wasn't a massacre — it wasn't even touched. All you did was murder an innocent scientist. You're nothing more than a common street thug."

"You cheated," the Gamemaster spat. My flare eyes detected a slight tic in his left cheek. Once. Twice. "Broke the rules."

"We never agreed to play!" Shelton shouted.

"*YES YOU DID!*" A snarl curled the Gamemaster's lips. "My first letter was an *invitation*. You accepted by seeking the next cache. It was *your* choice."

"It was a trick," I said. "A coward's setup."

"I gave you a chance to be great!" The playful tone was long gone. "An opportunity to shed the trappings of your pathetic, boring lives. You should be *thanking* me."

"You're insane," I snapped. "Playing God to mask whatever's broken inside you."

The Gamemaster's face was granite, but the tic was a giveaway. I could tell he struggled to contain his fury.

"The *world* is insane," he hissed. "I just help it dance."

"We have your computer!" Shelton crowed. "It's going straight to the cops."

"Everything on that drive is public record." Dismissive. "I'm not so reckless that I'd keep evidence connecting me to a crime. You don't even know who I am, Mr. Devers. *None* of you do. There's nothing on that laptop that can harm me."

His arrogance infuriated me. "How many have you killed? Do you even know?"

"*I've* killed no one." Almost offended. "Those unfortunates lost The Game."

"The Game is rigged!" Hi barked. "They never had a chance."

"*LIE.*" The Gamemaster leaned close to the camera. "Every clue had an answer, each puzzle a solution. Those people *failed.*"

"Has anyone escaped?" I asked. "Any player survived?"

"No." The brown-clad shoulders rose and fell. "But everyone had the chance."

"How can you live with yourself? So many dead."

"We're all just meat, Victoria Brennan." Spoken quietly. "Fragile bags of fluid and bone, drifting aimlessly, plodding through life until something ends it. I provide an escape from that dreadful reality. A chance to shine once in a drab, miserable existence, before facing the abyss."

"You're a hot, steaming ball of crazy," Hi said. "You know that, right? Freaking Looney Tunes. How have you gotten away with this for so long?"

"Bad things happen, Hiram." Strangely, he giggled. "Car brakes fail. A bridge gives way. A house explodes during a violent storm. Most times, no one suspects a thing. 'Unlucky,' they say. Bad karma. Fate. Even when the authorities confirm foul play — when I've left behind one of my toys, like that wonder box at The Citadel — it makes no difference. I follow no patterns. Leave no signature. I'm a ghost."

He flourished one hand. "I'm the Gamemaster."

"We tracked you here," I said. "We'll find you again."

"Doubtful. Though I admit, you've impressed me. Nearly caught me off guard. That *never* happens."

The image blurred. I sensed the Gamemaster was rising to his feet. Then his face filled the screen once more. "Now tell me, where is young Benjamin Blue?"

Ben froze mid-pace. Senses amplified, I heard his breath catch. Scented a burst of perspiration.

"Tell Ben thank you," the Gamemaster continued. "I've never worked with a partner before. It made this Game more exciting than others, being able to get so close —"

"*NO!*"

Ben sprang and grabbed the Dell, then flung it across the room.

The laptop hit the wall and exploded into pieces.

The rest of us shot to our feet. Coop bounded to stand between Ben and me, a confused growl rumbling in his throat.

No. It's not possible.

"What was he talking about, Ben?" I watched him with flare intensity. "Why did he call you his partner?"

"He's a liar!" Ben's chest was heaving. "I never tried to —"

He didn't finish.

At that moment, a series of powerful gusts struck the row house, rattling the walls and shaking the foundation. Water pounded the windows and roof. Outside, Katelyn was shrieking to new heights.

My focus never shifted from my friend. I needed answers.

"Explain. Now."

Shelton raised a trembling hand. "Ya'll hear that?"

"Hear what?" Eyes still on Ben, who was staring at the floor.

"Hissing," Shelton said. "Like the sound I heard in the basement of the Citadel."

There was a thump outside, but I ignored it.

Shelton's warning had tripped an alarm. But why?

I thought furiously. The Gamemaster's recent words flashed in my brain.

Bad things happen, Hiram. Car brakes fail. A bridge gives way. A house explodes during a violent storm. Most times, no one suspects a thing.

A house explodes during a violent storm.

Hissing.

"Oh my God."

I closed my eyes and drew deeply through my nose. Noted a hint of something harsh. Oily. The odor was subtle, but intensifying by the second. *Gas.* Without my flare I'd never have caught it.

I swung my head, testing for a scent trail.

The smell was trickling down the hallway.

A house explodes.

Gas.

The kitchen!

Headlights swept the room.

Hi shot forward and pressed his face to a window. "The driveway!"

I bolted for the kitchen. There the stench was overpowering.

My eyes shot to the stove. Saw the severed gas line.

The fireplace!

I tore back down the hall, terrified I was too late. "Everybody out!"

Hi tried the front door. "Locked! Deadbolt. No key!"

Ben shoved Hi aside. Golden eyes smoldering, he backed up three steps and charged, shoulder-slamming the door from its hinges. The forward motion tumbled him out onto the waterlogged grass.

The wind screamed as it swept into the living room, carrying a noxious perfume of salt, dead vegetation, garbage, and oil. Driving rain began drenching the carpet and furniture.

I frantically gestured to Hi and Shelton. "Go go go!"

They needed no urging. We shot out into the storm, Coop a half step behind us.

I heard a soft whiff, like an intake of breath.

Fire exploded from every window.

The force of the blast launched bricks and wooden slats high into the churning sky, tossing me forward like a Wiffle ball. I hit the ground and rolled, instinctively covering my head.

The boys were already sprawled across the lawn.

"Everyone okay?" I shouted. Three nods. The calmest corner of my mind noted the other Virals were still flaring.

Coop was circling me protectively, ears flat, fur wet and dancing in the gale.

Behind me, the house burned like a bonfire, defying the gallons of water plunging from the sky.

Slightly dazed, I glanced at the street.

The black F-150 was idling by the curb.

My flare vision pierced the truck's rain-streaked windshield. I saw the Gamemaster, eyes wide, mouth a black oval of shock. He lips formed a single word: *impossible.*

Six canvas duffels were piled in the truck bed.

Facts snapped into place. *How could I have been so blind?*

The fire in the living room. The Dell. Headlights in the driveway.

We'd hoped the Gamemaster might return. Never suspected he hadn't left.

The storage shed! We didn't check the damn shed.

"Bastard!" Ben charged the truck.

Startled, the Gamemaster stomped the accelerator. Rainwater sluiced up from his tires as the F-150 careened down to the intersection and turned left.

Ben sprinted after, wet jeans molded to his legs, jacket sleeves flapping in the vicious wind. I watched truck and boy disappear around the corner.

"Ben, wait!"

My scream was swallowed by the storm.

Then a gray blur fired past me.

"Cooper, no!"

Ignoring me, the wolfdog charged in pursuit.

Shelton and Hi ran to my side.

"What should we do?" Hi was hunching to hold his ground in the swirling wind.

Shelton grabbed my arm. Shouted. "What did the Gamemaster mean about Ben?"

"I don't know! We have to catch them!"

A trash can barreled down the street. Shingles flew from nearby roofs.

It was lunacy to be outside, but what choice did we have?

"Let's go!" Rounding the corner, I spotted Ben a block ahead, running full tilt. Coop was loping a few yards behind. Even flaring, I couldn't see the F-150.

Hurricane Katelyn was wholly unleashed.

Trees thrashed and writhed. Garbage and palm fronds swirled in the street and plastered walls and buildings. A fence post rolled down the sidewalk, followed by a plastic mailbox, a boot, and a clump of sodden magazines.

Horizontal rain filled my mouth and needled my skin.

Even flaring it was hard to see, to breathe.

We need every scrap of power. All we can access.

I motioned for Hi and Shelton to draw close.

Eyes shut, I focused on my flare. On the flaming cords linking our minds, the root of our psychic connection. Reaching deep, I drew from the hidden well of power I'd tapped to escape the grate.

Warmth permeated my limbs. The wind seemed slightly less murderous.

Instinctively, I spread the heat to my pack. Hi. Shelton. Coop. Even Ben.

Hi's back straightened. Shelton stopped shivering.

"Stick close," I yelled. "Harness your power."

"Don't burn out!" Hi shouted. "Without flares, we won't make it ten feet."

Together, we staggered to Spring Street, but Ben and Coop were nowhere to be seen. I watched dumbstruck as a gas station canopy ripped free and somersaulted into a Hardee's drive-through.

"There!" Hi pointed toward the hospital. Flaring, he had best eyes. "I saw Ben!"

"Why didn't the Gamemaster turn?" I yelled. "This road leads to the highway!"

"He can't use the bridges!" Shelton shielded his glowing eyes from the downpour. "The police have them blocked. The Gamemaster can't drive off the peninsula!"

He's trapped. And we have the scent.

So we forged ahead, retracing our steps from an hour before.

It seemed a lifetime ago. A different age, when I could still trust Ben.

It can't be true.

Then why would Ben panic? Why destroy the computer and run away?

For an instant, I'd caught his eye. Seen agony behind his golden irises.

Ben has *a secret.*

I have to learn what it is.

Three arduous blocks brought us back to Charleston Memorial Hospital. A doctor emerged from the lobby door and waved wildly for us to shelter inside. We pounded past.

Hi's finger stabbed left, inland, away from the harbor. "They ran down Calhoun!"

Another block and I spotted them.

The F-150 was stopped in the middle of the street. Ben and Coop were fifty yards behind it and closing.

"Downed trees are blocking the road," Hi panted. "The Gamemaster must've bailed."

In the distance I glimpsed a brown-robed figure lugging a drenched duffel bag on one shoulder. The Gamemaster turned and stared in our direction. I could almost taste his wrath at being pursued.

We're coming.

Ahead, Ben shot past the truck, vaulted a fallen palm tree, and fired up the street. Coop paused at the truck's open driver's side door, sniffed the interior, then spun and zipped after Ben.

Shelton, Hi, and I were approaching the F-150.

The Gamemaster watched, one hand tapping his leg in a regular rhythm.

What's he doing?

"The truck's got a CB antenna!" Shelton yelled. "I'll radio for help!"

Shelton and Hi beelined for the vehicle. I didn't. Bypassing the truck and downed palm, I continued the chase.

Ahead, Coop skidded to a stop. Turned. Howled back at me.

Intent on the Gamemaster, I nearly missed his message.

Fragmented images formed in my brain.

Black truck. Open door. Plastic brick on the seat. Blinking red light.

Danger. Bad smell. Bad thing.

I whirled.

Hi and Shelton were level with the truck's rear bumper.

Eyes closing, I screamed.

CHAPTER 56

The flaming cords sizzled in my subconscious.

They crackled with intensity, larger and more vibrant than ever before.

I fired a message to Hi and Shelton.

Get away from the truck!

On instinct I forwarded Coop's mental picture, overlaid with my own fear.

The force of my sending staggered them. They didn't think, didn't hesitate. Both turned and dove for the bushes bordering the road.

The truck exploded in a titanic fireball, lifting five feet into the air. Shards of metal and plastic blasted in every direction. The concussion knocked me to the pavement. Ignoring the pain, I streaked to where I'd last seen my friends.

Please be okay, please be okay, please be okay . . .

Coop raced past me and bounded into the singed and burning shrubs.

This time water conquered fire. As the hammering rain extinguished the flames, a choking cloud of smoke billowed across the street.

"Hi? Shelton?" I slogged into a knee-deep stream racing alongside the street. "Where are you?"

"Get this mutt off me!" A voice yelled from somewhere just ahead.

The smoke shifted to reveal Hi, on his back, sunk to his chin in a gathering creek. Coop had two paws on his chest and was licking his face.

A groan sounded to my right. I turned to see Shelton drag himself from the water.

"An exploding truck almost drowned me," he wheezed. "What are the odds?"

Despite their dousing, both boys still had fire in their eyes.

"Are either of you hurt?" I shouted.

Head shakes.

"Then get up! We have to catch Ben!"

I struggled back to the road, heard Shelton and Hi close behind. Coop shot ahead once more, but this time I called him back.

Heel. Wait.

Coop's ears perked. He checked his sprint and circled to my side.

"We do this together," I ordered aloud.

I paused to let my soggy companions catch their breath. Shelton coughed. Hi blew a mammoth snot-rocket from his nose. Finally, they both gave a thumbs-up. We raced up the block, alert for any sign of Ben or the Gamemaster.

Minutes passed. Not a trace.

"The wind is dropping," Shelton said, gasping for air. "I think the storm has blown out."

"Katelyn's not done." Hi pointed to a giant hole in the clouds. "The eye is passing over us. The backside of this baby is still to come."

As we approached the shopping district, the wind died altogether. An eerie quiet blanketed the city. After the last hour's mayhem, the still-ness was unnerving.

We watched Katelyn's eye slide over our heads.

"The hurricane's moving super fast," Hi said. "This break won't last."

We crossed King and were passing The Gap when a hand shot from the doorway. Terrified, I lashed out, punching and kicking with all my strength.

"Take it easy!" Ben's yellow eyes shone from the gloomy recess.

"What are you doing?" I demanded.

"Shh. He's just ahead." Ben slipped from the alcove and crept to the corner of the building, forcing us to follow at his heels.

"He's waiting for us." Ben peeked around at the open expanse of Marion Square. "I saw him cut across the plaza."

"Then let's get him." Angry. At Ben. At the Gamemaster. At myself for not confronting Ben then and there. "He could escape while we stand here talking."

"The scumbag we're chasing is a master marksman." Ben kept his eyes on the plaza. "What do you think is in that duffel?"

"That field is a perfect ambush site." Hi was also peering ahead. "And the wind just died."

Shelton pointed a finger at Ben. "The Gamemaster called you —"

"Not now!" Ben snapped. "He's a liar and a killer! We have to catch him first."

Shelton crossed his arms, clearly dissatisfied with Ben's response.

I wavered, unsure. Ben *was* hiding something.

But he was right. We had a job to do. A murderer to stop.

Answers would have to wait.

"Please." Ben's eyes practically begged. "I'll explain everything later."

"Okay," I said coolly. "But you *will* explain."

Ben nodded, then snuck another look at the square. "We need a plan."

I cleared my mind to focus on the problem. "What are our assumptions?"

"There's a sniper in the park," Ben said.

"He's heavily armed and highly skilled," Shelton said.

"He's had time to find an effective field of fire," Hi said. "Create an ambush."

I nodded. "And he'll want to settle this while the eye is overhead and the wind isn't a factor."

"Options?" Shelton asked.

Ben's hand slashed the air. "We flush him out, then take him down."

"Great work," Hi deadpanned. "Any idea how to do it?"

Ben shook his head. They all looked at me.

What did I know? Flush out a sniper? The only military strategy I'd ever learned was from watching *Band of Brothers*.

"I should've bought Call of Duty," Hi moaned. "But my stupid mother doesn't let me play first-person shooter games."

Coop brushed my leg. As I reached to rub his ears, the answer hit me.

"We use our edge. Stalk him like a wolf pack."

Hi took a deep breath. "Okay, but if you scan my brain's hard drive, stay away from the Internet search history. You won't like what you find."

Ignoring that, I shut my eyes and dove into my subconscious.

On impulse I held out both hands. Hi took one, Shelton the other. I felt Ben join the circle. And there was Coop, standing in the middle.

Focusing our strength.

The cords appeared, pulsing with energy.

Five sparking lines connected us together.

With our pack huddled so close, the lines rippled and thrummed with power.

I pushed.

The lines suddenly expanded, hollowed, and became tunnels.

That's never happened before.

Sweat joined the rain drenching my brow.

Acting on reflex, I forced my thoughts into the nearest tunnel.

Hiram.

There was a floating sensation, then I felt something click.

Eyes snapped open. A head turned.

I stared at a rain-soaked redhead standing to my right. A girl.

Me. I'm looking at me.

Hi gasped. Startled, I retreated from his mind.

Opening another pair of eyes, I found myself back in familiar skin.

"Wow," Hi breathed. "Oh wow."

"Amazing," I said. "But that's not what we need."

Concentrate. You've done this before.

I visualized the glowing cords. This time, I grabbed one but did not enter it.

Light pulsed its length. Fragments of thought assaulted me. Images. Emotions.

Shelton.

I reached for another line, forcing the power outward. More fragments appeared.

Hi.

Another. The neural chaos grew as Ben joined the circle.

I was bombarded by their feelings and impressions. By their fears. But I felt in control. I could touch their minds. Send thoughts or images to all of them.

Then I noticed a void, like a missing limb. The circle was incomplete.

Cooper's silhouette materialized in my mind. Every cord ran through him.

Coop's the key. Center of the pack.

Reaching out, I drew the wolfdog into the mix.

Flash of light. Fusion. Five minds melded into one.

Coop howled with canine delight.

Our pack was finally whole.

I felt a telepathic link to each of the Virals.

The missing level. This is it.

The boys grasped it, too. They sent and exchanged thoughts, blown away by this new level of connection. By our effortless communication. It was the rush of a lifetime.

Without thinking, I narrowed my focus to Ben. Peeked behind his shield.

My brain captured a single image: Ben, aboard *Sewee,* deep in conversation.

Noooooooooooooo!

I looked up. Ben cocked his head, unsure what was happening. Then a mental wall slammed into place, blocking access to his thoughts.

Too late. I'd seen the truth. Recognized Ben's companion.

The stolen memory seared my brain.

Ben had been speaking with the Gamemaster.

CHAPTER 57

The shock nearly extinguished my flare.

I stared at Ben, aghast, incapable of speech.

My friend. My confidant. Trusted above all others on earth. The pain of his betrayal sent tears to my eyes.

Coop nipped my hand, pulling me back from the brink.

Pack, Coop sent with crystal clarity. *Pack.*

The wolfdog had it right. Whatever Ben had done, I needed him at that moment. The pack had to be whole for what we were about to attempt.

Shelton and Hi were cautiously poking each other's chest.

Amazing, sent Hi.

No doubt, Shelton thought back.

I heard them both. Our union of minds was seamless, not the strained, incomplete connections of the past. A blink, and I could adopt another Viral's perception. See through his eyes. We could communicate telepathically without interference.

I looked at Coop. *Is this what a pack truly is?*

Coop looked back with feral intensity. I sensed contentment. Excitement. As if his family had finally arrived home.

"We should attack," Ben said aloud. "Flush out the Gamemaster before . . . whatever *this* is fades away."

Yes, I sent. *And no more words.*

The awesome power flowed through me. Filled me with confidence.

I sent the pack a series of images and instructions.

No more was needed. Single file, we stalked toward the plaza.

Marion Square occupies a full city block — a wide, flat expanse often used for concerts and festivals. Dirt paths run from corner to corner, forming a giant X on the lawn. Oaks and low bushes border the perimeter, but there is no cover inside the square.

We approached the southwest corner and slipped in among the trees, each ducking behind a giant truck. Coop crouched at my side, ears perked, tail pointed outward. Moving warily, I crouched and crab-stepped to my left to get a clean look at the terrain.

Across the plaza loomed a hotel designed to look like a fortress. The roofline was styled as a battlement, topped with false towers and indented crenellations.

A perfect shooting platform, Ben sent. He was watching through my eyes.

Agreed, I replied. *We need to revise our plan.*

CRACK.

Something stung my arm.

I dropped to my belly, trying to pinpoint the source of the noise. Not the hotel.

TORY! Shelton pushed so hard it made me dizzy.

Coop whined in distress.

Then Hi was dragging me back behind the oak. Shelton and Ben were staring with panicked eyes.

"Oh God," Hi panted. "How bad is it?"

How bad is what? I sent. *Why are you speaking?*

"Your arm!" Hi took a deep breath. *You've been shot.*

I looked down. My jacket and shirtsleeve were neatly sliced. A scarlet blossom was streaking the outside of the nylon. *Huh.*

"She's in shock." Ben's voice was shaky. "Hi, check the wound."

I'm fine. But I let Hi probe the rip in my sleeve.

Seconds ticked by. Then color returned to Hi's cheeks. "It's okay. Just a graze."

My finger traced the shallow slash on my upper arm. *Close.*

"Did anyone see the shot?" Shelton whispered.

No more talking! I mind-shouted, tugging off the windbreaker and ripping away my shirtsleeve.

The wound was neat, straight, and parallel to the ground. It sliced horizontally across my left biceps, angling neither up nor down.

He's level with us, I sent. *Not on a roof.*

I considered my body position at impact — facing forward, shoulders square to the park. To graze my left arm, the bullet had to have originated either directly ahead or from somewhere to our left.

I scanned the left side of the plaza. Settled on a trio of live oaks crowding the northeast corner. *There.*

Shelton spreads his hands. *That's all the way across the square!*

Coop nudged my thigh. When our eyes met, he transmitted a series of images: Shelton and Ben circling left. Coop, Hiram, and I swinging right. Then snapping jaws, our prey caught squirming between.

Overcoming my shock, I relayed the wolfdog's plan. *He would know.*

Thunder cracked. A lone squall swept the block, sprinkling us with briny drops. The eye was passing. Katelyn was about to rage again.

Go! I sent.

Everyone reacted at once. Coop, Hi, and I shot down Calhoun. Using the tree line as a screen, we sprinted to the end of the block and slid into the bushes.

Running west, I was aware of Ben and Shelton sprinting north along King. They hit the corner and took cover in the trees.

Both groups paused, panting, sharing points of view.

No shots. No movement. I worried the Gamemaster had already fled.

Glancing east, I saw a wall of rain marching across the peninsula. A blast of wind nearly knocked me on my butt as Katelyn stormed back. Howling and spitting, she fired branches across the plaza like matchsticks.

Close the jaws, I sent.

Simultaneously, we began to converge on the northeast corner.

Lightning flashed. For an insane moment I heard the wind scream my name. Then I danced sideways to avoid a tire tumbling down the sidewalk.

CRACK. CRACK.

Hot metal buzzed my ear.

Hi dove for the hedge. I crashed in after him, and together we army-crawled to a stand of live oaks. Coop scurried to join us.

I shifted my perception to Shelton. He and Ben had ducked behind an outcropping of the hotel wall. As I watched, Shelton buried his face in the back of Ben's sweatshirt.

Everyone okay? Struggling to catch my breath.

Coop yapped.

Beside me, Hi flashed a shaky grin. *Not shot, if that's what you mean.*

Check. Ben was staring at a stand of pines twenty yards from his position.

I'm okay. Shelton had wedged himself farther behind Ben. *Think I'll stay here.*

Hi tapped my shoulder and pointed.

A form was emerging from the shadows in the corner of the plaza, rifle trained on the hotel. Unaware of where Hi and I were positioned, the Gamemaster stepped into the square and began circling for a clean shot at Ben and Shelton.

In seconds they'd be in his crosshairs.

I beamed the danger. *Move!*

Ben didn't hesitate. Pushing Shelton before him, he darted up the block.

For a terrifying moment the two were totally exposed.

The Gamemaster tensed. Raised his weapon. Fired.

CRACK. CRACK.

Sparks flew from the hotel wall.

Ben and Shelton reached a stone bench and dove behind it.

The Gamemaster hurried forward, rifle trained on their position, back to where Hi and I crouched beside Coop.

Panic bubbled in my chest. He had the boys pinned down.

Before I could react, Hi rose and burst from the trees, lumbering straight for the Gamemaster's back.

No! I sent.

Coop streaked after Hi.

I shot from the trees in pursuit.

Focused on his target, the Gamemaster failed to notice the action behind him. He closed to within a dozen yards of the bench.

I felt Ben enter my headspace. Look through my eyes.

Then, to my shock, he popped up and started waving his arms.

The Gamemaster froze, momentarily surprised. Recovering quickly, he leveled the barrel to fire. Ben dropped back behind the bench.

Hi kept bombing toward the Gamemaster. Thirty yards. Twenty.

At ten yards, Katelyn betrayed him.

Lightning flashed. The Gamemaster caught movement in the corner of his eye.

He spun. Centered Hi in his crosshairs.

Hi stumbled and fell in the pouring rain. Slid to a stop on his knees.

A smile split the Gamemaster's mouth.

Oh damn, Hi sent.

I screamed, helpless.

Then a shadow exploded from the center of the plaza, rushing directly for the Gamemaster. He turned, astonished by this new attack.

The figure was familiar. I thought I was hallucinating.

Kit lowered one shoulder. Bellowing like a madman, he reached the Gamemaster and swung a wild haymaker.

The Gamemaster dropped his rifle and stepped sideways, ducking the blow and tossing Kit forward with one arm. Kit toppled and rolled across the slick grass.

Laughing, the Gamemaster pulled a Glock from his robe.

Too late.

Coop struck first, upending the Gamemaster and sending him sprawling.

The Glock went flying.

As the Gamemaster staggered to one knee, my foot connected with his jaw.

His eyes rolled back. Then Ben and Shelton tackled as one, driving him face-first into the muddy lawn.

"You freak!" Ben was hammering our enemy with his fists. I needed Shelton's help to drag him off.

"Now that's what I call backup!" Hi searched the Gamemaster's robe and removed three more handguns. "Never doubted you guys for a second." He jammed the weapons into his pockets. "Okay, that's not really true. But you came through anyway!"

As we regained our breath Katelyn raged on, pounding our group with renewed ferocity.

No matter. It was over. The Gamemaster lay unconscious at my feet. We'd won.

Then, a moment of panic. Kit was there.

I quickly fired a message: *Kill the lights!*

Four flares snuffed in rapid succession.

I turned to find Kit staring at me, lungs heaving, water coursing down his face.

He wore a look of total bewilderment.

"Hi, Dad."

CHAPTER 58

Outside, the hurricane thundered and churned.

Inside, my emotions did the same.

We sat in a hallway of Charleston Memorial Hospital, one group among many seeking shelter.

Though staffed by a skeleton crew, the building still bustled with doctors, patients, and stragglers caught by the storm. A medical center is never fully evacuated, and CMH was one of the few places downtown with its own generator.

I picked at my bandage, still avoiding the reality that I'd been shot. I certainly hadn't told Kit. Neither had the exhausted medical staff — an oversight I'd let run as long as possible. Coop napped at my side, exhausted by the day's events.

Shelton and Hi were spilling everything. Kit had demanded the story from me, but I'd remained stubbornly silent until the dynamic duo took up the tale. Kit's eyes widened as they related an *almost* complete version of our last two weeks.

Kit had already explained how *he* found *us*.

After discovering my note, Kit had run outside only to see *Sewee* motoring into the Atlantic. A full-blown panic had ensued, with every father demanding a spot on *Hugo* to chase us down.

Finally, playing the boss card, Kit had ordered his employees to evacuate Morris. Then he'd sped toward downtown in his 4Runner after browbeating the police into letting him cross the bridge. Once on the peninsula he'd stalled, having no idea where to look.

Then Katelyn closed in.

Fearing the worst, Kit tried the hospital, where an MD swore he'd seen a group of teens sprinting down Calhoun Street. Having no other plan, Kit hurried back out to his 4Runner and drove as far as the downed trees and smoking black truck.

That's when he'd heard gunshots. Terrified, he'd raced ahead on foot, eventually stumbling into Marion Square.

Spotting me, Kit had shouted my name.

I hadn't turned. Instead I'd run the other way.

Kit was about to pursue when a flying trash-can lid clocked him from behind. He'd dropped to a knee, momentarily stunned. When he'd recovered, I was gone. Then he'd spotted a gunman in the plaza aiming at Hi. The headlong assault had been pure reflex.

Super Dad hadn't let me out of his sight since.

I barely listened to Hi and Shelton's recitation. I was watching Ben.

He didn't speak. Avoided my gaze. Then he stood and strode down the hall.

I popped up and started after him. Coop rose to follow, but I gently shooed him back with one hand. Though displeased, he lay down beside Hi and closed his eyes.

"Don't go anywhere!" Kit called to my back. "You're not to leave this hospital!"

I turned. "Dad, it's over."

Kit stared at me intently, then nodded.

An hour earlier, we'd flagged an emergency vehicle sent to investigate the exploding F-150. The police had loaded everyone into vans and driven to CMH. Hearing our story, and seeing the guns, they'd taken the Gamemaster into custody. A full investigation would have to wait until after Katelyn passed.

There'd be questions. Statements. The whole shebang.

My interrogation couldn't wait.

I found Ben on a stool in an empty examining room, head in his hands.

He was waiting for me.

"I saw." No point mincing my words.

Ben didn't look up. "In my head?"

"Yes. You met with the Gamemaster aboard *Sewee*."

"Twice." Ben sat back, but didn't meet my eye. "His name is Simon Rome. At least, that's the name he used at LIRI."

I'd thought myself prepared. Was wrong.

"Ben, no! Why?" I felt the walls caving in around me.

"No one was supposed to get hurt!" Ben lashed out and kicked a trash can across the room. "It was just a stupid game!"

He spun away, shoulders trembling. I sensed that he was crying.

I took a deep breath. "Tell me everything."

Ben sniffed. Ran both hands over his eyes. Then he faced me, wearing a look of total devastation.

"Tell me," I whispered, close to tears myself.

Ben slumped on his stool. Said nothing.

I positioned a chair opposite him, sat, and leaned forward. "Tell me," I repeated for the third time.

"I met Rome on the LIRI dock," Ben said dully. "He was the new mechanic, had only been working at the institute a few months. I'd see him every few days, and we kinda got to be friends."

"Why did you never mention him?"

"I don't know." Ben scuffed at the floor with his sneaker. "I don't have a lot of friends, not like you. I guess it was just nice hanging with someone else. Someone older."

Not like me? What was Ben talking about?

"I . . . told him things." Ben's face reddened. "Personal things. After that he came up with this big idea."

Though I wanted to know what *things* Ben had told the Gamemaster, I needed to keep him talking. "The big idea. Was it The Game?"

"It was going to be fun," Ben said bitterly. "A series of codes and puzzles. And the best part was, *I'd* look smart and cool. We'd set up these tricky games, then I'd solve the clues and be a hero."

"But why?" I couldn't understand his thinking. "You didn't have to impress *us*. We know you. We're your friends. Your *family*."

For a long moment Ben didn't speak. Then, "I'm so stupid."

I was about to respond, but he cut me off.

"I pushed Hi to buy that metal detector. He thinks it was his idea. It wasn't. Then I started making fun of geocaching, all the time *knowing* he'd end up wanting to play the game. It worked, too. In no time I'd led everyone to the Loggerhead cache."

"The puzzle box. The coded message."

"The box was simple, and I knew Shelton would crack the cipher. But I saved the shining moment for myself." His voice become mocking. "Look at Ben! He solved the altered coordinates. He's so wonderful. On to Castle Pinckney!"

His sneaker slammed a nearby cabinet. "What a moron!"

"The second cache exploded." My tone sharpened. "Cooper was hurt."

Ben shook his head miserably. "That's when I knew the jerk had double-crossed me."

I waited for Ben to go on. He did.

"The Game wasn't supposed to be dangerous. Then Pinckney

happened. That monster rigged the cache with diesel fuel, then deto-nated a frigging *bomb* in Battery Park. It was all totally off script. I'd never seen that iPad before, and didn't know the pictogram or the chemical equation. Now Rome was threatening to *hurt* people. That wasn't part of the deal!"

My palms flipped up. "Why didn't you say something? Warn us?"

"I was shocked. Embarrassed. I tried to contact Rome the minute we got back, but the cell number he'd given me was disconnected. When I called LIRI, they said he was on vacation. I didn't know what to do."

I thought of the times Ben had gone missing lately. Had acted distant. How badly he'd freaked when I'd touched his mind at Castle Pinckney.

I'd chalked it all up to his natural moodiness, or his running feud with Jason. I never suspected something more sinister.

"Everything spiraled out of control." Ben's knee started bouncing up and down. "I . . . I thought . . . hoped that maybe I could stop it some-how. Make it all go away."

"The snare gun. Kit just said LIRI never owned one."

"I was as shocked as you. Rome and I never discussed *guns*. When you told me what Marchant said at the coffee shop, I didn't know what to think. I figured Rome *could've* stolen the weapon from LIRI, since he worked there. But I'm not surprised he was totally lying. Not now."

"The Gamemaster *murdered* a man, Ben." I forced him to meet my eye. "Eric Marchant was executed in cold blood. For no other reason than to mess with our heads."

"*Never.*" Ben's hands began to shake. "No one was supposed to ever, *ever* . . . It was a freaking *game*!"

I thought of something. "You *saw* Marchant. At the firing range."

He snorted without humor. "Why do you think I puked?"

"That was *after* Castle Pinckney." The realization stoked my anger. "*After* a cache burned Coop's mouth. *After* the Gamemaster blew up the wedding gazebo. *After* the snare gun fired at me!"

Ben looked away.

"You *scoffed* when I suggested the Gamemaster might work at LIRI."
My fury grew as more pieces fell into place. "And when I worried we'd
been specifically targeted for the Game? You *knew,* and lied to my face!
To all of us!"

"I panicked!" Ben shot to his feet and began pacing the small room.
"I didn't know what to do. When we got back I tried one last time to
reach Rome, to *demand* he end the game. I even tried to access his per-
sonnel file on that LIRI terminal. That why I sent you guys to check the
lobby. It was useless. The records were gone."

"You should've told us!"

"You wouldn't have let me help!" Ben shot back. "This whole nightmare was my fault. I needed to find that psycho and stop him. If I'd told
you guys the truth, you'd have shut me out. Then we found the corpse,
and . . . and . . ." He shook his head. "It was too late. Things were crazy.
All I could do was try to prevent whatever evil Rome had planned."

I held up a hand. Couldn't handle any more of his confession.

Unwittingly or not, Ben had assisted a monster. A killer. He'd known
the truth for days, and never told us. He'd lied. Even when The Game
had threatened our lives.

"Tell me why, Ben. Why would you want to trick us in the first place?"

Ben stopped pacing. Looked directly at me. "Don't you know?"

I shook my head, confused.

"To impress you, Victoria Brennan." His voice cracked. "I wanted
you to think I was special."

The words rocked me.

Oh, Ben.

He'd started this madness . . . for me?

"You were spending all that time with Jason," Ben said softly, staring at his shoes. "Skipping around town with your new perfect guy.
Cotillion *this.* Fund-raiser *that.* I *hated* it. Hated *him.* When I finally

told Rome, he said I needed to amaze you. Said I needed to figure out a way to make you see me."

"I see you, Ben." I rose and grabbed his hand. "I always have. You're in my pack."

He pulled away. "What if being packmates isn't enough for me?"

I was speechless.

The room froze in uncomfortable silence.

Then Kit stuck his head through the door. "Tory?"

"Uh-huh."

"The worst of the hurricane has passed. The police want to interview us now." Kit's eyes bounced between Ben and me. I was sure he could sense the tension, perhaps even hear my heart pounding in my chest. "You guys up for that?"

Was I? What would I say?

I made a decision.

"Yes." Stepping to the door. "But I have nothing to add to what we've already told you."

I heard Ben pivot. Felt his eyes on my back.

I could never turn you in. Not even for this.

"Okay." Kit sounded skeptical. "But we still have to make statements."

I was about to agree when Ben gripped my shoulder.

"No, Tory." His voice was tired, but firm. "It's time to tell the truth. All of it."

I spun to face him.

"There's no need to!" Tentacles of fear squeezed my heart. "It won't make any difference."

"It will to me." Squaring his shoulders, Ben nodded to Kit. "Lead the way, sir?"

My friend strode from the room, one step ahead of my tears.

Good-bye, Ben.

CHAPTER 59

"How long are we stuck in Charlotte?"

Hi tossed a stick across the patio beside Aunt Tempe's townhouse. It arced through slanting shafts of afternoon sun before vanishing into a stand of magnolias. Coop fired after with delight.

"A few days," I answered from my deck chair. "The bridge from Folly to Morris washed out, and there's no power or running water at our complex. Kit says we're lucky the building is still standing."

Hi dropped into the chaise longue beside me. "I'm worried about the bunker."

"So am I. We'll have to wait and see."

Hi yawned, stretched. "All in all, we got pretty lucky."

I nodded. "Katelyn blasted across Charleston in less than three hours."

The hurricane had moved much faster than anticipated. After unexpectedly turning toward land, she'd accelerated rapidly, catching the prognosticators off guard and disrupting the evacuation. Thousands had been caught in their cars, forced to hunker in while trapped bumper to bumper on bridges and highways. The Morris Island caravan had been part of that unhappy crew.

Katelyn had rolled over the city like a rampaging pachyderm. The damage had been dreadful. Then she'd raced inland, stalled over Columbia, veered northeast, and wobbled through central North Carolina and Virginia. A day later, she was nothing more than an ugly rainstorm dousing New England.

"The weather guy described Katelyn as unstable," Hi said. "One side of her was way bigger than the other. The skinny edge struck the city first — that's why the hurricane blew for less than an hour before the eye appeared. Thankfully, the leading edge also had the lower wind speeds. If we'd been caught outside for the trailing half . . ."

No need to finish. The winds that struck as we'd huddled at CMH had topped 130 mph. Safely tucked inside the hospital, we'd been shielded from the worst of the storm.

"It's cool Tempe took everyone in," Hi said. "Though we're crammed like backpackers in a hostel."

"The parentals are working on that. Your family and the Devers clan are relocating to my uncle Pete's house. It's much bigger."

"Great." Hi grinned. "You and Whitney can be even closer."

"Ugh, don't remind me. And Kit just told me her place in Charleston was flattened by a tree. She's a wreck. Guess who'll be bunking with us when we get back?"

"Bonding time. Ladies' nights."

Hi dodged my foot jab. Coop bounded up and dropped the saliva-coated stick at my feet. I hurled it back into the magnolias.

"How long are you grounded for?" I asked.

"For me, I don't think there's such a thing as 'not grounded' anymore."

"Same. This one's gonna sting."

Hi leaned back and laced his fingers behind his head. "Anything new on the Gamemaster?"

"Just what we heard last night." I summarized what Kit had been told by the police. "Simon Rome's real name is Anthony Goodwin. He was a Marine Corps munitions expert, honorably discharged after sustaining combat injuries in Iraq. He's already facing dozens of charges. Murder. Attempted murder. Arson. Terrorism. Yada yada yada."

"Hope he likes living in a box."

"The authorities haven't publically identified the body they found in Goodwin's shed, but everyone's sure it's Eric Marchant. No cause of death yet."

"My money's on poison. Shelton said *Dateline* is planning a two-hour special."

"Lovely."

Coop returned and begged for another round of fetch. I complied.

"I have some new info," Hi said. "Some blog published Goodwin's military file. Apparently he was on a routine patrol in Ramadi when one of our smart bombs hit a school. Killed dozens. Goodwin was first on the scene. It was really bad. The villagers turned on him, kept screaming that he was responsible."

I straightened in my chair. "That's awful."

"Then, on his way back to base, his Humvee struck a roadside IED."

"My God."

"I know, right? The records say Goodwin was all messed up about it. He had what they described as 'severe emotional trauma.' Some kind of personality split. The file used phrases like 'reversion to childlike state,' and, 'periodic disconnect with reality.' Sounds like he totally lost his marbles. Posttraumatic stress disorder all the way."

I thought of my meetings with Goodwin. He'd seemed so capable and self-assured in public. But he'd been a different man during our last confrontation. Childish. Erratic. Grandiose. I had no trouble believing Hi's report.

I examined how this new information made me feel. Decided it changed nothing. The Gamemaster may have experienced horrors, but that didn't excuse his becoming one.

"What happened to Goodwin after Iraq?" I asked.

"No one knows. He bailed on counseling and dropped off the grid."

"So he began assuming new identities." The pieces fit. "Using fake names to travel the country and set up his games. But how could he afford it?"

"Nothing used in The Game was all that expensive," Hi said. "And Goodwin had a steady paycheck. *I'm* curious about those machines he built. He must've developed the expertise in the service."

"Makes sense. I guess we'll learn more at his trial."

"Whoopee."

The boys and I would almost certainly be called to testify, with Ben as star witness.

Ben.

Nope. Not ready for that.

"How'd Goodwin get a job on Loggerhead, anyway?" Hi asked.

"LIRI hired—" I used air quotes, "—'Simon Rome' as an assistant mechanic four months ago, during the period last summer when the institute had no director. Kit said he didn't know much about it. I guess they didn't run a background check."

"Goodwin was probably using a stolen social security number. If so, he'd have passed the basic check for a mechanic's job. I bet Goodwin had a whole set of false Simon Rome papers."

"Isn't that hard to pull off?"

"Naw. Don't you watch *Cops*? Faking an identity is easier than you think."

"Still, Kit's having Hudson revamp the institute's screening procedures."

"Security Chief Hudson." Hi made a face. "What a douche."

"Kit admitted having Hudson spy on us. He suspected we were up to something when we asked for a lab. I tried to get all indignant, but it didn't fly. Since we really *were* up to something."

Hi snorted. "Future trips to Loggerhead should be a joy."

"At least the animals are okay. Kit said every monkey is accounted for, and someone saw Whisper's pack this morning, sniffing through trash washed up on Turtle Beach."

The sliding door opened and Shelton stepped out. Coop padded over and offered the slobber-stick. Shelton grimaced, but took the branch and flung it toward the tree line.

"What'd you learn?" I held my breath, afraid of Shelton's answer.

"Ben isn't going to be charged."

I exhaled slowly. "Thank God."

Shelton plopped down in the last open chair. "The cops believe that he didn't know about the Gamemaster's crimes."

"Of course he didn't!" Hi said at once.

I looked away.

Shelton and Hi had already forgiven Ben. So far, I couldn't.

He should have told us.

"Ben's testimony will be key to the prosecution's case," Shelton continued. "He can establish how Goodwin planned The Game, and link him to the original Loggerhead cache. Add in *our* testimony, plus the evidence we collected along the way, and there's no way Goodwin walks."

"No charges for Ben," Hi said. "That's the important thing."

Shelton's eyes dropped. "It's not all good news."

"What?" Again the fear.

"I heard my parents talking. Ben's getting expelled."

"From Bolton?" Not at all what I'd expected. "That makes no sense."

"The school's already contacted Kit, since he manages our scholarships. It's a done deal."

"But Ben is cooperating!" I couldn't believe it. "How can they expel him if he isn't been charged with a crime?"

"You know the administration," Shelton said. "Blueblood prigs with giant rods up their butts. They don't want scandal anywhere close to their *pristine* academy."

"It's a private school," Hi said glumly. "They can do what they want."

"Kit will fight this." I'd make him.

"My dad said he already tried. Kit even offered a sizable donation, but Bolton turned it down. Ben's as good as gone."

We sat silently, digesting the terrible news.

"So what do we do?" Hi finally asked.

I had no answer.

Ferry rides. Classes. Lunches. I couldn't imagine them without Ben.

My mind leaped back to the hospital. Our confrontation.

Ben's brokenhearted confession.

I'd resisted every impulse to consider his words. Or how they made me feel.

Nope.

Nope nope nope.

Not yet.

Now that I was safe, Kit was furious with me. All my worldly possessions might be drenched in seawater. Chance and Jason had seen way too much, and could cause trouble. I'd have to testify at the trial of our insane tormentor, an event sure to trigger a media frenzy.

I had enough problems.

Affairs of the heart would have to wait.

So I leaned back and let the silence linger. The slobber-stick made several more flights.

Then *it* started again.

Something had changed since Marion Square. It'd taken days for me to notice. I didn't think the boys were aware, though I suspected Coop might be. When the wolfdog looked at me now I could almost hear his thoughts.

Nothing I could point to. Just a knowing. An instinctive understanding. Unlike anything I recalled feeling before.

Was I more sensitive than the rest of my pack? Why?

Because I was Alpha? *Was* I Alpha?

My powers were dormant, tucked away inside my DNA. Still, I felt a . . . connection. Some lingering remnant of the pure union we'd experienced while fighting the Gamemaster.

I sensed the bond to my pack, even now, without a flare.

Hi. Shelton. Coop. Even Ben, somewhere to the southeast.

We'd never be apart again, even when we were. Not anymore.

The realization warmed me.

As I shifted my weight something jabbed me in the leg. I fished in my pocket. Pulled out a red plastic bar.

"Karsten's flash drive." Hi shot a quick glance at Tempe's sliding door. "You keep it on you?"

"Of course. It might have the answers we need. I can't risk losing it."

I studied the slim drive lying on my palm. Wondered what secrets it held.

Mapped DNA? The metabolic truth of our mutations? A cure?

"You asked what next, Hi?" I placed the drive on the patio table.

Shelton and Hi turned to face me.

Coop trotted over and sat at my feet.

"We find out what happened to us." I scratched behind my wolfdog's ears. "The whole story. Then we figure out what comes next."

I probed the new awareness swirling in recesses of my mind. Felt tantalizingly close to understanding. Then the feeling slipped away.

"It's time to discover what makes us Viral."

EPILOGUE

Chance Claybourne glared at the man standing before him.

He was sitting at the desk in his study. The colossus reminded him of his father, and he loathed using it, but the gleaming mahogany had a certain intimidation value he found useful.

Right then, he wanted to intimidate.

"Nothing else?" Chance spoke loud enough to be heard over the hammering in the courtyard below.

Claybourne Manor had weathered yet another hurricane. Though Katelyn had not left the property unscathed. Broken windows. Uprooted trees. An outbuilding reduced to a pile of rubble.

But the main house stood, strong as ever. Chance scoffed at the idea of evacuation. He'd lounged in his wine cellar, reading his Kindle, insulated from even the noise of the storm. The whole thing had been much to-do about nothing.

Chance reflected on a prior trip down those steps.

Tory Brennan. I was shot in that cellar, for God's sake.

The man before him shifted. Chance didn't offer a seat.

He needed this worm, but didn't like him.

"They should not have been up there," Mike Iglehart said. "The only person to ever work upstairs in Building Six was our former director, Marcus Karsten."

Chance kept his face blank. "Karsten?"

Iglehart nodded. "He's gone now. Murdered. It was awful."

Chance regarded the devious scientist with distaste. He was the perfect mole, his allegiance purchased for next to nothing. It still surprised him. Iglehart obviously had some personal grudge against his employer.

"Why is that relevant?" Chance asked.

"I think those brats stole something," Iglehart answered. "I'm certain the girl was hiding her hands. It might relate to the research Karsten was doing."

Chance's pulse quickened, but his tone remained flat. "Research?"

"No one knows. Karsten destroyed all the files."

Chance considered the new information. Iglehart knew nothing about his connection to the project, or his role in the events surrounding Karsten's death. Chance intended to keep it that way.

Karsten's secret research. Tory and her obnoxious friends.

Was there a link? How? What kind?

He thought back to his talks with Madison. To his own odd experiences with those four.

The wine cellar three stories below him.

A deserted beach.

The basement of The Citadel.

Something is amiss.

"Ah . . . Mr. Claybourne?" Iglehart fidgeted. "Is there anything else?"

Chance shook his head tightly. "Dismissed. Keep your eyes open."

Chance felt anger radiate from the man. Resentment that he, an accomplished scientist, was forced to run and fetch for a boy barely eighteen.

Chance smiled coldly. *Money talks.*

When the door closed, Chance opened a drawer and removed a large key ring. Then he rose and crossed to an ancient bureau against the far wall.

His father's private cabinet.

He'd never seen inside it before the old man went away.

Chance unlocked the door, removed a stack of files, and returned to the desk.

For a long moment he stared at the folders.

His father had never mentioned their existence. He'd found them only a few weeks earlier.

One finger traced the lettering stamped onto each one.

Candela Pharmaceuticals.
Dr. Marcus Karsten—Research Notes.
Top Secret.

"I *will* get answers," Chance whispered.

He began reading for the hundredth time.

ACKNOWLEDGMENTS

Code would not have been possible without the patient-yet-prodding efforts of our super-editor Arianne Lewin at G. P. Putnam's Sons. Thank you for your tireless work in shaping this story, and for providing solid direction for the Virals series going forward. We are in your debt. Thanks also to Ben Schrank and Anne Hetzel for their thoughtful contributions to both this manuscript and the series. We appreciate you all.

More thanks to Don Weisberg at Penguin and Susan Sandon at Random House UK, who have backed these crazy Virals from the beginning, a fact for which we are eternally grateful. We also must thank Jennifer Rudolph Walsh, and the entire staff at William Morris Endeavor Entertainment, for everything that they do. You keep the electricity humming.

Last, but certainly not least, a hearty thank-you to our loyal readers. We are at your service.